U0097839

語言學習‧叢書01

英檢pass定心丸

◌英檢重要基礎觀念攻略◌

◎王璟琪　著◎

謹以此書
獻給我親愛的學生們
因為你們專注於上課的眼神
為我們老師也注入無比的活力與鼓勵
我們因此希望透過本書的出版
能夠幫助你們在人生的路上
贏得更多的掌聲與喝采

金星出版社 http://www.venusco.com.tw
E-mail: venusco@pchome.com.tw

金星出版

英檢pass定心丸

序 學語言是很有趣的，這個觀念我從小大到都深信不疑。當然這樣的信念難免也有動搖的時候。你覺得呢？當壓力造成的時候，興趣往往都似乎被迫放棄了。不管社會狀況如何，景氣怎麼樣，其實我們在大學教書時，一直面對的都是同學對於畢業後該何去何從的問題。許多學校為了幫同學克服這樣的恐懼，希望在同學們畢業前提升大家的戰鬥值，也就是競爭力，所以設起了畢業門檻，相信『有要求，就會進步。』

　　同學們的看法呢？壓力，自然是的。但其實我往往鼓勵同學們往好處看，往國際的職缺需求來看，並且同學之間應該互相鼓勵，達到同儕一起進步的效果。這是在學校才有，而出了社會就失去的學習環境。於是，面對各式各樣的英檢考試，應該將它們視為測試及表現自己能力的工具，證明自己是有勝任在職場的工作挑戰的能力。不管是全民英檢、CSEPT 大學能力測驗 TOEIC 多益測驗、托福 iBT、劍橋英語測驗或者是雅思 IELTS 的考試，平時在英語學習上有持續的學習進步，只要選對適合自己的檢測工具，不僅可以做為未來學習的指標，最重要的也是取得升學及就業的語言能力證明。

　　此書是融合了老師在課堂教學時的重點整理及學生

學習需求觀察而著，為了很多因大考小考考不完的同學，為了準備初、中級英檢一個頭兩個大的同學而著。所以本書所匯整的主題，均為目前各式英檢中常考的主題，常出現在聽、說、讀、寫的題目內容。語言是溝通的工具，既然是工具，當然著重於要能用。有了工具還要有創意、有想法，否則要說什麼？要寫什麼呢？所以本書透過主題式內容，引導同學們思考並進而學習該主題所需要的相關單字。讓用功的同學唸起來，不僅有了骨架（清楚的概念），也要有靈魂，也就是自我的想法。每個大主題區後都有一個複習單元，老師也根據前文中所提到的一些語句，針對八大詞性做一個清楚的概念解說。讓同學們在複習之餘，能夠靈活使用句法。這是一本結合字彙、文法、閱讀、基礎寫作及考試準備的英語教材，希望達到讓同學們讀起來有興趣，很容易入門，那麼準備考試這件事不就變得快樂又輕鬆許多了嗎？

《英檢 Pass 定心丸》的書名，就是為此而生。希望同學服用過後，內功與信心大增，因而覺得學習英語，面對英檢考試不再是那麼令人慌張的事，以積極開放的態度，來學習語言，接觸多采多姿的世界文化。

Instruction 本書使用說明

　　本書前後分為兩大主軸，前半部為主題課文學習，後半部為文法概念解說及練習。

1. 主題課文學習：

　　本部份收錄了三大主題，分別是人我關係、興趣與休閒及生活與工作。主要目的在幫助同學以主題式累積字彙實力與相關句型及會話練習。每章的架構為：

A. Language box 語言框：

　　分為 2 個 Focus 焦點。通常 Focus 1 的問題比較被廣泛使用，屬於比較大的問題，回答的方式也比較多元。而 Focus 2 的問題多半範圍會縮小，屬於比較 detail 細節的問題，能回答的內容範圍也比較少。同學們可以藉由回答這些問題時，整理自己的口說表達內容。要試著講完整的句子，而不是只講對或錯而已。每個章節有提供一些不同的口語統整練習，引導同學講出屬於自己的答案。『語言注意面』則是整理同學們比較常誤用的句子，從比較的過程中，學習者會更清楚在何種狀況下應使用何種句子來表達不同的意思。

B. Conversation 會話練習：

　　會話練習則是依時事或日常生活常發生的場景、事物所編寫。每課提供兩段會話內容。同學們也可以透過這裡的會話內容，練習流利的口語表達。習慣成自然，

多唸幾課自然就會朗朗上口了。在本書的會話練習中，通常會注意到片語、句型的反覆運用，以加強學習者的印象。使用這裡做練習時，可以先不要看會話最上面一開始所提示的場景。同學們先看內容並朗讀練習，從內容中可猜猜看會話發生的背景是什麼，這兩個人是什麼關係？在哪裡發生？發生了什麼事？語氣應該是急切還是輕鬆？在第二次練習時就可以加入語氣來說看看，同學們可進行角色扮演。

C. Word bank 字彙隨身錠：

字彙表依字彙主題集合相關的字詞，同學們可利用此處的字彙表來做每課的代換練習，也可直接背誦練習，或用來檢查自己還有哪些單字沒背到。每章最後都會有幾題字彙練習題來做複習。如果在課堂教學時，老師也可以指派其為回家作業，上課時再講解題目意義。每個字彙除了音標外，母音的部份都會劃線，同學們也可試試見字發音，可以比較出發音及拼字的規則，有利於背字彙的形、音結合。

D. Reading Passage 閱讀測驗：

每課會收錄一篇或兩篇的閱讀測驗，長文章是為了複習單字所編寫，短篇的多半和英檢考試的題型類似。除了多樣化的閱讀形式外，還有克漏字測驗的練習，加強同學段落填空的弱點。閱讀測驗中有時候會出現的本

課所提到字彙以外的『新字彙』，是為了增加挑戰性，同學應該先依前後文推測該字的意義，訓練閱讀能力。我們通常看一篇文章時，不認識的字彙如果超出 20%到 30%的時候，整篇文章就會造成我們閱讀上的壓力，會感到挫折感很大。但考試時我們經常會碰到這樣的問題，所以需要來練習依前後文推測的功夫。

E. Vocabulary Challenge 字彙挑戰時間：

　　和閱讀測驗一樣，我們相信同學接觸該主題字彙愈久，愈能掌握到關聯字的學習要領，在每章最後的字彙測驗，通常和閱讀一樣，也希望題目內容靈活一點，可以讓同學學到這裡，又可以藉由做題目多體會一些這些單字可以運用的範圍，達到深度學習的目的。

2. 文法概念解說：

　　以縱貫線的方式來依詞類整理文法概念，本書編寫的方式是由初級到中級的文法，由淺入深，所以從最基本，同學常混淆的觀念開始解惑，加上一層層由簡易到複雜的練習，可以幫助同學們穩固基礎，一路清楚到底。文法部份有用一些比較俏皮的說法幫助同學記憶，還有語言實驗室用邏輯推理的方式，幫助同學更有效學習。在課堂上實際教學時，這樣的教法也得到很大的迴響。以推理的方式一旦懂了核心觀念，很多都可觸類旁通了。

目錄

第二部份：文法觀念解析

第一部份
主題式課文學習

人我關係 ➡ 興趣休閒 ➡ 生活工作

Lesson 1 | 個性與嗜好
Personality and hobbies

🗣 Language box 🗣

| Focus One |

What are you like? (你是怎麼樣的人？)

What's your personality like? (你的個性是怎麼樣的？)

What is your best friend like? (你最好的朋友如何？)

Is your personality similar to your families?
(你的個性和你的家人相似嗎？)

Are you different from your friends?
(你和你的朋友不一樣嗎？)

Are you similar or not? (你們相像還是不相像？)

✎ 語言注意面 Language Caution ✎

A: <u>What's your father like?</u> (你爸爸的個性如何?)

B: He is quite sociable. (他相當善於交際。)

**有別於 How's your father? (你爸爸如何？)—問最近的狀況。

**有別於 What does your father like?(你的爸爸喜歡什麼？)

••

❤愛的筆記貼❤ 這裡所提到的 What's your father like? 和 What does your father like?分別的關鍵就在於 like 這個字本身的詞性與意義。like 當一般動詞時，意思是『喜歡』，動詞三態為：like/ liked/ liked。like 當作介系詞及形容詞時都當『相像』的意思。而我們平常說的 just like『就

像』這裡的 like 是當做連接詞來用。很明顯的,如果是動詞的用法就是

『喜歡』之意,如果是其他詞性就是『相像』的意思。

Focus Two

What do you like doing? (你喜歡做什麼?)

What do you do in your free time? (你閒暇時都在做什麼?)

What do you and your friends do together?

(你和你朋友平常在一起會做什麼?)

✔ 語言注意面 Language Caution ✔

What do you like doing? (你喜歡做什麼?)

What are you doing? (你正在做什麼?)

How are you doing? (你最近如何啊?)

♥ **愛的筆記貼** ♥　❶以上語言注意面所提到的三句同學們容易混淆的句子,雖然語句中均有 doing,是 do 的現在分詞,但 What do you like doing?這裡的 doing 是因為直接接在 like 這個動詞之後,而不是現在進行式所用的 doing。所以主要動詞還是 like,造問句時需要用 do 這個助動詞。What are you doing?及 How are you doing?兩句都有問現在狀況的意思故用現在進行式 Be 動詞加 Ving 現在分詞。

❷語言的使用和前後文是什麼有關係。所以 What do you do?這句話,如果是在剛見面,彼此表明身份時,是問『工作』,你現在在做什麼(工作)。如果是好朋友見面時,應該是在問你最近在做些什麼。這個情形在一般電影或影集裡常見。

◎ Conversation 1 ◎

Addie: Hello, are you new here?　　　哈囉,你是新來的嗎?

Doris: Oh, yes. My name is Doris.　　喔,對。我的名字是朵莉

　　　　Are you new here, too?　　　絲。你也是新來的嗎?

Addie: No, I used to work in the accounting department. Actually, I just transfer to here. Nice to meet you.

不，我過去曾經在會計部工作。事實上，我剛調任這裡。很高興認識你。

Doris: Oh, really?
So, we will be colleagues in the same place. May I know your name?

喔，真的？這樣，我們將會在同一個部門當同事囉。我可以知道一下妳的名字嗎？

Addie: Oh, yes. Addie. A-d-d-i-e, not E-d-i-e.

喔，好的。艾迪。是拼成 A-d-d-i-e 不是 E-d-i-e。

Doris: Okay, I see.

好，我知道。

⊘ Conversation 2 ⊘

Doris: Tell me more about you. What do you like to do? Or what's your personality like?

跟我說一些有關你的事。你平常喜歡做些什麼？或你的個性是像怎樣的？

Addie: I think I am quite outgoing and sociable. My friends said I am a party animal, but actually I only like being with my friends together. I like to make friends.

我覺得我相當外向及喜歡交際。我朋友說我是個熱愛聚會的人，但實際上我只是喜歡和我的朋友在一起。我喜歡交朋友。

Doris: Are your friends all similar to you?

你的朋友們都和你很像嗎？

Addie: I don't think so. Most of them are like me, but sometimes I stay with quiet people and enjoy reading. What's about you? What do you do in your free time?

我不覺得這樣。他們大部份和我很像，但有時候我會和安靜的人在一起享受閱讀。你呢？你有空都在做什麼？

Doris: Oh, that's great. I love reading, too. Guess what? We may share the ideas in the future. How do you think?

Addie: Perfect. If you like, you may also join our reading club.

喔，太好了。我也喜歡閱讀。你猜怎麼著？以後我們也許可以分享一些讀書心得。你覺得怎樣？

好極了。如果你喜歡，你也可以加入我們的讀書會。

⊘Work Bank⊘ 隨時補充一錠，你在會話及閱讀理解必備的單字！

❀	**punctual** [ˈpʌŋktʃʊəl] 守時的	❀	**honest** [ˈɑnɪst] 誠實的
❀	**sincere** [sɪnˈsɪr] 誠摯的	❀	**sociable** [ˈsoʃəbl] 擅於交際的
❀	**outgoing** [ˈaʊtˌgoɪŋ] 外向的	❀	**loyal** [ˈlɔɪəl] 忠心的
❀	**easygoing** [ˈizɪˌgoɪŋ] 隨和的	❀	**careful** [ˈkɛrfəl] 小心的
❀	**kindly** [ˈkaɪndlɪ] 和善的	❀	**creative** [krɪˈetɪv] 有想像力的
❀	**friendly** [ˈfrɛndlɪ] 友善的	❀	**tender** [ˈtɛndə] 溫柔的
❀	**organized** [ˈɔrgənˌaɪzd] 有組織的		
❀	**enthusiastic** [ɪnˌθjuzɪˈæstɪk] 熱心的		
❀	**talkative** [ˈtɔkətɪv] 健談的；多話的		
❀	**confident** [ˈkɑnfədənt] 負責任的		
❀	**responsible** [rɪˈspɑnsəbl] 負責任的		
❀	**thoughtful** [ˈθɔtfəl] 細心的；體貼的；考慮周到的		
❀	**considerate** [kənˈsɪdərɪt] 體貼的；思慮周詳的		
❀	**humorous** [ˈhjumərəs] 幽默的 **with a sense of humor		
❀	**straightforward** [ˌstretˈfɔrwəd] 坦率的		
❀	**energetic** [ˌɛnəˈdʒɛtɪk] 精神飽滿的		
❀	**aggressive** [əˈgrɛsɪv] 侵略的；好鬥的；進取精神的；有幹勁的		
❀	**ambitious** [æmˈbɪʃəs] 有野心的		
❀	**sophisticated** [səˈfɪstɪketɪd] 世故的		
❀	**experienced** [ɪkˈspɪrɪənst] 有經驗的；經驗老道的		
❀	**blissful** [ˈblɪsfəl] 樂而忘憂的;帶來福氣的		
❀	**content** [kənˈtɛnt]、**self-satisfied** [ˈsɛlfˈsætɪsˌfaɪd] 知足的；自滿的		
❀	**patient** [ˈpeʃənt] 有耐心的	❀	**impatient** [ɪmˈpeʃənt]沒耐心的

❀ **extrovert** [`ɛkstrovɝt] 外向的	❀ **introvert** [`ɪntrəˏvɝt] 內向的
❀ **active** [`æktɪv] 主動的	❀ **passive** [`pæsɪv] 被動的
❀ **positive** [`pɑzətɪv] 積極的	❀ **negative** [`nɛgətɪv] 消極的
❀ **optimistic** [ˏɑptə`mɪstɪk] 樂觀的	❀ **pessimistic** [ˏpɛsə`mɪstɪk] 悲觀的
❀ **cautious** [`kɔʃəs] 謹慎的	❀ **serious** [`sɪrɪəs] 嚴肅的
❀ **demure** [dɪ`mjur] 端莊的	❀ **stubborn** [`stʌbən] 頑固的
❀ **dogmatic** [dɔg`mætɪk] 武斷的	❀ **dull** [dʌl] 無聊；乏味的
❀ **disgustful** [dɪs`gʌstfəl] 令人作嘔的	
❀ **blunt** [blʌnt] 遲鈍的；直率的	❀ **candid** [`kændɪd] 公正的
❀ **determined** [dɪ`tɝmɪnd] 果斷的,堅定的	
❀ **bashful** [`bæʃfəl] 羞怯的	❀ **quiet** [`kwaɪət] 沉靜的
❀ **reliable** [rɪ`laɪəbl̩] 守時的	❀ **shy** [ʃaɪ] 害羞的
❀ **sensitive** [`sɛnsətɪv] 敏感的	❀ **sensible** [`sɛnsəbl̩] 察顏觀色的
❀ **charming** [`tʃɑrmɪŋ] 迷人的	❀ **humble** [`hʌmbl̩] 謙虛的
❀ **stay-at-home** [`steəˏhom] 足不出戶的；經常待在家裡的	
❀ **childish** [`tʃaɪldɪʃ]、**childlike**[`tʃaɪldˏlaɪk]孩子氣	
❀ **innocent** [`ɪnəsn̩t] 天真的；單純的；無罪的	
❀ **ingenuous** [ɪnˋdʒɛnjʊəs]、**naïve** [nɑ`iv] 天真無邪的	
❀ **emotional** [ɪ`moʃənl̩] 情緒化的	
❀ **bossy** [`bɑsɪ] 愛指揮他人的；跋扈的；頤指氣使的	
❀ **miserable** [`mɪzərəbl̩] 悽慘的;悲哀的	
❀ **open-minded** [`opən`maɪndɪd] 心胸開朗的	
❀ **narrow-minded** [`næro`maɪndɪd] 心胸狹隘的	
❀ **stingy** [`stɪndʒɪ] 小氣的	❀ **miserly** [`maɪzəlɪ] 吝嗇貪婪的
❀ **greedy** [`gridɪ] 貪婪的	❀ **idiotic** [ɪdɪ`ɑtɪk] 白癡的
❀ **forgetful** [fə`gɛtfəl] 健忘的	❀ **picky** [`pɪkɪ] 挑剔的
❀ **irritable** [`ɪrətəbl̩] 易怒的	❀ **jealous** [`dʒɛləs] 妒忌的
❀ **anxious** [`æŋkʃəs] 焦慮的	❀ **selfish** [`sɛlfɪʃ] 自私的
❀ **sluggish** [`slʌgɪʃ] 懶散的	❀ **arrogant** [`ærəgənt] 自大的

♥愛的筆記貼♥ 以上單字都是對敘述個性的形容詞。同學們學得愈

多，形容人就可以形容的愈貼切。這時也可以想想哪些形容詞是比較適合來形容自己的。哪些形容詞可以用來形容朋友。可以跟朋友一起練習：Are your friends like you? My friends are much like me. We are all sensitive and thoughtful.這樣的句型。也可以問彼此喜歡的明星？為什麼喜歡他？Who is your favorite star? Why do you like him or her? My favorite star is Andy Liu. I think he is charming and humble.

Reading Passage 1

 Maria, 17, young lady from California. Outgoing, always with a sweet smile. Like singing, dancing and parties very much. Just moved in the town for the new semester. Want to make friends who are crazy like me. Send me an E-mail soon via mariaca@ciao.com! Let's go party together!

_____1. What is the main idea of the passage above?

　　(A) A house rental ads.　　　(B) A girl's diary.

　　(C) An invitation to a party.　　(D) A friends matching ads.

_____2. What kind of people might be Maria's friends like?

　　(A) Shy　　(B) Sociable　　(C) Introvert　　(D) Stay-at-home

♥愛的筆記貼♥ 這一篇是一篇短篇的廣告。既然是廣告，就像歌詞一樣往往句子簡短，甚至不成句。解題要看重點訊息。瑪莉亞是個17歲來自加州的女孩。外向，總是有著甜美的笑容。很喜歡唱歌、跳舞、參加聚會。為了新學期剛搬進這鎮上。(來就學的)想要交一些跟我一樣瘋狂的朋友。寄電子郵件給我到mariaca@ciao.com。讓我們一起去舞會。

解答：1.(D)這篇是徵友廣告。　2.(B)瑪莉亞的朋友都是擅於交際的。

Reading Passage 2

Please tell me what I should do now.

Dear Katherine,

I read your column on Glory Times every day and I am your big fan. Your warm ideas always cheer my mind. Actually, there is something that bothers me for quite a long time. My husband works as a cashier. His work is all about money and he loves money very much, especially the coins. His hobby is to collect the coins from different countries all over the world. I wish you won't say "well, not bad. It sounds like a great hobby." as most people react. The annoyance is whatever he collects; he shouldn't put every cent to satisfy with his hobby. And the worst is, with the convenience of the Internet, he started spending every minute reading, posting, and responding on the blogs with those coins fans. Hello! He totally forgets our children and I. I wonder if you have any good ideas to solve this problem. >_< I don't want to fight with a coin psycho anymore. It really drives me crazy!

I am looking forward to your reply.

Faithfully,
Gina

_____1. What seems to be Gina's problem?

(A) Gina misses Katherine too much and wants to see her.

(B) Gina's children don't listen to her anymore.

(C) Gina's husband has a great hobby and makes a great fortune by it.

(D) Gina's husband spends less and less time staying with his families.

_____ 2. According the passage, what might be Katherine's job?

(A) A housewife.　(B) A free lance.　(C) A singer.　(D) A fire fighter.

(　) 3. What do most people do when they heard of Gina's husband's hobby?

(A) They think it is a good hobby. (B) They think it costs a lot of money.

(C) They think he is out of mind. (D) They think it is an unusual hobby.

♥ 愛的筆記貼 ♥

這是一篇讀者寫給專欄作家的信。親愛的凱薩琳，我每天都讀你在榮耀時報上的專欄，而我是你的忠實讀者。你溫暖的主意總是鼓舞我的心。事實上，最近有件事煩擾我好久了。我的丈夫是一個出納員。他的工作都和錢有關而他也很愛錢，尤其是硬幣。他的嗜好就是收集世界各國的錢幣。我希望你不會說『好的，不錯啊！這聽起來像是一個好興趣。』像大部份的人所反應的。惱人的事是不管他收集什麼，他不應該把每一分錢都拿去滿足他的嗜好。最糟的是，隨著網路的便利性，他開始花每一分鐘都在閱讀、張貼，以及回應那些硬幣迷在部落格的文章。拜託！他完全忘記了我們的小孩和我。我在想你會不會有任何的好主意來解決這個問題。我不希望再跟一個硬幣瘋子吵架了。這問題真的把我逼瘋了！我期待你的回應。忠實地，吉娜。

解答：1.(D) 問題是吉娜的丈夫花愈來愈少的時間跟家人相處。

　　　2.(B) 凱薩琳的工作是自由作家。

　　　3.(A) 一般人聽到她丈夫的嗜好都覺得是好的。

◎ 有關 Hobbies 嗜好的補充詞彙 ◎

○ reading books, newspapers, magazines	閱讀書、報紙、雜誌
○ seeing a movie, or watch DVDs at home	看電影，或在家看 DVD
○ listening to some music	聽音樂
○ playing the guitar, piano, violin, or flute	彈吉他、鋼琴、小提琴或長笛
○ playing basketball, baseball, soccer	打籃球、棒球或踢足球
○ taking photos	攝影
○ going swimming, cycling, or hiking	去游泳、騎車、健行
○ surfing the Internet / reading the blogs	瀏覽網頁或看部落格
○ playing online games	玩線上遊戲
○ chatting with people on the Internet chatting with people on the MSN, Yahoo Messenger, or chatroom	在網路上和人們聊天 和人們在 MSN、Yahoo 通訊軟體或聊天室聊
○ going shopping	去購物
○ sketching, drawing and painting	素描、徒手繪、繪畫
○ collecting stamps, cans, coins, or cards	收集郵票、鐵罐、錢幣、或卡片

Vocabulary Review

_____1. Joanna shows her _____ interests in the competition of the higher position.

(A) sociable   (B) active   (C) loyal   (D) reliable

_____2. Nobody likes Harris in the company because he is too _____ and easy to irritate people.   (A) organized   (B) responsible (C) careful   (D) straightforward

_____3. I am really afraid to stay with Sandra in a room. I don't know how to talk to her because she is so _____.

(A) dull   (B) punctual   (C) easygoing   (D) talkative

_____ 4. Don't be so _____. I think you should try to think and act

as an adult.

(A) sluggish   (B) open-minded   (C) candid   (D) childish

_____ 5. My sister is really _____ and she always makes us do everything

for her.   (A) dull   (B) sluggish   (C) bossy   (D) tender

_____ 6. Chuck, remember to arrive on time tomorrow. Mr. Frank is

quite _____. He doesn't like waiting for the late bugs. (A)

open-minded   (B) punctual   (C) responsible   (D) patient

_____ 7. A: Do you know how old Sally is?   B: Why do you ask?

A: Nothing. Her speech and act seem _____. I can't

believe that she is the age showed on the form.

(A) anxious   (B) stingy   (C) jealous   (D) sophisticated

_____ 8. A: Sorry, I am a little _____. Could you say it again for me?

(A) blunt   (B) narrow-minded   (C) candid   (D) ambitious

_____ 9. A: Don't you think your boss is sometimes crazy and irritable?

B: Well, he is kind of _____ but he is creative as a

commercial genius.

(A) sophisticated   (B) emotional   (C) naïve   (D) tender

_____ 10. A: Why did you split up?

B: He is so _____ and wants to save every cent. It's quite

different from my generous values.

(A) blissful   (B) jealous   (C) stingy   (D) punctual

解答：(1) B (2) D (3) A (4) D (5) C (6) B (7) D (8) A (9) B (10) C

Lesson 2 | 外觀與穿著
Appearance and dressing

🎤 Language box 🎺

Focus One

What do you look like? (你長得像什麼樣子？)

How do you look? (你看起來怎樣？)

What does your brother look like? (你哥哥長相是怎麼樣？)

✏ 語言注意面 Language Caution ✏

A: <u>What</u> do you <u>look like</u>? (你看起來像什麼樣子？)

B: I <u>look like</u> a big bear. (我看起來像一隻大熊。)

A: <u>How</u> do I <u>look</u>? (我看起來如何？)

B: You <u>look</u> elegant! (你看起來很優雅。)

A: What do you <u>look at</u>? (你看什麼看？)

B: Nothing. I didn't <u>look at</u> you. (沒事。我不是在看你。)

❤愛的筆記貼❤ 拜網路之賜，現在好多人都透過網路結交新朋友，和以前筆友時代差不多，大家都抱著緊張又好奇的心態，想知道文字背後的那個人究竟長得如何？於是這句話 How do you look?就常發生在網路上的對話中。look 一字動詞就是『看』的意思。但當名詞時，就是指『外貌長相』。要注意的是，how 是問情況，通常回答的是形容詞。例如 How is your father?回答：He is fine.(他很好)。How do you look?就回答：I look short but smart.(我看起來矮但聰明。)fine, short, smart 都是形容詞。如果要問長得像誰？長得像什麼？就可以說 Who do you look like? What do you look like? like 後多接名詞。回答：I look like Arnold Schwarzenegger.I look like the green giant.(我看起來像阿諾

史瓦辛格。我看起來像一個綠巨人。)注意 look 在此的用法為連綴動詞,當做『看起來』的意思。look 後加形容詞,而 look like 後加名詞。問句 how 後面不加 like,問句 what 後面才跟 like。這個和問天氣一樣。例:How is the weather in Canada now?與 What is the weather like in Canada now?兩者問句形式些微不同,但其實意思都在問加拿大的天氣如何?有關 look 的用法,在後面有關動詞的章節會特別為同學說明。

<練習> 有人問你 How do you look?你會怎麼回答呢?以下是一位同學的回答,劃線部份可依標號來找對應的字彙群組,可以幫助你練習講講有關自己的長相敘述喔!

I am underline{average tall}[1]. I have underline{big}[2] eyes, short brows, and a underline{snob}[3] nose. My cheeks are always pink and my face is underline{a little chubby}[4]. I think I am quite underline{normal}[5], and how about you?

1. Height 身高	2. Eyes 眼睛	3. Nose 鼻子	4. Face 臉型	5. Look 長相
☐ tiny	☐ small	☐ normal	☐ chubby	☐ normal
☐ short	☐ big	☐strawberry	☐ small	☐ unusual
☐ average tall	☐ shiny/ bright	☐ aquiline/ hook	☐ big	☐ usual
☐ quite tall	☐ fierce/ sharp	☐ snob	☐ long	☐ so-so
☐ 165 cm tall	☐ deep	☐ small	☐ an oval face	☐ beautiful
	☐charming	☐ big	☐ quite rectangular	☐ stylish
		☐ thin	☐ round	☐handsome
			☐ square	☐ like an alien
			☐triangular	

♥愛的筆記貼♥ 這個練習主要是幫同學們擬一份自我的外觀敘述草稿,例題的內容是:我是一般高。我有大眼睛、短眉毛和一個朝天鼻。我的臉頰總是粉紅色而我的臉有點胖胖的。我覺得我相當地普通,那你呢?同學們可以循劃線部份的數字來找每一欄位中的代換單詞,可以先檢視一下自己懂得外觀單字有哪些?其他的就到 Word Bank 去一解心中疑惑吧!

┤ **Focus Two** ├

What do you like to wear? (你喜歡穿什麼？)

Do you prefer dressing in a casual style or a formal style? (你較喜歡休閒穿著還是正式穿著？)

Do you know the girl standing there with a blonde and curly hair? (你認識站在那有著一頭棕色捲髮的女孩嗎？)

語言注意面 Language Caution

I am with a black and straight hair and a big mouth.

(我有著黑色直髮及大嘴巴。)

I am in a black jacket, a pink shirt, and a miniskirt.

(我穿著黑夾克、粉紅襯衫和迷你裙。)

**with →有著　　in →穿著

♥愛的筆記貼♥　外觀除了我們本身的長相外，也可以從一個人的穿著打扮來敘述這個人。例如這邊主要的練習句：Do you prefer dressing in a casual style or a formal style? 是說一個人平常比較喜歡的穿著形式。dress 當名詞時是洋裝，當動詞時有『打扮穿著』之意。這裡常考的重點是：with 和 in 這兩個介系詞的運用。通常形容我們身上的部份是用 with，講穿著衣物時是用 in。

⊙ **Conversation 1** ⊙

(網友 Kitten 小貓和 Dreamer 夢想家在 MSN 上第一次聊天。)

Dreamer: ^O^ Are you there?	哈囉，你在嗎？
Kitten: Yeah. Do I know you?	是啊。我認識你嗎？
Dreamer: Maybe, maybe not. If you want, you will know me soon.	也許是，也許不是。如果你想你很快就會認識我。

Kitten: Oh, yeah? Sounds interesting. OK, Dreamer. How do you look?	喔，是嗎？聽起來很有趣。好吧，夢想家。你長得如何？
Dreamer: Oh, I see. Shallow.	喔，我知道了。只重視表面的人。
Kitten: Warning! Hey, watch your words. I just wonder how you look. That's all. Is that something embarrassing for you?	警告！嘿，注意你的話。我只是好奇你的長相罷了。這樣而已。難道這對你有什麼難為情的嗎？
Dreamer: Please don't mind. Just kidding. I am much like an alien, so I have to keep my secret.	請別介意。只是開個玩笑。我很像一個外星人所以必需保密。
Kitten: Oh, really? Cold joke. And I am tiny like a kitten. How do you think?	喔，真的嗎？冷笑話。那我就像一隻貓一樣嬌小。你覺得怎麼樣？
Dreamer: This time is true! I am bald with big eyes, and I am so skinny and tiny.	這次是真的！我禿頭有著大眼睛，而且我很皮包骨般的瘦小。
Kitten: Really? Wow, I can't believe I meet my species. I am also bald, skinny and I have a big beer belly. Would you like to have beer with me?	真的？哇！我真不敢相信我遇到了同類。我也是禿頭、皮包骨而且我還有個大脾酒肚。你想要和我一起喝杯啤酒嗎？
Dreamer: *O* Well, so, you're not a chick, pal? I guess I am too drunk tonight.	嗯…好的，這樣，原來你不是個小妞，朋友？我想我今晚真是喝太醉了。

◎ Conversation 2 ◎

(Doris 和 Addie 一起共事了一星期了，情人節快到了，這天中飯時她們一起聊天。)

Doris: Addie, what's your plan for the coming Valentine's Day?

艾迪,情人節快到了你有什麼計劃?

Addie: Well, Doris. I don't have a boyfriend yet. How about you? What present will you give your boyfriend?

是這樣的,朵莉絲。我還沒有男朋友。你呢?你將要送你男朋友什麼禮物?

Doris: I am sorry, and I don't mean it. My boyfriend is quite outgoing and likes being with friends together. I guess we will have a party with our friends again this year.

我很抱歉,我不是故意的。我的男朋友相當外向而且喜歡和朋友在一起。我想我們今年又會和朋友在一起聚會。

Addie: Really? But don't you think the Valentine's Day should be for couples only? I mean you should stay with you two.

真的嗎?但你不覺得情人節應該只是給情人的嗎?我的意思是你們應該兩個人在一起。

Doris: Of course not. That's why I love my boyfriend. I love his personality more than his look.

當然不是囉。這就是為什麼我愛我的男朋友。我愛他的個性甚過於長相。

Addie: Interesting. What does he look like?

有趣。他長得像什麼樣子?

Doris: He is like my polar bear. Actually, he is a dentist with a sweet smile. His job is so stressful, so he always prefers the casual dressing. He has hundreds of Hawaiian shirts.

他很像我的北極熊。事實上,他是一位有著甜美笑容的牙醫。他的工作壓力很大,所以他總是偏好休閒穿著。他有上百件的夏威夷衫。

◎Work Bank◎ 隨時補充一錠,你在會話及閱讀理解必備的單字!	
㉕ **head** [hɛd] 頭	㉕ **forehead** [ˈfɔrˌhɛd] 前額

⊛ **hair** [hɛr] 頭髮	⊛ **face** [fes] 臉
⊛ **eye** [aɪ] 眼睛	⊛ **tear** [tɪr] 眼淚
⊛ **eyebrow** [ˋaɪˏbraʊ] 眉毛	⊛ **eyelid** [ˋaɪˏlɪd] 眼皮；眼瞼
⊛ **eyelash** [ˋaɪˏlæʃ] 眼睫毛	⊛ **eyeball** [ˋaɪˏbɔl] 眼球；眼珠
⊛ **nose** [nos] 鼻子	⊛ **nostril** [ˋnɑstrɪl] 鼻孔
⊛ **snub nose** [snʌb nos] 朝天鼻	⊛ **long nose** [lɔŋ nos] 長鼻子
⊛ **short nose** [ʃɔrt nos] 短鼻子	⊛ **thin nose** [θɪn nos] 瘦鼻子
⊛ **flat nose** [flæt nos] 扁鼻子	⊛ **Grecian nose** [ˋgriʃən nos] 挺直鼻
⊛ **brandy nose** [ˋbrændɪ nos] 白蘭地鼻；酒糟鼻	
⊛ **aquiline nose** [ˋækwəˏlaɪn nos] / **hook nose** [hʊk nos] 鷹勾鼻	
⊛ **strawberry nose** [ˋstrɔbɛrɪ nos] 草莓鼻	
⊛ **temple** [ˋtɛmpl] 太陽穴；鬢角	⊛ **cheek** [tʃik] 臉頰
⊛ **ear** [ɪr] 耳朵	⊛ **wax** [wæks] 耳垢；蠟
⊛ **mouth** [maʊθ] 嘴部	⊛ **lip** [lɪp] 嘴唇
⊛ **tooth** [tuθ] 牙齒	⊛ **tongue** [tʌŋ] 舌頭
⊛ **dimple** [ˋdɪmpl] 酒窩	⊛ **chin** [tʃɪn] 下巴
⊛ **neck** [nɛk] 頸部；脖子	⊛ **shoulder** [ˋʃoldɚ] 肩膀
⊛ **arm** [ɑrm] 手臂	⊛ **elbow** [ˋɛlbo] 手肘
⊛ **collarbone** [ˋkɑlɚˏbon] / **clavicle** [ˋklævɪkl] 鎖骨	
⊛ **wrist** [rɪst] 手腕	⊛ **hand** [hænd] 手
⊛ **finger** [ˋfɪŋgɚ] 手指	⊛ **nail** [nel] 指甲
⊛ **knuckle** [ˋnʌkl] 指關節	⊛ **body** [ˋbɑdɪ] 身體
⊛ **breast** [brɛst] 胸部	⊛ **belly** [ˋbɛlɪ] 肚子
⊛ **waist** [west] 腰部	⊛ **bottom** [ˋbɑtəm] 屁股；底部
⊛ **back** [bæk] 背部	⊛ **leg** [lɛg] 腿部
⊛ **lap** [læp] 膝上；腿上	⊛ **knee** [ni] 膝蓋
⊛ **foot** [fʊt] 腳	⊛ **toe** [to] 腳趾頭
⊛ **bone** [bon] 骨頭	⊛ **skin** [skɪn] 皮膚
⊛ **wrinkle** [ˋrɪŋkl] 皺紋	⊛ **freckle** [ˋfrɛkl] 雀斑
⊛ **double eyelid** [ˋdʌbl ˋaɪˏlɪd] 雙眼皮	
⊛ **beard** [bɪrd] 山羊鬍；大鬍子	⊛ **moustache** [məsˋtæʃ] 八字鬍
⊛ **oval face** [ˋovlˏfes] 鵝蛋臉	⊛ **round face** [raʊnd fes] 圓臉
⊛ **square face** [skwɛr fes] 方臉	⊛ **heart face** [hɜt fes] 心型臉

人我關係	興趣與休閒	生活與工作	文法解析

名 **triangular face** [traɪˋæŋgjələ] 三角臉			
名 **rectangular face** [rɛkˋtæŋgjələ] 方臉			
形 **tall** [tɔl] 高的		形 **average tall** [ˋævərɪdʒ ˌtɔl] 一般高的	
形 **height** [haɪt] 身高		形 **short** [ʃɔrt] 矮的	
形 **big** [bɪg] 大的		形 **fat** [fæt] 胖的	
形 **small** [smɔl] 小的		形 **shiny** [ˋʃaɪnɪ] 發光的；閃耀的	
形 **bright** [braɪt] 明亮的		形 **gleamy** [ˋglimɪ] 發光的；閃耀的	
形 **fierce** [fɪrs] 兇猛的		形 **sharp** [ʃɑrp] 尖銳的；銳利的	
形 **deep** [dip] 深沉的；深邃的		形 **charming** [ˋtʃɑrmɪn] 迷人的	
形 **heavy** [ˋhɛvɪ] 重的；胖的		形 **overweight** [ˋovɚˌwet] 過重的	
形 **slim** [slɪm] 苗條的；瘦的		形 **fit** [fɪt] 身材適中的	
形 **bony** [ˋbonɪ]/ **skinny** [ˋskɪnɪ] 骨瘦如柴的；皮包骨的			
形 **hairy** [ˋhɛrɪ] 多毛的		形 **sluggish** [ˋslʌgɪʃ] 懶散的	
形 **handsome** [ˋhænsəm] 英俊的		形 **beautiful** [ˋbjutəfəl] 美麗的	
形 **elegant** [ˋɛləgənt] 優雅的		形 **chubby** [ˋtʃʌbɪ] 胖胖的；豐腴的	
形 **normal** [ˋnɔrml̩] /**usual** [ˋjuʒʊəl] / **so-so** [so so] 一般的			
形 **stylish** [ˋstaɪlɪʃ] 時髦的			

♥愛的筆記貼♥ 以上單字都是身體的各部份及敘述長相的形容詞。同學們可以配合前面 Focus 1 的部份，再做一次整理，可以試著敘述自己的長相，也可以試著敘述一下家人、朋友的長相喔！

Reading Passage 1

Jeff: Ben, do you prefer the casual wear or the formal wear?

Ben: Well, it depends. Most of time I prefer dressing in the mix style, which means I could wear a formal shirt with a casual blue jeans. You know, people sometimes feel you are too __(1)__ when you dress well __(2)__ a black suit. The fashion masters once suggested that the pink color may soften your image. Anyway, the bright and light colors mostly mean friendly to people. My job is to introduce some good products to my customers and I need to be not only very friendly but persuasive to them. So I am always __(2)__ a __(3)__ shirt with a pair of casual pants. What's about you?

____ (1)	A. chubby	B. crazy	C. serious	D. sluggish
____ (2)	A. with	B. of	C. on	D. in
____ (3)	A. dark	B. bright	C. black	D. long

____ (4)   What is the "mix style"?
          A. A tie with a suit   B. A jacket with a cap
          C. A sneakers with a jeans   D. A shirt with a jeans

____ (5)   Why does Ben like the "mix style"?
          A. He wants to be friendly.   B. He wants to be sharp.
          C. He wants to be serious.   D. He wants to be smart.

♥愛的筆記貼♥ 這是一篇朋友回答穿著喜好的對話。整篇是說Jeff問Ben：你喜歡休閒穿著還是正式的服裝？Ben回答要看情形。大多數時間他都是穿混搭的型式。這指得是他上面穿一件正式的襯衫下面穿一件休閒的牛仔褲。你知道的，當你穿戴整齊穿著黑色西裝時，人們有時候會覺得你太嚴肅。有一次時尚大師們有建議粉紅色可能使你的形象柔軟化。反正就是大部份亮和淡的顏色對人們來說是代表友善的。我的工作是介紹一些好產品給我的顧客，對他們而言，我不只是需要表現得非常友善而且要有說服力。所以我總是穿一件亮色的襯衫配休閒長褲。你呢？ 解答：1.(C)穿黑的帶給人嚴肅的形象。 2.(D) 穿衣服的介系詞用in。 3.(B) 所以他穿亮的帶給人友善的形象。 4.(D)襯衫配牛仔褲是『混搭』型態。 5.(A)他喜歡混搭是因為帶給人友善的形象。

Reading Passage 2 ► This is a critic survey on super stars. Guess who they are talking about.

(這是一份對明星的批評調查。猜猜看他們在討論誰？)

_____ Will Smith 威爾史密斯 ┆ _____ Nicole Kidman 妮可基嫚

_____ Bruce Willis 布魯斯威利 ┆ _____ Renee Zellweger 蕊妮齊薇格

Hint A Well, how to start? I think she is a bit skinny for me. Not everyone can have such a five fingers forehead like hers. She sometimes looks fierce because of her sharp eyes. Do you remember one of her movies which talked about the witch? That is. Her nose is small but sharp, just like a hook. However, many people like her because she has certain bewitchment, you know, sometimes people like half evil and half pure personality. Who knows? Anyway, I pretty like her blonde hair and lips. I think both are sexy.

Hint B She is definitely born to be a comedy star! Look at her cheeks! They make her look so funny but friendly. Come on, I am not teasing her! I wish I have such a charming face like her. The most impressive thing is her weight! It confuses me. How could she lose weight efficiently? I really want to know her ways! She was quite different in Bridget Jones's Diary and Chicago. When I saw Chicago in the movie theater, I couldn't believe she was so slim! She is just like a balloon!

Hint C　Ha, ha. You've tried the wrong person. I didn't like him at all. Don't you think he is much like a sly fox with the small eyes? Well, bald is not the main problem. At least, he is somebody. Well, many people said "bald" means somebody in man's talk. The worst thing is, I don't think people should be a big hero all the time. And he should avoid acting as the way and thinking he is so charming. After all, nobody can stay young forever and times goes by, the hero should be others.

Hint D　He is the best in my heart! I drive Audi because of him. Does it sound silly? I almost spent all my cents! But I really want to be cool like him. He is stylish and charming. I like to listen to his voice and rap songs. I like his oval face with the warm eyes and his smile is just like the sunshine. He is cool but hot inside. And his dark skin makes

♥愛的筆記貼♥

❶提示 A 是位女性，五指寬的高額頭、很瘦、眼神銳利、鼻子尖、金髮，所以是 Nicole。❷提示 B 是位女性，喜劇演員、臉很迷人友善、演過 BJ 單身日記及芝加哥、體重忽胖忽瘦，所以是 Renee。❸提示 C 是位男性，是光頭、英雄主義、不年輕了、給人感覺自己覺得自己很迷人，所以是 Bruce。❹提示 D 是位男性，代言奧迪跑車、很酷、唱饒舌歌、鵝蛋臉、眼神溫暖、陽光般的笑容、外表酷但內心熱情、深顏色的皮膚讓他看起來更酷。所以是 Will。同學都猜對了嗎？

Vocabulary Challenge

_____ 1. Debbie got a pair of _____ as a Christmas present last year.

(A) jacket　(B) necklace　(C) gloves　(D) belt

_____ 2. People sometimes wear _____ to walk in the snow.

(A) slippers　(B) boots　(C) sandals　(D) socks

_____ 3. Rita always attracts people very much because her charming eyes and beautiful _____.

(A) mustache　(B) mascara　(C) nostril　(D) eyelashes

_____ 4. Any _____ dressing is not allowed in our company.

(A) uniform　(B) informal　(C) beautiful　(D) formal

_____ 5. She went to Hawaii for vacation last week, so her skin got _____ recently.

(A) sunscreen　(B) sunburned　(C) sunglasses　(D) sunrise

_____ 6. Ellie, today I'd like to trim my hair a little and _____ with the brown color.

(A) perm　(B) make some layers　(C) shorten　(D) dye

_____7. Frank cherishes each of his hair so much. After all, he is almost _____.

(A) a man　(B) bald　(C) slim　(D) blond

_____ 8. Some people were born to be curly hair, so they want to _____their hair to be straight.

(A) perm　(B) make some layers　(C) shorten　(D) dye

_____ 9. I didn't sleep well recently, so I have some pimples on my _____.

(A) legs (B) forehead (C) eyebrows (D) aquiline

(　　) 10. We used to be required to wear _____ at school, but not anymore at college now.

(A) wigs (B) underwear (C) sportswear (D) uniform

(　　) 11.Sally is the girl _____ a purple dress sitting on the sofa.

(A) with (B) on (C) at (D) in

(　　) 12. You should _____ a jacket when you go out in such a chilly weather.

(A) put on (B) put down (C) take in (D) take off

(　　) 13. _____ such a beautiful heart, she devoted her whole life to help those who need to be taken good care of.

(A) with (B) on (C) at (D) in

(　　) 14. She always wears the t-shirts and the sport shoes for work. Her special taste of _____ was not allowed in her workplace.

(A) food (B) driving (C) painting (D) dressing

(　　) 15. Ayumi is really the most _____ Japanese singer. Her dressing always leads the fashion.

(A) average tall (B) stylish (C) selfish (D) bossy

B (15) D (14) A (13) A (12) D (11)
D (10) B (9) A (8) B (7) D (6)
B (5) B (4) D (3) B (2) C (1) : 解答

Lesson **3** | # 朋友和夢想
Friends and dreams

🎤 Language box 🗨

| **Focus One** |

Who is your best friend? (你最好的朋友是誰？)

What is your best friend like? (你最好的朋友是怎樣的人？)

Are you and your friends alike? (你和你的朋友們相像嗎？)

What do you usually want to do with your friends together? (你通常會想和你的朋友們一起做些什麼事？)

Do you and your friends share the same interests?
(你和你的朋友有共同的興趣嗎？)

Where do you and your friends usually hang out?
(你和朋友通常去哪裡呢？)

How do you keep in touch with your friends?
(你和你的朋友們如何保持連繫呢？)

Have you ever lost contact with your friends?
(你曾經和朋友失去連繫嗎？)

Why do you lose contact with your friends?
(為什麼你會和朋友失去連繫呢？)

✎ 語言注意面 Language Caution ✎

以上問句中有些常用動詞片語需要注意：

○ **hang out** 閒逛。

○ **keep in touch with someone** 和某人保持連繫。

○ **lose contact with someone** 和某人失去連繫。

♥愛的筆記貼♥ 繼前兩課我們練習過個性及外表的說法後，在這課我們來講講我們身旁周遭的人。練習敘述自己的朋友及自己和朋友之間的關係。Are you and your friends alike?意義和 Are you similar to your friends?相似。是問你和你的朋友相像嗎？alike 是形容詞表示『相像』之意。

Focus Two

What kind of things will make you feel angry with your friends? (什麼樣的事會讓你對你的朋友們生氣？)

What will you do when you have something unpleasant with your friends?
(你和朋友有不開心的事時通常你會做什麼？)

What do your friends usually do when you get in trouble? (你的朋友在你遇到困難或麻煩時通常會怎麼做？)

What do you do when your friends feel unhappy?
(當你的朋友感到不開心時你會怎麼做？)

語言注意面 Language Caution

以上問句中有些常用動詞片語需要注意：

○ **make you feel+形容詞** 讓你感到…。

○ **get in trouble** 遇上問題或麻煩。

♥愛的筆記貼♥ make 這個字本身有許多意思，在此處是使役動詞的用法，意思是『使、讓』。使役動詞後接動詞原形。feel『感覺』後直接加形容詞，如果是 feel like 連用，『感覺像…』，後面就要加名詞。例如：Your words make me feel warm. / Your words make me feel like having the hot chocolate in winter. 你的話語使我感到溫暖。／你的話語使我感到像是在冬天喝上一杯熱巧克力。

⊘ Conversation 1 ⊘

(Raymond 老師和學生 Tim。)

Mr. Raymond: Tim, are you interested in English songs?

提姆,你對英文歌曲有興趣嗎?

Tim: Sure, and why do you ask? What's new?

當然啦!怎麼問這個問題?有什麼新鮮事嗎?

Mr. Raymond: There is going to be an English karaoke competition next month. I wonder whether you want to join it.

下個月將會有一場英語卡拉 OK 比賽。我想知道你想不想參加。

Tim: Sounds interesting. Would you give me some advice on the selection of the song? And what should I notice?

聽起來很有趣。你會給我一些建議來選歌嗎?我還要注意哪些事情?

Mr. Raymond: Wow, take it easy! I think the first thing is to find your partner. Do you have friends who can sing with you?

哇,放輕鬆點!我覺得第一件要做的事是找好你的伙伴。你有朋友可以和你合唱的嗎?

Tim: May I sing with my friends together?

我可以和我的朋友合唱嗎?

Mr. Raymond: Sure. I think it's much better than singing alone. You know, you can encourage each other just like what you do every day.

當然,我覺得比自己獨自唱要好許多。你知道的,你們可以互相鼓勵就像你們每天在一起那樣。

Tim: Joanna might be the one. She sings well and likes English so much. I like her soft voice and we

瓊安娜也許可以。她唱得很好而且很喜歡英文。我喜歡她柔和的嗓音,而且

share the same interests.	我們有共同的興趣。

⊘ Conversation 2 ⊘

(Dreamer 和 Kitten 在網上用 MSN 聊天。)

Dreamer: Hey, Buddy. I need your suggestion.	嘿！老弟！我需要你的建議。
Kitten: Are they trying to attack us?	他們準備要攻打我們了嗎？
Dreamer: Who? Are you talking to me?	誰？你在跟我說話嗎？
Kitten: I mean the aliens, haha. OK, what's your problem? Try me if you trust me.	我是指外星人，哈哈！好啦，你的問題是什麼？如果你相信我的話你可以試試看。
Dreamer: Come on. Be serious. Haven't you ever had such a problem before?	拜託。正經一點啦！你難道以前沒有過這樣的問題嗎？
Kitten: U__U Go ahead, hurry!	(想睡的符號)有話直說，快點！
Dreamer: I just got the wedding invitation card from my old friend, but I don't know what to do.	我剛剛接到來自我老朋友的囍帖，但我不知道怎麼。
Kitten: Are you out of mind? Of course you should go and aim at the single girls in the party. Oh, I see. You don't want to spend a lot. Stingy.	你瘋了嗎？當然你應該去而且要瞄準婚宴中的單身女郎啦！喔，我懂了。你不想花很多錢。小氣鬼。
Dreamer: Hey, it's NOT what you think. He used to be my good friend in high school, but we didn't keep in touch for ages!	喂，不是你想得那樣！他過去在高中時曾是我的好朋友，但是我們已經好久沒有連絡了。

Kitten: Well, what an OLD friend he was. Are you sure you still know him right now?

是喔，他還真是一個『老』朋友。你確定你現在還認識他嗎？

Dreamer: Right, brilliant. Thank you for your advice.

對，好聰明。謝謝你的建議！

◎Work Bank◎ 隨時補充一錠，你在會話及閱讀理解必備的單字！	
⑧ **friend** [frɛnd] 朋友	⑪ **friend or foe** 是敵是友
⑧ **foe** [fo] 敵人	⑧ **enemy** [ˋɛnəmɪ] 敵人
⑧ **companion** [kəmˋpænjən]伙伴	⑧ **mate** [met] 同伴
⑧ **schoolmate** [ˋskuⱢˏmet] 同學	⑧ **roommate** [ˋrumˏmet] 室友
⑧ **classmate** [ˋklæsˏmet] 同學	⑧ **partner** [ˋpartnɚ] 伙伴；拍檔
⑧ **crony** [ˋkronɪ] 密友；好朋友	⑧ **associate** [əˋsoʃɪɪt] 伙伴；同事
⑧ **colleague** [ˋkɑlig] 同事	⑧ **buddy** [ˋbʌdɪ] 朋友；老兄
⑧ **pal** [pæl] 好友；伙伴	⑧ **chum** [tʃʌm] 好友；室友
⑧ **confidant /confidante** [ˋkɑnfəˏdænt] 知己、知己女友	
⑱ **close** [klos] 親密的；靠近的	⑱ **best** [bɛst] 最好的
⑱⑧ **inseparable** [ɪnˋsɛpərəbⱢ] 不可分開的；形影不離的朋友	
⑩ **misunderstand**[ˋmɪsʌndɚˋstænd] 誤會；曲解	
⑧ **friendship** [ˋfrɛndʃɪp] 友誼	⑧ **fellowship** [ˋfɛloˏʃɪp]伙伴關係
⑧ **relationship** [rɪˋleʃənˏʃɪp] 親屬關係；戀愛關係	
⑧ **hardship** [ˋhardʃɪp] 艱難	⑧ **intimate** [ˋɪntəmɪt]密友；好朋友
⑧ **brotherhood** [ˋbrʌðɚˏhud] 兄弟情；手足情	
⑧ **sisterhood** [ˋsɪstɚhud] 姐妹情	⑪ **have something in common**
⑱ **solid** [ˋsɑlɪd] 堅固的	⑱ **firm** [fɝm] 堅定的
⑱ **strong** [strɔŋ] 堅固的	⑱ **weak** [wik] 脆弱的
⑱ **fragile** [ˋfrɛdʒəl] 脆弱的	⑪ **tear apart** 撕裂；分裂；折磨
⑩ **share** [ʃɛr] 分享	⑩ **esteem** [ɪsˋtim] 尊重
⑩ **respect** [rɪˋspɛkt] 尊敬	⑩ **support** [səˋport] 支持
⑩ **fight** [faɪt] 打鬥；爭吵	⑩ **quarrel** [ˋkwɔrəl] 吵鬧；爭吵
⑩ **encourage** [ɪnˋkɝɪdʒ] 鼓勵	⑩**communicate** [kəˋmjunəˏket]溝通

♥愛的筆記貼♥ 以上都是和友情相關的單字，同學們可以配合前面的會話焦點句型來試著回答，也可以複習一下前兩課形容個性和外表的單字喔！

Readin g Passage 1

Dear Bill,

How are you? It has been a long time since we met on the graduation of the Glen Ridge high school. I hope that you still remember me, your best friend in high-school age. Guess what? I am getting married on June 16th that means next month. I can't wait to share my happiness with you, my best friend. Do you remember that we ever made a wish about the future? My dream comes ture! I have become a robot designer, and the beauty I am going to marry is a programer, too. We work in the same company. How about you, my friend? Hope your dreams also come true and will you come to my wedding? Sure you will. See you soon.

The big day for Frank & Marissa!

Monday, June 16th, 2008, at 103, Palace Avenue

Please attend our cocktail party. Let's share the happiest moment.

Please respond the invitation before June 1st.

Sincerely yours,

Frank

_____ (1)　　What is the purpose of the letter?
　　　　　　(A) A graduation invitation　　(B) A baby shower invitation.
　　　　　　(C) An open day invitation.　　(D) A wedding invitation

_____ (2)　　What might Frank call Marissa?
　　　　　　(A) My old friend.　　　　　　(B) My robot.
　　　　　　(C) My fiancée.　　　　　　　(D) My mom.

_____ (3)　　When did Frank write the letter?
　　　　　　(A) March　　(B) May　　(C) June　　(D) September

_____ (4)　　Why did Frank say that his dream has already come true?
　　　　　　(A) He got married.　　　　　　(B) His wife is a beauty.
　　　　　　(C) He found his friend.　　　　(D) He is satisfied with his job.

_____ (5)　　What should Bill do if he wants to attend the party?
　　　　　　(A) Reply it before June 1st.　　(B) Attend the party on June 1st.
　　　　　　(C) Call the palace.　　　　　　(D) Call the high school.

♥愛的筆記貼♥　這是一篇婚禮邀請函，內容是由一位好久不見的朋友法蘭克 Frank 寫給比爾 Bill 的。親愛的比爾你好嗎？自從我們上次在格蘭瑞治高中畢業典禮上見面已經好久了。我希望你仍然記得我，這個高中時期的好友。你猜怎麼著？我在 6 月 16 日，也就是下個月要結婚了。我等不及要和你，我最好的朋友來分享我的喜悅。你還記得我們曾經許過一個關於未來的願望嗎？我的夢想成真了！我已經成為一個機器人設計師，而將要和我結婚的美人也是個軟體設計師。我們在同一家公司工作。我的好友，你呢？希望你的夢想也都能實現。你會來參加我的婚禮嗎？你當然會囉！希望很快就能見到你。這個屬於法蘭克和瑪莉莎的大日子在 2008 年 6 月 16 日星期一，皇宮大道 103 號。請來參加我們的雞尾酒派對。讓我們分享這幸福開心的一刻。請在 6 月 1 日前回覆這邀請函。誠摯的法蘭克。解答：1.(D)這封信的主要目的是婚禮邀請。　2.(C)法蘭克可能會叫瑪莉莎為未婚妻。　3.(B)因為信中寫到 6 月 16 日也就是下個月婚禮要舉行，所以寫信月份應該在五月。　4.(D)法蘭克說他的夢想已達成的後句接說他已經變成了機器人設計師，是他的工作。所以是他很滿意他的工作。　5.(A)信的內容最後一句說如果 Bill 想參加請在 6 月 1 日前回覆。respond 等於 reply，回覆的意思。

Reading Passage 2

Friend or Foe, it's up to you.

Today, the two interviewers will share their experience with you about how they saved their friendship. What will you do if you were they?

Sally from California. There is no pure friendship between men and women. But a fool as I, I almost broke my best friend, Daniel's heart. He always trusts me and supports me.

Every time when I was sad or want to talk to someone, he was always there for me. Until that day, he told me that he didn't only want to be my friend. I totally understood what he said but felt so surprised, so I said "are you out of mind?" He kept silence for a while and then I knew I made a big mistake. We didn't get in touch for few weeks. He didn't answer my calls and had a long vacation far away from our town. I was so regretful and I missed him so much. The feeling almost tore me apart. Finally, I asked his best friend Tom to take me to where he was. Believe it or not, when the first time I saw him again, I burst out tearing and no more words to describe my love. Now we are still good friends, and we may be a couple in the near future. We just need some time.

Barbara from New Jersey. Well, I know I am quite straightforward but really kind in my mind. However, I just lost my best friend Lucy last month. She got married and trusted her husband more than I.

Come on, we have been friends for 10 years. 10 years, my god. Why would she rather trust the man that she just met last year? I always respect her and believe her smart and kind mind until she wanted to open a bookshop in such a hard time. Now she hangs up my calls, and removed me from her friends list on MSN. My e-mails  are always returned. I am also heart-broken, ten years, you know. How could she treat me like this? That's great. Now I have another **foe** in the world. My gosh! Aren't my enemies many enough?

_____ (1)　What was the problem between Daniel and Sally?
(A) Sally is selfish.　　(B) Daniel is blunt.
(C) They don't know each other well.
(D) Daniel might misunderstand Sally's response.

_____ (2)　What did Sally do to solve the problem?
(A) Make other friends instead.　(B) Be honest to herself.
(C) Her tears explained it all.　(D) She yelled at Daniel.

_____ (3)　What might be the main reason to break the friendship between Barbara and Lucy?
(A) Barbara's personality.　(B) Lucy's misunderstanding.
(C) Lucy's husband.　　(D) All of the above.

____ (4)　　According to the passage, how many ways did Barbara try
　　　　to contact her friend, Lucy?
　　　　(A) 10　(B) 2　(C) 3　(D) 4

____ (5)　　What does the word "foe" mean in the reading?
　　　　(A) A friend.　　　　　　　　(B) A roommate.
　　　　(C) An enemy.　　　　　　　(D) A husband.

❤愛的筆記貼❤ 這篇閱讀的標題是 Friend or foe，不是朋友就是敵人。內容是：今天有兩位受訪者要和大家分享他們如何挽救友誼的經驗。如果你是他們你會怎麼做呢？❶來自加州的莎莉。在男女之間根本沒有純友誼。但是像我這樣的傻子，我差點就傷害了我最好的朋友，丹尼爾的心。他總是相信我而且支持我。每次當我難過或想要和誰說說話，他都在我身邊。直到那一天，他告訴我他不只想做我的朋友。我完全了解他在說什麼但是覺得很驚訝，所以我說『你瘋了嗎？』他沉默了一會兒然後我就知道我犯了個大錯。我們彼此沒有連絡上好幾個星期。他沒有接我的電話而且離開我們鎮上很遠的地方去渡假。我很後悔而且非常想念他。這種感覺幾乎把我快撕裂了。最後，我要求他的摯友湯姆帶我到他去的地方。信不信由你，當我再次看到他的第一眼，我突然大哭，不需要任何話語來描述我對他的感情了。現在我們仍然是好朋友，而我們在不久的將來可能會成為情侶。我們只是需要一些時間。❷來自紐澤西的芭芭拉。好吧，我知道我個性上相當直率，但是我心裡真的很和善。然而，我剛剛才在上個月失去了我最好的朋友露西。她結婚了而且相信她的老公更甚過於我。得了吧，我們都已經當朋友十年了。為什麼她寧願相信這個她在去年才遇到的男人呢？我總是尊重她而且相信她聰明及和善的心，直到她想要在這樣一個艱困的時期開一家書店。現在，她掛斷我的電話，而且把我從 MSN 通訊軟體的好友名單刪除。我寄給她的電子郵件總是被退信。我也很傷心，十年了，你知道的。她怎麼能這樣對我？真是太好了，現在我在世上又多了一個敵人。我的老天啊！我的敵人還不夠多嗎？解答：1.(D)丹尼爾和莎莉之間的問題是丹尼爾可能誤解了莎莉的意思。 2.(C) 莎莉的眼淚就說明了一切，解決了問題。 3.(D)以上皆是，因為芭芭拉提到影響她和露西友誼的可能是她的個性太直，露西相信她的老公甚過於她，還有她反對露西開店的事是因為現在景氣不好，這都是可能造成露西不高興的理由。 4.(C)芭芭拉提到她電話被掛斷、MSN 好友名單被刪、電子郵件被退，所以是三種連絡方式。 5.(C)依照整篇文章及最後一句，foe 就是 enemy 敵人。

Vocabulary Challenge

_____ 1. I can't believe the friendship between you and I is so _____.
Why don't you trust me at all?

    (A) firm   (B) fragile   (C) strong   (D) solid

_____ 2. We _____ every customer's suggestion and your kindly
help make us better!

    (A) forget   (B) remind   (C) notice   (D) respect

_____ 3. Roxanne needs our _____. We certainly will stand on her side.

    (A) debate   (B) arguement   (C) support   (D) hardship

_____ 4. No matter what I want to do, my friends always _____ me.

    (A) encourage   (B) lie on   (C) betray   (D) leave

_____ 5. She is my best friend because she is a nice and _____ girl.

    (A) bewitched   (B) reliable   (C) unfair   (D) stingy

_____ 6. I made him mad because I _____ his birthday party and
went to see the movie with my girl friend.

    (A) remembered   (B) forgot   (C) went   (D) held

_____7. I can't stand Jeff anymore because of his _____ temper. He
always gets angry easily.

    (A) happy   (B) calm   (C) impatient   (D) patient

_____ 8. A: How did you keep contact when you study abroad?
B: I responded her e-mails every day and _____ with her on
Yahoo messenger.

    (A) cheated   (B) chatted   (C) cheesed   (D) cheapened

_____ 9. The true friends are the people who give you a hand when you are in the _____.

(A) relationship　(B) friendship　(C) scholarship　(D) hardship

(　　) 10. Peter is my best friend because we _____. Both of we enjoy watching and discussing the soccer games.

　　(A) get in touch　　　　　(B) tear ourselves apart

　　(C) have different interests　(D) have something in common

(　　) 11.Good skills on _____ will help you have good relation.

　　(A) irritation　　　(B) location

　　(C) communication　(D) substitution

(　　) 12. A: Do you know anything about Hanna?　B: No, _____.

　　(A) I remember her.　　(B) I lost contact with her, either.

　　(C) I sometimes talk with her.　(D) she mentioned you.

(　　) 13. A: Is Ben your boyfriend?　B: No, he is just a ____ friend.

　　(A) close　(B) open　(C) near　(D) like

(　　) 14. You may trust Kenny. He is a _____ man.

　　(A) sly　(B) tricky　(C) sincere　(D) childish

(　　) 15. The best medicine to cure the crack in your friendship is to listen to your friends' words carefully and you'll <u>realize</u> their heart.

　　(A) misunderstand　(B) understand　　(C) fool　(D) support

Lesson 4 喜歡和不喜歡
Like and dislike

🗣 Language box 🗣

Focus One

Do you like apple? (你喜歡蘋果嗎？)

Do you like cake or pie? (你喜歡蛋糕還是派？)

Which one do you like? Cake or pie?

(你喜歡哪一個？蛋糕還是派呢？

I like cake most./ I most like cake. (我最喜歡蛋糕。)

Cake is my favorite. (蛋糕是我的最愛。)

My favorite dessert is cake. (我最喜歡的甜點是蛋糕。)

Why don't you like pie? (為什麼你不喜歡派？)

I dislike the taste of pie. (我不喜歡派的味道。)

I like grape more than any other fruit.

(我喜歡葡萄甚過於任何水果。)

Why do you like grape most? (你為什麼最喜歡葡萄呢？)

✎ 語言注意面 Language Caution ✎

<u>What fruit</u> do you like? 你喜歡什麼水果？

Do you like <u>apple</u>? 你喜歡蘋果嗎？

<u>Don't</u> you <u>like</u> apple? / <u>Do</u> you <u>dislike</u> apple?

你不喜歡蘋果嗎？你討厭蘋果嗎？

- 44 -

♥愛的筆記貼♥ ❶在喜歡和不喜歡這一類型的問句裡，只要是問到類別，例如 Do you like apple?這樣的問句，問句中的名詞屬於類別，講得是蘋果這種水果，而不是單顆的水果時，我們不用 the 這個冠詞來指定限定哪一顆，所以不加 the。What fruit do you like?也是一樣。除非是拿著一顆蘋果問朋友：Do you like the apple?你喜歡這顆蘋果嗎？這時候我們就要加 the 來指定限定描述的範圍。 ❷Do you like…?表示你喜歡某事物嗎？like 後接的是事物的名詞。這是預設立場的問法。就是預設你喜歡什麼，更具體的問法，適合已經知道對方喜好時，節省時間的問法。因為回答通常是一翻兩瞪眼，不是 yes 就是 no。What fruit do you like? 這樣的問題就相對的開放許多。 ❸dislike 和 like 一樣是動詞，表示『不喜歡；討厭』，是否定的用法，所以通常我們會用否定問句直接問 Don't you like…? 或是說 Do you dislike…?用 dislike 來問『討厭』的語意，後面這句就不能用否定了，不然就會變成 Don't you dislike…? 你不討厭蘋果嗎？在語意上有負負得正的效果。 ❹回答我最喜歡某事物，可以用 I like …most. "most"這個字在這裡是當做副詞用，副詞通常用來修飾動詞，可以放在句末加強語氣，也可以放在動詞的前後，例：I most like…。

│ **Focus Two** ├

Do you like to go bungee jumping? (你喜歡高空彈跳嗎？)
Would you like to try bungee jumping?
(你想要嘗試高空彈跳嗎？)
Do you prefer having the drink before or after the meal? (你喜歡飲料在餐前上還是餐後上？)

♥愛的筆記貼♥ ❶ Do you like to+原形動詞和 Do you like+Ving 動名詞的問句，在語意上有些差別。like to do 是指沒有做過或不確定有沒有做過這件事時用，而 like+Ving 動名詞是說已經有了這件事的體驗。例：Do you like to go bungee jumping?是不確定或對方沒有跳過高空彈跳，這時問他喜歡高空彈跳這項運動嗎？Do you like going bungee jumping?對有高空彈跳運動經驗的人，可以用這句來問他喜歡與否。

❷很多同學會將 Do you like to 和 Would you like to 兩種問句形式搞混。would like to 指得是『想要』之意。Would you like to dance with me? 其實就是 Do you want to dance with me?『你想要和我跳舞嗎?』之意。

◎ Conversation 1 ◎

(Tim 約 Joanna 吃中飯,和她討論英語卡拉 OK 比賽的事。)

Tim: Hey, Joanna. Sorry, I am a little late.	嘿!瓊安娜。抱歉,我有點晚到。
Joanna: Well, Mr. Big is always late.	好吧,大人物總是會遲些。
Tim: All right, my fault. It's my treat, OK?	好吧,我的錯。這次我請,好嗎?
Joanna: Wow, that's unbelievable. I must be a lucky star. Ok, what's the point?	哇!太不可思議了。我一定是個幸運星。好啦,到底是要談什麼事?
Tim: Which one do you prefer? Steak or seafood meal? Let's order our lunch first, and then I will tell you specifically.	你喜歡哪一套餐?牛排還是海鮮餐?我們先點午餐,然後我再詳細地告訴你。
Joanna: Do they have anything with tuna? I don't touch meat.	他們有鮪魚做的餐點嗎?我不碰紅肉類。
Tim: Are you a vegetarian? I don't know you dislike meat.	你是素食者嗎?我不知道你討厭肉類。
Joanna: Yeah, I hate the smell and the taste of meat. It makes me ill. I may even feel dizzy sometimes. Could you do that for me?	是啊,我討厭紅肉聞起來和嘗起來的味道。它讓我不舒服。我有時甚至會昏眩。你可以配合我一下嗎?
Tim: Sure. How about Modanna?	好。瑪丹娜怎麼樣?

Joanna: What are you talking about? Is that a name for the set?

你在說什麼啊？那是套餐的名字嗎？

Tim: Do you like her songs? We may choose one of her songs to join the English karaoke competition together. By the way, I heard that she is also a vegetarian.

你喜歡她的歌嗎？我們也許可以選一首她的歌一起去參加英語卡拉 OK 比賽。順便一提，我聽說她也是素食者。

⊘ Conversation 2 ⊘

(Phoebe 和 Rudolph 在餐廳見面，這是他們第一次約會。)

Phoebe: Do you like keeping pet? I mean dog or cat, not fish, spider or parrot.

你喜歡養寵物嗎？我指得是狗或貓，而不是魚蜘蛛或鸚鵡。

Rudolph: Sorry, no offense. What's the matter of fish?

抱歉，無意冒犯。魚又怎麼了？

Phoebe: Nothing, I just think they are cold-blooded, and people who love them may dislike my Labrador as well.

沒事，我只是認為他們是冷血的，喜愛他們的人也許也不會喜歡我的拉不拉多犬。

Rudolph: No worries. I love dogs as well as my fish. I don't keep any dogs because the rental rules of my apartment. What's his name?

不用擔心。我愛狗和愛我的魚一樣。我不養狗是因為我住的公寓有租房規定。他的名字叫什麼？

Phoebe: Dora, the gift from god.

朵拉，名字的涵義是上帝恩賜的禮物。

Rudolph: Oh, a young lady with a wonderful name.

喔，一位有著美好名字的年輕女士。

Phoebe: Dora and I are allergic to the smell of cigarette.

朵拉和我對煙味過敏。

Rudolph: I don't like smoking, either. There is no smoking in both my office and my apartment, but I like to have some wine after my work. | 我也不喜歡抽煙。在我的辦公室和我的住處都禁煙，但我喜歡在工作後喝點小酒。

Phoebe: Which bar do you usually go? | 你通常都去哪個酒吧？

Rudolph: No, you misunderstood. I don't drink a lot like a heavy drunker. I like to have some wine alone at home. I have a wine collection. Would you like to try some? | 不，妳誤會了。我沒有像一個酒鬼般喝得那樣多。我喜歡在家獨自喝點酒。我收藏了一些酒。你想不想來嘗嘗？

Phoebe: Sure, why not? You dislike smoking, drunker, but love dogs. Qualified. Dora and I would like to visit you someday. | 好啊，有何不可？你不喜歡抽煙、酗酒者，但是愛狗。符合資格。朵拉和我會想要找天去拜訪你。

◇Work Bank◇ 隨時補充一錠，你在會話及閱讀理解必備的單字！

- 働 **like** [laɪk] 喜歡
- 働 **prefer** [prɪˋfɝ] 較喜歡；寧願
- 形 **favorite** [ˋfevərɪt] 最愛
- 名 **fruit** [frut] 水果
- 名 **cake** [kek] 蛋糕
- 名 **sweet** [swit] 甜的；甜點；糖
- 名 **bagel** [ˋbegəl] 培果；硬麵包圈
- 名 **toast** [tost] 吐司；烤麵包片
- 名 **taco** [ˋtako] 玉米餅；玉米捲
- 名 **submarine hamburger** [ˋsʌbməˏrin] [ˋhæmbɝɡɚ] 潛艇堡
- 名 **croissant** [krwɑˋsɑn] 可頌；牛角麵包
- 名 **dumpling** [ˋdʌmplɪŋ] 餃子
- 名 **fast food** [fæst] [fud] 速食

- 働 **dislike** [dɪsˋlaɪk] 不喜歡
- 名 **preference** [ˋprɛfərəns]
- 名 **dessert** [dɪˋzɝt] 甜點
- 名 **food** [fud] 食物
- 名 **donut** [ˋdoˏnʌt] 甜甜圈
- 名 **pie** [paɪ] 派；餡餅
- 名 **bread** [brɛd] 麵包
- 名 **sandwich** [ˋsændwɪtʃ] 三明治
- 名 **pita** [ˋpitə] 圓麵餅；口袋餅
- 名 **sugar** [ˋʃugɚ] 糖
- 名 **steamed bun** [stimd] [bʌn] 包子
- 名 **instant noodle** [ˋɪnstənt] [ˋnudl] 泡麵

㊷ **h<u>a</u>mb<u>urger</u>** [ˈhæmbɝˈgə] 漢堡	㊷ **fr<u>ie</u>s** [ˈfraɪz] 炸薯條
㊷ **fr<u>ie</u>d ch<u>icke</u>n** [fraɪd] [ˈtʃɪkɪn] 炸雞	㊷ **fr<u>ie</u>d r<u>ice</u>** [fraɪd] [raɪs] 炒飯
㊷ **sn<u>ack</u>** [snæk] 點心	㊷ **<u>ice</u> cr<u>ea</u>m** [aɪs] [krim] 冰淇淋
㊷ **v<u>a</u>n<u>illa</u>** [vəˈnɪlə] 香草	㊷ **s<u>u</u>nd<u>ae</u>** [ˈsʌnde] 聖代冰淇淋
㊷ **str<u>a</u>wb<u>erry</u>** [ˈstrɔbɛrɪ] 草莓	㊷ **m<u>a</u>ngo** [ˈmæŋgo] 芒果
㊷ **d<u>u</u>r<u>ia</u>n** [ˈdurɪən] 榴槤	㊷ **st<u>a</u>rfr<u>uit</u>** [ˈstɑrˌfrut] 楊桃
㊷ **<u>apple</u>** [ˈæpl̩] 蘋果	㊷ **ch<u>erry</u>** [ˈtʃɛrɪ] 櫻桃
㊷ **dr<u>a</u>gon fr<u>uit</u>** [ˈdrægən] [frut] / **p<u>i</u>t<u>aya</u>** [pɪˈtɑjɑ] 火龍果	
㊷ **b<u>a</u>n<u>a</u>n<u>a</u>** [bəˈnænə] 香蕉	㊷ **p<u>i</u>n<u>eapple</u>** [ˈpaɪnˌæpl̩] 鳳梨
㊷ **w<u>a</u>t<u>e</u>rm<u>e</u>l<u>o</u>n** [wɑtɚˌmɛlən] 西瓜	㊷ **m<u>e</u>l<u>o</u>n** [ˈmɛlən] 哈蜜瓜；甜瓜
㊷ **<u>o</u>r<u>a</u>nge** [ˈɔrɪndʒ] 柳橙	㊷ **t<u>a</u>ng<u>e</u>r<u>i</u>ne** [ˈtændʒəˌrin] 橘子
㊷ **l<u>e</u>m<u>o</u>n** [ˈlɛmən] 檸檬	㊷ **p<u>o</u>m<u>e</u>l<u>o</u>** [ˈpɑməlo] 柚子
㊷ **l<u>i</u>me** [laɪm] 萊姆	㊷ **p<u>ea</u>ch** [pitʃ] 桃子
㊷ **g<u>ua</u>v<u>a</u>** [ˈgwɑvə] 芭樂	㊷ **k<u>i</u>w<u>i</u> fr<u>uit</u>** [ˈkiwɪ] [frut] 奇異果
㊷ **gr<u>a</u>pe** [grep] 葡萄	㊷ **gr<u>a</u>pefr<u>uit</u>** [ˈgrepˌfrut] 葡萄柚
㊷ **l<u>itchi</u>** [ˈlitʃi] 荔枝	㊷ **s<u>u</u>g<u>e</u>rc<u>a</u>ne** [ˈʃugɚˌken] 甘蔗
㊷ **p<u>e</u>rs<u>i</u>mm<u>o</u>n** [pɚˈsɪmən] 柿子	㊷ **pl<u>u</u>m** [plʌm] 李子
㊷ **p<u>a</u>ss<u>io</u>n fr<u>uit</u>** [ˈpæʃən] [frut] 百香果	㊷**wax <u>apple</u>** [wæks] [ˈæpl̩] 蓮霧
㊷ **d<u>a</u>te** [det] 棗子	㊷ **p<u>a</u>p<u>aya</u>** [pəˈpaiə] 木瓜
㊷ **m<u>e</u>n<u>u</u>** [ˈmɛnju] 菜單	㊷ **m<u>ea</u>l** [mil] 餐食
㊷ **d<u>i</u>sh** [dɪʃ] 一盤；一道菜	㊷ **fl<u>a</u>v<u>or</u>** [ˈflevə] 味道；風味
㊷ **s<u>au</u>ce** [sɔs] 醬汁	㊷ **dr<u>e</u>ss<u>i</u>ng** [ˈdrɛsɪŋ] 填料；沙拉調料
㊷ **s<u>ea</u>s<u>o</u>n<u>i</u>ng** [ˈsiznɪŋ] 調味料	㊷ **t<u>o</u>pp<u>i</u>ng** [ˈtɑpɪŋ] 填料
㊷ **m<u>ai</u>n c<u>our</u>se** [men] [kors] 主菜	㊷ **<u>e</u>ntr<u>ée</u>** [ˈɑntre] 主菜
㊷ **<u>appe</u>t<u>izer</u>** [ˈæpəˌtaɪzə] 開胃菜	㊷ **s<u>i</u>de d<u>i</u>sh** [saɪd] [dɪʃ] 小菜
㊷ **s<u>a</u>l<u>a</u>d** [ˈsæləd] 沙拉	㊷ **s<u>ou</u>p** [sup] 湯
㊷ **n<u>oo</u>dle** [ˈnudl̩] 麵條	㊷ **r<u>i</u>ce** [raɪs] 米飯
㊷ **l<u>asagna</u>** [ləˈzɑnjə] 千層麵	㊷ **p<u>a</u>st<u>a</u>** [ˈpɑstə] 通心粉
㊷ **sp<u>aghetti</u>** [spəˈgɛtɪ] 義大利麵	㊷ **p<u>i</u>zz<u>a</u>** [ˈpitsə] 比薩
㊷ **b<u>e</u>v<u>e</u>r<u>a</u>ge** [ˈbɛvərɪdʒ] 飲料	㊷ **dr<u>i</u>nk** [drɪŋk] 飲料
㊷ **j<u>ui</u>ce** [dʒus] 果汁	㊷ **sm<u>oo</u>th<u>ie</u>** [ˈsmuðɪ] 濃果汁；冰沙
㊷ **C<u>o</u>ke** [kok] 可樂	㊷ **s<u>o</u>d<u>a</u>** [ˈsodə] 汽水
㊷ **m<u>i</u>lk** [mɪlk] 牛奶	㊷ **soy m<u>i</u>lk** [sɔɪ] [mɪlk] 豆漿
㊷ **c<u>offee</u>** [ˈkɔfɪ] 咖啡	㊷ **tea** [ti] 茶

- 名 **ginger beer** [ˈdʒɪndʒɚ] 薑汁汽水
- 名 **milkshake** [ˌmɪlkˈʃek] 奶昔
- 名 **alcohol** [ˈælkəˌhɔl] 含酒精飲料
- 名 **liquor** [ˈlɪkɚ] 酒；烈酒
- 名 **beer** [bɪr] 啤酒
- 名 **whiskey** [ˈhwɪskɪ] 威士忌酒
- 名 **brandy** [ˈbrændɪ] 白蘭地酒
- 名 **gin** [dʒɪn] 琴酒
- 名 **light beer** [laɪt] [bɪr] 淡啤酒
- 名 **tequila** [təˈkilə] 龍舌蘭酒
- 名 **beef** [bif] 牛肉
- 名 **pork** [pork] 豬肉
- 名 **turkey** [ˈtɝkɪ] 火雞；火雞肉
- 名 **rib** [rɪb] 肋排；排骨
- 名 **fish** [fɪʃ] 魚；魚肉
- 名 **salmon** [ˈsæmən] 鮭魚
- 名 **seafood** [ˈsiˌfud] 海鮮
- 名 **shrimp** [ʃrɪmp] 蝦
- 名 **clam** [klæm] 蛤蜊
- 名 **clam chowder** [klæm] [ˈtʃaʊdɚ] 蛤蜊濃湯
- 名 **corn chowder** [kɔrn] [ˈtʃaʊdɚ] 玉米濃湯
- 名 **vegetable** [ˈvɛdʒətəbl] 蔬菜
- 名 **garlic** [ˈgɑrlɪk] 大蒜
- 名 **onion** [ˈʌnjən] 洋蔥
- 名 **spring onion** [sprɪŋ] [ˈʌnjən] 青蔥
- 名 **cabbage** [ˈkæbɪdʒ] 甘藍；包心菜
- 名 **mushroom** [ˈmʌʃrʊm] 蘑菇
- 名 **bean** [bin] 豆子
- 名 **carrot** [ˈkærət] 紅蘿蔔
- 名 **spinach** [ˈspɪnɪtʃ] 菠菜
- 名 **pepper** [ˈpɛpɚ] 胡椒粉
- 名 **mayonnaise** [ˌmeəˈnez] 美乃茲
- 名 **yoghurt** [ˈjogɚt] 優酪

- 名 **root beer** [rut] [bɪr] 沙士
- 名 **hot chocolate** [hɑt] [ˈtʃɑkəlɪt] 熱可可
- 名 **soft drink** [sɔft] [drɪŋk] 無酒精飲料
- 名 **cocktail** [ˈkɑkˌtel] 雞尾酒；調酒
- 名 **wine** [waɪn] 葡萄酒；酒
- 名 **cream liquor** [krim] [ˈlɪkɚ] 奶酒
- 名 **rum** [rʌm] 蘭姆酒；烈酒
- 名 **draft beer** [dræft] [bɪr] 生啤酒
- 名 **dark beer** [dɑrk] [bɪr] 黑啤酒
- 名 **meat** [mit] 肉類
- 名 **steak** [stek] 牛排；肉排
- 名 **chicken** [ˈtʃɪkɪn] 雞肉
- 名 **ham** [hæm] 火腿
- 名 **lamb** [læm] 羊肉
- 名 **cod** [kɑd] 鱈魚
- 名 **tuna** [ˈtunə] 鮪魚
- 名 **crab** [kræb] 蟹肉；螃蟹
- 名 **lobster** [ˈlɑbstɚ] 大龍蝦
- 名 **oyster** [ˈɔɪstɚ] 牡蠣；蠔
- 名 **vegetarian** [ˌvɛdʒəˈtɛrɪən] 素食者
- 名 **tomato** [təˈmeto] 番茄
- 名 **potato** [pəˈteto] 洋芋；馬鈴薯
- 名 **egg plant** [ɛg] [plænt] 茄子
- 名 **Chinese cabbage** 大白菜
- 名 **ginger** [ˈdʒɪndʒɚ] 薑
- 名 **pea** [pi] 豌豆
- 名 **turnip** [ˈtɝnɪp] 蕪菁；白蘿蔔
- 名 **lettuce** [ˈlɛtɪs] 萵苣；美生菜
- 名 **curry** [ˈkɝɪ] 咖哩
- 名 **Thousand Island** 千島醬
- 名 **Caesar sauce** [ˈsizɚ] [sɔs] 凱薩醬

[名] **Japanese sauce** 和風醬
[名] **ketchup** [ˋkɛtʃəp]
[名] **chili sauce** [ˋtʃɪlɪ] [sɔs] 辣醬
[名] **butter** [ˋbʌtɚ] 奶油
[名] **jam** [dʒæm] 果醬
[名] **peanut butter** 花生醬
[名] **cheese spread** [tʃiz] [sprɛd]起司抹醬
[名] **cream** [krim] 鮮奶油
[名] **whipping cream** 打發奶油
[名] **double cream** 濃奶油
[名] **salt** [sɔlt] 鹽
[名] **soy sauce** [sɔɪ] [sɔs] 醬油
[名] **vinegar** [ˋvɪnɪgɚ] 醋
[名] **wine vinegar** 酒醋
[名] **spice** [spaɪs] 香辛料
[名] **herb** [h”b] 香草；草本植物
[形] **sweet** [swit] 甜的
[形] **sour** [ˋsaʊr] 酸的
[形] **bitter** [ˋbɪtɚ] 苦的
[形] **hot** [hɑt] 辣的

♥愛的筆記貼♥ 以上幫同學統整了食材和水果類必備單字，如果遇到敘述自己喜歡吃什麼的問題，都可以運用以上字彙配合本章的重點句型來練習對話。這些生活單字，有些並不常在課本上學到，但對於即將出國遊學、留學、旅遊、打工，要在外國生活一段時間的同學，都非常的有用，所以盡量收錄在此章，希望能幫助到同學在國外一切生活順利喔！如果在餐廳打工遇到講英語的外國人，也可以用這些單字來介紹說明菜肴及口味，加強自己的口語表達能力。

Readin g Passage 1

HAPPY HOURS CAFÉ

Customer Feedback Analysis

The following charts are the result of a survey on the customers' favorite visit time and the satisfaction about the menu.

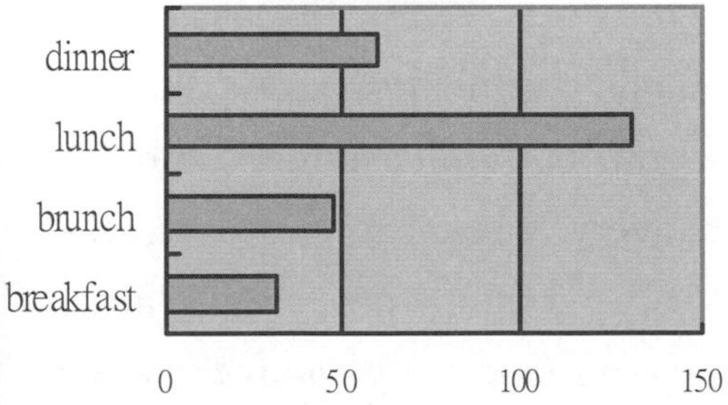

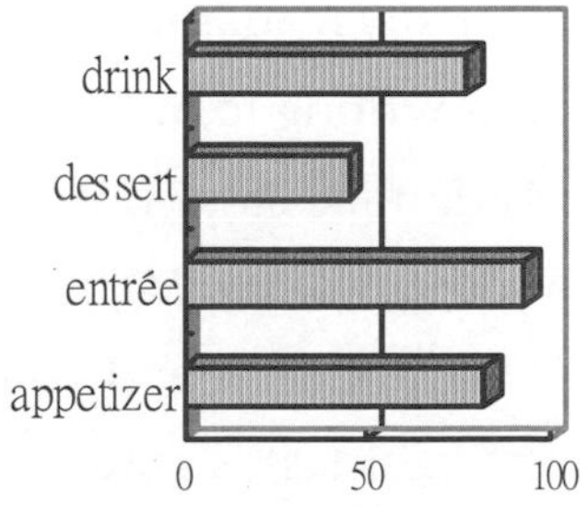

_____ (1)　What time do most customers like to visit?
　　　　　(A) breakfast　　(B) brunch　　(C) lunch　　(D) dinner
_____ (2)　What part of the menu do most customers support?
　　　　　(A) Appetizer　　(B) Entrée　　(C) Dessert　　(D) Drink
_____ (3)　What part of the menu should be improved?
　　　　　(A) Appetizer　　(B) Entrée　　(C) Dessert　　(D) Drink
_____ (4)　If the the shop owner wants to shorten the open hours,
　　　　　what will be the best open-hour session?
　　　　　(A) 6 a.m. to 10 p.m.　　　　(B) 11 a.m. to 9 p.m.
　　　　　(C) 6 a.m. to 10 a.m.　　　　(D) 6 p.m. to 10 p.m.

♥愛的筆記貼♥　這是一份餐廳的顧客回函報告分析結果。這兩張圖表是顧客最愛造訪的時間，以及顧客對於菜單的滿意度。左圖中由下往上可以看到早餐 breakfast、早午餐 brunch、午餐 lunch、晚餐 dinner，最多人的時段是午餐及晚餐。右圖中由下往上是開胃菜 appetizer、主菜 entrée、甜點 dessert 以及飲料 drink。從右圖中可以看到顧客最支持的是主菜和開胃菜，最需要改進的是甜點部份。**解答：1.(C)最多顧客喜歡造訪的時段是午餐時段。 2.(B)在菜單上顧客最支持的部份是主菜。 3.(C)菜單上最需要被改進的是甜點。 4.(B)如果老板想要縮短營業時間，最好的開店時段應為中午 11 點至晚上 9 點，也就是做午、晚餐時段就好。**

Reading Passage 2

Dear sir / madam,

I am writing to make comments on your food service.

My families and I used to be your faithful customers, and we almost visited *Happy Hours* every weekend. However, we found the taste and your service is getting worse since March. The beef tasted rotten, and it even made my nephews sick for weeks. Unfortunately, it's not the only case. Not only us but also the neighbors all consider the cakes you offered as the out-of-date problem. The cream tasted sour and hard. We are curious about the reason of your careless. Since *Happy Hours* was ever our best choice to enjoy our family day, we think that it would be better to let you know our feelings. Hope you will respect our feedback, and improve your service as soon as possible. We will be glad to see your great improvement, or we are afraid that you may lose the support in our community.

Thank you for your attention.

Faithfully,

James

16th May

_____ (1) What's the main idea of the letter?
(A) Apology   (B) Advertisement
(C) Complaint   (D) Invitation

_____ (2) What is Happy Hours?
(A) A travel agency.   (B) A bakery.
(C) A real estate.   (D) A restaurant.

_____ (3) According to the letter, what happened to Happy Hours?
(A) The food is not fresh.   (B) The service is bad.
(C) The neighbors hate them.
(D) They make a lot of noise.

_____ (4) How long does the problem last so far?
(A) A couple weeks.   (B) About half a year.
(C) Just few days.   (D) Two months.

_____ (5) What do James and his family want Happy Hours do?

(A) Reply the letter.　　　(B) Close the shop.
(C) Do some changes.　　　(D) Cut down the price.

♥愛的筆記貼♥ 這篇閱讀是一封信件，內容為：先生或女士好，我寫信是為了要給你們一些有關餐飲服務的意見。我的家人們和我過去都是你們忠實的客戶，我們幾乎每個週末都去快樂時光用餐。然而我們發現餐點的味道和你們的服務從三月以來都愈來愈糟。牛肉嘗起來是腐壞的，而且甚至讓我的姪子們病了好幾個星期。不幸的，這還不是唯一發生的事。(不是偶發事件)不只我們還有鄰居們都認為你供應的蛋糕是過期的問題。鮮奶油吃起來有酸味而且硬掉了。我們對你這樣漫不經心的理由感到好奇。因為快樂時光曾經是我們家族聚會的首選，我們應該要讓你們了解一下我們的感受。希望你們會尊重我們的意見回覆，並且盡快改善你們的服務。我們很樂意看見你們的改善，否則我們恐怕你將會失去我們社區裡的支持。謝謝你的注意。忠實的詹姆士，五月 16 日。
解答：1.(C)這封信主要是一封顧客抱怨信函。 2.(D)根據信的內容所言，快樂時光是一家餐廳。 3.(A)根據這封信，快樂時光發生了食物不新鮮的問題。4.(D)這個問題從三月持續到詹姆士寫信這天是五月，所以是兩個月。 5.(C)詹姆士和他的家人希望快樂時光能夠做些改變。

Vocabulary Challenge

_____ 1. Jessica prefers the Garden Salad only, because she is a _____.

(A) sugar lover (B) vegetarian　(C) couch potato　(D) big fan

_____ 2. A: What _____ do you offer?

B: We have some alcohol and soft drinks.

(A) beverages　(B) food　(C) snacks　(D) desserts

_____ 3. We need some _____ to make the omelet(歐姆蛋).

(A) tomatos　(B) potatoes　(C) juices　(D) soy milks

_____ 4. Please pass me the white _____. I like to add some flavor in

my soup. (A) paper　(B) pager　(C) piper　(D) pepper

_____ 5. She _____ some peanut butter on a piece of toast.

　　(A) threw　(B) filled　(C) spread　(D) poured

_____ 6. Kathy is allergic to the shrimps, fish, and crabs, so she

　　dislikes the _____.

　　(A) seafood　(B) vegetable　(C) beverages　(D) fruit

_____7. The _____ is a kind of fruit. Both of its peel and fruit are

　　yellow. It tastes a little salty and sweet. It's good for your

　　throat. Most of all, you may make a wish because of its shape.

　　(A) litchi　(B) passion fruit　(C) star fruit　(D) wax apple

_____ 8. It would be better to understand what one's _____ is

　　before we choose the present.

　　(A) favorite　(B) sweets　(C) birthday　(D) expired date

_____ 9. Sam prefers _____ a pet more than having a family. He

　　thinks it makes life simpler.

　　(A) feeding　(B) offering　(C) keeping　(D) serving

(　) 10. When I do what I _____ to do, I will feel so painful.

　　(A) like　　(B) dislike　　(C) enjoy　　(D) am willing

B (10) C (9) A (8) C (7) A (6)

解答 : (1) B (2) A (3) B (4) D (5) C

Lesson 5　成長和成家
Milestone and Marriage

🎤 Language box 🎙

| Focus One |

How old are you? (你幾歲了？)

When is your birthday? (你生日幾號？)

When did you have your first car? (你何時擁有第一台車？)

When did you have your driver's license? (你何時領駕照？)

What's your education background? (你教育背景是什麼？)

What degree do you have? (你擁有什麼學位？)

What certificate do you have? (你擁有什麼證照？)

What's your major at college? (你在大學的主修是？)

You got a bachelor's degree in accounting at college, didn't you? (你在大學得到的是會計系學士學位，是嗎？)

What's your first job? (你第一份工作是什麼？)

Have you ever worked in a big company before?
(你以前曾經在大公司工作過嗎？)

♥愛的筆記貼♥　本課是人我關係的最後一課，特別統整了對人生各階段的一些常用問句，不管是在日常生活聊天，英檢或移民的口試，或者是工作面試時，都是必會的問句，每個同學也可以在心裡整理一下自己的答案，看看英文要怎麼說。除了最基本的 What, When, How 問句以外，像附加問句的問法也是很常見的，例：You got a bachelor's degree in accounting at college, didn't you? 造附加問句有三個注意點,以逗點來分前後句:(1) 注意前句的主詞是第幾人稱,選擇適當的代名詞,因為後句(附加問句)一定用代名詞。(2)依前句主要動詞的時態決定後句(附加問句)的助動詞。(3)前句是肯定,後句就是否定;前句是否定,後句就是肯定句。例:Nancy and her young brother went to the zoo, didn't they? Nancy and her young brother 是複數要選代名詞 they 他們。主要動詞 went 是過去式,造問句要用助動詞 did。前句是肯定,所以附加問句用否定,所以附加問句是 didn't they。意思是南西和他的弟弟去了動物園,是嗎?要回答附加問句的時候,要以前句主要句子為準來回應。例:Yes, they did. 是,他們去動物園了。若主要句子是否定句,例:Mr. Lin didn't come this morning, did he? 林先生今早沒來,不是嗎?回答若是對,他沒來,就答 No, he didn't. 否定句的回答比較容易混淆,同學只要抓準了回答時,『對就對到底,錯就錯到底』的準則。Yes, he did./ No, he didn't. 語意以 yes/ no 後面的回答為準。例如這句因應否定句的回答為 No, he didn't.就是『是的,他沒來』的意思,重點在 he didn't 他沒來。

<附加問句練習> 試著依以下問句,造附加問句,然後和你的朋友做問答練習:

1. You remember Linda, _____?

2. Linda is your cousin, _____?

3. Linda won the first price of the lottery, _____?

4. Linda and her husband moved to Canada, _____?

5. Their parents don't agree with it, _____?

6. They have lost contact for three years, _____?

♥愛的筆記貼♥ ❶你認識琳達,是嗎?答案是:do you? ❷琳達是你的表姐,是嗎?答案是:isn't she? ❸琳達中了樂透頭彩,是嗎?答案是:didn't she? ❹琳達和她的老公已搬到了加拿大,是嗎?答案是:didn't they? ❺他們的父母親不同意這樣(指搬到加拿大這事),不是嗎?答案是:do they? ❻他們已經失去連繫三年了,是嗎?答案是:haven't they? have 在此句後面接的是 lost 的過去分詞,所以 have 是助動詞,have+過去分詞是現在完成式,問句直接用助動詞 have 來造句。

| 人我關係 | 興趣與休閒 | 生活與工作 | 文法解析 |

Focus Two

Are you engaged? (你訂婚了嗎？)

Are you married? (你結婚了嗎？)

Did you get married? (你結過婚了嗎？)

How long have you been married? (你們結婚多久了？)

How many children do you have? (你有幾個小孩？)

Do you have your own family yet? (你成家了嗎？)

Why do they want to divorce? (他們為什麼要離婚？)

✗ 語言注意面 Language Caution ✗

A: Are you married?　B: No, not yet. I am single.

(A: 你結婚了嗎？　B:不，還沒。我單身。)

**Did you get married?–你結婚了嗎？你結過婚了嗎？

**The couple is getting married.–這對情侶將要結婚了。

♥**愛的筆記貼**♥通常我們問一個人結婚了沒？會用 Are you married?問未婚或已婚的狀態。有些人會回答 single，但可能的狀況有很多，也許是結過婚又離婚了(divorce)，有的人是因為一些事件失去了另一半，也是結過婚但另一半不在了，鰥夫叫 wifeless man 或 widower，寡婦叫做 widow。所以當然要學 Did you get married?你結過婚了嗎？這種句型來了解清楚了。婚姻生活(marriage)通常要公證辦婚禮以後才算數，證婚或婚禮算是一個人生的里程碑，跨過才算，所以問結過婚了沒要用過去式。

⊗ **Conversation 1** ⊗

(主管 Truman 和應徵者 Roy 進行面試。)

Truman: Have a seat, Roy. I am Truman, the manager of R & D department.

請坐，洛伊。我是楚門，研究開發部經理。

Roy: Nice to meet you.

很高興見到你。

Truman: My secretary told me that you also graduated from my college. What degree did you get?

我的秘書告訴我你也是和我同一個大學畢業的。你拿的是什麼學位？

Roy: Master of science, from the Electronic Engineering department.

工學碩士，電子工程系。

Truman: Good. Do you have any working experience related to the R & D?

很好。你有沒有研發相關的工作經驗？

Roy: I used to work in Kenny Brothers' company, and I did many great proposals on the tableware.

我過去曾在肯尼兄弟公司做事，我在餐具方面有很好的提案。

Truman: Yes, that's famous in their chain stores. However, our works are mainly about applying the chips to develop some useful gadgets. How do you think?

是，那在他們連鎖店很有名。然而，我們的工作主要是有關應用晶片來開發一些有用的小器具。你覺得如何？

Roy: Great, that will meet my interests and profession more. Actually, most of the items that I have dealt with are quite successful so far. I just mentioned the top one on my list. I have won the top R&D staff price for three years.

太好了，那將會比較符合我的興趣及專長。事實上，大部份我經手的項目到目前為止都相當的成功。我剛剛只是提到了我清單上表現最佳的一個。我已經贏得最佳研發員工獎三年了。

Truman: Really? That's great. So, do you have your family yet?

真的？那太好了。這樣，你有自己的家庭了嗎？

Roy: Yes, I'm married and just have a baby this year. A girl, so adorable.

是的，我結婚了而且今年才剛有了小嬰兒。一個女

孩,很可愛。

Truman: I also have a daughter, Fiona. Indeed, I know what you meant. Fathers always treasure their daughters like pearls.

我也有個女兒叫做費歐娜。的確,我了解你說的。爸爸總是把他們的女兒當做珍珠一般寵愛。

Roy: Right, and she's worth my effort doing everything to give her a better life.

對啊,而且她值得我努力為她做所有事來得到更好的生活。

Truman: Young man, you'll be a good father.

年輕人,你會是一個好爸爸的。

♥愛的筆記貼♥ 這是一篇面試時常遇到的狀況,婚姻及家庭狀況的對話內容其實常常會出現在面試題目裡,因為都會影響一個人在工作上的表現,所以同學在準備面試英文前,應該也要想到一些基本的對應以及個人的狀況是否適合這份工作等問題,這都會影響到面試的成功與否。一般常加班、工時較長、常出差、工作時間地點不定的工作,會比較希望用單身人士。一般比較重視機密、忠誠度及工作穩定性的工作,會比較需要已婚人士。以上提到的 R & D 就是 Research and Development 研究及發展部門的簡稱,是常見的名稱要記起來喔!

◎ Conversation 2 ◎

(記者 Suzanna 訪問一位歌星 Christine。)

Suzanna: Welcome to Suzanna's studio. We are so happy with Christine today!

歡迎來到蘇珊娜播音室。今天我們很開心請到克莉絲汀跟我們一起。

Christine: Hi, haha, yes, it's me, Christine.

嗨!哈哈,對,是我,克莉絲汀。

Suzanna: Why was it so long that we didn't hear anything about you? I thought you suddenly disappeared or were kidnapped by the aliens!

為什麼我們這麼久都沒有聽到關於妳的任何消息?我以為你突然消失了或者是被外星人綁架

Where have you been?	了！你到底去哪了呢？
Christine: Kind of! I was kidnapped by my babies!	有點算是吧！我被我的小孩綁架了。
Suzanna: Yeah, where did you hide? Why didn't the paparazzi find you? That's amazing.	對，你藏哪裡去了？為什麼狗仔隊沒有找妳呢？真是神奇。
Christine: Actually, they're really something in my life after joining in the American Idol.	事實上，在我參加美國偶像後，影響我最大的就是我的孩子們。
Suzanna: Yes, you said twins, right? They must be much more important than the competition.	是，你說是雙胞胎，對嗎？他們一定是比這場比賽還來得重要許多。
Christine: Certainly. They're just like angels. When I was so depressed, they suddenly came to save me from the mess. I mean, a loss may turn out to be a gain.	確實是。他們就像天使一樣。當我那麼沮喪時，他們突然就把我從一團糟中拯救出來。我的意思是，塞翁失馬焉知非福。
Suzanna: That's right. Christine, your fans may want to know what happened after your failure in the game.	對。克莉絲汀，你的歌迷朋友也許想要知道關於妳在比賽失敗後究竟發生了什麼事。
Christine: Ok, it's still really hard for me to tell. Standing on the stage to sing for millions of people is never an easy thing for me. The competition means a lot to me so far.	好，對我來說還是很難講出來。站在舞台上為數百萬人唱歌，對我來說從來不是件容易的事。到目前為止，這比賽對我來說意義還是很重大。
Suzanna: What happened to you then?	然後發生了什麼事？
Christine: I was so frustrated and even tried to kill myself. Stanley and I moved to Las Vegas. We	我很挫折，甚至想自殺。史丹利和我搬到拉斯維加斯。我們發現我懷孕

found that I got pregnant, so we had the shotgun wedding.

Suzanna: In the sin city?

Christine: Haha. I know your point. Everything was too hasty for me to worry, but thanks god, all the things are just in god's hands. I did learn to be stronger like a mom, and I got the chance to sing for my fans again. Hope you will love me more.

Suzanna: Sure we will!

了，所以我們就奉子成婚了。

在這罪惡之都？

哈哈！我知道你的意思。所有事都太倉促以致於我根本來不及操心，但是感謝上帝，所有事都像是由上帝安排好的。我的確學著像一個母親一樣更加堅強，而且我再次得到了再為我的歌迷們唱歌的機會。希望你們會更愛我。

我們當然會囉！

♥愛的筆記貼♥ 每個人在人生中都會有人生的里程碑 milestone，也就是一些事件，讓自己印象深刻。跨過了，就學會成長，還沒跨過，就在心裡，慢慢沉澱。這是一篇明星接受訪問的對話，同學們可以學到表達自己人生過程的一些說法，也可以注意一下時下流行的事件像 American Idol 美國偶像是全美流行的選秀節目。會話中提到了 Las Vegas 拉斯維加斯是著名的賭城，也有 Sin City 萬惡之都的封號。In god's hand 指得是一切由上天安排。

⊘Work Bank⊘ 隨時補充一錠，你在會話及閱讀理解必備的單字！

图 **milestone** 里程碑；人生階段		图 **infancy** [ˈɪnfənsɪ] 嬰兒期	
图**adolescence** [ˌædlˈɛsns]青少年期		图**maturity** [məˈtʃurətɪ] 成人期	
图 **old age** [old][edʒ] 老年期		图 **birth** [bɝθ] 出生；誕生	
图 **death** [dɛθ] 死亡		图 **disease** [dɪˈziz] 疾病	
图働 **date** [det] 約會		图 **blind date** [blaɪnd] [det] 相親	
图 **love affair** [lʌv] [əˈfɛr] 戀情；外遇		图**split up** [splɪt] [ʌp] 分手	
圈 **married** [ˈmærɪd] 已婚的		圈 **engaged** [ɪnˈgedʒd] 訂婚的	
圈 **divorced** [dəˈvɔrst] 離婚的		圈 **widowered** [ˈwɪdəwəd] 喪妻的	

[形] **widowed** [ˋwɪdod] 喪夫的 [形] **pregnant** [ˋprɛgnənt] 懷孕的
[名] **engagement** [ɪnˋgedʒmənt] 訂婚 [名] **marriage** [ˋmærɪdʒ] 婚姻
[名] **sudden marriage** [ˋsʌdn̩] [ˋmærɪdʒ] 閃電結婚
[名] **hasty marriage** [ˋhestɪ] [ˋmærɪdʒ] 草率；匆忙成婚
[名] **shotgun wedding** [ˋʃɑtˏgʌn] [ˋwɛdɪŋ] 奉子成婚
[名] **arranged marriage** [əˋrendʒd] [ˋmærɪdʒ] 婚禮籌辦
[動] **two-time** [ˋtuˏtaɪm]劈腿
[名] **two-timer** [ˋtuˏtaɪmɚ]劈腿、對愛情不忠的人
[片] **sit on the fence + Ving** 劈腿；腳踏兩條船(坐在圍欄上的人)
[名] **turning point** [ˋtɝnɪŋ] [pɔɪnt]轉戾點 [名]**climax** [ˋklaɪmæks]高潮；高峰
[名] **fame** [fem] 名聲 [名] **honor** [ˋɑnɚ] 榮耀
first day at school 第一天上學 **get the driver's license** 拿到駕照
have the first baby 有了第一個小孩 [名] **first time** 第一次
travel around the world 環遊世界 **achieve one's goal** 達成目標
meet one's Mr. Right 遇到適合的對象
one's dreams come true 某人的美夢成真
one's big day 某人的重要日子 [名]**award-winner** [əˋwɔrdˏwɪnɚ]獲獎人
[名] **education** [ˏɛdʒʊˋkeʃən] 教育 [名] **career** [kəˋrɪr] 職業；職涯
[名] **license** [ˋlaɪsn̩s] 執照 [名] **certificate** [sɚˋtɪfəkɪt] 執照；證書
[名] **experience** [ɪkˋspɪrɪəns] 經驗 [名] **event** [ɪˋvɛnt] 事件；活動
[名] **celebration** [ˏsɛləˋbreʃən]慶祝 [名]**graduation**[ˏgrædʒʊˋeʃən]畢業典禮
[名]**anniversary** [ˏænəˋvɝsərɪ]紀念日 [名] **farewell** [ˋfɛrˋwɛl] 歡送會
[名] **retirement** [rɪˋtaɪrmənt]退休 [名] **menopause**[ˋmɛnəˏpɔz]更年期
[名] **baby shower** 新生兒送禮會[名]**bachelor party** 婚前告別單身漢聚會
[名]**bride shower** 新娘告別單身聚會 [名]**ceremony** [ˋsɛrəˏmonɪ]儀式；典禮
[名] **belief** [bɪˋlif] 信仰 [形] **baptized** [bæpˋtaɪzd] 受洗的
[名] **Christian** [ˋkrɪstʃən]基督教徒 [名] **Catholic** [ˋkæθlɪk] 天主教徒
[名] **Buddhist** [ˋbudɪst] 佛教徒 [名] **Muslim** [ˋmʌzlim] 回教徒
[名] **funeral** [ˋfjunərəl] 喪禮 [名] **shock** [ʃɑk] 衝擊；震撼
[名] **hardship** [ˋhɑrdʃɪp] 艱難；困苦 [名] **frustration** [ˏfrʌsˋtreʃən] 挫折
[名] **difficulty** [ˋdɪfəˏkʌltɪ] 困難；難題 [名] **obstacle** [ˋɑbstəkl̩] 障礙
[名] **crisis** [ˋkraɪsɪs] 危機 [名] **challenge** [ˋtʃælɪndʒ] 挑戰
[名] **accident** [ˋæksədənt] 意外 [名] **disaster** [dɪˋzæstɚ] 災難；不幸

- ⊛ **war** [wɔr] 戰爭
- ⊛ **tsunami** [tsuˋnɑmɪ] 海嘯
- ⊛ **tornado** [tɔrˋnedo] 龍捲風
- ⊛ **contagious disease** [kənˋtedʒəs] [dɪˋziz] 傳染病
- **commit a crime** [kəˋmɪt] [ə] [kraɪm] 犯罪
- ⊛⊛**murder** [ˋmɝdɚ] 謀殺
- **kill oneself** 自殺
- ⊛ **fortune** [ˋfɔrtʃən] 財富；好運
- ⊛ **wealth** [wɛlθ] 財富
- **have mental problem** [ˋmɛntl̩] [ˋprɑbləm] 有心理問題
- ⊛ **unforgettable** [ˌʌnfɚˋgɛtəbl̩] 難忘的
- ⊛ **incredible** [ɪnˋkrɛdəbl̩] 不可置信的
- ⊛ **unbelievable** [ˌʌnbɪˋlivəbl̩] 令人不可置信的
- ⊛ **unacceptable** [ˌʌnəkˋsɛptəbl̩] 難以接受的

- ⊛ **earthquakes** [ˋɝθ͵kwek] 地震
- ⊛ **hurricane** [ˋhɝɪ͵ken] 颶風
- ⊛ **horror attack** 恐怖攻擊
- ⊛⊛ **suicide** [ˋsuə͵saɪd] 自殺
- ⊛ **a sudden death** 猝死
- ⊛ **health** [hɛlθ] 健康
- **stressful** [ˋstrɛsfəl] 壓力大的

♥愛的筆記貼♥ 人生幾何，以上都是和人生經歷相關的單字，同學們學習單字時，也可以回憶一下到目前為止，你覺得最有自信的那一刻是什麼時候呢？最自豪的時光和自己最糟糕的時光，可以運用這裡所學的單字，敘述看看。不管各式英檢，對於政治、種族以及宗教這些比較敏感的話題是比較少碰觸的，一個公正的考試必需要避免因內容而引起的誤會與影響，所以通常這類的單字比較少考，但因為是生活中常用的單字，屬於歐美人士的常識，所以也是必學的喔！

Reading Passage

Memo

Date:　June 21st, 2007

Subject:　Hamilton's Harvest Farewell and Thanks

From:　Mike Raymond

Some of you may be aware that my retirement has been approved, and it is going to be effective on 29th, next Friday. This is bittersweet for me as I have enjoyed working with you all on the great manufacture team.

35 years here in such a vibrant company are never long for me. The big day that we produced the first bottle of HH lemon bubble juice was especially unforgettable for me. Some of the unique highlights that I'm pleased to take part in and those creative commercials and great success on the market share all make me feel so proud with you together. Certainly, none of the above would have been possible without your efforts. I'd like to thank you all for your support in achieving all the "missions impossible". I will miss working for the company.

Rudy Williams is going to be the successor to my position. All the documents and proposals will be taken over by her from next Monday. Hope you all give her kindly assistance as how you support me.

I wish you all will be successful and happy in your career and family. See you on my farewell party on Thursday. My secretary Linda will inform all of you via your e-mails.

_____ (1)　What is the main idea of the memo?
　　　　(A) Someone wants to say goodbye to the colleagues.
　　　　(B) Celebrate one's promotion.
　　　　(C) Someone wants to apply for the retirement.
　　　　(D) Someone transfers to other department.

_____ (2)　When will be the last day for Mike at work?
　　　　(A) One week later.　　　　(B) 8 days later.
　　　　(C) Next month.　　　　　(D) Today.

_____ (3)　What kind of company does Mike work for?
　　　　(A) An import firm.　　　　(B) A publisher.
　　　　(C) A beverages factory.　　(D) A food processor.

_____ (4)　Who will continue Mike's works in the company?
　　　　(A) Mr. Raymond　　　　(B) Ms William
　　　　(C) Linda　　　　　　　(D) Mike, himself.

_____ (5)　What product did impress Mike in his career?
　　　　(A) A kind of bottle.　　　(B) A commercial.
　　　　(C) The stocks of HH.　　(D) A kind of drink.

♥愛的筆記貼♥　這是一篇備忘錄。發文時間是 2007 年 6 月 21 日。主旨是漢米頓的收穫公司的歡送會及感謝。發文者是麥克雷蒙。你們有些人可能已經知道我的退休案已被批准，而此案將在 29 日也就是下星期五生效。這對我來說是既甜又苦的尤其是很喜歡跟你們這麼棒的製造團隊在一起工作。在這麼有活力的公司工作了 35 年對我來說一點也不算久。我們製作出第一瓶檸檬汽泡果汁那個大日子對我來說永難忘懷。我很榮幸可以參與很多重要事件中的部份，那些有想像力的廣告及在市場佔有率上的大成功都讓我為能和你們一起工作而感到驕傲。如果沒有你們的努力以上所講到的事一定無法完成。我想要再次感謝你們完成了這麼多『不可能的任務』。我會很想念在公司工作的日子。露比威廉絲將會來接替我的職位。從下個星期一開始，所有的文件和企劃案都會由她來接手。希望你們會給她親切的協助就像你們支持我一樣。我祝你們將會在職涯和家庭都會很成功而且開心。星期四的送別會上再見囉！我的祕書琳達會透過電子郵件來通知你們。**解答：1.(A)** 這封備忘錄的主要內容是麥克要向大家道別。　**2.(A)** 備忘錄是 21 日發的，而 29 日麥克的退休生效，所以是一星期後是他的最後一天上班日。　**3.(C)** 檸檬汽

泡果汁是一種飲料，所以麥克應該是在一家飲料工廠上班。4.(B)繼續
麥克的工作的人是露比威廉絲，所以是威廉絲小姐。 5.(D)讓麥克印象
深刻的產品是檸檬汽泡果汁，所以是一種飲料。

Vocabulary Challenge

_____ 1. The survey shows that the number of _____ people is increasing because the worse and worse economy.

  (A) deserted (B) divorced (C) deleted (D) defended

_____ 2. Some couples will have the _____ to announce them as fiancé and fiancée before their arranged wedding.

  (A) bride shower   (B) shotgun wedding

  (C) engagement   (D) bachelor party

_____ 3. 8 years ago, the 911 _____ happened and took many lives away. (A) tsunami (B) fire (C) horror attack (D) hurricane

_____ 4. _____ are nature disasters and unpredictable.

  (A) Car accidents (B) Murders (C) Earthquakes (D) Wars

_____ 5. She felt dizzy and uncomfortable because she was _____.

  (A) out of mind (B) married (C) pregnant (D) vibrant

_____ 6. Malinda has some _____ problem because of the stressful life.

  (A) financial (B) mental (C) educational (D) natural

_____7. We may be requested to have a body check when we come from the warning area of _____ diseases.

  (A) heart (B) continue (C) gene (D) contagious

解答：(1) B (2) C (3) C (4) C (5) C (6)B (7) D

Lesson **6** | 電影
Movies

🗣 Language box 🗣

Focus One

Do you like seeing movies? (你喜歡看電影嗎?)

How often do you go to see a movie?

(你多久去看一次電影?)

Would you like to see a movie? (你想要看電影嗎?)

What kind of movie do you like? (你喜歡看什麼電影?)

What's your favorite movie? (你最喜歡的電影是哪一部?)

What movie did impress you a lot?

(哪一部電影令你印象深刻?)

Who are your favorite actor and actress?

(你最喜歡的男演員和女演員是誰?)

Do you like any directors? (你有喜歡任何導演嗎?)

✎ 語言注意面 Language Caution ✎

A: <u>Do you like</u> seeing movies? (你喜歡看電影嗎?)

B: Sure. I love seeing movies very much! I go to the movie
theaters twice a week!
(當然。我很熱愛看電影。我每個星期要去電影院兩次。)

A: <u>Would you like</u> to see a movie? (你想要看電影嗎?)

B: Oh, yeah. That's a great idea. Which one?
(喔,好啊。好主意。要看哪一部呢?)

♥愛的筆記貼♥ 以上所比較的兩種句型，Do you like 是問『平常的喜好』，Would you like to 是問『你想要…嗎？』兩個問句意思不同，當然回答也就不一樣，同學們需注意用法。

---| **Focus Two** |---

Where do you prefer watching movies?

(你喜歡在哪看電影？)

How did you find the movie? (你覺得這部電影如何？)

Have you ever seen the same movie for several times?

(你曾經看過同一部電影好幾次嗎？)

What habits do you have when you see a movie?

(你看電影時有什麼習慣？)

✎ 語言注意面 Language Caution ✎

A: <u>How do you find</u> the movie? (你要如何找到這部電影呢？)

B: I will check the library on campus first. If they do have it, I will go to the Blockbuster to rent it.(我會先到學校圖書館先查一下是否有。如果他們沒有這部電影，我會到百事達去租這部片。)

A: <u>How did you find</u> the movie? (你有找到這部電影嗎？)

B: It's a long story. I checked several DVD rental shops. They always told me that it's a very old film. Finally, I found its VCD in a second hand shop. (說來話長。我查了好幾家 DVD 出租店。他們總是告訴我它是一部非常老的片了。最後，我在一家二手店找到它的 VCD。)

A: <u>How did you find</u> the movie? (你覺得這部電影如何？)

B: Crap movie with terrible jokes. Strongly recommend you to delete it on your wish list. (有著爛笑話的爛電影。強烈建議你從想要看的清單中刪除掉這部片。)

❤愛的筆記貼❤ 以上探討了 How do you find+something 及 How did you find+something 的問句，find 這個字就是『找尋』的意思，但隨著過去式和現在式時態的不同，How did you find 用過去式表示『已經找到了』所以問句的意思就會是『你怎麼找到的？』用現在式的 How do you find 表示『你要怎麼找呢？』還有在日常生活會話中，常常用 How did you find 來問你對人事物的感覺。通常用過去式，因為如果是問對某人的感覺，也得相處過後才知道。如果是像以上所述，問對一部電影的感覺，也得對方有看過這部電影才會回答。所以一般這樣的問句會問 How did you find+something?用過去式時態來問。

∞ Conversation 1 ∞

(網友 Kitten 小貓和 Dreamer 夢想家在 MSN 上第一次聊天。)

Dreamer: Have you seen the trailer of "Fall in love with Jody's dog"?
你看過了『愛上裘蒂的狗』的預告片了嗎？

Kitten: The name sounds interesting. How did you find it?
這名字聽起來很有趣。你看過覺得如何？

Dreamer: The trailer was hilarious. It looks like a romantic comedy.
預告片很好笑。它看起來像是一齣浪漫的喜劇。

Kitten: Who are starring in the movie?
誰在這部電影裡演出？

Dreamer: Oh, the actor and actress are not famous. I can't even remember their names, but they look so familiar. They might star in some popular soap opera before.
喔，男主角和女主角都不有名。我甚至無法記得他們的名字，但是他們看起來好面熟。他們以前可能有在一些受歡迎的連續劇中演出。

Kitten: Do you want to go to see the movie in the movie theater?
你想要去電影院看這部電影嗎？

Dreamer: Yeah, why not? Do you want to go with me?
是啊，有何不可？你想要跟我一起去嗎？

Kitten: I don't know. Most of recent comedies showed their most hilarious part in the trailers. They turned out to be boring because we have already known the plots. My friends and I feel regretful and lose our faith in the new releases.

我不知道。大部份最近的喜劇都在預告片中播出他們最好笑的部份。因為我們已經都知道情節了，最後反而令人感到無聊。我的朋友們和我都覺得很後悔而且對新的電影感到失去信心。

Dreamer: Well, pal. Then you may find your faith back from this one.

好的，朋友。那你也許可以從這部開始找回你的信心啊。

⊙ Conversation 2 ⊙

(Doris 和 Addie 一起共事了一星期了，情人節快到了，這天中飯時她們一起聊天。)

Addie: Doris, have you seen the movie "Chicago"? Well, I mean that famous opera, which was starred by Richard Gere.

朵莉絲，你看過芝加哥這部電影嗎？是，我指得就是那部很有名的歌劇，由李察吉爾演的那部。

Doris: Right, that one. Sure I did. It's a musical and so ironic. I did remember the lyric "You can like the life you're living. You can live the life you like." How do you think?

對，就是那部。當然我有看過。是一部音樂劇而且很諷刺。我很記得這段歌詞『你可以喜歡上你正在過得生活，你也可以過你喜歡的生活。』你覺得怎麼樣？

Addie: Yeah, that's so impressive. I just had the soundtrack CD, but can you believe it? I haven't seen the movie before.

是啊，那很令人印象深刻。我只有原聲帶 CD，但是你相信嗎？我以前還沒有看過這部電影。

Doris: Why? The musical is so well-known, so almost everyone in the company has seen it!

為什麼？這部音樂劇好有名，所以幾乎公司裡每個人都已經看過了！

Addie: I just missed it! Few days ago, Gina mentioned the movie with me, and I was just like a fool there with no response.

我就是錯過了！幾天前，吉娜和我聊天時提到這部電影，而我就像一個呆子一樣沒有回應。

Doris: If you like the film, I can lend you my DVDs.

如果你喜歡這部電影，我可以借給你我的 DVD。

Addie: You have the DVDs?

你有 DVD？

Doris: Yeah, of course. That's one of my favorites. You may enjoy it in your lovely living room or... if you don't mind, maybe we can watch it together someday.

是啊，當然。那是我的最愛之一喔！你可以在你可愛的客廳享受這部片，又或者…如果你不介意的話，也許我們可以找一天一起看這部片啊！

◎Work Bank◎ 隨時補充一錠，你在會話及閱讀理解必備的單字！

- ㉝ **movie** [ˈmuvɪ] 電影
- ㉝ **film** [fɪlm] 影片
- ㉝ **title** [ˈtaɪtl̩] 片名
- ㉝ **timetable** [ˈtaɪm‚tebl̩] 時刻表
- ㉝ **showing time** 放映時間
- ㉝ **Now showing** 今日上映
- ㉝ **Next change** 下期放映
- 動㊫ **book the tickets** 預訂票
- ㉝ **box office** [ˈbɑks‚ɔfɪs] 票房
- ㉝ **HBO=Home Box Office** 家庭票房電影院
- ㉝ **movie theater** [ˈθɪətɚ] / **cinema** [ˈsɪnəmə] 電影院
- ㉝ **screen** [skrin] 螢幕
- ㉝ **curtain** [ˈkɝtn̩] 簾幕
- ㉝ **stage** [stedʒ] 舞台
- ㉝ **sound effects** [saund][ɪˈfɛkts] 音效
- ㉝ **Dolby** [ˈdolbɪ] 杜比環繞音效
- ㉝ **seat** [sit] 座位
- ㉝ **row** [ro] 排
- ㉝ **odd** [ɑd] 單號
- ㉝ **aisle** [aɪl] 通道
- ㉝ **even** [ˈivən] 雙號
- ㉝ **house** [haus] / **room** [rum] 電影廳
- ㉝ **full house** [ful][haus] 客滿

㊉ **sold out** [sold][aʊt] 票賣完了   ㊏ **ticket** [ˋtɪkɪt] 票

㊏ **ticket stub** [ˋtɪkɪt] [stʌb] 票根   ㊏ **scalper** [ˋskælpɚ] 黃牛

㊏ **first run** [fɝst][rʌn]首輪戲院   ㊏ **second run** [ˋsɛkənd][rʌn]二輪戲院

㊏ **poster** [ˋpostɚ] 電影海報   ㊏ **soundtrack** [ˋsaʊndˌtræk] 原聲帶

㊏ **trailer** [ˋtrelɚ] 預告片   ㊏ **premier** [primɪɚ] 首映

㊏ **theme song** [θim][sɔn] 主題曲

㊏ **subtitle** [ˋsʌbˌtaɪtl] 字幕   ㊏ **script** [skrɪpt] 腳本；劇本

㊏ **adapt** [əˋdæpt] 改編   ㊏ **voice-over** [ˋvɔɪs ˋovɚ] 旁白

㊏ **cast** [kæst] 卡司；演員表   ㊏ **star** [stɑr] 演出

㊏ **guest star** [gɛst] [stɑr] 客串   ㊏ **story** [ˋstorɪ] 故事

㊏ **genre** [ˋʒɑnrə] 類型   ㊏ **comedy** [ˋkɑmədɪ] 喜劇片

㊏ **romance** [roˋmæns] 浪漫愛情片 ㊯ **touching** [ˋtʌtʃɪŋ]

㊯ **popular** [ˋpɑpjəlɚ] 受歡迎的   ㊯ **romantic** [roˋmæntɪk] 浪漫的

㊏ **laughter** [ˋlæftɚ] 歡笑；笑聲   ㊐ **laugh** [ˋlæf] 大笑

㊏㊐ **tear** [tɪr] 眼淚；流淚   ㊑ **burst into tears** 突然哭出來

㊏ **tragedy** [ˋtrædʒədɪ] 悲劇   ㊏ **drama** [ˋdrɑmə] 劇情片

㊏ **horror** [ˋhɔrə] 恐怖片   ㊏ **thriller** [ˋθrɪlɚ] 驚悚片

㊏ **science fiction** [ˋsaɪəns ˋfɪkʃən] 科幻小說片(簡稱 sci-fi)

㊏ **war movie** 戰爭片   ㊏ **fantasy** [ˋfæntəsɪ] 奇幻片

㊏ **western** [ˋwɛstɚn] 西部片   ㊏ **martial arts** [ˋmɑrʃəl] 武俠片

㊏ **musicals** [ˋmjuzɪkl] 音樂劇   ㊏ **crime** [kraɪm] 犯罪片

㊏ **cartoon** [kɑrˋtun]/ **comic** [ˋkɑmɪk] 卡通片

㊏ **animation** [ˌænəˋmeʃən] 動畫片

㊏ **documentary** [ˌdɑkjəˋmɛntərɪ] 記錄片

㊏ **disaster** [dɪˋzæstɚ] 災難片   ㊏ **adventure** [ədˋvɛntʃɚ] 冒險片

㊏ **popcorn** [ˋpɑpˌkɔrn] 爆米花   ㊏ **plot** [plɑt]情節

㊏ **actor** [ˋæktɚ] 男演員   ㊏ **actress** [ˋæktrɪs] 女演員

㊏ **director** [dəˋrɛktɚ] 導演   ㊏ **scenarist** [sɪˋnɛrɪst] 電影編劇

㊐ **lend** [lɛnd] 借出   ㊐ **borrow** [ˋbɑro] 借入

Reading Passage 1

Have your ever seen the *Jaws* and found that you couldn't sleep all night? Have you ever heard people screaming in a movie theater and felt thrilled then? Have you ever laughed with tears or burst into tears with your friends together while seeing a great film?

Well, many people think seeing a movie in the cinema or watching DVDs at home is a great choice to relax after an exhausting day from the work or the school. There are many types of films that you can choose up to your mood or interests. Different people reflect various demands on movies. It makes the movie industry boom all the time.

Why do most people like movies? What kind of movie attracts what kind of people? Psychologists have recently pointed out that people, who like seeing movies, could release their emotion and pressure with those touching plots. Even more, they could learn the philosophy or ideas from the films. That is, the characters in the film might sometimes present people's real stories in their daily life, so they are just like looking at the mirror. In the real life, people don't know what will happen tomorrow. However, in the films, they may see and guess the results at the end. Most people look forward to seeing the good endings with happiness. After all, people don't always get the happy endings for everything. It's just a little contentment in their life.

Different people have various preferences. Some of them prefer the comedies while others prefer the thrillers. Teenagers enjoy something really exciting. For example, *Saw* and *Creep* are really something in the thrillers, and both of them were popular and had the sequels. However, same as a thriller, the *Mist* directed by Stephen King mainly focused on the discussion on the humanity when people face the extreme terror. The thriller fans often give a higher mark on *Mist* than other disgustful thrillers because it arouses more

Stephen King

issues to think. For those stressful office gentlemen and ladies, sometimes they just want to laugh and forget all the worries. Therefore, Jim Carrey and Stephen Chow play the very important roles in comedies from west to east. They are sometimes compared with each other by the comedy fans all over the world. The comments on them usually said that they both have the similarities and the differences in their works.

Some movies get popular and successful because of their materials. Take drama for

© Picture from the Universal Studio

example, *The Devil Who Wears Prada* told us what the relation between the fascinating dressing and the success in career is. The sequel made by the same film team led us to think about the truth of happiness, marriages, and weddings through the *27 Dresses*. We may learn how to "*hitch*" our ideal lover in Will Smith's love comedy. For the gay issue, Adam Sandler and Kevin James will take you to experience a "gays or friends" journey in *I now announce you Chuck and Larry*. No matter we agree or disagree with those thoughts mentioned in a drama, we experience a thinking tour while we are laughing or tearing during the film.

_____ (1)　What is the main idea of the article?
　　　　　A. There's a discussion on different kinds of people.
　　　　　B. There's a discussion on different movie theaters.
　　　　　C. There's a discussion on different types of films.
　　　　　D. There's a discussion on different actors and
　　　　　　　actresses from different countries.

_____ (2)　According to the passage, why do many people think
　　　　　seeing a movie as a good way to relax?
　　　　　A. Movies are different.
　　　　　B. Movies meet their interests and feelings.
　　　　　C. The movie industry attracts them.
　　　　　D. Movies are always hilarious.

_____ (3)　Which of the following statement is **NOT** true?
　　　　　A.　People could relax themselves by screaming for the
　　　　　　　scary plots.
　　　　　B.　The stories in a film may reflect people's real life.
　　　　　C.　Most people expect good endings.
　　　　　D.　Young adults prefer a drama more than a thriller.

_____ (4)　Why do most thriller fans give Mist a higher mark?

A. It was directed by Stephen King.

B. Jim Carrey also played a role in it.

C. It questions the humanity.　　D. It is not scary at all.

____ (5) If we want to see a movie which mainly talks about the welfare issue, what kind of movie types should we find in a DVD rental shop?

A. Thriller　　B. Romance　　C. Series　　D. Drama

♥愛的筆記貼♥ 本篇文章有些長，主要是為了幫同學複習有關電影主題的單字，以及表達意見時需要到的一些單字。內容翻譯：你曾經看過『大白鯊』然後發現你整晚都睡不著嗎？你曾經聽過人們在電影院尖叫然後覺得很刺激嗎？你曾經和你的朋友們在看電影時一起笑出眼淚或者是突然哭出來過嗎？

是的，很多人認為在電影院看電影或者是在家看 DVD 是工作和上學辛苦了一天後放鬆的好選擇。你可以依照你的心情或者是興趣來選擇好多類型的電影。不同的人反應出對電影的不同需求。這使得電影工業總是興盛。

為什麼大部份的人都喜歡電影呢？什麼樣的電影會吸引什麼樣的人們？心理學家們最近已經指出那些喜歡看電影的人們，可以透過那些感人的情節來釋放他們的情緒和壓力。甚至，他們可能從影片中學到一些哲理或想法。那也就是，在電影中的角色們有時候呈現了人們日常生活中真實的故事，所以他們就像在照鏡子。在真實生活中，人們不知道明天會發生什麼事。然而，在電影裡，他們可以看到和猜到結局。畢竟，人們不會總是事事都如意。這只是在他們生活中的小小滿足感而已。

不同的人有不同的喜好。有人喜歡喜劇就有人喜歡驚悚片。青少年喜歡一些真的很刺激的電影。舉例來說：『奪魂鋸』和『噬血地鐵站』都是驚悚片的代表，而且兩者都是很受歡迎且有續集。然而，同樣也是驚悚片，由史帝芬金執導的『迷霧驚魂』主要強調對人性面對極恐懼時會有什麼反應的討論。驚悚片迷們常給這部片比其他噁心的驚悚片更高的評價，因為它引發更多的議題來思考。對那些壓力很大的上班族來說，有時候他們只想要大笑然後忘記所有煩惱。因此，金凱瑞和周星馳扮演了從西方到東方喜劇中的重要角色。他們有時會被全世界的喜劇迷拿來彼此做比較。對他們的評論通常是他們在作品中彼此有相似點和不同點。

有些電影變得受歡迎而且成功是因為他們的題材。舉劇情片為例：

『穿著 Prada 的惡魔』告訴我們令人著迷的服裝和事業成功之間的關係。由同樣的電影團隊拍出的續集『27 件禮服的秘密』，引導我們繼續想想有關真正的幸福、婚姻和婚禮是什麼。我們可以在威爾史密斯的愛情喜劇中學到怎麼『釣』我們的理想情人。(Hitch 剛好就是這部片名，翻譯為『全民情聖』。)關於同性戀的議題，在『當我們假在一起』這部片中，亞當山德勒和凱文詹姆士將帶你體驗一場『是同性戀還是純友誼』的旅程。不管我們同意或不同意這些劇情片中提到的想法，當我們看電影而大笑或流淚的同時，我們體驗了一場思想旅程。**解答：1.(C)這篇文章主要是談論電影的形式。 2.(B) 很多人認為電影可以放鬆情緒是因為電影符合他們的興趣與感覺。 3.(D) 根據這篇文章中所述，青少年喜歡驚悚片甚過劇情片。 4.(C)大部份的人會給『迷霧驚魂』這部片較高的評價是因為它質疑人性的劇情。 5.(D)如果我們想找與社會福利制度相關的電影，我們可以到 DVD 出租店中找 Drama 劇情類的片子。**

Reading Passage 2

When you enjoy the movie, please remember to switch your mobile to the vibratile or mute mode. Most people enjoy the fine music with the films rather than the ring from your mobile phone. Moreover, if you want to answer the phone, please go out of the house with your ticket stub, and answer it quietly. Nobody would like to understand your own story better than the movie. Your convenience could be everybody's inconvenience. Please respect the enjoyable time without any possible disturbance.

_____ (1) What's the best title for the passage?
A. Fun with your mobile.　　B. Quiet is inconvenient.
C. The manner of seeing a movie.
D. Don't leave your seat frequently.

_____ (2) Where might the notice appear?
A. The door of a restaurant. B. The counter of the bank.
C. The rear glass of a car.　D. The screen in a theater.

_____ (3) Why should we switch off the ring of our mobiles during a movie?
A. The ring is noisy.
B. Most people don't like the theme songs.
C. So we can keep talking on the phone in the room.
D. We don't want others to know our phone number.

_____ (4) What should we do if we get a call during the movie?
A. Leaving the room is allowed.
B. Keep staying at your seat.　C. Cut off it right away.
D. Answer the phone call in the room.

♥愛的筆記貼♥ 本篇是一篇提醒的告示文。有時候我們會在電影開始放映前，看到這樣的文字。常看電影的同學，應該都不陌生。內容是：當你享受看電影時，請記得把你的手機調成震動或靜音模式。大部份的人享受電影的精緻配樂而不是從你手機傳出的手機鈴聲。再者，如果你想要接電話，請帶著你的票根走出電影廳，小聲地講電話。沒有人想要了解你自己的故事甚過於電影情節。你的方便可能會是大家的不便。請尊重這享受的一刻，避免任何可能的打擾。

解答：1. (C) 最符合這篇文章的主題是『看電影的禮貌』。
2. (D) 這篇告示可能會出現在電影院的螢幕上。
3. (A) 因為手機鈴聲很吵會干擾到別人，所以看電影時要關掉手機。
4. (A) 如果看電影中想接聽手機，應該離開電影廳去接聽。離開電影廳是被允許的。

Lesson 7 | 音樂 Music

🎤 Language box 🎤

| Focus One |

Do you like listening to the music? (你喜歡聽音樂嗎？)

How often do you go to a concert?
(你多久去聽一次音樂會/演唱會？)

Would you like to listen to some music?
(你想要聽音樂嗎？)

What kind of music do you like? (你喜歡聽哪一類型的音樂？)

What's your favorite song? (你最喜歡的歌是哪一首？)

Who is your favorite singer? (你最喜歡的歌手是誰？)

Which band do you support? (你支持哪一個樂團？)

✎ 語言注意面 Language Caution ✎

A: <u>How often</u> do you go to a concert? (你多久去一次演唱會？)
B: About half a year, so it's <u>twice a year</u>.
　 (大概是半年，也就是一年兩次。)

A: <u>How long</u> was the concert? (這場演唱會的時間是多久？)
B: It lasted for three days! The popular singers performed in relays, so we can listen to all the hits. (它居然持續了三天！流行歌手們就輪流上陣表演，所以我們可以聽到所有的當紅歌曲。)

A: <u>Do you often</u> go to a concert? (你常常去看演唱會嗎？)
B: No, I usually listen to the radio. (沒有，我通常聽收音機。)

A: <u>Did you go</u> to Jolin's concerts <u>before</u>?
(你以前有去聽過蔡依琳的演唱會嗎？)

B: Yes, once. My friends got the tickets for me.
(是啊！有一次。我朋友有票給我。)

♥愛的筆記貼♥ 以上比較了四個同學們比較會混淆的問題。How often 是問頻率，所以回答時我們通常是回答多久一次 once a month(一個月一次)、twice a year(一年兩次)、three times a week(一星期三次)。次數放前面，時間期放後面，來表示頻率。How long 其實是在問『持續多久的時間』，所以回答多為幾分鐘(minutes)、幾小時(hours)、幾天(days)、幾週(weeks)、幾月(months)、幾年(years)等等。Do you often … 是在問『你常常…』其實也是問頻率，可是這是屬於 yes/no question，所以一定要回答 yes 或 no，或者是回答類似意思的 sure 或 not really。這種問題我們也常用頻率副詞總是(always)、通常(usually)、經常(often)、有時候(sometimes)、很少(seldom)、極少(rarely)、從不(never) 來回答此類問題。而 Did you go…before?完全是用過去式的問法，問對方過去是否有過這樣的經驗？也可以用 Have you been to…來問對方是否有去過…？

│ Focus Two ├

Do you play any instruments? (你會演奏任何樂器嗎？)

Do you like singing? (你喜歡唱歌嗎？)

How do you like your voice? (你覺得你的聲音如何？)

Have you ever joined in any singing competitions?
(你曾經參加過任何歌唱比賽嗎？)

Do you like to buy CDs or download the music?
(你喜歡買 CD 還是喜歡下載音樂？)

Do you create your own songs? (你會自己創作歌曲嗎？)

Do you have your own band? (你有自己的樂團嗎？)

How do you show/ publish your own music?

(你如何表演/出版你自己的音樂呢?)

How often do you visit the music shop?

(你多久去一次唱片行?)

♥ 愛的筆記貼 ♥ Have you + 過去分詞(p.p.)的問法都是指從過去到現在,你是否有過這樣的經驗?所以 Have you joined in...就是『你曾經參加過…』。

<Practice> 這是一位同學對自己音樂喜好的介紹。請依照自己對音樂的喜好,將劃線部份的字彙代換,練習講出自己對音樂的喜好吧!(相關字彙請同學參考本課的 Words Bank 字彙庫來做代換練習。)

I prefer the <u>lounge</u>[1] music. It always helps me relax a lot. Besides, I also like some <u>pop</u>[2] music. The <u>Taiwanese</u>[3] singers like <u>Jay Chow and Jasmine Leong</u>[4], and the <u>western</u>[5] singers like <u>Jason Mraz and Robbie Williams</u>[6] are my favorites. I often download the mp3 to my <u>mobile</u>[7] so that I can enjoy my favorite music any time. I always support them by <u>buying their album CDs</u>[8] but I <u>rarely</u>[9] share or lend the CDs to my friends and put them <u>on my shelves</u>[10] as my collections.

◦ **Conversation 1** ◦

(兩位大學同學 Isaac 和 Jackie 在下課時聊音樂。)

Issac: Hey, Jackie. What's up?　　嘿,傑奇。今天怎麼樣?

Jackie: Where have you been? The classes in the morning were boring as usual. I would rather have studied in the library and enjoyed the music.

你跑到哪去了？今天早上的課還是跟往常一樣地無聊。早知道的話我還寧願在圖書館唸書，享受我的音樂。

Issac: Dude, what are you listening to? It sounds like the heavy metal.

朋友，你正在聽什麼？聽起來好像是重金屬音樂。

Jackie: No, it's Tupac.

不是，是吐派克。

Issac: What's that?

那是什麼？

Jackie: Man, don't tell me that you don't know about Tupac.

老兄，不要告訴我你不知道吐派克。

Issac: I would like to know the music if you don't mind.

如果你不介意的話我想知道一下這音樂。

Jackie: He was really a talented rapper in hip pop. The beats, the vocals, and the lyrics all impressed me. In brief, his songs reflect the societal problems.

他真的是一個天才嘻哈饒舌歌手。節奏、語言流暢感、還有歌詞都讓我印象深刻。簡單的說，他的歌反映了社會問題。

Issac: Wow, you're much like a big fan of Tupac. I like some rap, but not much like you. Actually, I prefer the folk music.

哇，你真的很像是吐派克的歌迷。我喜歡一些饒舌歌，但是沒有像你那麼喜歡。事實上，我比較喜歡民謠。

Jackie: You do? Don't you think they are a little similar? Both of them tell stories or reflect the issues people care about.

你喜歡民謠？你不覺得他們有點像嗎？兩種音樂都會講故事或反映了人們關心的事情。

Issac: Well, maybe. But I prefer the folk music because it sounds much pleasant and the singers sometimes told local jokes in the

是啊，也許。但是我喜歡民謠是因為它聽起來愉快多了，而且民謠歌手有時候會在歌裡講一些當

songs.   地的笑話。

⊘ Conversation 2 ⊘

(Nancy 找 Harris 參加校慶的音樂表演。)

Nancy: Harris, the school day is coming. We're going to have a show for it.   哈里斯，校慶要到了。我們將要為校慶準備一個表演。

Harris: Oh, what show is it?   喔？是什麼樣的表演？

Nancy: A concert. Do you play any instruments?   音樂會。你有玩什麼樂器嗎？

Harris: I can play the drums. How do you think?   我會打鼓。你覺得如何？

Nancy: Bad luck. Jeff said it first. Can you play other instruments?   不幸地。傑夫先說了。你會其他的樂器嗎？

Harris: Well, that's OK. I am good at keyboard, too. Don't you remember it?   好，沒關係。我也很擅長鍵盤樂器。你不記得了嗎？

Nancy: Oh, yeah. That's why I ask you. I heard that you even wrote some songs. Do you ever play them in public?   喔，對。這就是為什麼我要問你啊。我聽說你甚至還寫了一些歌。你曾經在公開場合彈過這些歌嗎？

Harris: Kind of. I shared my ideas and songs on my blog. Then, some bloggers listened to my works and made comments on them. I even have fans now!   算是吧。我在我的部落格上分享我的想法和歌。然後，有些部落客聽過我的作品後還會給些意見。我現在甚至有歌迷了呢！

图 **music** [ˋmjuzɪk] 音樂	图 **song** [sɔŋ] 歌曲
图 **rhyme** [raɪm] 韻腳；押韻	图 **beat** [bit] 節奏
图 **lyric** [ˋlɪrɪk] 歌詞	图 **vocal** [ˋvokl̩] 口白
图 **chorus** [ˋkorəs] 合唱	動 **repeat** [rɪˋpit] 重覆
图 **tune** [tjun] 曲調；旋律	图 **melody** [ˋmɛlədɪ] 主旋律；音樂
動 **sing** [sɪŋ] 唱歌	動 **play** [ple] 演奏
图 **singer** [ˋsɪŋɚ] 歌手	图 **player** [ˋpleɚ] 演奏者
图 **audio** [ˋɔdɪˏo] 音響；聲音	图 **audience** [ˋɔdɪəns] 聽眾；觀眾
图 **conductor** [kənˋdʌktɚ] 指揮	图 **composer** [kəmˋpozɚ] 作曲家
图 **lyricist** [ˋlɪrɪsɪst] 作詞家	動 **remix** [riˋmɪks] 混音
图 **instrument** [ˋɪnstrəmənt]樂器	图 **accompaniment** [əˋkʌmpənɪmənt]伴奏
图 **band** [bænd] 樂團	图 **concert** [ˋkɑnsɚt] 音樂會；演奏會
图 **unplug** [ˏʌnˋplʌg] 不插電；小型音樂會	图 **record** [ˋrɛkɚd] 唱片
图 **album** [ˋælbəm] 專輯	图 **collection** [kəˋlɛkʃən] 精選集
图 **musician** [mjuˋzɪʃən] 音樂家	图 **bass** [ˋbes] 低音樂器；低音吉他
图 **guitar** [gɪˋtɑr] 吉他	图 **guitarist** [gɪˋtɑrɪst] 吉他手
图 **flute** [flut] 長笛	图 **flutist** [ˋflutɪst] 長笛家
图 **piano** [pɪˋæno] 鋼琴	图 **pianist** [pɪˋænɪst] 鋼琴家
图 **keyboard** [ˋkiˏbord]鍵盤；鍵盤手	图 **soundboard** [ˋsaundˏbord] 響板
图 **recorder** [rɪˋkɔrdɚ] 直笛	图 **accordion** [əˋkɔrdɪən] 手風琴
图 **drum** [drʌm] 鼓	图 **drummer** [ˋdrʌmɚ] 鼓手
图 **violin** [ˏvaɪəˋlɪn] 小提琴	图 **violinist** [ˏvaɪəˋlɪnɪst] 小提琴手
图 **cello** [ˋtʃɛlo] 大提琴	图 **cellist** [ˋtʃɛlɪst] 大提琴家
图 **viola** [vɪˋolə] 中提琴；中提琴家	图 **trumpet** [ˋtrʌmpɪt] 喇叭；小號
图 **organ** [ˋɔrgən] 風琴	图 **pipe organ** [paɪp][ˋɔrgən] 管風琴
图 **clarinet** [ˏklærɪˋnɛt] 黑管；豎笛	图 **oboe** [ˋobo] 雙簧管
图 **clarinetist** [klærəˋnɛtəst] 豎笛手	图 **oboist** [ˋoboɪst] 雙簧管家
图 **saxophone** [ˋsæksəˏfon] 薩克斯風	图 **xylophone** [ˋzaɪləˏfon] 木琴
图 **harp** [hɑrp] 豎琴	图 **harmonica** [hɑrˋmɑnɪkə] 口琴
图 **percussion** [pɚˋkʌʃən] 打擊樂器	图 **aerophone** [ˋɛroˏfon] 管樂器
图 **stringed instrument** [strɪŋd] [ˋɪnstrəmənt] 弦樂器	
图 **orchestra** [ˋɔrkɪstrə] 管弦樂團	图 **symphony** [ˋsɪmfənɪ] 交響樂團
图 **Apple ipod** 蘋果掌上型電腦	图 **USB disk** 隨身碟
图 **mp3 player** mp3 播放器	图 **mobile** [ˋmobɪl] 手機(cell phone

- 名 **alternative** [ɔl'tɝnətɪv] 非主流
- 名 **blues** [bluz] 藍調
- 名 **classical** ['klæsɪkl̩] 古典樂
- 名 **country** ['kʌntrɪ] 鄉村音樂
- 名 **disco** ['dɪsko] 迪斯可音樂
- 名 **samba** ['sæmbə] 森巴舞曲
- 名 **jazz** [dʒæz] 爵士樂
- 名 **Mediterranean** [ˌmɛdətə'renɪən] 地中海音樂
- 名 **chill-out** ['tʃɪlaʊt] 輕鬆音樂
- 名 **Caribbean** [ˌkærə'biən] 加勒比海音樂
- 名 **eclectic** [ɛk'lɛktɪk] 融合音樂
- 名 **folk** [fok] 民謠
- 名 **golden oldie** ['goldn̩]['oldɪ] 經典老歌
- 名 **adult contemporary** 成人抒情歌曲
- 形 **contemporary** [kən'tɛpəˌrɛrɪ] 當代的
- 名 **contemporary Christian** 當代基督教音樂
- 名 **gospel** ['gɑspl̩] 福音；基督教音樂
- 名 **rap** [ræp] 饒舌歌曲
- 名 **hip hop** [hɪp][hɑp] 嘻哈音樂
- 名 **R&B** 節奏藍調樂
- 名 **funk** [fʌŋk] 放克音樂
- 名 **latino** [lɑ'tino] 拉丁音樂

- 名 **ambient** ['æmbɪənt] 氛圍音樂
- 名 **rock and roll** [rɑkn̩rol] 搖滾樂
- 名 **crossover** ['krɔsˌovɚ] 跨界音樂
- 名 **dance** [dæns] 舞曲
- 名 **bossa nova** [ˌbɑsə'novə] 森巴爵士
- 名 **cha-cha** ['tʃɑ'tʃɑ] 恰恰舞曲
- 名 **lounge** [laʊndʒ] 沙發音樂
- 名 **Newage** ['nju'edʒ] 新世紀音樂
- 名 **electronic** [ɪlɛk'trɑnɪk] 電子樂
- 名 **hit** [hɪt] 當紅流行歌曲
- 名 **religious** [rɪ'lɪdʒəs] 宗教音樂
- 名 **popular** ['pɑpjələ] 流行樂(pop)
- 名 **reggae** ['rɛge] 雷鬼搖擺樂
- 名 **soul** [sol] 靈魂樂
- 名 **holidays** ['hɑləˌdez] 假日音樂
- 名 **international** [ˌɪntɚ'næʃənḷ] 國際音樂

♥愛的筆記貼♥ 以上單字都是根據音樂的組成要項、樂器、表演人以及音樂類型所整理出來。其中音樂類型是根據一個很流行的音樂分享及播放軟體：蘋果電腦的 iTune，這個軟體對目前時下的音樂類型所作的詳細分類來做介紹。Tune 這個字本身是『曲調；調頻』的意思，所以 iTune 還可以聽線上廣播。根據音樂類型分類，同學們可以體驗不同的音樂廣播。以上有關音樂的單字，可以配合前面的代換口語練習，講出屬於你自己的音樂喜好喔！

Reading Passage ➤

ANNUAL SALE COMES AGAIN!

You may find all the great music here.

Satisfy your wish list with an unbelievable low price.

Double weeks' sales to your double wishes.

Visit us before May 14th, and you will have the special discount:

- Buy one get one free for all the albums with green tags
- Buy one with green tag get one with red tag half price
- All the items in lounge, reggae, religions, and classical areas are 80% off the original price.
- All of the pop, R&B, and rock-and-roll items are 10% off the tagged price.

  Mok's Soulmates, the best choice to your wish list.

Any visitors will get a FREE copy of POPnROCK music magazine during the sales.

_____ (1) What is the "Mok's Soulmates"?
A. A karaoke audio shop.   B. A book shop.
C. A supermarket.   D. A music shop.

_____ (2) According to the poster, how often do they have the sales?
A. Once a year.   B. In the summer.
C. Twice a year.   D. Few months.

_____ (3) Sally wants to buy a symphonic CD during the sales. What discount will she get?

A. No discount.　　　　　B. Totally free.

C. 80 % off the price　　　D. 10% off the price

_____ (4)　If I want to buy the Elvis Presley's CD with a green tag on May 7th, what discount will I have?

A. Buy two green tags for one, 10% off the price, and a free magazine.

B. Buy two green tags for one, 80% off the price.

C. Half price with the green tag CD, and a free magazine

D. 10% off the price on the Elvis Presley's CD, and free charge for a CD with the red tag and a magazine.

_____ (5)　When do they offer the free music magazine?

A. Anytime you visit the shop. B. During the 2 weeks.

C. Every Christmas.　　　　D. Only on weekends.

●愛的筆記貼● 從標題可以看出，這是一篇大減價的廣告。整篇是說一年一度(Annual 每年的)的大拍賣又來了！在這裡你可以找到所有的好音樂。用難以置信的低價格滿足你的需求清單。兩個禮拜的大減價對你雙重的願望。在 5 月 14 日前來店，你會享有這樣的特別折扣優惠：● 有綠色標籤的所有專輯都買一送一。● 買一件綠色標籤的即可享有一件紅色標籤半價優惠。● 所有在沙發音樂、雷鬼樂、宗教音樂以及古典樂區域的專輯都打 2 折。● 所有在流行音樂、節奏藍調以及搖滾樂區的商品都是標籤價再打 9 折。老莫的心靈伴侶，滿足你需求清單的最好選擇。**任何在減價期間來店的客人都會得到一本免費的 POPnROCK 音樂雜誌喔！** 解答：1.(D) 從音樂類型的單字可以知道，老莫的心靈伴侶是一家唱片行的名字。 2.(A) 根據標題可以看到 Annual 每年這個字，也就是一年一次。 3.(C) 莎莉想要在大拍賣期間去買一張交響樂CD，交響樂屬於古典音樂，可享有扣掉原價的百分之 80 也就是原價的 2 折價。 4.(A) 如果我想買這張貓王的綠標專輯，綠標可享有的折扣優惠是可免費獲得另一張綠標專輯，或可享有另一張紅標專輯半價優惠。而且貓王的歌屬於搖滾樂，可享扣掉原價的百分之 10，也就是打 9 折。拍賣期間每位來店的客人都可以獲得一本免費的音樂雜誌。所以較符合的答案是 A。 5.(B) 在此拍賣的雙週期間，來店即可獲得一本免費的音樂雜誌。

Vocabulary Challenge

_____ 1. All the _____ were moved by his great violin skills.

   (A) music   (B) audience   (C) audio   (D) instruments

_____ 2. John is a cellist, and his wife is a composer. Both of them are

_____. (A) instruments (B) music   (C) symphony   (D) musicians

_____ 3. Violins, guitars, and the harps are all the _____ instruments.

   (A) percussion   (B) stringed   (C) keyboard   (D) aerophone

_____ 4. Do you know how to _____ the music from the websites to

   my cell phone?

   (A) download (B) remove (C) remember (D) recall

_____ 5. Hank is the original _____ of this song. He wrote the lyrics

   and the melody by himself.

   (A) conductor (B) orchestra   (C) director   (D) composer

Question 6-10

Did you go to their __(6)__ last night? The rock music __(7)__ all

night. The acoustics ___(8)___ because of their loud music! They

__(9)__ for the disturbance, __(10)__. I really dislike being one of

the neighbors living by the stadium.

_____ 6.   (A) exhibition (B) concert (C) soccer game (D) sales
_____ 7.   (A) rocks   (B) was rocking   (C) rocked   (D) to rock
_____ 8.   (A) break   (B) broke   (C) broken   (D) were broken
_____ 9.   (A) fine   (B) fines   (C) fined   (D) were fined
_____10.   (A) too   (B) either   (C) neither   (D) even

解答：(1) B (2) D (3) B (4) A (5) D
(6) B (7) C (8) D (9) D (10) A

Lesson 8 | 旅遊與冒險
Travel and adventures

✿ Language box ✿

⊢ Focus One ⊣

Where have you traveled to? (你去過哪裡旅行？)

Have you been to Paris before? (你以前去過巴黎嗎？)

Have you gone to Paris? (你去巴黎了嗎？)

Have you traveled abroad? (你有到國外旅行過嗎？)

Do you like to travel? (你喜歡旅遊嗎？)

Do you like to travel alone, with your friends, or join tour groups?

(你喜歡獨自旅遊，和你的朋友們一起旅遊，還是參加旅行團？)

Where do you most like to travel to? (你最喜歡去哪旅行？)

How often do you have a trip? (你多久去旅行一次？)

⚡ 語言注意面 Language Caution ⚡

A: Have you been to Paris before? (你以前去過巴黎嗎？)

B: Yes, few years ago. I was with a tour group. It's my first time visiting there.

(是啊，幾年前。我和一個旅遊團去的。這是我第一次造訪那。)

A: Have you gone to Paris? (你去巴黎了嗎？)

B: Yes, I have been here for 3 months.
(是啊，我已經來這裡3個月了。)

♥愛的筆記貼♥ 語言注意面在這裡為同學說明的是 Have you been to 及 Have you gone to 兩個問句的意義。been 是 be 動詞的過去分詞，而 gone 是 go 這個動詞的過去分詞。這兩個動詞本身的差異即為 be 沒有動作，功能是繫詞，連繫名詞和名詞，連繫名詞和形容詞。句子裡沒有動作時我們用 be 動詞。例：She is beautiful. She is my mom. be 動詞還有表示『存在』的意義。所以 Have you been to 是在問『經驗』，你曾經去過…？現在人可能已經回來了，不在所問的當地。Have you gone to 則是問：你去了嗎？強調『去』的動作。也有『你已去到那裡了嗎？』的意思。所以人還在所問的當地。

Focus Two

Do you often arrange the itinerary by yourself?
(你經常自己安排行程的嗎？)

Do you prefer bringing a brief case or a lot of luggage with you? (你較喜歡帶簡易行李還是很多行李？)

Do you often get carsickness/ airsickness/ seasickness?
(你經常暈車/暈機/暈船嗎？)

Do you often get jet lag after a long flight?
(在一段長途飛行後，你常有時差嗎？)

How long do you like to travel around? (你喜歡旅行多久？)

Do you prefer a long journey or a short trip?
(你較喜歡長期旅行還是短期旅行？)

Do you like the well-arranged tour or adventures?
(你喜歡安排妥當的旅遊還是冒險？)

Are good companions important to you?
(好的旅遊伴侶對你來說重要嗎？)

<練習> 有人問你 **Do you like traveling?** 你會怎麼回答呢？以下是一位同學的回答，劃線部份可依標號來找對應的字彙群組，可以幫助你練習表達有關自己對於旅行的喜好。

I <u>like</u>[1] traveling <u>very much</u>[2]. I <u>have</u>[3] been to <u>several countries</u>[4]. I prefer <u>the well-arranged tour</u>[5], so I always travel <u>with the tour groups</u>[6]. Staying at comfortable hotels is <u>quite</u>[7] important to me. I prefer taking the <u>airplanes</u>[8] to travel around, but sometimes I also have to travel by <u>train or bus</u>[8]. My favorite <u>city</u>[9] is <u>Edinburg</u>[10]. I <u>have</u>[11] been to there <u>once</u>[12]. I want to visit there <u>again</u>[13].

♥愛的筆記貼♥

①喜歡 like，不喜歡 dislike 或 don't like。②喜歡或不喜歡的程度。very much 表示『非常』，也可以不講。③已經去過 have，沒有去過 haven't。④去過好幾個國家 several countries，去過一個國家，就直接把國家名講出，例如我去過日本，整句話說 I have been to Japan.我還沒出過國是 I haven't been abroad.⑤喜歡的旅遊型態，well-arranged tour 安排妥善的旅行、backpacker routes 背包客路線、jump on and off 跳上跳下行程(依巴士開車路線，定點接送的自由行旅遊)、camping 露營。⑥和旅行團一起去 with the tour groups，和家人一起去 with my family，和朋友一起去 with my friends，獨自旅行 alone。⑦住舒服的旅館對自己重不重要？quite 表『相當』，如果不重要就代換成 not。⑧喜歡搭乘的交通工具，一般有 airplane 飛機、train 火車、bus 巴士、rental car 出租汽車、cruise ship 遊輪、motorcycle 機車、bike 腳踏車、甚至是 hot air balloon 熱氣球。『搭乘』這個動詞可用 take。也可用 by 這個介系詞表示。⑨最喜歡的地方可以是 city 城市、country 鄉村、village 村莊、town 小鎮、mountain 山、sea 海、place 地方。⑩地名可依照自己喜好來代換。⑪曾經去過自己最喜歡的地方嗎？曾去過選 have，不曾去過選 haven't。⑫去過的次數，如果前面是不曾去過，此處就不用講。去過一次是 once，兩次 twice、三次以上說 three times, four times…以此

類推。好幾次是 several times。⑬想要再去這個地方的意願與時機。again
再一次、in the near future 在不久的將來、next year 明年。範文內容：
我很喜歡旅行。我曾去過好幾個國家。我喜歡安排妥當的旅行，所以
我總是跟旅行團去旅行。住舒服的旅館對我來說很重要。我較喜歡搭
飛機去旅行，但有時候我也必需要坐火車和巴士。我最喜歡的城市是
愛丁堡。我曾經去過那裡一次。我想再去一次。

◎ Conversation 1 ◎

(兩位好朋友 Brian 布萊恩和 Stella 史黛拉在看照片。)

Brian: What are you looking at?	妳在看什麼？
Stella: My photos of the trip in Prague.	我在布拉格旅行的相片。
Brian: Really. Could you show me some?	真的嗎？妳可以給我看一些嗎？
Stella: Sure, but I don't feel well with these photos.	好啊，但是看這些相片我心裡不太舒服。
Brian: Why? I think they are wonderful. At least, the views are wonderful in the pictures. But you are too small in them. Who did take the pictures for you?	為什麼？我覺得他們很棒。至少，相片中的景色很美好。但是妳在照片中太小了。是誰幫你拍的相片呢？
Stella: George, my companion in the trip. This was the first time he went to Europe.	喬治，我此行的旅伴。這是他第一次到歐洲。
Brian: How about you? You look experienced in the backpacker's life.	那妳呢？妳看起來對於背包客的生活很有經驗。
Stella: You know me quite well. I think I prefer traveling alone after this experience. He complained a	你真得很瞭解我。在這次體驗後，我覺得我比較喜歡獨自旅行。他在旅程中

lot in the trip, and he was with a bad mood all the time. It really depressed me a lot.

Brian: Sounds terrible. Companions are always important if you don't want to travel alone. Especially when you go to an unfamiliar area, you have to count on each other. He might encounter the culture shock.

Stella: Yes, maybe. But his selfish ruined most of my time and even the photos in Prague. Next time, I would rather visit there alone.

抱怨很多，而且總是心情不好。這真的讓我覺得很沮喪。

聽起來很糟。如果妳不想一個人旅行，旅伴總是很重要的。尤其是當你到了一個不熟悉的地方，你們必需信賴依靠彼此。他可能遭遇了文化衝擊吧！

是的，可能吧！但他的自私已經毀掉了我在布拉格大部份的時間而且甚至是相片。下一次，我寧願自己一個人去。

⊙ Conversation 2 ⊙

(Doris 和 Addie 在聊員工旅遊的事。)

Doris: Addie, have you filled out the survey?

艾迪，妳填問卷了沒？

Addie: What's that for?

什麼問卷？

Doris: Company tour, don't you know it yet?

員工旅遊，你還不知道嗎？

Addie: Oh, yeah. I heard that we are having an overseas tour, right?

喔，對。我聽說我們將會有個國外旅遊，對嗎？

Doris: Yeah, maybe. It's up to the result of the survey. I heard that the oversea tour is getting more support so far.

是啊，可能。這要看問卷調查的結果。我聽說到目前為止國外旅遊得到較多支持喔！

Addie: How many days are we going to be on vacation?

我們將要去渡假幾天？

Doris: 5 days only. If the tour requires more days to stay, we will have to apply for no more than another 5 days from our paid vacation.

只有五天。如果這趟旅行需要停留更多天的話，我們將必需請不超過5天的年假(有薪假)。

Addie: So it means we will probably have 5 to 14 days, includes a double weekend, for the oversea tour. Where do you most like to go?

所以這指得是我們大概將會有5到14天，包括2個週末，去國外旅行。那你最想去的地方是哪裡？

Doris: Turkey, actually. The country and culture seem much mysterious so the country attracts me a lot.

其實很想去土耳其。這個國家和文化似乎很神祕 ，所以這國家非常吸引我。

Addie: Well, do we have other choices?

是喔，那我們還有別的選擇嗎？

Doris: Oh, yes, darling. Scotland, France, Australia, Turkey, and Japan.

喔，有啊，親愛的。蘇格蘭、法國、澳洲、土耳其和日本。

Addie: Why not Scotland? In August, they will have the Edinburg Festival and Military Tattoo. I always want to visit there some day.

為什麼不去蘇格蘭呢？在八月份，他們將會有愛丁堡國際藝術節和軍樂表演。我總希望有一天可以去那。

Doris: Sounds great. I changed my mind. Scotland sounds more suitable for a 14-day tour.

聽起來很棒。我改變心意了。蘇格蘭聽起來更適合14天的行程。

Addie: Do you think so? OK, so will you go with your boyfriend?

你也這麼想嗎？好，這樣你將和你的男友去嗎？

Doris: No. I hope I can be in the same group with you, so we can stay

不會。我希望我可以和你同一團，所以我們可以住

together.

Addie: Oh, that's great. But, is he too busy to be on vacation?

Doris: Not really. He preferred outdoor activities more than a comfortable journey. He really misses the bungee jumping in Australia. I can't imagine where my heart will be at that moment.

一起。

喔，那很好啊。但是，他太忙了無法渡假嗎？

不是的。他較喜歡戶外活動甚過於舒服的旅程。他真的很想念澳洲的高空彈跳。我不敢想像在那一刻我的心臟會在哪裡。

◎Work Bank◎ 隨時補充一錠，你在會話及閱讀理解必備的單字！

- ⊛ **travel** [ˈtrævl̩] 旅行
- ⊛ **tour** [tʊr] 觀光旅行；巡迴演出
- ⊛ **journey** [ˈdʒɝnɪ] 長途旅行
- ⊛ **tour agency** [tʊr][ˈedʒənsɪ] 旅行社
- ⊛ **tour guide** [tʊr][gaɪd] 導遊
- ⊛ **itinerary** [aɪˈtɪnəˌrɛrɪ] 旅遊路線
- ⊛ **route** [rut] 路線
- ⊛ **backpacking** [ˈbækˌpækɪŋ] 自助旅行
- ⊛ **traveler** [ˈtrævlə] 旅行者；旅客
- ⊛ **safari** [səˈfɑrɪ] 狩獵旅行
- ⊛ **arranged tour** [əˈrendʒd][tʊr] 安排妥當的旅行
- ⊛ **visa** [ˈvizə] 簽證
- ⊛ **boarding pass** [ˈbordɪŋ][pæs] 登機證
- ⊛ **vacation** [veˈkeʃən] 假期
- ⊛ **holiday** [ˈhɑləˌde] 假日；假期
- ⊛ **airplane** [ˈɛrˌplen] / **aircraft** [ˈɛrˌkræft] / **plane** [plen] 飛機
- ⊛ **airport** [ˈɛrˌport] 機場
- ⊛ **bus** [bʌs] 公車；巴士
- ⊛ **train** [tren] 火車
- ⊛ **shuttle bus** [ˈʃʌtl̩][bʌs] 接駁公車
- ⊛ **cruise** [kruz] 遊輪；航程

- ⊛ **trip** [trip] 短程旅行
- ⊛ **outing** [ˈaʊtɪŋ] 郊遊；短程旅遊
- ⊛ **voyage** [ˈvɔɪɪdʒ] 航海旅行
- ⊛ **tour group** [tʊr][grup] 旅行團
- ⊛ **guide book** [gaɪd][bʊk] 旅遊書
- ⊛ **map** [mæp] 地圖
- ⊛ **plan** [plæn] 計劃
- ⊛ **backpacker** [ˈbækˌpækə] 背包客
- ⊛ **pleasure boat** [ˈplɛʒə][bot] 遊輪
- ⊛ **theme tour** [θim][tʊr] 主題旅行
- ⊛ **passport** [ˈpæsˌport] 護照
- ⊛ **suitcase** [ˈsutkes] 旅行箱
- ⊛ **luggage** [ˈlʌgɪdʒ] 行李
- ⊛ **flight ticket** [flaɪt][ˈtɪkɪt] 飛機票
- ⊛ **train station** [tren][ˈsteʃən] 火車站
- ⊛ **bus stop** [bʌs][stɑp] 巴士站牌
- ⊛ **high speed train** [haɪ][spid][tren] 高鐵
- ⊛ **terminal** [ˈtɝmən l̩] 航廈
- ⊛ **ship** [ʃɪp] 船

⊛**yacht** [jɑt] 遊艇；快艇　⊛**transportation** [ˌtrænspɚˋteʃən]交通工具

⊛ **flight** [flaɪt] 班機；飛行航程　⊛ **transfer** [ˋtrænsfɝ] 轉機

⊛ **arrival** [əˋraɪvl] 到達；入境　⊛**departure** [dɪˋpɑrtʃɚ] 離開；離境

⊕ **on time** 準點；準時　　　⊛⊛ **delay** [dɪˋle] 延遲；誤點

⊛ **baggage claim** [ˋbægɪdʒ][klem] 行李提領處

⊛ **baggage declaration** [ˋbægɪdʒ][ˌdɛkləˋreʃən] 行李申報

⊛ **flight attendant** [flaɪt][əˋtɛndənt] 空服員 ⊛ **service** [ˋsɝvɪs] 服務

⊛ **duty free** [ˋdjutɪ][fri] 免稅商品　⊛ **menu** [ˋmɛnju] 菜單

⊛⊕ **fasten your seat belt** [ˋfæsn][juɚ][sit][bɛlt] 扣緊安全帶

⊛⊕ **unbuckle your seat belt** [ʌnˋbʌkl][juɚ][sit][bɛlt] 打開安全帶

⊛**window seat** [ˋwɪndo][sit]靠窗座位⊛**aisle seat** [aɪl][sit] 靠走道座位

⊛ **check-in** [ˋtʃɛkɪn] 入住；登機手續　⊛ **airline** [ˋɛrˌlaɪn] 航空公司

⊛ **security check** [sɪˋkjurətɪ][tʃɛk]安全檢查

⊛**air recreation** [ɛr][ˌrɛkrɪˋeʃən]機上娛樂⊛**tax refund** [tæks][rɪˋfʌnd]退稅

⊛ **souvenir** [ˋsuvəˌnɪr] 紀念品　　⊛ **postcard** [ˋpostˌkɑrd] 明信片

⊛ **key ring** [ki][rɪŋ] 鑰匙圈　　　⊛ **camera** [ˋkæmərə] 照相機

⊛**notebook**[ˋnoˌbuk]/ **laptop**[ˋlæptɑp]筆記型電腦⊛**stay**[ste]停留；住宿

⊛**converter** [kənˋvɝtɚ] 變壓器⊛**plug adapter**[plʌg][əˋdæptɚ] 轉換插頭

⊛**accommodation**[əˌkɑməˋdeʃən] 住處 ⊛**hotel**[hoˋtɛl] 旅館；飯店

⊛ **hostel**[ˋhɑstl] 旅舍；青年旅舍　⊛ **villa** [ˋvɪlə] 別墅；渡假村

⊛ **B&B (Bed & Breakfast)/ home stay** 民宿

⊛ **restaurant** [ˋrɛstərənt] 餐廳　⊛ **food stand**[fud][stænd] 小吃攤

⊛ **night market** [naɪt][ˋmɑrkɪt]夜市 ⊛ **carnival** [ˋkɑrnəvl] 嘉年華會

⊛ **spa** [spɑ] 溫泉水療池　　　⊛ **casino** [kəˋsino] 賭場

⊛ **shopping mall** [ˋʃɑpɪŋ][mɔl] 購物中心　⊛ **park** [pɑrk] 公園

⊛ **amusement park** [əˋmjuzmənt] [pɑrk]　⊛ **zoo** [zu] 動物園

⊛ **museum** [mjuˋzɪəm] 博物館　⊛ **art gallery** [ɑrt][ˋgælərɪ] 美術館

⊛ **cash** [kæʃ] 現金　　　⊛ **credit card** [ˋkrɛdɪt][kɑrd] 信用卡

⊛ **exchange rate** [ɪksˋtʃendʒ][ret] 匯率 **traveler's check** 旅行支票

⊛ **currency exchange** [ˋkɝənsɪ][ɪksˋtʃendʒ] 貨幣匯兌

⊛ **scenery** [ˋsinərɪ] 景色　　⊛ **oasis** [oˋesɪs] 綠洲

⊛ **desert** [ˋdɛzɚt] 沙漠　　　⊛ **hill** [hɪl] 丘陵；小山

⊛ **cliff** [klɪf] 峭壁；懸崖　　⊛ **valley** [ˋvælɪ] 山谷

⊛ **gorge** [gɔrʒ] 峽谷　　　⊛ **waterfall** [ˋwɔtɚˌfɔl] 瀑布

㊝ **island** [ˋaɪlənd] 島嶼　　㊝ **jet lag** [dʒɛt][læg] 時差不舒服感

㊵㊉ **get lost** 迷路　㊵㊉ **ask for direction** 問路；問方向

㊝㊵ **adventure** [ədˋvɛntʃɚ] 冒險　㊝ **surfing** [ˋsɝfɪŋ] 衝浪

㊝ **bungee jumping** [ˋbʌndʒɪ][ˋdʒʌmpɪŋ] 高空彈跳

㊝ **climbing** [ˋklaɪmɪŋ] 攀岩　　㊝ **diving** [ˋdaɪvɪŋ] 潛水

㊝ **hot air balloon** [hɑt][ɛr][bəˋlun] 熱氣球　㊝ **cycling** [ˋsaɪklɪŋ] 自行車旅行

Reading Passage 1

Date: Sep. 22nd, 12:24 p.m.

Sender: Sunshine Airline Online Service

Subject: Order Confirmation OP1542136609221115003

Dear Mr. Jones,

　　Thank you for using the Sunshine Airline Online Service, your best travel companion wherever you are. Your order for the flight tickets and room reservations has been placed on September 22nd.

　　Please confirm the following information of your order. If you have any question, please call the hotline: 1-800-341-341.

Flight information:

Return tickets from Seattle to San Francisco

Date: Sep. 26th, Thursday　Airport: SEA　　Flight No.: NY 530
Departure Time: 7:30 a.m.　　　　Arrival Time: 9:40 a.m.
Terminal 1　　Gate 7　　Seat C25　　　Economy Class

Date: Sep. 28th, Saturday　Airport: SFO　　Flight No.: NY 608
Departure Time: 8:45 p.m.　　　　Arrival Time: 11:00 p.m.
Terminal 1　　Gate 2　　Seat C27　　　Economy Class

Accommodation: 2 nights, a single room in Queen Palace Hotel
**Please check in after 3 p.m. with the letter and your credit card. They will return you the deposit after your check-out.

Pick-up Service: $1 City Express from the terminal to your hotel. We much appreciate you again and hope you enjoy your trip.

_____ (1)   What is the main idea of the e-mail?

A. A complaint.   B. A confirmation.

C. A brochure.   D. An invitation.

_____ (2)   If Mr. Jones has some questions, what suggestion is made to him?

A. Call the police.   B. Reply the e-mail.

C. Call the customer service.   D. Turn off the Internet.

_____ (3)   What is **NOT** true about the trip?

A. Mr. Jones ordered the tickets through the Internet.

B. 4 days later, Mr. Jones is going to start off.

C. Mr. Jones is having an oversea business trip.

D. The order includes the flight tickets, a room for two nights, and a bus ticket as well.

_____ (4)   Why will Mr. Jones have to use his credit card when he checks in the hotel?

A. He has to pay for the rent.

B. He has to pay the insurance.

C. He has to pay for the handling fee for check-out.

D. He has to pay nothing and it's just for the safekeeping.

_____ (5)   What will Mr. Jones take on his way back to the airport on Sep. 28th?

A. A shuttle bus.   B. A rental car.

C. The subway.   D. Not mentioned above.

♥愛的筆記貼♥ 這是一篇商業服務信函，內容為：日期：九月 22 日，下午 12 點 24 分。發信人：陽光航空線上服務。信件主旨：訂單確認 OP154213660922115003(此為訂單編號)。親愛的瓊斯先生：謝謝您使用陽光航空線上服務，你不管你在何處都是你最好的旅遊同伴。您的飛機票及訂房的訂單已經在 9 月 22 日確認下單了。請確認以下的訂單資訊。如果您有任何的疑問，請撥打熱線(服務專線)：1-800-341-341。(美國的免付費電話號碼)。班機資訊：西雅圖到舊金山的來回機票。日期：9 月 26 日，星期四。機場：西雅圖。班次：NY530。起飛時間為早上 7:30。抵達時間為早上 9:40。第一航廈，7 號閘門，座位是 C25。經濟艙。日期：9 月 28 日，星期六。機場：舊金山。班次：NY608。起飛時間為晚間 8:45。抵達時間為晚間 11 點。第一航廈，2 號閘門，座位

是 C27。經濟艙。住處：在皇后宮殿旅館的一間單人房入住兩晚。**
請在下午3點後用這封信及你的信用卡辦理入住手續。他們將會退還給
你這筆押金在你辦理退房手續後。接送服務：1元的城市快捷(旅遊巴士)
從航廈開往你的旅館。我們再次感謝您而且祝您旅途愉快。
解答：1.(B)這是一封確認信函。 2.(C)如果瓊斯先生有些疑問，這封
信給他的建議是撥電話給客戶服務部門。 3.(C)從西雅圖到舊金山均在
美國本土，所以這趟行程是國內旅行而非 overseas 海外旅行。 4.(D)
瓊斯先生將必需用到信用卡來付住房保證的押金，但會在退房手續時歸
還，所以其實不會付此費用。 5.(D)瓊斯先生在9月28日回機場要搭
什麼交通工具訂單上並無顯示，他只訂了26日從機場到旅館的單程特
價巴士接送服務。所以選『沒有提到』。

Reading Passage 2

Some people think taking a trip __(1)__ a relaxing and
enjoyable thing while __(2)__ prefer more exciting ways to
challenge __(3)__. __(4)__ to punting in a peaceful river with
the geese and swans, windsurfing and riding the personal
watercraft are much more __(5)__.

____ 1.　A. as　　　　B. to　　　　C. for　　　　D. about
____ 2.　A. any other　B. the others　C. another　　D. others
____ 3.　A. them　　　B. itself　　　C. themselves D. one
____ 4.　A. To compare B. Compared C. Comparing C. Compares
____ 5.　A. excites　　B. excited　　C. exciting　　D. excite

♥愛的筆記貼♥ 段落填充內容：當有些人認為旅行是一種放鬆和
享受的事，也有些人較喜歡更刺激的方法來挑戰他們自己。和在平靜
的河裡和雁鴨及天鵝一起撐船比起來，風浪板衝浪和騎水上摩托車是
更為刺激。解答：1.(A)think as 是『認為』之意。 2.(D)Some...others...
一些...另一些...是常用不定代名詞用法。以空格後接的動詞不加 s 亦
可看出此為複數名詞。 3.(C)應用反身代名詞『他們自己』，專指後面
的。 4.(B)此句主詞均是事物，因此事物是被拿來比較的，所以此處

用有被動語氣的過去分詞當形容詞用，原句中的關係代名詞 which 和被動語氣的 be 動詞 was 被省略。 **5. (C)**戶外活動屬事物，所以形容詞用 Ving 的 exciting，令人感到刺激的。

Vocabulary Challenge

_____ 1. Attention, every passenger. The train number 1034 from Pington to Keelung will be _____ for 14 minutes. Thank you for your patience. (A) on time (B) in time (C) delayed (D) visited

_____ 2. The famous rock band is on _____ in Asia now! The tickets were sold out in a very short time.
(A) tour (B) cycle (C) vacation (D) time

_____ 3. This is the _____ of the route. Where is your destination? You might have missed your stop or you should change to another route.
(A) terminal (B) transportation (C) flight (D) start

_____ 4. We will be passing through turbulent air. For your safety, please remain seated and _____ your seat belts.
(A) unbuckle (B) loose (C) take off (D) fasten

_____ 5. Excuse me. I think I got lost. Could you show me the _____ to the train station?
(A) destination (B) direction (C) point (D) square

_____ 6. The tourists may not be able to have their own Eiffel Tower, but they could buy the clay models as the _____.
(A) accommodation (B) itinerary (C) souvenirs (D) voyage

解答：(1) C (2) A (3) A (4) D (5) B (6) C

Lesson 9 | 運動和遊戲
Sports and games

🗨 Language box 🗨

┤ **Focus One** ├

What sports do you play? (你有從事哪些運動？)

What sports do you like? (你喜歡哪些運動？)

Do you like watching sports on TV?
(你喜歡收看電視的運動節目嗎？)

What sports do you like to watch? (你喜歡收看何種運動？)

Do you like any athletes or players?
(你喜歡任何運動員或者是球員嗎？)

Which team do you support? (你支持哪隻球隊？)

Are you a soccer/ baseball/ basketball fan?
(你是足球/棒球/籃球迷嗎？)

Why do you like basketball? Why do you like Kobe?
(你爲什麼喜歡籃球呢？你爲什麼喜歡科比？)

What's the most popular sport in your country?
(你們國家最受歡迎的運動是什麼？)

✎ 語言注意面 Language Caution ✎

A: <u>Do you like</u> any sports? (你喜歡任何運動嗎？)

B: Yes, I like tennis, billiards and figure skating.
　 (有啊，我喜歡網球、撞球和花式溜冰。)

A: <u>Do you play</u> any of the sports you like?
(你有從事任何你喜歡的運動項目嗎？)

B: Yes, I play tennis well, but I can't play billiards and skating. I only like to watch the games on TV.
(有，我打網球打得很好，但是我不會打撞球和溜冰。我只喜歡看電視轉播的比賽。)

♥愛的筆記貼♥ 以上所比較的兩種句型，do you like 是問『喜好』，喜好的運動項目卻不一定會從事，所以如果問『你都做哪些運動？』還是要問 What sports do you play? 關於動詞方面，通常球類運動名稱前是搭配 play 這個動詞，而動名詞 Ving 形態的運動名稱，例如 swimming 游泳、hiking 健行、climbing 攀岩前面，是搭配 go 這個動詞。yoga 瑜珈、exercises 運動、gymnastics 體操通常前面是搭配 do 這個動詞。

Focus Two

Do you do some exercises regularly?(你有規律地做運動嗎？)

Do you often go to the gym? (你常去健身房嗎？)

How do you like yoga? (你覺得瑜珈如何？喜歡嗎？)

Do you prefer playing sports with friends or doing exercises alone? (你較喜歡和朋友一起運動還是自己做運動？)

⊘ Conversation 1 ⊘

(網友 Kitten 小貓和 Dreamer 夢想家在 MSN 上聊運動。)

Kitten: Are you there?	你在嗎？
Dreamer: Yap. How are you doing?	在。你過得如何？
Kitten: Did you watch the game tonight?	今晚看過那場球賽了嗎？

Dreamer: Which game do you mean, soccer or basketball? I have no idea about which one you said.

你指得是哪一場,足球還是籃球?我不知道你在說哪個。

Kitten: No way. I think you also like soccer, don't you?

不會吧。我想你也喜歡足球,不是嗎?

Dreamer: Bingo. So, do you mean last Manchester United's match?

賓果!所以,你說得是上一場曼聯的比賽嗎?

Kitten: Right. Christiano Ronaldo was just so perfect!

對啊!C.羅那度真是太棒,太完美了!

Dreamer: I think that was really an excellent game. 5 nil to the champion so far. They are really unbeaten!

我覺得那真是一場精采的球賽。到目前為止,5個0沒有敗績,一路打到冠軍。他們真是無敵!

Kitten: Do you also want to have such an exciting game this weekend?

你週末也想來一場這麼精采的比賽嗎?

Dreamer: You mean, go to the sports bar to watch soccer games together?

你指得是,一起去運動酒吧看球賽嗎?

Kitten: No. Seriously, pal, do you want to play a soccer game with my friends? How do you think?

不。認真一點啦,朋友,你想要和我的朋友們來踢一場足球賽嗎?你覺得怎麼樣?

Dreamer: Oh, yeah? Thanks anyway. I prefer watching games with my favorite beer.

喔,是嗎?不管怎樣先謝了。我還是比較喜歡和我最愛的啤酒一起看球賽。

Kitten: Oh, come on. No wonder you have a big beer belly!

喔,拜託。難怪你有一個大啤酒肚!

◎ Conversation 2 ◎

(Doris 和 Addie 在廁所遇見,兩人對健身話題聊了起來。)

Doris: Oops. Oh, that's too bad. A crack on my Armani?

咦？噢，真糟。一個裂縫在我的亞曼尼上？

Addie: Well, that's a sign.

好吧，那是一個徵兆。

Doris: I see. A reminder for a keeping fit plan. I think I had better start my diet right away.

我知道。一張上面寫著『減肥計劃』的便條紙。我想我最好馬上開始節食。

Addie: Personally, I think you are fit. Do you often go to gyms? You just need some exercises to make your legs thinner. Diet couldn't help shape your figure after all.

我個人認為你身材適中。你常去健身房嗎？你只是需要一些運動來讓你的腿更纖細。節食對雕塑身材曲線畢竟是沒有多大幫助的。

Doris: Wow, you sound like my boyfriend. Last night, I complained my bottom with him. I heard there is a body-sculpting set which works and many people recommended it on websites. Do you know what he said?

哇！你聽起來真像我的男朋友。昨天晚上，我和他抱怨我的屁股。我聽說有一種塑身套餐很有用而且很多人在網站上推薦它。你知道他怎麼說？

Addie: Baby, I love your bottom as much as your heart?

寶貝，我愛你的屁股就像愛你的心一樣多？

Doris: Awful. He might forget to say that. He tried to call my personal instructor and requested for an intensive training on my ass.

可怕。他可能忘了說這句。他試著打給我的個人健身教練然後要求一個針對我的屁股來個密集的訓練。

Addie: Oh, my god. Was he serious?

喔，我的天啊。他是認真的嗎？

Doris: He was mad on my idea. He thinks regular exercises and a well-balanced diet lead us to a better life.

他對我的想法感到很生氣。他認為規律的運動和均衡的飲食會帶領我們有個更好的生活。

人我關係	興趣與休閒	生活與工作	文法解析

Addie: Wonderful. It's good to have a doctor as your boyfriend.

所以有個醫生當男朋友還真好。

◎Work Bank◎ 隨時補充一錠，你在會話及閱讀理解必備的單字！

- ⊛ **sport** [sport] 運動
- 働 **go** [go] 從事運動+Ving
- ⊛ **soccer** [ˋsakɚ] 足球
- ⊛ **rugby** [ˋrʌgbɪ] 橄欖球
- ⊛ **basketball** [ˋbæskɪtˏbɔl] 籃球
- ⊛ **table tennis** [ˋtebl] [ˋtɛnɪs] 桌球
- ⊛ **golf** [gɑlf] 高爾夫球
- ⊛ **dodge ball** [dɑdʒ] [bɔl] 躲避球
- ⊛ **cricket** [ˋkrɪkɪt] 板球
- ⊛ **bowling** [ˋbolɪŋ] 保齡球
- ⊛ **volleyball** [ˋvɑlɪˏbɔl] 排球
- ⊛ **swimming** [ˋswɪmɪŋ] 游泳
- ⊛ **diving** [ˋdaɪvɪŋ] 潛水
- ⊛ **snorkelling** [ˋsnɔrklɪŋ] 浮潛
- ⊛ **sailing** [ˋselɪŋ] 航行
- ⊛ **climbing** [ˋklaɪmɪŋ] 攀岩
- ⊛ **skating** [ˋsketɪŋ] 溜冰
- 働 **go for a walk** 散步
- ⊛ **dancing** [ˋdænsɪŋ] 跳舞
- ⊛ **bungee jumping** [ˋbʌndʒɪ] [ˋdʒʌmpɪŋ] 高空彈跳
- ⊛ **cycling** [ˋsaɪklɪŋ] 騎自行車
- ⊛ **exercise** [ˋɛksɚˏsaɪz] 運動
- ⊛ **gymnastics** [dʒɪmˋnæstɪks] 體操
- ⊛ **stadium** [ˋstedɪəm] 體育場
- ⊛ **field** [fild] 野外；棒球場
- ⊛ **court** [kort] 網球場、籃球場
- ⊛ **gym** [dʒɪm]/ **gymnasium** [dʒɪmˋnezɪəm] 體育館；健身房
- ⊛ **playground** [ˋpleˏgraʊnd] 操場
- 働 **play** [ple] 打、踢(球類運動)
- 働 **do** [du] 做(體操、瑜珈)
- ⊛ **football** [ˋfʊtˏbɔl] 足球；橄欖球
- ⊛ **American football** 美式足球
- ⊛ **baseball** [ˋbesˏbɔl] 棒球運動
- ⊛ **ping pong** [ˋpɪŋˏpɔn] 乒乓球
- ⊛ **tennis** [ˋtɛnɪs] 網球
- ⊛ **badminton** [ˋbædmɪntən] 羽毛球
- ⊛ **hockey** [ˋhɑkɪ] 曲棍球
- ⊛ **billiards** [ˋbɪljɚdz] 撞球
- ⊛ **pool** [pul] 撞球/ 游泳池
- ⊛ **surfing** [ˋsɝfɪŋ] 衝浪
- ⊛ **scuba-diving** [ˋskubəˏdaɪvɪŋ] 潛水
- ⊛ **windsurfing** [ˋwɪndˏsɝfɪŋ] 風帆衝浪
- ⊛ **hiking** [ˋhaɪkɪŋ] 健行
- ⊛ **skiing** [ˋskiɪŋ] 滑雪
- ⊛ **jogging** [ˋdʒɑgɪŋ] 慢跑
- ⊛ **car racing** [kar] [ˋresɪŋ] 賽車
- ⊛ **aerobics** [ˏeəˋrobɪks] 有氧運動
- ⊛ **riding** [ˋraɪɪŋ] 騎馬、騎車
- ⊛ **practice** [ˋpræktɪs] 練習；訓練
- ⊛ **yoga** [ˋjogə] 瑜珈
- ⊛ **equipment** [ɪˋkwɪpmənt] 設備
- ⊛ **facility** [fəˋsɪlətɪ] 設備；工具
- ⊛ **track** [træk] 軌道；跑道
- ⊛ **team** [tim] 團隊；球隊

㊝**bat** [bæt] 棒球、板球球棒、桌球球拍　㊝ **net** [nɛt] 網子
㊝**racket** [ˋrækɪt] 網球、羽毛球拍　㊝ **golf club** [gɑlf][klʌb] 高爾夫球桿
㊝**ball** [bɔl] 球　㊝**point** [pɔɪnt] /**score** [skor] 得分
㊝**player** [ˋpleɚ] 球員　㊝**athlete** [ˋæθlit] 運動員
㊝**coach** [kotʃ] 教練　㊝**umpire** [ˋʌmpaɪr] /**judge** [dʒʌdʒ] 裁判
㊝**runner** [ˋrʌnɚ] 跑者　㊝**match** [mætʃ] 比賽
㊝**Olympics** [oˋlɪmpɪks] 奧林匹克運動會　㊝**game** [gem] 比賽
㊝**tournament** [ˋtɝnəmənt] 比賽；巡迴賽事
㊰ **dribble** [ˋdrɪbl̩] 運球　㊰ **shoot** [ʃut] 射球
㊰ **crossover dribble** [ˋkrɔsˏovɚ][ˋdrɪbl̩] 交叉運球
㊰ **slam dunk** [slæm][dʌŋk] 灌籃　㊰ **defend** [dɪˋfɛnd] 防守
㊰ **pitch** [pɪtʃ] 投球　㊰ **catch** [kætʃ] 接球
㊰ **serve** [sɝv] 發球　㊰ **return** [rɪˋtɝn] 擊球
㊝**singles** [ˋsɪŋglz] 單打　㊝**doubles** [ˋdʌblz] 雙打
㊰ **win the triumph** [ˋtraɪəmf] 勝利　㊰ **defeat** [dɪˋfit] 擊敗
MLB/ Major League Baseball 美國職棒大聯盟
NBA/ National Basketball Association 美國國家籃球協會
WNBA/ Women National Basketball Association
美國女子國家籃球協會
Wimbledon championships 溫布頓網球錦標賽
Open championships 公開賽
LPGA/ Ladies Professional Golf Association 女子職業高爾夫協會
PGA/ Professional Golf Association 職業高爾夫協會
FIFA/ Federation International Football Association 國際足球協會

Reading Passage 1

Notice

The fitness center doesn't come with any instructors.
Please read the instructions carefully before you use the
facilities. Children under the age of 12 or 130 cm are
NOT allowed to enter the swimming pool and SPA
area. Thank you for your cooperation.

_____ (1) Where might we see the notice?
A. A baseball field.　　B. A playground on campus.
C. A tennis court.　　D. A gymnasium.

_____ (2) Why do we have to read the instructions?
A. There will be no one that can help us use the machines.
B. The machines are too expensive for us to use.
C. Children are always troublesome.
D. We have to pay for the extra fee to hire an instructor.

_____ (3) When should we read the instructions?
A. Before we start to use it.　　B. When we get hurt.
C. When we check out.　　D. After we swim.

_____ (4) According to the notice, who can enter the SPA area?
A. Anyone who is above 12 years old.
B. Anyone who has no instructor.
C. Anyone who is under 130 cm.
D. Anyone who can swim.

♥愛的筆記貼♥ 本篇閱讀是一個告示。主要是告訴大家：這個健身中心沒有任何的健身教練，所以請在使用這些器材前仔細地閱讀指引說明。未滿12歲或是在130公分以下的兒童不許進入游泳池及水療區域。感謝您的合作。解答：1. (D) 我們可能在一個健身房看到這樣的告示。2. (A) 因為可能沒有任何人來幫助我們使用這些器材，我們必需先閱讀這些指引。 3. (A) 我們必需要在使用前閱讀說明文字。 4. (A) 根據這篇告示，任何在12歲以上的人都可以進入水療區。

Reading Passage 2

Do you want to dance with me online? Let's go bowling on Wii tonight. Through the motion sensors and simulators, today, we can also play an exciting baseball game alone at home. Any time, anywhere, and even any kinds of weather, you can just do any sports if you want. Sports are not limited by the time, weather, and skills anymore. Anybody could be Chien-Ming Wang, Kobe Bryant, Elena Dementieva in the online world. Some people really enjoy the convenience from the new technology while others think neither TV games nor online games are able to **replace** the importance of doing REAL exercises. "People need to burn their calories by the real motions more than shaking or waving." said by a doctor, William. Another psychologist Lisa suggests that "sometimes we do sports not only for ourselves but also with friends. We may know friends more and learn the experiences to share the triumph or failure results through a game." Sports are not only for fun and relaxing. It can also offer us some entertainment when we watch the games. After all, whatever the forms we choose to access sports, both of our mental and physical condition will be well-balanced because of the regular exercises. Are you happy with today's game on TV? Do you do any exercises today? Let's just do it now!

_____ (1) What is the main idea of the passage?
A. The importance of sport.   B. Sport spirit.
C. Different ways of doing sports.
D. The ways to be a top athlete one day.

_____ (2) According to the passage, why can we slam dunk if we don't have such a skill?

A. It's possible in an online game.   B. It's just a dream.

C. The instructor will teach us.

D. We can slam ourselves anytime.

_____ (3)   What does "replace" mean?

    A. take turns   B. instead of

    C. take place   D. use something again

_____ (4)   What does Dr. William mean?

    A. He doesn't agree with Lisa's opinion.

    B. Doing too much exercise is harmful.

    C. Playing online sports game doesn't burn enough calories.

    D. Through doing sports, people share their feelings with others to balance and comfort their mind.

_____ (5)   Which one is **TURE** about the passage?

    A. Whether you do sports or not is good for your health.

    B. Watching the baseball game is harmful to our hearts.

    C. Go jogging in the morning every day is good to us.

    D. It's impossible to be someone like Kobe.

●愛的筆記貼● 本篇內容:你想要和我在線上跳舞嗎?我們今晚一起打 Wii 的保齡球遊戲吧!透過動作感應器和模擬器,現在,我們也可以獨自一人在家打一場刺激的棒球賽。任何時間、任何地方、而且甚至是何種天氣,只要你想的話你可以從事任何型態的運動。運動不再受到時間、天氣和技巧的限制了。任何人在線上世界裡都可能是(棒球名將)王建民、(籃球名將)寇比布萊恩特、(網球名將)伊莉娜狄曼提娃。有些人很享受來自新科技的便利性,在此同時其他人認為電視遊戲或線上遊戲都不能取代從事真正的運動的重要性。『人們需要透過真正的動作來燃燒他們的卡洛里甚過於只是搖搖或揮手。』一位威廉醫生這麼說。另一位心理學家麗莎建議『有時候我們從事運動並不只是為了我們自己,也是為了和朋友一起。我們可能透過一場球賽更加地認識我們的朋友,也可以從分享勝利或失敗的結果中學習經驗。』運動不只是為了有趣和放鬆而已。它也可以提供我們一些娛樂當我們看比賽的時候。畢竟,不管我們選擇什麼形式來接觸運動,因為規律的運動我們的心靈和身體狀況將會均衡。你滿意今天電視轉播的球賽嗎？你今天有做任何運動嗎？讓我們現在就做做運動吧！

解答：**1. (C)** 最符合這篇文章的主題是『從事運動不同的方法』。**2. (A)** 即使我們沒有灌籃的技巧但我們還是可以在線上遊戲裡灌籃。 **3. (B)** replace 這個字是『代替』的意思，所以選 instead of。take turns 輪流、take place 發生、舉行，using something again 再利用一次，可以是 reuse 或 recycle 回收之意。**4. (C)** 威廉醫生的意思是玩線上遊戲並不會燃燒足夠的卡洛里。**5. (C)** 每天早上慢跑是一種規律的運動所以對我們健康有益。

Vocabulary Challenge

_____ 1. _____ is a water sport.

  (A) Hiking   (B) Scuba-diving   (C) Bowling   (D) Hockey

_____ 2. The Williams sisters are famous for their strong _____ in

  tennis. (A) defending (B) pitching (C) serving (D) shooting

_____ 3. Six players were banned for the following games because

  they disobeyed the _____ in the match.

  (A) team player   (B) athlete   (C) coach   (D) umpire

_____ 4. 9 to 5 as the result. The Bears team was _____ for 4 points

  behind.   (A) won   (B) defeated   (C) lost   (D) got

_____ 5. All the most excellent _____ are on ESPN channel, the best

  choice for sports fans!

  (A) literary works   (B) tournaments

  (C) master pieces   (D) equipments

_____ 6. Regular exercises and a healthy diet help us _____.

  (A) keep fit   (B) lose jobs   (C) give away   (D) get weight

解答：(1) B (2) C (3) D (4) B (5) B (6) A

Lesson 10 | 閱讀 Reading

🎙 Language box 🎙

Focus One

Do you like reading? (你喜歡閱讀嗎？)

If yes, why do you like reading? (如果是，為何喜歡閱讀呢？)

What do you like to read? (你喜歡讀些什麼？)

What's your favorite book? (你最喜歡的書是什麼書？)

Do you like to read alone or join in a reading club?
(你喜歡自己看書還是參加閱讀社團？)

Do you prefer reading magazines or books?
(你較喜歡看雜誌還是看書？)

Who's your favorite author? (你最喜歡的作者是誰？)

What's your favorite book? (你最喜歡的書是什麼書？)

How often do you go to the library? (你多久去一次圖書館？)

**Do you prefer borrowing books from other people or
buying new books?** (你較喜歡和別人借書還是買新的書？)

**Do you like to buy books in a bookstore or through
shopping online?** (你喜歡去書店買書還是上網買書？)

✎ 語言注意面 Language Caution ✎

A: <u>Would you like to</u> have a look in this book?
(你想要看一下這本書的內容嗎？)

B: Yes, may I? I've waited for the author's latest work so long.
(是啊，我可以看一下嗎？我已經等這個作者的最新作品等了好久了。)

A: Can you help me close the door?
I've gotten too many stuff in my hands.
(你可以幫我關一下門嗎？我手上拿太多東西了。)

B: Yes, I would love to. (好，我樂意幫你。)

A: Do you want to go out to see a movie with me?
(你想不想和我一起出去看場電影？)

B: In such a typhoon day? No, I would rather stay at home.
(在這樣一個颱風天？不了，我還是寧願待在家裡。)

♥愛的筆記貼♥ 以上是為同學們整理了 would 的三種說法。第一種 would like to 和第二種 would love to，同學們會發覺語意上有時挺相像的。因為 like 喜歡和 love 愛，兩個字的感覺本來就很接近。但我們通常用 would like to 來表示『想要』做某件事，類似 want to 的用法，而 would love to 是『樂意、心甘情願，願意』的意思。語氣上有些差別。至於 would rather+原形動詞的用法，則是指比起某件事來說，我『寧願』做某件事。

Focus Two

Do you prefer fiction or non-fiction books?
(你較喜歡小說還是非小說類的書？)

Do you write some reviews after reading?
(在閱讀過後你會寫一些評論/讀後感想嗎？)

If I would like to start from some horror stories, what will you recommend?
(如果我想要從一些恐怖故事開始看起，你會推薦什麼給我看呢？.)

How did you find the digital publications?
(你對數位出版品有什麼看法？)

Where do you enjoy reading mostly?

(你大部份時間都在哪裡享受閱讀時光？)

Have you ever made any comments on blogs?

(你曾經在部落格上發表過評論嗎？)

<練習> 有人問你以上關於閱讀的問題?你會怎麼回答呢？以下整理一位同學的回答當作範例，劃線部份可依標號來找對應的字彙群組，可以幫助你練習講講有關自己的閱讀喜好喔！

Sure[1], I love[2] reading. Reading for me is really an enjoyable moment[3]. I prefer the traditional things more than the digital publications[4]. I enjoy reading the true stories[5] which make me feel warm and passionate[6]. I read[7] newspaper every morning[8]. And I also prefer[9] the biographic and encouraging kindle books[10]. I go to the book shops twice a month[11].

❤愛的筆記貼❤ 這個練習主要是幫同學們擬一份自我的閱讀興趣草稿，例題的內容是：當然，我熱愛閱讀。閱讀對我來說真是一個享受的時刻。我較喜歡傳統的事物甚過於數位出版品。我最喜歡讀真實的故事，他們總是使我感到溫暖且充滿熱情。我每天早上都看報，而且我也喜歡傳記類的和勵志類的書籍。

　　同學們可以循劃線部份的數字來找每一欄位中的代換單詞，可以先檢視一下自己懂得閱讀相關單字有哪些？以下是為了不喜歡閱讀的同學，提供一些代換的答案。試著講講看自己對閱讀的看法吧！

1. Not really　2. dislike　3. a torture　4. the digital publications more than the traditional things　5. gossips and ghost stories　6. relaxed and pleasant 7. don't read　8. at all　9. dislike　10. the science, history, and some serious books　11. Sometimes, I go to the library to get done my papers. But be honest, I would rather check something useful through the Internet. It's fast and efficient.

如果照以上代換的回答來說，語意即為：不會，我不喜歡閱讀。閱讀對我來說真是一種折磨。我較喜歡數位出版品甚過於傳統的事物。我最喜歡看八卦消息和鬼故事，他們總是使我感到放鬆且愉快。我從不看報，而且我不喜歡科學、歷史和嚴肅的書籍。有時候，我去圖書館只是完成我的報告。但是說老實話，我寧願透過網路來查一些有用的資訊。它快又有效率。

⊙ Conversation 1 ⊙

(Collin 和 Laura 在圖書館找書。)

Laura: What are you looking for?	你在找什麼？
Collin: The Perfect Murders. Volume 4.	完美謀殺案，第四冊。
Laura: Have you checked the fiction section?	你查過小說區了嗎？
Collin: Of course I did. The other 9 volumes are still on the shelf, but the Vol. 4 is just missing.	我當然查過了。其他的 9 冊都仍然在架上，但是第四冊就是不見了。
Laura: That's a pity, but why are you looking here? I thought it's the science and nature section.	真是遺憾，但為什麼你在這找呢？我還以為這是科學和自然區呢。
Collin: I knew but I think someone who loves the series so much as me will probably hide it somewhere out of logic.	我知道但是我在想這人如果和我一樣這麼喜歡這系列，大概會把它藏在一個沒什麼邏輯的地方。
Laura: All right. Tell me, did you do the same thing before?	好吧。告訴我，你以前做過同樣的事嗎？
Collin: That's a good question. Let's solve it some other day. Now, just be a detective. Where could he hide it?	那真是個好問題。讓我們改天再來解答。現在，只要做一個偵探就好。他到底把它藏在哪呢？

Laura: Come on! You seem to be way too far. Maybe it's simply borrowed by somebody and hasn't been returned back.

Collin: I've checked the due date was yesterday. Wait a minute. You're right. What if he didn't return it back? Nice, let's ask the librarian. May I request the book "The Perfect Murders Volume 4", written by Peter Rockefeller? I've checked everywhere but fail.

Librarian: Yes, it's overdue. We will call it back for you in no time. Would you like to reserve it?

Collin: Yes, please.

Librarian: Your name and account, please.

Collin: Jason B. Malcolm JBM106632.

Librarian: Are you kidding me? It's not fun at all. The guy who is occupying the book now is exactly yourself, Jason Malcolm!

Laura: Oh, that's really the funniest mystery I've ever seen.

拜託！你似乎有點太超過囉！也許它只是單純被某人借走，而且還沒被還回來而已。

我已經確認過期限是昨天了。等一下。你是對的。那如果它沒有還回來呢？真好，我們去問圖書館員好了。我可以問一下這本由彼得洛克斐勒寫的完美謀殺案第四集嗎？我已經到處找過但是找不著。

是的，它過期了。我們將會為你盡快把它召回。你想要預訂它嗎？

是的，麻煩你。

你的名字和帳號，麻煩給我一下。

傑森 B 麥爾康。帳號是 JBM106632。

你在跟我開玩笑嗎？一點都不好玩。現在佔有這本書的傢伙的確是你自己沒錯，傑森麥爾康！

喔，那真是我曾看過最奇怪的謎了。

Conversation 2

(Doris 和 Addie 一起邊看雜誌邊聊天。)

Doris: Look at these models! Do they eat anything?

看看這些模特兒！他們有吃任何東西嗎？

Addie: Sure, darling. They have brownies all the time and pick their throats to throw up again and again.

當然囉，親愛的。他們總是吃布朗尼然後不斷地挖喉嚨把它們吐出來。

Doris: Yuck! Who told you that?

好噁心！誰跟你說是這樣的？

Addie: Well. Some gossip newspapers or you may find them time to time on some websites.

有些八卦小報或者你有時在一些網站上也可以找到這些消息啊。

Doris: Seriously, the designer dressings are gorgeous, but I just can't get rid of the "Armani nightmare".

說實在的，這些設計師品牌的服裝真的好棒喔，但是我就是沒辦法擺脫上次的『亞曼尼夢魘』。

Addie: Oh, right. Why not read some qigong, yoga, or recipes of healthy diets instead? Forget about the fashion magazines.

喔，對喔。你為什麼不看一些氣功、瑜珈或是健康飲食的食譜來代替呢？忘了那些時尚雜誌吧！

Doris: You want me to run away from the RUNWAY? No way, it's one of my shiny dreams.

你要我逃離『伸展台』？不行，這是我閃亮亮的夢想中的其中之一呢！

Addie: Does your boyfriend like reading those magazines?

你男朋友喜歡讀那些雜誌嗎？

Doris: Of course not. We have different collections. His favorites are OUTDOORS and EXPLORER. For such an image lover like me, they are really brilliant to have so many spectacular photos inside.

當然不會。我們有不同的收藏。他的最愛是戶外生活及探險家雜誌。對像我這樣一個影像愛好者來說，他們在雜誌裡放了那麼多壯觀的照片真是聰明。

Addie: That's really a good way to bribe a man's girlfriend.

那真是個好方法來賄賂一下男人的女友。

Doris: Yeah, that's why we are big subscribers for so many magazine publishers, and they also rewarded us with the annual discounts and hundreds of gifts so far.

是啊,那就是為什麼我們是那麼多家雜誌社的大訂戶了,而且到目前為止他們也用每年的折扣及數百件禮物來回報我們。

◎Work Bank◎ 隨時補充一錠,你在會話及閱讀理解必備的單字!

- 名 **book** [buk] 書
- 名 **magazine** [ˌmægəˋzin] 雜誌
- 名 **newspaper** [ˋnjuzˌpepɚ] 報紙
- 名 **DM=Direct Mail** [dəˋrɛkt] [mel] 大量投遞的廣告信函
- 名 **flyer** [ˋflaɪɚ] 傳單
- 名 **editor** [ˋɛdɪtɚ] 編輯
- 名 **free lance** [fri][læns] 自由作家
- 名 **royalty** [ˋrɔɪəltɪ] 版稅
- 名 **publisher** [ˋpʌblɪʃɚ] 出版商
- 動 **subscribe** [səbˋskraɪb] 訂購
- 名 **subscription** [səbˋskrɪpʃən] 訂閱
- 名 **fiction** [ˋfɪkʃən] 小說
- 名 **genre** [ˋʒɑnrə] 文藝作品類型
- 名 **writer** [ˋraɪtɚ] 作家;撰稿人
- 名 **book store** 書店
- 名 **publication** [ˌpʌblɪˋkeʃən] 出版品
- 名 **composition** [ˌkɑmpəˋzɪʃən] 作文
- 名 **passage** [ˋpæsɪdʒ] 短篇文章
- 動 **copy** [ˋkɑpɪ] 複製;抄襲
- 名 **copyright** [ˋkɑpɪˌraɪt] 版權
- 形 **interesting** [ˋɪntərɪstɪŋ] 有趣的
- 形 **funny** [ˋfʌnɪ] 奇怪的;好笑的
- 形 **serious** [ˋsɪrɪəs] 嚴肅的
- 名 **category** [ˋkætəˌgorɪ] 分類

- 名 **blog** [blog] 部落格;網誌
- 名 **webpage** [ˋwɛbˌpedʒ] 網頁
- 動 **read** [rid] 閱讀

- 動 **edit** [ˋɛdɪt] 編輯
- 名 **flat fee** [flæt][fi] 版稅
- 形 **advanced** [ədˋvænst] 預先的
- 動 **publish** [ˋpʌblɪʃ] 出版
- 動 **release** [hed] 出版;發行
- 名 **subscriber** [səbˋskraɪbɚ] 訂戶
- 名 **nonfiction** [nɑnˋfɪkʃən] 非小說類
- 名 **column** [ˋkɑləm] 專欄
- 名 **author** [ˋɔθɚ] 作家;創始人
- 形 **digital** [ˋdɪdʒɪtl] 數位的
- 名 **article** [ˋɑrtɪkl] 文章
- 名 **masterpiece** [ˋmæstɚˌpis] 名作
- 名 **paragraph** [ˋpærəˌgræf] 段落
- 名 **plagiarism** [ˋpledʒɚˌrɪzəm] 抄襲
- 動 **plagiarize** [ˋpledʒɚˌraɪz] 抄襲
- 形 **sad** [sæd] 難過的
- 形 **boring** [ˋborɪŋ] 無聊的
- 名 **catalog** [ˋkætələg] 目錄
- 名 **periodical** [ˌpɪrɪˋɑdɪkl] 期刊

名 physics [ˈfɪzɪks] 物理學
名 chemistry [ˈkɛmɪstrɪ] 化學
名 biology [baɪˈaˌlədʒɪ] 生物學
名 technology [tɛkˈnaˌlədʒɪ] 技術
名 science [ˈsaɪəns] 科學
名 art [ɑrt] 藝術
名 literature [ˈlɪtərətʃɚ] 文學
名 history [ˈhɪstərɪ] 歷史
名 mathematics [ˌmæθəˈmætɪks] 數學
名 etiquette [ˈɛtɪkɛt] 禮節；禮儀
名 politics [ˈpaˌlətɪks] 政治
名 law [lɔ] 法律
名 education [ˌɛdʒʊˈkeʃən] 教育
名 communication [kəˌmjunəˈkeʃən] 通訊
名 transportation [ˌtrænspɚˈteʃən] 運輸；交通
名 photography [fəˈtɑɡrəfɪ] 攝影術
名 audiobooks 有聲書
名 memoir [ˈmɛmwɑr] 自傳；回憶錄
名 business [ˈbɪznɪs] 商業；生意
名 investment [ɪnˈvɛstmənt] 投資
名 graphic [ˈɡræfɪk] 圖解；圖畫
名 computer & Internet 電腦網路
名 crafts [kræft] 手工藝
名 entertainment [ˌɛntɚˈtenmənt] 娛樂
名 recreation [ˌrɛkrɪˈeʃən] 消遣
名 gay [ɡe] 同性戀；男同性戀
名 health [hɛlθ] 健康
名 body [ˈbadɪ] 身體
名 mystery [ˈmɪstərɪ] 神秘小說；推理小說
名 thriller [ˈθrɪlɚ] 恐怖；探險小說
名 outdoors [ˈaʊtˌdorz] 戶外生活
名 Parenting & Families 為人父母親及家人
形 professional [prəˈfɛʃənl̩] 專業的
名 puzzles & games 拼圖及遊戲

名 generality [ˌdʒɛnəˈrælətɪ] 總論
名 philosophy [fəˈlasəfɪ] 哲學
名 religion [rɪˈlɪdʒən] 宗教
形 social [ˈsoʃəl] 社會的；社交的
名 social science 社會科學
名 language [ˈlæŋɡwɪdʒ] 語言
名 geography [ˈdʒɪˈagrəfɪ] 地理
名 psychology [saɪˈkaˌlədʒɪ] 心理學
名 custom [ˈkʌstəm] 習俗
名 folklore [ˈfokˌlor] 民俗
名 economics [ˌikəˈnamɪks] 經濟
名 military [ˈmɪləˌtɛrɪ] 軍事
名 commerce [ˈkamɝs] 商業
名 kindle [ˈkɪndl̩] 心靈勵志類
名 biography [baɪˈagrəfɪ] 傳記
名 comic [ˈkamɪk] 卡漫；漫畫
名 novel [ˈnavl̩] 小說
名 cooking 烹飪 名 cuisine 美食
名 hobbies 嗜好
名 lesbian [ˈlɛzbɪən] 女同性戀
名 mind [maɪnd] 心智
名 home & garden 家及花園美化
名 Nature [ˈnetʃɚ] 大自然
名 reference [ˈrɛfərəns] 參考書

㊜ **spirituality** [ˌspɪrɪtʃʊˈælɪtɪ] 精神；靈性 ㊜ **self-help** [ˈsɛlfˈhɛlp] 自助
㊏ **sports** [spɔrts] 運動的　　　㊜ **textbook** [ˈtɛkstˌbʊk] 教科書；課本
㊏ **teens** 青少年的　　　　　　　㊜ **travel** 旅遊

♥愛的筆記貼♥ 以上的單字，大部份是關於閱讀書籍的分類名稱，
提供同學們在講到自己對於閱讀的興趣時，可以用上的一些單字。以上
除了介紹一般在圖書館常見到的分類名稱，也為同學介紹了 Amazon 亞
瑪遜書店的分類名稱，所以同學們會看到一些似乎不像類別的單字出現
在這張字彙表上，但亞瑪遜網路書店的分類是有其指標性的，表示現在
最熱門常見的書種，所以大家可以參考看看。

Reading Passage 1

Reading becomes quite different from time to time. It could be discussed in mainly three points, the publishing channels, the genres, and the attitude. Do you prefer reading magazines or blogs? What kind of topics does attract you more? Romance or nonfiction? Are you a critical reader or a yes-person when you are reading? These questions above are worthy to consider and they could help you understand yourself better!

Media

Every day in the modern life, there are many media presenting the updating or everlasting, useful or useless, real or just gossip information to us. Whatever you like or not, information goes into your life anywhere and anytime through varied media, i.e. the news reported on TV, newspapers, magazines, websites and blogs, forums and chat rooms, fliers, brochures and booklets, books, e-mails, newsletters, etc.. With the development of the new technology, some of the media boom while others are less demanded. Take newspapers and magazines for example, the sales amount of both of the traditional media apparently reduced because of the popular and efficient media through the Internet.

Genre

Mostly, we divide the reading topics into two types, fiction and non-fiction. The most famous series of fiction books are "The Ring of Lord" and "Harry Potter". Those two series are neither real nor relevant to our daily life. They are just fantasy but the talented authors presented their great imagination and

creative. Both of the master piece series meant a lot as an important section in the literature field. On the other hand, if you like to read some facts and true stories, something practical to your mind and life, you may walk to the non-fiction section in a bookstore quite often. Any computer instructions, an encouraging autobiography of a successful celebrity, a persuasive financial suggestion or economic problems analyzing book may be your favorites. No matter your favorites belonged to either of them, those books

did inspire you a lot. Besides sorting by fiction and non-fiction, there is one special topic namely "gossip". Despite the fact that gossip is nothing about true or false, practical or unrealistic, people like and want to know about the celebrities' personal and public life. Gossip becomes a common topic whenever we are with our families, friends, and colleagues.

Attitude

To be a critical reader is not so easy for most people. We usually do reading because we want to learn something interesting, new, or even useful. Mostly, readers accept the authors' ideas and concepts from the articles. However, not everything they told is all right and perfect. People all have their own views and emotion, so everyone could see things in different ways. Some of the views could be objective and acceptable while others could be dogmatic and arguable. Anything ridiculous yesterday could be something normal today. Holding a critical thinking is a good way to maintain you as a wise reader rather than being a yes-man to all the information. To be a wise reader, you may have to think about why I want to read and what I want to know from the article first. Then, you start setting up few questions in your mind. After your reading, you may

check your questions and try to define if the book has given you what you need or not. Maybe you will get more than your expectation! Let's start exploring a new world and enjoy our reading from now on!

_____ (1) What is the main idea of the article?
   A. Be a wise reader.
   B. Fiction is more creative.
   C. Know how to read, read to know more things.
   D. Digital media may substitute the traditional media totally.

_____ (2) Which one is **NOT** a nonfiction book?
   A. Chicken soup for inspiring your potential.
   B. Yoga, anytime and anywhere.
   C. Speech master: achieving better presentation.
   D. Romeo and Juliet.

_____ (3) According to the article, what kind of topics do most people talk about all the time?
   A. Literature master pieces.
   B. Celebrities' personal life.
   C. How to fix the crack in the economic crisis.
   D. Critical readers are always irritable.

_____ (4) What does the sentence "*Anything ridiculous yesterday could be something normal today.*" mean in the article?
   A. The readers should think carefully when they read.
   B. The readers should believe every word the authors said.
   C. The readers should learn how to quarrel with each other.
   D. Anybody could be an author some day.

_____ (5) According to the article, what's **NOT** true about a wise reader? A wise reader will…
   A. pick the topics to read.
   B. set up some goals before reading.

C. check what he or she has already learned after reading.
D. choose the books up to the cover design.

❤愛的筆記貼❤　閱讀不時地改變成相當不同的模式。這情形主要可以分為三點來被討論：出版方式、類型，以及態度。你較喜歡看雜誌還是網誌(部落格)？什麼樣的主題比較吸引你呢？浪漫的故事還是非小說的類別？當你在閱讀時，你是一個批判性思考的讀者還是唯命是從的讀者呢？以上這些問題都值得我們來想想，而且這些問題可以幫助你更了解自己！媒體：在現代生活的每一天裡，有很多的媒體來呈現不斷更新的或者是永恆的、有用的或沒用的、真實的或者只是八卦訊息給我們。不管你喜歡或不喜歡，資訊從不同的媒體在任何地點任何時間進入了你的生活。例如：在電視、報紙、雜誌、網站和部落格、討論區和聊天室、廣告傳單、廣告手冊、書、電子郵件、商業通訊上報告的新聞，等等。隨著新科技的發展，這些媒體其中的一些繁榮、快速成長了起來，而其他的可能就相對地需求減少。舉報紙和雜誌為例，這兩個傳統媒體的銷售量因為這些透過網路而受歡迎且效率高的媒體而明顯地減少。類型：大部份來說，我們將閱讀主題分為兩個型態：小說類和非小說類。最有名的小說類的系列就是『魔戒』及『哈利波特』。這兩個系列既不是真實的也不是和我們日常生活有關。他們只是幻想的但是這些有天份的作者展現出他們極佳的想像力和創造力。兩個大師系列都對文學領域意義重大且佔有一個重要的區域。在另一方面，如果你喜歡閱讀一些事實和真實的故事，一些對你的心靈和生活有實際影響的，你也許會常常走到書店中的非小說類區。任何電腦的指引手冊、一位成功名流激勵人心的自傳、一本有說服力的財務建議，或者是經濟問題的分析書可能會是你的最愛。不管你的最愛是小說還是非小說類其中的一種，這些書都的確激發你很多。除了由小說和非小說來分類，還有一種特別的主題就是『八卦』。儘管事實是八卦是無關是非對錯、真實或不真實，人們喜歡而且想要知道名流私底下或公領域的生活。八卦變成了一種不管何時我們和家人、朋友、同事聊天的共通常見話題。態度：要當一位批判性思考的讀者對大部份人來說不是很容易的事。我們通常從事閱讀是因為我們想要學到一些有趣、新穎或者是有用的事。大部份來說，讀者從文章裡接受了作者的想法和概念。然而，他們講得不是每件事都是對的和完美的。人們都有他們自己的觀點和情緒，所以每個人可以用不同方法來看事情。有些觀點是客觀而可以接受的，而有些觀點則可能是武斷的或具有爭議性的。任何昨天覺得很荒謬的事可能在今天是件很正常的事。持有一種批判性的思考是種好方法來維持自己是個明智的讀者甚過於當個接受所有資訊的唯命是從的人。要成為一個明智的讀者，你可能必需在一開始時就要想想為什麼我要讀這篇文章和我從這篇文章中想要學到哪些東西。然後，你在心中開始設定一些問題。在閱讀後，你可以檢視一下自己的問題而且試著定義這本書有沒有給你你所需要的。也許你將會獲得超乎你想像的更多東西。讓我們開始探索一個新世界而且從現在開始享受閱讀吧！**解答：1.(C)這篇文章的主旨是『知道怎麼閱讀，閱讀幫你學到更多事』。 2.(D) 羅蜜歐和茱莉葉不是非小說類。 3.(B) 根據這篇文章所述大部份的人都在討論名流的私生活。 4.(A) 讀者應想清楚他們在讀什麼(做個批判性思考的讀者)。 5.(D)從封面設計來挑書不是文章中所提到明智的讀者會做的事。**

Vocabulary Challenge

_____ 1. Jamie Oliver donates part of his _____ from his best-selling cooking books to promote a diet innovation in UK.

(A) royal   (B) free lances   (C) subscribers   (D) royalty

_____ 2. Some celebrities like to publish their _____, but they sometimes therefore irritate their friends or foes.

(A) memoir   (B) newspapers   (C) scandals   (D) leases

_____ 3. There is too much _____ in your ads. Could you simplify it and people will understand your purposes better.

(A) news   (B) information   (C) tricks   (D) folklore

_____ 4. Vincent is always rude to girls. I bet that he doesn't have an _____ instruction on his bookshelf.

(A) etiquette   (B) unit   (C) animation   (D) biology

解答：(1) D (2) A (3) B (4) A

Lesson **11** | 租屋與傢俱
Renting a house and furnishings

🗣 Language box 🗣

| **Focus One** |

Where do you live? (你住在哪裡？)

Where do you want to live? (你想要住哪？)

Do you like your neighborhood? (你喜歡你家的周遭環境嗎？)

Do you know any of your neighbors?
(你認識任何一位鄰居嗎？)

Do you live alone, share an apartment with other friends, or live with your family?
(你自己住，還是跟朋友們分租一間公寓，或是跟家人住一起？)

Is your neighborhood convenient? (你家附近便利嗎？)

How long does it take from your house to your workplace/ school? (從你家到工作地方或學校要多久時間？)

What's your favorite book? (你最喜歡的書是什麼書？)

✎ 語言注意面 Language Caution ✎

A: <u>How long does it take</u> from your house to your school?
　　(你從家裡到學校要花多久時間？)

B: <u>It</u> usually <u>takes me</u> 30 minutes if there is no traffic jam.
　　(通常都要花我 30 分鐘，如果沒有塞車的話。)

A: <u>How far</u> is your house from our school?
　　(你家離我們學校有多遠？)

B: It is about 5 blocks away. It is about a 30-minute way by
   bus. (大概在 5 條街遠的地方。坐公車大概是一趟 30 分鐘的路程。)

♥愛的筆記貼♥ 以上是為同學們整理了 How long 和 How far 兩
個問題的用法。第一種問句形式 How long 是指時間的『多久』。第二
種問句形式 How far 是指距離的『多遠』。How long 通常會指一件事
物花了人多久的時間，所以和『花費的四大動詞 spend、pay、cost、take』
中的 take 常一起使用。How long does it take you to complete the work?
此類句型中的 it 虛主詞，指得就是後面『to complete the work』完成
工作這件事。這件事當主詞，花時間用『take』這個動詞。有關花費
的四大動詞，在本書後半部的文法解析第二章動詞單元有詳細介紹，
請同學要多練習。第二個問句是 How far 問『多遠』，對於距離我們通
常會說長度有多少，但我們也可以用『乘坐交通工具』多久來說明對
距離的感覺。

┤ **Focus Two** ├

Please describe your house. (請敘述一下你的住家狀況。)

Do you have a house for rent? (你有房子要出租嗎？)

Is it a suite/studio or a room? (是套房還是雅房？)

How many rooms are there in your house?
(在你的房子裡有多少間房間？)

How is the furnishing in the house? (房裡的設備如何？)

Do you offer some appliances/ utilities?
(你有提供一些電器設備嗎？)

Do I have to share the house with other people?
(我必需和其他人分租這間房子嗎？)

How much do I have to pay for the deposit?
(我必需付多少押金？)

> **Do I have to pay for any other cost first?**
> (我必需要先付其他任何的費用嗎？)
> **Does the rent include the water, gas, electricity or Internet fee?** （房租有包含水、瓦斯、電或網路的費用嗎？）
> **Do you offer parking space?** (你有提供停車位嗎？)

<練習> 有人問你以上關於『居住環境』的問題?你會怎麼回答呢？以下整理一位同學的回答當作範例，劃線部份可依標號來找對應的字彙群組，可以幫助你練習講講有關自己對住家的看法！

I want to live in the <u>suburb</u>[1], but I live <u>with my family</u>[2] in the <u>downtown</u>[1] now. We have <u>our own</u>[3] <u>apartment</u>[4]. There are <u>a living room, two bedrooms, a dining room, a bathroom, a kitchen and a lovely balcony</u>[5] in my house. It's <u>small but nice</u>[6]. Although living in the <u>downtown</u>[1] is much <u>noisier</u>[7] than the <u>suburb</u>[1], the neighborhood is much <u>more convenient</u>[7]. It takes me <u>15 minutes</u>[8] to the <u>workplace</u>[9] every day. People here are quite <u>kindly</u>[10], (though we only greet when we met. We didn't know each other, but did anybody know someone here? It's quite normal in such a big city, isn't it?)

1. ☐ downtown   ☐ suburb   ☐ urban/city
   ☐ country/rural   ☐town
2. ☐ alone   ☐ with my family   ☐ with friends
3. ☐ have our own   ☐ share the   ☐ rent the
4. ☐ apartment   ☐ house   ☐ dormitory
5. ☐ living room   ☐ bedroom   ☐ dining room   ☐ bathroom
   ☐ kitchen   ☐ recreation room   ☐ balcony

6. □ garage □ garden □ laundry room □ swimming pool
6. □ small □ narrow □ big □ huge
7. □ noisier □ quieter □ more convenient □ less convenient
8. □ 10-15 minutes □ half an hour □ few hours
9. □ workplace □ supermarket □ bus stop/ Metro station
   □ school □ gym □ movie theater
10. □ kindly □ just like strangers □ always in a hurry
   □ polite □ warmhearted □ acquainted with each other

♥愛的筆記貼♥ 這個練習主要是幫同學們擬一份自己對住家敘述的草稿，例題的內容是：我想要住在近郊，但我現在是跟家人一起住在鬧區裡。我們有自己的公寓。在我們家裡有一間客廳、兩間臥室、一間餐廳、一間浴室、一間廚房和一個可愛的陽台。我們家小但很好。雖然住在鬧區比起郊區來得更吵雜，附近是比較方便的。我每天去公司只要 15 分鐘。在這裡的人們都很友善，(雖然我們只是見面時打個招呼。我們不認識彼此，但這裡有誰認識某人嗎？這在這樣一個大城市不是很常見嗎？)

同學們可以循劃線部份的數字來找每一欄位中的代換單詞，可以先檢視一下自己懂得閱讀相關單字有哪些。

⊘ Conversation 1 ⊘

(Jason 和 Real estate agent 房地產仲介講電話。)

Agent: Anderson Housing, may I help you?

安德森房屋您好，有什麼我可以為您效勞的嗎？

Jason: Hello, this is Jason. Do you have some houses for rent?

哈囉！我是傑森。你有房子在出租嗎？

Agent: Sure, what's your demand?

當然，你的需求是什麼？

Jason: Well, we are a small family, so basically we will ask for two bedrooms, a living room, a kitchen and the laundry facilities.

是的，我們是個小家庭，所以基本上我們會要求兩間臥房、一間客廳、一個廚房和洗衣設備。

Agent: Let me see. Fine, we now have 2 apartments which meet your requirements.

讓我看看。很好，我們現在有兩間公寓符合你的需求。

Jason: Excuse me. I said I am interested in houses instead.

抱歉。我說我是對獨棟的房子感興趣。

Agent: Oh, sorry. Just a second.

喔，對不起。等我一下。

Jason: That's all right. I can't stand the rude neighbors upstairs.

沒關係。我只是無法忍受樓上無禮的鄰居。

Agent: Yes, understandable. Okay, there is a nice and quiet one on the Maple street. Do you want to visit it?

是的，可以理解。好了，有一間很好很安靜的房子在楓樹街。你想去參觀一下嗎？

Jason: Is it far from the town center?

它離市中心遠嗎？

Agent: It only takes you 15 minutes if you drive. Do you drive to work?

如果你開車的話只要 15 分鐘的路程。你開車上班嗎？

Jason: Luckily, yes. Do they offer any furniture and appliances?

幸運的，沒錯。他們有提供任何傢俱和電器嗎？

Agent: Oh, yes, but the furniture can be changed up to your demand. Why not visit it first then you can consider it later? Are you available at 2 p.m.?

喔，有的，但是傢俱可以依照你的需求來改變。為何不先去看一下然後等下再想這個問題？你下午兩點有空嗎？

⊗ Conversation 2 ⊗

(Jason 看完房子回家和太太 Gillian 討論租屋的事情。)

Gillian: Darling, how is everything doing?

親愛的，事情進行的怎麼樣啊？

Jason: Not bad. Today, Anderson Housing's Sam showed me the house around.	不錯啊。今天，安德森房屋的山姆帶我看過房子了。
Gillian: Really? How does it look like?	真的？那間房子看起來怎麼樣？
Jason: A pretty nice house with a small garden as your wish.	一間相當好的房子有著你想要的小花園。
Gillian: Wow, how big is it?	哇！它有多大？
Jason: Small but warm. The number of rooms distributed in two levels also meets our demand.	小但是溫暖。分布在兩層樓的房間數也符合我們的需求。
Gillian: Sounds great, and then? I mean where it is?	聽起來好棒，然後呢？我是說它在哪裡？
Jason: Don't worry. It's right on the Maple street. The view is wonderful and it's near the supermarket and the gym as well. The best thing is that it only takes 10 minutes to town center if we drive.	不要擔心。它就在楓樹街上。景觀很美而且它也靠近超市和健身中心。最好的是開車只要 10 分鐘就到市中心了。
Gillian: How is the furnishing?	裝潢設備怎麼樣？
Jason: Fantastic! All included. There is even a study room with the wireless Internet access. The laundry room is also equipped.	很棒！全都包括在內。甚至還有一間有著無線網路的書房。洗衣房也都設備完善。
Gillian: Have you decided yet?	那你決定了嗎？
Jason: The thing is, the rent is much more than our budget. I'm afraid that we can't afford it.	問題是，房租超出我們預算很多。我恐怕我們住不起這樣的房子。

| 人我關係 | 興趣與休閒 | 生活與工作 | 文法解析 |

⊗Work Bank⊗ 隨時補充一錠，你在會話及閱讀理解必備的單字！

- 動⊗ **rent** [rɛnt] 租用；租出；租金
- ⊗ **house** [haʊs] 房子
- ⊗ **apartment** [ə`partmənt] 公寓
- ⊗ **land** [lænd] 土地
- ⊗ **fortune** [`fɔrtʃən] 財產
- ⊗ **contract** [`kɑntrækt] 契約；合同
- ⊗ **architecture** [`arkətɛktʃə] 建築物
- ⊗ **agreement** [ə`grimənt] 協議；合約
- ⊗ **landlord** [`lænd,lɔrd] 房東；地主
- ⊗ **regulation** [,rɛgjə`leʃən] 規則
- ⊗ **rule** [rul] 規則
- 形 **polite** [pə`laɪt] 禮貌的
- 形 **behaved** [bɪ`hevd] 守規矩的
- 形 **rude** [rud] 粗魯無禮的
- ⊗ **nuisance** [`njusns] 討厭、麻煩事
- ⊗ **annoyance** [ə`nɔɪəns] 煩惱；生氣
- 介 **underneath** [,ʌndə`niθ] 在下面
- ⊗ **downstairs** [,daʊn`stɛrz] 樓下
- ⊗ **upstairs** [`ʌp`stɛrz] 樓上
- 動 **repair** [rɪ`pɛr] 修理
- ⊗ **elevator** [`ɛlə,vetə] 電梯
- ⊗ **stair** [stɛr] 樓梯
- 動 **fall apart** [fɔl][ə`part] 分離
- 動 **afford** [ə`ford] 買得起
- ⊗ **appliance** [ə`plaɪəns] 器具；電器
- ⊗ **electricity** [,ɪlɛk`trɪsətɪ] 電力
- ⊗ **furnishing** [`fɝnɪʃɪŋ] 傢俱；室內裝潢
- ⊗ **gas** [gæs] 瓦斯；天然氣；汽油
- ⊗ **fee** [fi] 費用
- 動 **be acquainted with** 和某然熟識
- 動 **get used to Ving** 習慣某事
- ⊗ **commute** [kə`mjut] 通勤

- 動 **buy** [baɪ] 買
- 動 **purchase** [`pɝtʃəs] 購買
- ⊗ **dormitory** [`dɔrmə,torɪ] 宿舍
- ⊗ **property** [`prɑpətɪ] 資產；房地產
- ⊗ **architect** [`arkə,tɛkt] 建築師
- ⊗ **lease** [lis] 租約
- ⊗ **lessor** [`lɛsɔr] 出租人
- ⊗ **landlady** [`lænd,ledɪ] 女房東
- ⊗ **real estate** [`rɪəl][ɪs`tet] 房地產
- ⊗ **agent** [`edʒənt] 代理人；仲介人
- ⊗ **agency** [`edʒənsɪ] 代理；仲介商
- ⊗ **tenant** [`tɛnənt] 房客；住戶
- 動 **annoy** [ə`nɔɪ] 使⋯生氣
- 形 **annoyed** [ə`nɔɪd] 氣惱的
- ⊗ **complex** [`kɑmplɛks] 綜合大樓
- ⊗ **location** [lo`keʃən] 位置
- ⊗ **tall building** [tɔl][`bɪldɪŋ] 高樓
- 動 **skyscraper** [`skaɪ,skrepə] 摩天大樓
- ⊗ **tower** [`taʊə] 高塔
- ⊗ **staircase** [`stɛr,kes] 樓梯間
- 形 **equipped** [ɪ`kwɪpt] 配備好的
- ⊗ **equipment** [ɪ`kwɪpmənt] 設備
- ⊗ **facility** [fə`sɪlətɪ] 設備；工具
- 形 **antique** [æn`tik] 古老的
- ⊗ **furniture** [`fɝnɪtʃə] 傢俱
- 形 **wireless** [`waɪrlɪs] 無線的
- 動 **own** [on] 擁有；自己的
- ⊗ **view** [vju] 景觀
- ⊗ **carpet** [`karpɪt] 地毯

❀ **budget** [`bʌdʒɪt] 預算	❀ **stain** [sten] 沾污；污點
❀ **neighbor** [`nebɚ] 鄰居	❀ **neighborhood** [`nebɚ͵hʊd] 鄰近地區
❀ **security guard** [sɪ`kjʊrətɪ][gɑrd] 保安人員	❀ **maid** [med] 女僕
❀ **housekeeper** [`haʊs͵kipɚ] 女管家	❀ **cleaner** [`klinɚ] 清潔工
❀ **living room** [`lɪvɪŋ][rum] 客廳	❀ **janitor** [`dʒænɪtɚ] 工友；看門人
❀ **study room** [`stʌdɪ] [rum] 書房	❀ **doorkeeper** [`dor͵kipɚ] 守門人
❀ **laundry** [`lɔndrɪ] 洗衣房	❀ **Laundromat** [`lɑndrəmæt] 自助洗衣店
❀ **ceiling** [`silɪŋ] 天花板	❀ **bedroom** [`bɛd͵rum] 臥室
❀ **kitchen** [`kɪtʃɪn] 廚房	❀ **dining room** [`daɪnɪŋ][rum] 餐廳
❀ **recreation room** [͵rɛkrɪ`eʃən] [rum] 娛樂房	
❀ **bathroom** [`bæθ͵rum] 浴室	❀ **town** [taʊn] 鎮
❀ **balcony** [`bælkənɪ] 陽臺	❀ **garage** [gə`rɑʒ] 車庫
❀ **garden** [`gɑrdn̩] 花園	❀ **yard** [jɑrd] 院子；後院
❀ **downtown** [͵daʊn`taʊn] 鬧區	⊛ **suburb** [`sʌbɝb] 近郊的
⊛ **urban** [`ɝbən] 城市的	❀ **city** [`sɪtɪ] 城市
⊛ **country** [`kʌntrɪ] 鄉下的；鄉下	❀ **citizen** [`sɪtəzn̩] 公民
⊛ **rural** [`rʊrəl] 農村的	❀ **resident** [`rɛzədənt] 居民

Reading Passage 1

Apartment Share

- Suitable for students in St. Mary College

- Only female, no pets, and single.

- The room is furnished with a fine wooden desk, closet, and a double bed. Two windows with nice Persian curtains.

- The Internet is shared with other three roommates.

- Kitchen is equipped, but we don't like any one to make a lot smoke here.

- Neither the laundry facilities nor telephone is available,

but the Laundromat is just around the corner.

If you are qualified and interested to be our roommate, please send us an e-mail via sunwoo@smc.edu.

_____ (1)　Who is suitable to be their roommate?
A. A cute couple.　　　B. An old man.
C. The principle.　　　D. A girl student.

_____ (2)　What is **NOT** mentioned in the ads?
A. Refrigerator.　　　B. Furnishing materials.
C. Telephone.　　　D. Television.

_____ (3)　What's **TRUE** about the kitchen?
A. Some appliances are broken.
B. Nobody knows how to cook.
C. No cooking because they don't like.
D. They don't have a kitchen.

_____ (4)　Which one is **TRUE** about the apartment?
A. The apartment now is shared by 4 roommates.
B. There is a twin bed.
C. The girls have to go out to do the laundry.
D. They are not able to use the Internet.

_____ (5)　Why do they want people to contact them by e-mail?
A. The phone call costs too much.
B. They are too busy.
C. They only have the Internet access.
D. The phone is set in the Laundromat only.

♥愛的筆記貼♥ 這是一篇徵室友、分租房間的廣告。意思是：公寓分租。適合就讀聖瑪麗大學的學生。只限女性，沒有寵物，且單身。房間裡配備很精緻的木製書桌、衣櫃和一張雙人床。還有兩扇裝有波斯窗簾的窗戶。網路是和其他三位室友來分享的。廚房配備完善，但是我們不喜歡任何人來製造很多的煙。沒有洗衣設備也沒有電話，但是自助洗衣就在街角而已。如果你符合以上資格而且你有興趣成為我們的室友。請寄電子郵件到sunwoo@smc.edu和我們連絡。 解答：1.(D)一位女學生是符合室友的條件。 2.(D) 電視沒有被提到。 3.(C) 不能烹飪因為他們不喜歡。 4.(C)這些女孩必需出去才能洗衣服。 5.(C)他們只有網路可以用。

Reading Passage 2

Rental Agreement

The agreement was signed ___1___ the tenant Roxanne Royce __1__ the house owner Donald Charles. __2__ of them agree the house for rent according to the follows,

• A monthly rent of $650. ___3___, a deposit of two-month rent will be charged along __4__ the first-month rent before the tenant's moving in.

• The keys will be given to the tenant as the amount is paid.

• The water and gas fee are included in the monthly rent already.

• Any accident or disaster caused by tenant's careless behavior ___5___ as the tenant's responsibility. The property insurance is to ensure the compensation for the damages caused by natural disasters.

_____ (1) A. both…and…   B. between…and…
           C. neither…nor…   D. either…or…
_____ (2) A. None   B. One   C. Both   D. Many
_____ (3) A. At once   B. In addition
           C. Unfortunately   D. In some cases
_____ (4) A. on   B. for   C. by   D. with
_____ (5) A. will be seen   B. is going to see
           C. was seen as   D. will see

♥愛的筆記貼♥ 這是一篇租房子的合約。意思是：這份合約是由房客 Roxanne Royce 和房子擁有者 Donald Charles 兩人之間所簽定。他們兩人都同意要依照以下約定來租房：每月房租為 650 元美金。除此之外，一筆兩個月房租的押金將會和第一個月的房租在房客搬入之前收取。在這筆金額付款後鑰匙即會被交給房客。水費及瓦斯費已包括在每月房租之內。任何因為房客不小心的行為所造成的意外或災害將會被視為是房客的責任。這房子的產物保險是為了保障因為天然災害所造成的損失而賠償。 **解答：1.(B) 2.(C) 3.(B) 4.(D) 5.(A)**

Vocabulary Challenge

This morning, I have some ___1___ with my ___2___. He promised me to rent his apartment through the phone call a week ago. After I moved in, he told me he made a mistake on my ___3___. The amount should be 100 dollars more than the original cost. He is really sly and dishonest. I was pissed off and argued with him but fail, because we haven't had a ___4___ yet. I didn't want to pay for another moving fare, and I didn't want to spend more time moving again, ___5___. Then, I looked out of my window, and went to stand on my lovely ___6___ to breathe some fresh air outside. The view was great and it did ___7___ my anger a lot. So, I decided to start my ___8___ life from ___9___ the cruel facts in such a big city. Not only ___10___ a lesson today but I should learn how to protect myself better.

_____ 1. (A) parties　　(B) jewels　　(C) quarrels　　(D) facts

_____ 2. (A) attorney   (B) parents   (C) colleagues   (D) landlord

_____ 3. (A) rent   (B) position   (C) allowance   (D) pension

_____ 4. (A) vomit   (B) lease   (C) leaser   (D) tenant

_____ 5. (A) too   (B) neither   (C) either   (D) nor

_____ 6. (A) balcony   (B) yard   (C) garage   (D) trunk

_____ 7. (A) irritate   (B) release   (C) return   (D) innovate

_____ 8. (A) suburb   (B) country   (C) rural   (D) urban

_____ 9. (A) forgetting myself from   (B) acquainting myself with

      (C) bringing myself up   (D) fleeing myself from

_____ 10. (A) I learned   (B) did I have learned

      (C) I did learned   (D) did I learn

解答：(1) C (2) D (3) A (4) B (5) C
(6) A (7) B (8) D (9) B (10) D

Lesson **12** | 交通工具與方向
Transportation and direction

🗣 Language box 🗣

| Focus One |

How do you get to school or work? (你怎麼去學校或上班的？)

What kind of vehicle do you have? (你有哪種車輛？)

Is taking a bus or taking the Metro more convenient to you? (對你來說搭公車還是坐捷運比較方便？)

What's the best way for me to get to the city hall?
(我要去市政廳最快的路是什麼？)

What kind of transportation do you most like to take?
(你最喜歡搭乘哪一種交通工具？)

What kind of transportation do you take most frequently? (哪一種交通工具是你搭乘最多次的？)

Is the public transportation in the city good?
(這個城市的公共交通運輸設施好嗎？)

<Practice> 有人問你以上關於『交通運輸』的問題?你會怎麼回答呢？以下整理一位同學的回答當作範例，劃線部份可依標號來找對應的字彙群組，可以幫助你練習講講有關自己搭乘交通工具的敘述！

    I hate[1] to take the taxi[2] because I am always sick in the car[3]. I don't like the close space[4]. It makes me hard to breathe[5].

(Besides, the expensive fare and my bad experiences caused by some rude drivers both stop me taking a cab to work.) Even when <u>the Metro system stops their service by accident</u>[6], I would rather go to work |by| <u>foot</u>[2].

1. ☐ like   ☐ dislike   ☐ enjoy   ☐ hate
2. ☐ taxi/cab   ☐ train   ☐ bus   ☐ plane   ☐ subway   ☐ boat
   ☐ foot   ☐ helicopter   ☐ car   ☐ horse   ☐ camel
3. ☐ sick in/on it   ☐ late for school/work   ☐ in a hurry
   ☐ tired to transfer
4. ☐ air/smell   ☐ close space   ☐ crowd   ☐ tempo   ☐ sound
   ☐ seat   ☐ pressure
5. ☐ hard to breather   ☐ feel uncomfortable   ☐ vomit
   ☐ feel dizzy   ☐ get headache
6. ☐ it rains heavily   ☐ I feel uncomfortable   ☐ I'm in a hurry

♥愛的筆記貼♥ 這個練習主要是幫同學們擬一份敘述自己喜歡搭乘什麼交通工具的草稿,例題的內容是:我討厭搭計程車,因為我坐車都會不舒服。我不喜歡密閉空間。它使我難以呼吸。(除此之外,昂貴的車資和我因為遇到一些無禮的司機的壞經驗都使我打消了坐計程車上班的念頭。)甚至當捷運突然停止服務時,我寧願走路去上班。

　　同學們可以循劃線部份的數字來找每一欄位中的代換單詞,可以先檢視一下自己懂得閱讀相關單字有哪些。以上括號中的字句是額外的理由,可依每個同學的喜好自行增刪。

✎ 語言注意面 Language Caution ✎

A: How do you usually <u>get to</u> work? (你通常是怎麼來上班的?)
B: I walk to the MRT station and |take| it to work.
　　(我走路到捷運站然後搭捷運來上班。)

A: How do you usually <u>travel to</u> Shanghai?
(你通常怎麼去上海的？)

B: Most people |take| the ship and the train to save money, but
I usually go there |by| plane. It saves more time and it is
much more comfortable. (大部份的人搭船和火車來省錢，但是
我通常坐飛機去。這樣省較多時間而且比較舒服些。)

❤愛的筆記貼❤ 搭乘交通工具可 take 這個動詞，也可用 by 這個
介系詞。通常我們用 travel to 來說到比較遠的地方，有『遠行』之意。

┤ **Focus Two** ├

Could you tell me how to get to the train station?
(你能告訴我怎麼去火車站嗎？)

Could you show me the direction? (你可以告訴我方向嗎？)

Is the way to the Maple Street? (這條路會到楓樹街嗎？)

Which route should I take? (我該搭哪條路線？)

Do you know where the post office is? (你知道郵局在哪？)

Can you drive me to the airport in 40 minutes?
(你能在 40 分鐘內開車載我到機場嗎？)

Where should I buy the tickets? (我應該到哪去買票呢？)

Which platform should I get on the train at?
(我該去哪個月台搭火車呢？)

Do I have to transfer to the other route?
(我必需轉乘其他路線嗎？)

✎ 語言注意面 Language Caution ✎

A: <u>Where</u> |is| <u>the post office</u>? (郵局在哪裡？)
B: You go straight and across the road. It is just over there.

(你直走然後過馬路。它就在那。)

A: Do you know <u>where the post office</u> is? (你知道郵局在哪？)

B: It just moved to three blocks away. You can take a bus to there if you like.
(它剛搬到三條街遠的地方。你可以坐公車如果你喜歡的話。)

♥愛的筆記貼♥ 以上是『直接問句』和『間接問句』的比較。同學可以看到在『直接問句』的 be 動詞位置夾在 Where 和 the post office 之間。本來是 The office is ＿＿＿. 造問句所以用 Where 這個疑問詞放在前面，然後 be 動詞 is 和名詞 the office 倒裝而成了問句 Where is the post office?但在『間接問句』的時候，因為前面多了一個問句 Do you know，所以後面的『間接問句』中，倒裝的 be 動詞及名詞 the office，就要還原成原本的次序，而成了 Do you know where the office is?

<練習>

❶ How do I get there? → Could you tell me ＿＿＿＿＿＿＿＿＿？

❷ What number should I call a taxi?
→ Do you know ＿＿＿＿＿＿＿＿＿＿＿＿？

❸ When do we have to start off?
→ Does anybody know ＿＿＿＿＿＿＿＿＿＿？

<解答> ❶ Could you tell me how I get there?

❷ Do you know what number I should call a taxi?

❸ Does anybody know when we have to start off?

◦ Conversation 1 ◦

(一位旅客 tourist 向本地人 local 詢問溫泉的方向怎麼去。)

Tourist: Excuse me. Could you tell me where the hot spring area is?	打擾一下。你可以告訴我溫泉區在哪嗎？
Local: Hot spring? Do you mean the hotels or the outdoors springs?	溫泉？你指得是旅館還是戶外的溫泉？
Tourist: Actually, I haven't gotten a plan. What will you suggest?	事實上，我還沒有任何計劃。你會怎麼建議呢？

Local: Well, wait a second. Are you out from the Metro system?

Tourist: Yes, I thought the springs are just here around.

Local: Have you gotten the guide brochure yet? They're right in the information desk in front of the entrance. You can choose whatever you want to stay from it, and there should be some useful maps inside.

Tourist: Oh, that's useful. I'll get one. What will you recommend me to do here?

Local: If you like the natural style, you can go for a walk. You will enjoy the views and fresh air, and get into the outdoors spring house on the way. It's much cheaper but makes you feel free.

Tourist: Wow, sounds interesting. So, what's the direction?

Local: You have to transfer to the other Metro station. It's just at the next stop from this one. Then, when you get out of the station, there will be a park just opposite to the station. There are roads on the both sides of the park. It would be better to choose the left

是喔，等一下。你是從捷運站出來的嗎？

是啊，我原本以為溫泉就在這附近。

你有拿旅遊手冊了嗎？他們就在入口前的詢問處裡。你可以從它裡面選擇你想待的地方，而且裡面應該有一些有用的地圖。

喔，那很有用。我會去拿一本。你會推薦我在這要做些什麼呢？

如果你喜歡自然的型態，你可以散散步。你將會享受到景觀和新鮮的空氣，而且你在途中可以進入戶外溫泉屋。它會比較便宜但是讓你感到很自由自在。

哇~聽起來很有趣。這樣，方向怎麼去？

你必需轉乘到其他的捷運站。它就在這個站的下一站。然後，當你走出捷運站時，那裡會有個公園就在捷運站的對面。這個公園的兩邊都有路。選左邊那條路走會比較好。

one.

Tourist: Is it far away? I'm a little tired. | 它很遠嗎？我有點累了。

Local: Or you can take a bus here. On your left, there are some bus stops. | 或者你可以在這搭公車。在你的左手邊，有一些公車站牌。

Tourist: May I go to the hotels by them? Which route should I take? | 我可以搭公車去旅館嗎？我該搭哪條路線？

Local: Oh, some hotels offer free shuttle buses. You can see them from time to time on your right. Over there, did you see them? | 喔，有些旅館提供免費的接駁巴士。你可以不時地看到他們在你的右手邊。就在那，你看見了嗎？

Tourist: Do you mean those vans? | 你指得是那些休旅車嗎？

Local: Definitely they are, and they are free. | 確定是他們，而且他們是免費的。

Tourist: Thank you very much. I've got to go. | 非常謝謝你，我必需走了。

Local: Have a nice day! | 祝你玩得愉快！

◎ Conversation 2 ◎

(火車誤點很久了，兩個原本不認識的旅客 Grace 和 Sam 聊了起來。)

Grace: What's wrong with the train? Why does it delay so long? | 火車怎麼了？為什麼它誤點那麼久？

Sam: It is said the train was stopped between last station and this one. | 據說是火車停在上一站和這一站之間。

Grace: Really? What happened? | 真的？發生什麼事了？

Sam: The conductors said there was a train accident. Two trains in the | 那些火車服務人員說有一件火車意外發生。兩列

| different directions crushed together. | 不同方向的火車撞在一起了。 |

Grace: Oh, that's too bad. Did anybody injure? I can't imagine how it happened.

喔，太糟了。有任何人受傷嗎？我想不到那是怎麼發生的。

Sam: Neither do I. People now take taxies instead. Do you want to share the ride?

我也想不到。人們現在都改搭計程車了。你想要共乘嗎？

Grace: Oh, great. Where are you going?

喔，好啊。你要去哪裡？

Sam: Taipei. Are you in the same direction?

台北。你是同樣的方向嗎？

Grace: Fortunately, yes. Hey, I am Grace, nice to meet you.

幸運地，是的。嘿，我是葛瑞絲，很高興見到你。

Sam: Sam. Are you here for a tour or business trip?

山姆。你是來這旅行的還是出差的？

Grace: Oh, neither of them. I live here. I just want to visit my friends in Taipei. Do you know how to get to San Chong? They just told me how to get there from the Ban chiao train station.

喔，兩者都不是。我住這。我只是想要去看我在台北的朋友。你知道怎麼去三重嗎？他們只告訴我怎麼從板橋火車站去那裡。

Sam: Yes, it's quite convenient if you get off the cab at Taipei main station. There are many buses to get there. Do you know where we can take a cab now?

是的，如果你在台北火車站下計程車的話會很方便。有許多公車會到那裡。你知道我們現在要去哪坐計程車嗎？

Grace: Go upstairs first. We are going to go across the platforms, and go straight along the corridor. Turn

先上樓。我們要穿過這先月台，然後沿著走廊直走。在門口右轉然後計程車站應該是在我們的右

right at the doorway and the taxi stops should be on our right. ┆ 手邊。

⊘Work Bank⊘ 隨時補充一錠，你在會話及閱讀理解必備的單字！

- ⊛ **scooter** [ˋskutɚ] 機車(前有腳踏板)
- ⊛ **motorcycle** [ˋmotɚˏsaɪkl̩] 摩托車(跨坐型)
- ⊛ **public transportation** 大眾交通工具
- ⊛ **bicycle** [ˋbaɪsɪkl̩] 自行車；腳踏車
- ⊛ **boat** [bot]/ **ship** [ʃɪp] 船
- ⊛ **bus** [bʌs] 公車；巴士
- ⊛ **taxi** [ˋtæksɪ]/**cab** [kæb] 計程車
- ⊛ **car** [kɑr] 汽車
- ⊛ **van** [væn] 休旅車；小卡車
- ⊛ **train** [tren] 火車
- ⊛ **Metro** [ˋmɛtro] 地鐵= **Metropolitan Railway** (都會區的鐵路)
- ⊛ **MRT=Mass Rapid Transportation** 大眾快捷運輸工具(捷運)
- ⊛ **traffic jam** [ˋtræfɪk][dʒæm] 塞車
- ⊛ **subway** [ˋsʌbˏwe] 地下鐵
- ⊛ **Tube** [tjub] 英國地下鐵；管狀物
- ⊛ **vehicle** [ˋviɪkl̩] 車輛
- ⊛ **jet** [dʒɛt] 噴射機
- ⊛ **helicopter** [ˋhɛlɪkɑptɚ] 直升機
- ⊛ **flight** [flaɪt] 班機
- ⊛ **airplane/ plane** [plen] 飛機
- ⊛ **aircraft** [ˋɛrˏkræft] 飛機
- ⊛ **truck** [trʌk] 卡車
- ⊛ **commute** [kəˋmjut] 通勤
- ⊛ **get around** 到處去
- ⊛ **helmet** [ˋhɛlmɪt] 安全帽
- ⊛ **seat belt** [sit][bɛlt] 安全帶
- ⊛ **airbag** [ˋɛrˏbæg] 安全氣囊
- ⊛ **brake** [brek] 煞車
- ⊛ **traffic** [ˋtræfɪk] 交通
- ⊛ **traffic light** 交通號誌燈

- ⊛ **transfer** [trænsˋfɝ] 轉乘
- ⊛ **fine ticket** 罰單
- ⊛ **ticket** [ˋtɪkɪt] 車票
- ⊛ **stub** [stʌb] 票根
- ⊛ **economic** [ˏikəˋnɑmɪk] 經濟的
- ⊛ **pollution** [pəˋluʃən] 污染
- ⊛ **save time** 省時間
- ⊛ **rush hour** 尖峰時間
- ⊛ **car accident** 車禍
- ⊛ **traffic regulation** 交通規則
- ⊛ **direct the traffic** 指揮交通
- ⊛ **volunteer** [ˏvɑlənˋtɪr] 義工；志願者
- ⊛ **speed limit** 速限
- ⊛ **track** [træk] 鐵軌
- ⊛ **platform** [ˋplætˏfɔrm] 月台
- ⊛ **high way** 高速公路
- ⊛ **token** [ˋtokən] 代幣
- ⊛ **passenger** [ˋpæsn̩dʒɚ] 乘客；旅客
- ⊛ **pedestrian** [pəˋdɛstrɪən] 行人
- ⊛ **conductor** [kənˋdʌktɚ] 指揮
- ⊛ **bus stop** 公車站牌
- ⊛ **driver** [ˋdraɪvɚ] 駕駛；司機
- ⊛ **driver's license** 駕駛執照
- ⊛ **route** [rut] 路線
- ⊛ **schedule** [ˋskɛdʒul] 時程表
- ⊛ **fare** [fɛr] 車資

图 **traffic sign** 交通標誌		图 **ferry** [ˈfɛrɪ] 渡輪	
图 **transportation** [ˌtrænspəˈteʃən] 交通工具			
图 **stair** [stɛr] 樓梯		働 **get on the train** 上火車	
图 **bridge** [brɪdʒ] 橋		働 **get off the train** 下火車	
旧 **out of gas** 沒有汽油了		働 **get into the taxi** 坐進計程車	
働 **fill the gas** 填滿汽油		働 **get out of the taxi** 從計程車出來	
图 **spare tire** [spɛr][taɪr] 備胎		图 **direction** [dəˈrɛkʃən] 方向	
图 **flat tire** [flæt][taɪr] 輪胎洩氣；爆胎		介 **straight** [stret] 直走	
图 **trunk** [trʌŋk] 行李箱		働 **go along** 沿著…走	
图 **gas station** 加油站		働 **go through the red light** 闖紅燈	
形 **handicapped** [ˈhændɪˌkæpt] 殘障的		働 **go ahead** 直走	
图 **parking space** 停車位		働 **go across** 跨越…	
图 **parking lot** 停車場；停車位		働 **cross** [krɔs] 跨越	
图 **railroad** [ˈreɪˌrod] 鐵路		图 **block** [blɑk] 街區	
图 **railroad crossing** 鐵路平交道		旧 **far away** [baɪ] 買	
图 **dead end** 死路		働 **turn left/ right** 左轉/右轉	
图 **child safety seat** 兒童安全座椅		旧 **at the corner** 在轉角處	
图 **priority seat** [praɪˈɔrətɪ][sit] 博愛座		图 **lane** [len] 小巷子	
旧 **on your left/ right** 在你的左/右手邊		图 **alley** [ˈælɪ] 弄	
图 **one way** 單行道		图 **U-turn** 迴轉道	
图 **street** [strit] 街道		图 **road** [rod] 路	
图 **avenue** [ˈævəˌnju] 大道		图 **boulevard** [ˈbuləˌvɑrd] 大道	

Reading Passage 1

Ladies and gentlemen, thank you for taking the Metro system. Due to a serious damage caused by the power shut, all the systems are not in service now. The technicians have been checking and trying to solve the problems in the meanwhile, but the precise time of recovering is uncertain. We offer the free shuttle buses at the bus stops outside the station. Please take other transportation instead. Thank you for your cooperation and deeply apologize for the inconvenience.

_____ (1)　What happened to the Metro system?
　　　　　A. Out of the track.　　　B. Car accident.
　　　　　C. Out of order.　　　　 D. A flood.
_____ (2)　What does the notice suggest the passengers?
　　　　　A. For safety, they should walk instead.
　　　　　B. Remain in their seats.
　　　　　C. Wait for the next train.
　　　　　D. Take other transportation.
_____ (3)　Where can we take the shuttle bus?
　　　　　A. In the lobby.　　 B. Go to the bus stops.
　　　　　C. Go downstairs.　　D. Transfer to other stations.

♥愛的筆記貼♥ 這是一篇捷運故障的告示。意思是：女士先生們，謝謝你們來搭乘捷運系統。因為電力中斷造成嚴重的損害，所有的系統現在都停止服務。技術人員已經正在檢查而且試著要解決這些問題，但是確切的修復時間還不確定。我們提供了免費的接駁公車就在車站外面的公車站牌。請改搭別的交通工具。謝謝您的合作，不便之處我們深感抱歉。**解答：1.(C)** 捷運因為電力中斷故障了。 **2.(D)** 告示建議乘客改坐其他的交通工具。 **3.(B)** 到公車站牌。

Reading Passage 2

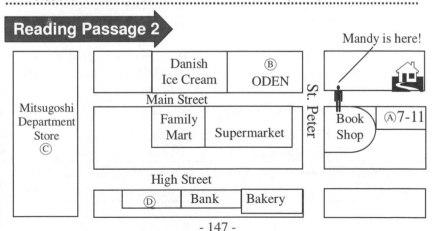

_____ (1) Mandy wants to collect the Hello Kitty dolls so she has to buy something in 7-11.
Can you point out the right direction for her?
(A) It's right here.　　(B) It is opposite to the bookshop.
(C) It is next to the bookshop.
(D) Just go across the road and it is on your right.

_____ (2) Mandy's mother wants her to buy some good fish roes in the supermarket of the department store.
How does she get there from here?
(A) She crosses the road, and it is on her left.
(B) She goes along the Main Street to the end.
(C) It is across from the Ice Cream Shop.
(D) It's three blocks away from here.

_____ (3) At 3 p.m., she will go to see a movie with her friend. The movie theater is across from the supermarket.
Where should she go?
(A) A　(B) B　(C) C　(D) D

_____ (4) She has to bring some flowers home and the florist is next to the bank on the High street.
(A) A　(B) B　(C) C　(D) D

_____ (5) What is the best order for her route on schedule?
(a) Enter the department store and turn left.
(b) She goes straight along the Main Road.
(c) Go straight to home.
(d) And then get the exit at High Street and go out.
(e) Turn left at the corner of the St. Peter and High Street.
(f) Turn right at the corner of the book shop.
(g) Go along the high street

(A) b>a>d>g>e>f>c　　　(B) b>g>e>f>d>a>c
(C) b>a>e>f>d>g>c　　　(D) b>e>d>a>f>g>c

♥愛的筆記貼♥ 這是一張 Mandy 家的周邊環境地圖。地圖題要注意的是尋找地標的問題。通常都是藉由方向的指示詞來定位：corner

角落、block 街區也就是走過了幾條街 street 的意思、turn left/right 左轉還是右轉、go straight/ along 直走或沿著某路走、across from/ opposite 是在對面，還有 on your left/ right 在你的左手還是右手邊。這些都是定位方向的關鍵字詞。**解答：1.(C)Mandy 想收集凱蒂貓的玩偶，所以她必需去 7-11 便利超商買東西。正確的位置就在書店旁邊。 2.(B) Mandy 的媽媽想要她去百貨公司的超市裡買一些上好的魚子回來。所以她沿著 Main Street 走到底就是百貨公司了。 3.(B) 在下午3點，她將和她的朋友去看電影，而電影院就在超級市場的對面，所以她應該去 B 地點。ODEN 就是這家電影院的名稱。4.(D) 她必需帶一些花回家，而花店就在 High Street 上的銀行旁邊。所以她應該到 D 地點。 5.(A)最後按照她的行程最適當的路線順序就是：b)沿著 Main Street 直走，a)進入百貨公司然後左轉，d)然後走到 High Street 的那個出口，走出百貨公司，g)沿著 High Street 走，e)在聖彼得街和 High Street 的交叉口轉角左轉，f)在書店那個轉角右轉，c)然後直走回到家。這樣走就可以先到電影院看電影，再到百貨公司的超市去買魚子，再去買花，然後要回家時，再去 7-11 買東西集凱蒂貓就好了。**

Vocabulary Challenge

_____ 1. It's quite hard to find a cab in such a _____.

    (A) traffic jam   (B) rush hour   (C) U-turn   (D) red light

_____ 2. The seat is the _____ for elder, pregnant women, and

    children. (A) priority   (B) property   (C) private   (D) prevent

_____ 3. All the cars should yield the _____ first on the crossing.

    (A) subway   (B) police   (C) helicopter   (D) pedestrians

_____ 4. We think we had better hurry up to catch on the _____.

    We almost run out of time.

    (A) route   (B) schedule   (C) project   (D) position

解答：(1) B (2) A (3) D (4) B

Lesson 13 | 工作態度與職場發展
Working attitude and Career development

🗣 Language box 🗣

Focus One

What do you do? (你是做什麼的？)

What's your job? (你的職業是什麼？)

What is Mr. Jones? (瓊絲先生是什麼職業的人？)

Do you have a full-time or part-time job?
(你有全職工作還是兼職工作？)

What's your position? (你的職位是什麼？)

How is your company? (你的公司如何？)

Do you get along with your colleagues/ supervisors?
(你和你的同事或主管相處得好嗎？)

What kind of work are you good at? (你擅長做什麼工作？)

What benefit/ welfare did your company offer to you?
(你的公司提供給你什麼樣的利益或福利呢？)

What kind of salary would you like? (你想要怎樣的薪水？)

How long are your paid holidays this year?
(你今年的給薪年假有多久？)

✐ 語言注意面 Language Caution ✐

<u>How</u> do you do? (久仰，好久不見了你好嗎？)

<u>What</u> do you do? (你的職業是什麼？)

♥愛的筆記貼♥ How do you do 其實算是個招呼語，而 what do you do 則是問『職業』。兩者有所不同，現在我們比較少講 How do you do 了。通常會講 How are you doing?一切還好嗎？來當問候語。

Focus Two

Do you have your own business? (你有自己的事業嗎？)

Are you self-employed or an employee?
(你是自營生意還是受雇者？)

Do you enjoy your current job? (你喜歡現在的工作嗎？)

Are you satisfied with your current job?
(你還滿意現在的工作嗎？)

Do you have any teamwork experiences?
(你有任何團隊合作的經驗嗎？)

How do you define "teamwork"? (你如何定義『團隊合作』？)

What is more suitable to you, to be a leader or to be a follower? (是當領導者還是當追隨者比較適合你呢？)

Do you often have to do some risky works?
(你必需常要做一些危險的工作嗎？)

What kind of works in your job does make you feel tired? (在你的工作中哪些工作會讓你感到疲累？)

Do you sometimes want to transfer to other fields?
(你時常想轉換到別的領域嗎？)

What's the worst part in your works?
(你工作中最糟的部份是什麼？)

What's the best part in your works?
(你工作中最好的部份是什麼？)

⊙ Conversation 1 ⊙

(Esther 到 Job center 求職中心諮詢工作機會。)

Agent: May I help you?	我可以幫你嗎？
Esther: Hi, my name is Esther Hamilton. I'm looking for an accountant job.	嗨，我的名字是伊瑟海米頓。我正在找一份會計師的工作。
Agent: Would you show me your resume and fill out the application form, please?	能請你給我看一下你的履歷表而且填寫一下這張申請表格嗎？
Esther: Sure. Here you go.	好的，在這裡。
Agent: Do you have the accounting certificate?	你有會計相關的證書嗎？
Esther: Not yet, but I'm preparing for the test.	還沒有，但我正在準備考試。
Agent: All right, so we can only search for some vacancies of accounting assistant for you. Do you agree with it?	好吧，這樣我們只能幫你找一些會計助理員的工作。你同意嗎？
Esther: Yes, no problem. I also need some practical experiences.	好，沒問題。我也需要一些實際的經驗。
Agent: And your degree and payment wish seem quite qualified to the two job opportunities. Please have a look on my screen.	你的學位和待遇要求似乎相當符合這兩個工作機會。請看一下我的螢幕。
Esther: Oh, OK. Let me see. Jason audit and financial consulting firm. Wow, I don't know they are recruiting.	喔，好的。讓我看一下。傑森帳務和財務資詢實業。哇，我不知道他們正在找人。
Agent: Yes, they are. The vacancy was just released this morning.	是的，他們有。這個職缺是早上才剛釋放出來。早

Early birds always got something great. Do you want to have a try?

Esther: Yes, I would love to. Wish me luck.

Agent: OK. I will send your application to their manpower department. Ms Robinson may contact you for an interview in the afternoon. Please keep your cell phone on.

起的鳥兒總是有好果子吃。你想要試試看嗎？

是啊，我樂意。祝我好運。

好。我會將你的申請表寄給他們的人力資源部。羅賓遜女士也許會在下午和你連繫面試的事情。請保持手機開機。

⊘ Conversation 2 ⊘

（兩個好朋友 Addie 和 Doris 在辦公室聊天。）

Addie: I heard that crazy Billy has been fired this morning.

Doris: Oh, that's great. It's definitely a start of another war.

Addie: What do you mean?

Doris: He must accuse the R & D director right away.

Addie: I've ever seen him coming to the office with his attorney. The lawyer was fighting for the confidential works and bonus for him. Is that true? Everybody said he has some mental problems.

Doris: I don't know, and I don't want to know. People said he was quite talented to develop good designs, and he was good at the marketing

我聽說瘋子比利今天早上已經被炒魷魚了。

喔，太好了。一定是另一場戰爭的開始。

你指得是什麼呢？

他一定會馬上告研發部的總監。

我曾看過他和他的律師到公司來。這位律師是來為他爭取保密的作品和紅利的。那是真的嗎？每個人都說他有一些心理問題。

我不知道，我也不想知道。人們說他對開發新設計很有天份，而且他對行銷策略也很擅長。然而，

strategies. However, he seemed too aggressive to some other guys. He required the promotion for several times but were all denied.

他似乎對某些其他人來說是太激進了一些。他要求升職了好幾次,但是都被否決了。

Addie: Really? Pool thing. Well, it will never happen to me again.

真的?可憐的傢伙。是啊,這樣的事將不會再發生在我身上了。

Doris: Pardon, I can't get your points.

你再說一遍?我不懂你的意思。

Addie: I mean, the job for me is a new start. I used to be aggressive like him. I always expect to be better, shimmery, rich, and in a higher position.

我是說,這份工作對我來說是個新開始。我過去曾經像他一樣都很激進。我總是期望好還要更好,發光發熱,有錢,而且到更高的職位。

Doris: Then, what did make you change?

然後呢?什麼使你改變的?

Addie: From a janitor's retirement. He had talked to me once in front of the toilet.

從一位清潔工的退休開始。他曾經有一次在廁所前跟我說過話。

Doris: No way. You're inspired in front of the toilet. Good job.

不會吧。你在廁所前被啟發?做得好。

Addie: He said working is just an opportunity to know more people and to experience more things and feelings. What have you experienced so far, chick? Then, I felt upset and weird.

他說工作只是一個認識更多人和體驗更多事情及感覺的機會。你目前為止體驗了什麼啊,小妞?然後我覺得很不舒服而且很怪。

Doris: Of course, what's his point? Frustrate you?

當然囉,他想幹嘛?打擊你嗎?

Addie: Ha, if that's truc, hc won. When I backed to my seat, the stacks of documents on my desk and the piles of e-mails on my screen all looked so ironic to my lovely surfing poster beside. What am I doing?	哈，如果那是真的，他贏了。當我回到我的座位，在我桌上成堆的文件，和螢幕上成排的電子郵件，和我桌旁美麗的衝浪海報相比，看起來真是諷刺。我到底在幹什麼？
Doris: For money to pay for your rent, darling.	為了繳房租的錢啊，親愛的。
Addie: True, so I quitted and took a long vacation in Australia. The experiences have changed my attitude.	沒錯，所以我辭職而且去澳洲渡了一個假。這樣的經驗已經改變我的態度很多。
Doris: And now you are here with me.	然後現在你就來這和我一起了。
Addie: Yes, dear. We are good friends and thank you to join in my life.	是啊，親愛的。我們是好朋友，謝謝你進入我的生命。
Doris: No way, I don't want to get married with you.	不行。我不想跟你結婚喔。
Doris & Addie: (giggled).	(兩人咯咯笑著。)

⊘Work Bank⊘ 隨時補充一錠，你在會話及閱讀理解必備的單字！

- 名 **occupation** [ˌɑkjəˈpeʃən] 職業
- 名 **job** [dʒɑb] 工作；職業
- 名 **work** [wɜk] 工作
- 名 **career** [kəˈrir] 職業；職業生涯
- 名 **profession** [prəˈfɛʃən] 專業
- 名 **specialist** [ˈspɛʃəlɪst] 專家
- 名 **lawyer** [ˈlɔjə]/ **attorney** [əˈtɜnɪ] 律師
- 名 **psychologist** [saɪˈkɑlədʒɪst] 心理學家
- 名 **psychiatrist** [saɪˈkaɪətrɪst] 精神科醫師
- 名 **ophthalmologist** [ˌɑfθælˈmɑlədʒɪst] 眼科醫師
- 名 **nurse** [nɜs] 護士
- 名 **nursing assistant** 看護
- 名 **doctor** [ˈdɑktə] 醫師
- 名 **dentist** [ˈdɛntɪst] 牙醫
- 名 **vet** [vɛt] 獸醫
- 名 **internist** [ɪnˈtɜnɪst] 內科醫師
- 名 **judge** [dʒʌdʒ] 法官；裁判
- 名 **umpire** [ˈʌmpaɪr] 裁判
- 名 **coach** [kotʃ] 教練

[名] **police officer** 警察　[名] **optometrist** [ɑp`tɑmətrɪst] 驗光師
[名] **fire fighter** 消防員　[名] **optician** [ɑp`tɪʃən] 眼鏡商
[名] **mailman/ postman** 郵差　[名] **audiologist** [ˏɔdɪ`ɑlədʒɪst] 聽力醫師
[名] **delivery person** 快遞員　[名] **driver** [`draɪvɚ] 司機
[名] **chiropractor** [`kaɪrəˏpræktɚ] 脊椎按摩；治療師
[名] **physical** [`fɪzɪkl̩] 身體的；物理的　[名] **intern** [ɪn`tɝn] 實習醫師
[名] **librarian** [laɪ`brɛrɪən] 圖書館員　[名] **therapist** [`θɛrəpɪst] 治療師
[名] **cashier** [kæ`ʃɪr] 出納員；收銀員　[名] **consultant** [kən`sʌltət] 顧問
[名] **pharmacist** [`fɑrməsɪst] 藥劑師 [名] **baby-sitter/nanny** [`nænɪ]保姆
[名] **waiter** [`wetɚ]/ **waitress** [`wetrɪs] 服務生/女服務生
[名] **camp counselor** [kæmp][`kaʊnsl̩ɚ] 營隊管理員
[名] **volunteer** [ˏvɑlən`tɪr] 志工；義工
[名] **manager** [`mænɪdʒɚ] 經理　[名] **accountant** [ə`kaʊntənt] 會計
[名] **director** [də`rɛktɚ] 導演；總監；樂隊指揮
[名] **actor** [`æktɚ] 男演員　[名] **actress** [`æktrɪs] 女演員
[名] **president** [`prɛzədənt] 總統；總裁　[名] **pension** [`pɛnʃən] 退休金
[名] **principle** [`prɪnsəpl̩] 校長　[名] **assistant** [ə`sɪstənt] 助理
[名] **interpreter**[ɪn`tɝprɪtə]/ **translator** [træns`letɚ] 翻譯
[名] **janitor** [`dʒænɪtɚ] 工友；管理員　[名] **architect** [`ɑrkəˏtɛkt] 建築師
[名] **cleaner** [`klinɚ] 清潔工　[名] **artist** [`ɑrtɪst] 藝術家；美術家
[名] **model** [`mɑdl̩] 模特兒　[名] **assembler** [ə`sɛmblɚ] 組裝工
[名] **designer** [dɪ`zaɪnɚ] 設計師　[名] **technician** [tɛk`nɪʃən] 技術人員
[名] **hairdresser** [`hɛrˏdrɛsɚ] 美髮師　[名] **engineer** [ɛndʒə`nɪr] 跨越
[名] **courier** [`kʊrɪɚ] 派信人　[名] **mechanic** [mə`kænɪk] 機械工
[名] **fisher** [`fɪʃɚ] 漁夫　[名] **operator** [`ɑpˏretɚ] 操作員；接線生
[名] **farmer** [`fɑrmɚ] 農夫　[名] **baker** [`bekɚ]] 麵包師傅
[名] **programer** [`prograemɚ] 程式設計師　[名] **cook** [kʊk] 烹調
[名] **businessman** [`bɪznɪsmən] 商人　[名] **chef** [ʃɛf] 主廚；大廚
[名] **sales person** 業務人員　[名] **sales assistance** 業務助理
[名] **florist** [`florɪst] 花商　[名] **project manager** 專案經理
[名] **attendant** [ə`tɛndənt] 服務員　[名] **leader** [`lidɚ] 領導人；隊長
[名] **crew** [kru] 全體船員；機上人員　[名] **butcher** [`bʊtʃɚ] 屠夫；肉販
[名] **flight attendant** 空少；空姐　[名] **worker** [`wɝkɚ] 工人；工作者

 🄐 **gas attendant** 加油站服務生   🄐 **carpenter** [ˋkɑrpəntɚ] 木匠

 🄐 **staff** [stæf] 全體工作人員   🄐 **musician** [mjuˋzɪʃən] 音樂家

 🄐 **faculty** [ˋfækl̩tɪ] 全體教職員   🄐 **painter** [ˋpentɚ] 油漆工；畫家

 🄐 **housekeeper** [ˋhausˌkipɚ] 女管家   🄐 **staff** [stæf] 工作人員

 🄐 **homemaker** [homˌmekɚ] 家庭主婦 🄐 **teacher** [ˋtitʃɚ] 教師

 🄐 **receptionist** [rɪˋsɛpʃənɪst] 接待員   🄐 **proposal** [prəˋpozl̩] 企劃案

 🄐 **porter** [ˋpotɚ] 提行李的服務員   🄐 **tutor** [ˋtjutɚ] 家教

 🄐 **reporter**[rɪˋportɚ]/ **journalist** [ˋdʒɝnəlɪst] 記者

 🄐 **instructor** [ɪnˋstrʌktɚ] 指導者   🄐 **sport instructor** 運動教練

 🄐 **secretary** [ˋsɛkrəˌtɛrɪ] 秘書   🄐 **travel agent** 旅行社

 🄐 **telemarketer** [ˌtɛləˋmɑrkɪtɪŋ] 電話銷售人員 🄐 **tour guide** 導遊

 🄐 **maid** [med] 女傭   🄐 **clerk** [klɝk] 店員

 🄐 **writer**[ˋraɪtɚ]/**author** [ˋɔθɚ] 作家   🄐 **editor** [ˋɛdɪtɚ] 編輯

 🄐 **paper work** 報告   🄐 **part-time** 兼職

 🄐 **document** [ˋdɑkjəmənt] 文件   🄐 **full-time** 全職

 🄥 **resume** [ˌrɛzjuˋme] 履歷   🄓 **inquire** [ɪnˋkwaɪr] 詢問；調查

 🄐 **application** [ˌæpləˋkeʃən] 申請書 🄓 **qualify** [ˋkwɑləˌfaɪ] 符合資格

 🄓🄐 **interview** [ˋɪntɚˌvju] 面試；訪談   🄐 **reward** [rɪˋwɔrd] 報酬

 🄐 **experience** [ɪkˋspɪrɪəns] 經驗   🄐 **agreement** [əˋgrimənt] 協議

 🄐 **background** [ˋbækˌgraund] 背景   🄐 **contract** [ˋkɑntrækt] 合約書

 🄐 **wage** [wedʒ] 週領或日領的報酬   🄐 **pay** [pe] 報酬

 🄐 **labor** [ˋlebɚ] 勞工；勞方   🄐 **salary** [ˋsælərɪ] 薪資

 🄓 **employ** [ɪmˋplɔɪ] 雇用   🄐 **benefit** [ˋbɛnəfɪt] 好處；津貼

 🄐 **employee** [ˌɛmplɔɪˋi] 員工   🄐 **welfare** [ˋwɛlˌfɛr] 福利

 🄐 **employer** [ɪmˋplɔɪɚ] 雇主   🄐 **supervisor** [ˌsupɚˋvaɪzɚ] 主管

 🄓 **hire** [haɪr] 雇用   🄐 **strategy** [ˋstrætədʒɪ] 策略

 🄐 **client** [ˋklaɪənt] 委託人；客戶   🄓 **transfer** [trænsˋfɝ] 轉任

 🄐 **customer** [ˋkʌstəmɚ] 顧客；買主   🄐 **sales skill** 銷售技巧

 🄐 **sick leave** 病假單   🄐 **budget** [ˋbʌdʒɪt] 預算

 🄐 **on vacation** 渡假   🄐 **performance** [pɚˋfɔrməns] 表演

 🄐 **paid holiday** 給薪假期   🄐 **goal** [gol] 目標

 🄐 **retirement** [rɪˋtaɪrmənt] 退休   🄐 **achievement** [əˋtʃivmənt] 成就

 🄓**retire** [rɪˋtaɪr] 退休   🄐 **development** [dɪˋvɛləpmənt] 發展

 🄓 **promote** [prəˋmot] 升職；促銷🄓 **quit** [kwɪt]/ **resign** [rɪˋzaɪn] 辭職

ⓝ **pr<u>o</u>m<u>o</u>t<u>i</u>on** [prəˋmoʃən] 升職；促銷 ⓥ **f<u>i</u>re** [faɪr] 跨越

Reading Passage

Few years ago, Nancy started her own business selling healthy supplements. Before this, she used to be a nurse in a public hospital. She quitted her job with a stable salary because the unstable night shift timetable made her health get worse. Then, she found that selling vitamins and some health care facilities aroused her interests. Not only can she apply her professional but also earn a better life for her family. And the best thing was to help more people get a healthier life. Dreams are always wonderful in the beginning. However, lacking of the budget management and accounting knowledge made her bankrupt and quit herself from her dream. She thought she was self-employed so that she couldn't apply for the subvention without the proved certificate. Nancy is not the only case in the society. Many of you may have the similar problem like her. If you need any help, please call 1-800-333-827. The government social care system assists you from time to time. What about Nancy now? She is fine with her subvention. Now she is taking a business training program hold by the labor department. She is ready for her second career, how about you?

____ (1)   What's the purpose of this passage?

A. Encourage people to develop their career.

B. Encourage people to use the public social assistance.

C. Encourage people to buy more vitamins.

D. Encourage people to help Nancy.

_____ (2) Why didn't Nancy want to be a nurse?

A. The job was stressful.

B. She had to take care of her family

C. She couldn't earn her life by this job.

D. She didn't feel well with the working hours.

_____ (3) What does "Dreams are always wonderful in the beginning." imply in the passage?

A. People like the job in the beginning but give up it very easily.

B. People prefer dreaming rather than practical things.

C. People didn't consider their dreams specifically in the beginning.

D. People always feel satisfied with their current job.

_____ (4) Why didn't Nancy apply for the unemployed aid?

A. She didn't know the information before.

B. She misunderstood the qualifications.

C. She was too sad to accept the failure.

D. She quitted her job again.

_____ (5) What will the government do if you call the hotline?

A. They may help you apply for a new job.

B. They may help you apply for the financial aid.

C. They may want you to give people a lesson.

D. They may help you buy some insurance.

♥愛的筆記貼♥ 這是一篇勞工局的政令宣導。主要是舉 Nancy 為例，來喚起勞工們對於失業津貼的需求。題意是：幾年前，Nancy 開了一家她賣營養食品的公司。在這之前，她曾是一位公立醫院的護士。因為不固定的排班時間表使她的健康愈來愈糟，她不辭去了她有著很好的薪水的工作。然後，她發現賣維他命和一些健康補給品引起了她的興趣。她不只可以應用她的專業而且她可以為她的家庭帶來更好的生活。最好的事是可以幫助更多人擁有更健康的生活。夢想在一

開始時總是美好的。然而，缺乏預算管理和會計知識都使她破產而且使她放棄了她的夢想。她原本以為她因為是自營商無法提供證明失業的文件所以無法申請失業給付。在社會上 Nancy 並不是個個案。你們之中很多人也許也和她一樣有著相似的問題。如果你需要幫助，請撥1-800-333-827。政府的社會照顧系統會不時的協助你。現在的 Nancy 怎麼了呢？她有了失業救濟金所以過得不錯。她現在正在上一個由勞工部門辦得商業訓練的套裝課程。她已準備好面對她的第二個職業生涯，那你呢？　**解答：1.(B)這段文章的意圖是『鼓勵人們利用社會協助』。2.(D) Nancy 對於工作時間不滿意所以她不想當護士。3.(C)『夢想在一開始總是美好的』這句話意味著『人們在一開始都沒有考慮到細節具體的地方』。4.(B) Nancy 不申請失業援助是因為她誤會了申請資格。5.(B) 如果你撥打這隻熱線電話，他們可能會幫助你申請財務援助。**

Vocabulary Challenge

_____ 1. An Asian-American _____ was missing in Korea and lost contact with her news agency suddenly. It is said she was under arrest by the local government because she has reported some big issues.

　(A) professor　(B) optician　(C) journalist　(D) interpreter

_____ 2. The boss wants to attend the big fair in Frankfurt but he doesn't understand German. He needs a _____ therefore.

　(A) transportation　　(B) interpreter

　(C) camp counselor　(D) flight attendant

_____ 3. You got the wrong medicine and seemed to be allergic to it. Don't you show the prescription to the _____?

　(A) optician　(B) dentist　(C) cashier　(D) pharmacist

_____ 4. Vincent was quite _____ to this position, but he didn't accept the job offer due to his study schedule.

(A) desired　(B) qualified　(C) designed　(D) assigned

_____ 5. Many people attempt to restart another _____ after their retirement.

(A) lifespan　(B) disappointment　(C) career　(D) assistance

_____ 6. After 10-year hard working, she finally got the _____ to be the CEO in the overseas business.

(A) potentials　(B) promotion　(C) allowance　(D) farewell

_____ 7. A: I want to report the leaking faucet and pipes in my suite.

B: OK, thank you for your calling. We will send a _____ to fix it in 5 minutes.

(A) cleaner　(B) volunteer　(C) janitor　(D) deliver

_____ 8. Just check in here with the receptionists, please. Your luggage will be sent to your room later by the _____.

(A) manager　(B) monitor　(C) elevator　(D) porter

_____ 9. Considering the rising cost, she decided not to _____ anyone but do her own business by herself.

(A) hire　(B) fire　(C) resign　(D) purchase

_____10. Any concrete _____ could be accepted in the boardroom and rewarded as a beautiful bonus. Please try hard.

(A) presentations　(B) professions

(C) proposals　(D) preferences

解答：(1) C (2) B (3) D (4) B (5) C (6) B (7) C (8) D (9) A (5) C

Lesson 14 | 健康與醫療
Health care

🗣 Language box 🗣

Focus One

What's wrong with you? (你怎麼了？)

What's the matter with you? (你發生什麼事？/你怎麼了？)

Are you all right? (你還好嗎？)

Do you need a break/ rest? (你需要休息一下嗎？)

Do you feel well? Do you feel better now?

(你感覺好點了嗎？)

Should I take some medicine? (我應該服用一些藥物嗎？)

Do you have a band-aid? I cut myself.

(你有 OK 繃嗎？我割傷了。)

Do you usually go to a clinic or a hospital?

(你通常去診所還是去醫院看病？)

Do I have to change my diet? (我需要改變我的飲食嗎？)

What's wrong with my teeth? (我的牙齒怎麼了？)

Do you take any vitamins or tonics?

(你有服用任何維他命或補藥嗎？)

Are you allergic to seafood? (你對海鮮過敏嗎？)

What do you usually do when you catch a cold?

(你通常感冒時會做些什麼事？)

Focus Two

What's your blood type? (你的血型是什麼？)

Do you have a health insurance? (你有健保嗎？)

May I see your insurance card? (我能看一下你的保險卡嗎？)

Have you ever tried acupuncture before?
(你以前試過針灸嗎？)

What are your symptoms? (你的症狀/病徵有哪些？)

Do you keep doing exercises regularly?
(你有持續規律地運動嗎？)

How often do you have a body check/health check-up?
(你多久做一次健康檢查呢？)

Are you able to try the Chinese herbal medicine?
(你可以試試看中藥嗎？)

When's your last treatment/ therapy?
(你上一次治療是何時？)

Do you feel stressful sometimes? (你有時會覺得壓力大嗎？)

Have you ever had a mental consulting before?
(你曾經去過心理諮商嗎？)

Can I avoid the surgery? I really don't want to experience an operation.
(我可以避免這個手術嗎？我真得不希望要經歷開刀。)

How long have you had a headache? (你頭痛多久了？)

Do you have a healthy diet? (你有健康的飲食嗎？)

Would you mind changing your diet?
(你介意改變你的飲食嗎？)

Are you used to staying up night? (你習慣熬夜嗎？)

⊙ **Conversation 1** ⊙

(Addie 在辦公室看到 Doris 不太舒服的樣子，於是問候她的狀況。)

Addie: What's wrong with your cheeks, Doris? There are some rashes on your cheeks!

朵莉絲，你的臉頰怎麼了？你臉頰上有一些紅疹子。

Doris: I knew! They are quite a mess, aren't they? Oh, pool I.

我知道！他們真的很糟，不是嗎？喔，可憐的我。

Addie: Have you put on some medicine?

你有擦些藥在上面嗎？

Doris: Not again. I've tried several so-called "Good advice" therapies. As you can see, they are getting worse now!

不要再來了吧！我已試過好幾個所謂的『好建議』療法。就像你看到的，他們現在愈來愈糟了。

Addie: Oh, sorry. I didn't mean it.

喔，抱歉。我不是故意的。

Doris: You're all right, Addie. I've caught everyone's eyes, but I realize your good will.

你還好啦，艾迪。我已經受到很多人的眼光注目了，但我了解你們的好意。

Addie: Have you gone to see the doctor?

你已經去看醫生了嗎？

Doris: That's the point. I should have seen the doctor first. In the beginning, there was only a small rash on my face. My colleagues

那就是重點。我早就應該先去看醫生才對。在一開始，我的臉上只是有一顆小疹子。我的同事們以為它會變成青春痘，所以他

thought it was going to be pimples, so they lent me some useful ointment.

Addie: Oh, yeah. They may be pimples. How was it going?

Doris: Gosh, it hurt a lot, and the rashes expanded. Then, my boyfriend said it's definitely sunburn, because we've just gone surfing last weekend. He put some mint ointment on my rashes. It was cool and comfortable but nothing happened to my rash.

Addie: Oh, that's interesting. Isn't he a doctor?

Doris: Yes, I'm so lucky that he isn't a vet. Come on, he is a dentist.

Addie: All right, never mind. So, did you go to see the doctor then?

Doris: It's for sure. I can't stand everyone's care, discussion, and bothering anymore, so I go to a skin clinic. The doctor said it's just an insect bite, and it expanded because it was infected and I'm allergic to it.

Addie: Oh, that's too bad. Did he give you the prescription?

Doris: Yes, quite a lot. I just take two

們借我一些有用的藥膏。

喔，是耶。他們可能是青春痘。那然後呢？

天啊，痛死了，然後這些疹子就擴散開了。然後，我男朋友說它一定是曬傷了，因爲我們上週末才剛剛去衝浪過。它擦了一些薄荷膏在我的疹子上。涼涼的很舒服但是疹子沒發生什麼變化。

喔，那挺有趣的。他不是醫生嗎？

是啊，好家在他不是個獸醫。拜託，他是牙醫好不好。

好啦，別在意。那麼，你後來有去看醫生嗎？

當然囉。我再也無法忍受每個人都要來關心、討論還有打擾了，所以我去一家皮膚科診所。這個醫生說它只是被昆蟲咬了，而且它會擴散開來是因爲被感染了，而且我又對它過敏。

喔，太糟了。他有給你處方箋嗎？

有，蠻多藥的。我只每餐

pills after every meal, three times a day. So far, it's not itchy at all.

Addie: Hope you recover soon.

後吃兩顆藥丸，一天三次。到目前為止，一點都不會癢了。

希望你很快地康復。

⊙ Conversation 2 ⊙

(一位 psychiatrist 精神科醫師在和 Mike 這位 patient 病人做諮商。)

Doctor: Mike, nice to see you today.

麥克，今天看到你來真好。

Mike: Yeah? What's about last Saturday and next Saturday?

是嗎？那上星期六和下星期六呢？

Doctor: Oh, great. Past is something we couldn't change. As for the future, we don't know it yet, Mike.

喔，好極了。過去是我們無法改變的事。而至於未來，我們還不知道呢，麥克。

Mike: That's really something told by a psychiatrist.

那還真像是個心理醫師會說的話。

Doctor: All right. So, how are you doing this week? Do you want to talk about your work or family?

好吧。這樣，你這星期過得如何？你想要談談你的工作或家人嗎？

Mike: No. You think my life is so boring, huh? Just work or family? Could we talk about something else, dull?

不想。你認為我的人生很無聊啊？只有工作和家人？我們可以說些別的事嗎？呆子。

Doctor: Take it easy, pal. Of course you can say anything about your life or tell me where your superman dressing room is. I would say it's a regular life rather than a boring life. At least, most

放輕鬆，朋友。當然你可以說任何有關你生活上的事，或者告訴我你的超人更衣室在哪？我會說那是一般人的生活而非無聊的生活。至少，大部

people do it all the time.

Mike: I'm sorry, pretty sorry. (Weeping.) I don't know what wrong I am? Sorry…I'm damn fine, no, I'm not good. What am I talking about?

Doctor: Are you all right? Your face looks so pale and you are trembling.

Mike: Nothing, oh, it's time to take pills. Where is my aspirin? I just can't get rid of the annoying headache. It has almost taken my life away.

Doctor: Wait, Mike. That's not aspirin. Let's see the tag. It's for curing the diabetic. How long have you taken the pills?

Mike: I don't know. Maybe few months, maybe few weeks. I am not sure.

Doctor: Mike, listen, it's quite serious. I would like you to think about it carefully. Where did you get the medicine?

Mike: Don't push me! I just felt better when I took them. I found them in my cabinet.

Doctor: Oh, Mike. You should throw them away. First of all, you're

份的人都是這樣過得。

對不起，真得很對不起。(哭泣著)。我不知道我怎麼了。對不起…我該死地很好(口語：極好的意思)，不，我不好。我到底在說什麼？

你還好嗎？你的臉看起來好蒼白而且你正在顫抖。

沒事，喔，是時候要吃藥了。我的阿斯匹靈在哪？我就是擺脫不了這惱人的頭痛。它幾乎要了我的命。

等一下，麥克。那不是阿斯匹靈啊。來看看這標籤。它是用來治療糖尿病的。你已經吃這些藥多久了？

我不知道。也許幾個月，也許幾星期。我不確定。

麥克，聽著，這相當嚴重。我想要你仔細地想想。你在哪裡拿到這些藥的？

不要逼我！當我吃這些藥時我就覺得比較好了一些。

喔，麥克。你應該把他們丟掉。首先，你沒有糖尿

healthy without the diabetic. As you can see, the tag said the pills were for your mother Lisa rather than you. And they were overdue 2 year ago. They are killing both your body and mind. Can't you feel it?

Mike: Really, were they? Oh, yes, they were overdue already. But why did I feel better then?

Doctor: Well, sometimes people feel better because they think they've taken some medicine. Your boss and wife called me and told me your situation is not good still. They're worrying about your health so much. We now understood what happened. Throw them away, Mike. And go back to your regular life. You don't need them, and you're healthy.

Mike: Really? Am I? Oh I thought I'll kill somebody if I don't take the pills.

Doctor: No, you won't, but you will if you keep taking them. You just overdosed.

Mike: Oh, you saved my life. Do I have to take other medicine?

病你是健康的。就像你看到的，標籤上說這些藥是給你母親麗莎而不是給你的。而且他們早就過期兩年了。他們正在傷害你的身心靈。你感覺不到嗎？

真的嗎？他們過期了嗎？喔，對耶。他們已經過期了。但是為什麼我覺得比較好些了呢？

是會這樣，有些人覺得比較好只是因為他們認為他們已經吃過了一些藥。你老闆和老婆打電話給我而且告訴我你的情況仍然不好。他們現在非常擔心你的健康。我們現在了解了到底發生了什麼事。把他們丟掉，麥克。然後回到你的正常生活。你不需要他們，你是健康的。

真的嗎？我是嗎？喔，我還以為我如果沒吃藥的話我會殺人。

不，你不會的，但你如果繼續吃這些藥就會。你只是服用過量的藥而已。

喔，你救了我一命。我必需吃別的藥嗎？

Doctor: DON'T TAKE MEDICINE. YOU DON'T NEED THEM NOW, YOUNG MAN.　不要吃藥！你現在不需要藥，年輕人。

⊘Work Bank⊘ 隨時補充一錠，你在會話及閱讀理解必備的單字！

- medicine [ˋmɛdəsn̩] 藥物
- temperature [ˋtɛmprətʃɚ] 溫度
- take the medicine 服用藥物
- take the temperature 量體溫
- pill [pɪl] 藥丸
- tablet [ˋtæblɪt] 藥片
- capsule [ˋkæpsl̩] 膠囊
- essential [ɪˋsɛnʃəl] 必要的；基礎
- essential oil 香精油
- herb [hɝb] 草藥
- spread out 散佈
- contagious [kənˋtedʒəs] 接觸傳染的
- cough syrup [kɔf][ˋsɪrəp] 咳嗽糖漿
- hospital [ˋhɑspɪtl̩] 醫院
- clinic [ˋklɪnɪk] 診所
- draw blood 抽血
- ice pack 冰袋
- eye contact 隱形眼鏡
- lens [lɛnz] 鏡片
- glasses [ˋglæsɪz] 眼鏡
- brace [bres] 牙套；義肢
- inject [ɪnˋdʒɛkt] 注射
- surgery [ˋsɝdʒərɪ] 手術
- operation [ˌɑpəˋreʃən] 手術
- injury [ˋɪndʒərɪ] 傷害
- flu [flu] 流行性感冒
- infection [ɪnˋfɛkʃən] 傳染；感染
- acupuncture [ˋækjʊˌpʌŋktʃɚ] 針灸
- CPR (cardiopulmonary resuscitation) 心肺復甦法

- medical [ˋmɛdɪkl̩] 醫學的
- thermometer [θɚˋmɑmətɚ] 溫度計
- solid [ˋsɑlɪd] 固體的
- fluid [ˋfluɪd] 流質的；液體的
- liquid [ˋlɪkwɪd] 液體的
- powder [ˋpaʊdɚ] 粉末
- gas [gæs] 氣體
- spray [spre] 噴霧；噴灑液
- nasal spray 鼻子噴劑
- eye drop 眼藥水(滴藥)
- ointment [ˋɔɪntmənt] 藥膏
- immunity [ɪˋmjunətɪ] 免疫力
- bandage [ˋbændɪdʒ] 繃帶
- band [bænd] 帶子；綑綁
- lozenge [ˋlɑzɪndʒ] 錠劑
- throat lozenges 喉糖
- antiseptic [ˌæntəˋsɛptɪk] 殺菌的
- without antiseptic 沒有殺菌
- panadol caplet 普拿疼吞劑
- aspirin [ˋæspərɪn] 阿斯匹靈
- band aid OK 繃
- first aid 急救
- first-aid kit 急救工具
- cure [kjʊr] 治療
- therapy [ˋθɛrəpɪ] 治療；療法
- treatment [ˋtritmənt] 治療
- allergy [ˋælɚdʒɪ] 過敏
- rescue [ˋrɛskju] 救援

名 **measles** [ˋmizl̩z] 麻疹		
名 **chicken pox** 水痘	形 **faint** [fent] 頭昏；暈眩
名 **mumps** [mʌmps] 腮腺炎	形 **dizzy** [ˋdɪzɪ] 頭暈目眩的
名 **disease** [dɪˋziz] 疾病	名 **cold** [kold] 感冒
名 **fever** [ˋfivə] 發燒	動 **hurt** [hɝt] 受傷
動 **catch a cold** 感冒	動 **bleed** [blid] 流血
動 **cough** [kɔf] 咳嗽	形 **tired** [taɪrd] 疲倦的
動 **sneeze** [sniz] 打噴嚏	名 **rash** [ræʃ] 疹子
名 **gout** [gaʊt] 痛風	名 **symptom** [ˋsɪmptəm] 症狀；徵兆
名 **sore throat** [sor][θrot] 喉嚨痛	名 **prescribe** [prɪˋskraɪb] 開藥方
名 **sore muscle** 肌肉酸痛	名 **prescription** [prɪˋskrɪpʃən] 處方
名 **headache** [ˋhɛdͺek] 頭痛	名 **check-up** 檢查
名 **toothache** [ˋtuθͺek] 牙痛	名 **insurance** [ɪnˋʃʊrəns] 保險
名 **earache** [ˋɪrͺek] 耳朵痛	形 **mental** [ˋmɛntl̩] 精神的
名 **stomachache** [ˋstʌməkͺek] 胃痛	形 **physical** [ˋfɪsɪkl̩] 身體的
名 **backache** [ˋbækͺek] 背痛	名 **health** [hɛlθ] 健康
名 **joint pain** [dʒɔɪnt][pen] 關節炎	形 **healthy** [ˋhɛlθɪ] 健康的
名 **constipation** [ͺkɑnsəˋpeʃən] 便秘	名 **mind** [maɪd] 心智
動 **pull a tooth** 拔牙齒	名 **body** [ˋbɑdɪ] 身體
動 **feel not good** 感覺不舒服	名 **condition** [kənˋdɪʃən] 狀況
動 **feel sick** 感覺不舒服	名 **situation** [ͺsɪtʃʊˋeʃən] 處境；情況
名 **cancer** [ˋkænsə] 癌症	名 **brain** [bren] 腦袋
名 **diabetic** [ͺdaɪəˋbɛtɪk] 糖尿病	名 **windpipe** [ˋwɪndͺpaɪp] 氣管
名 **heart attack** 心臟病發作	名 **heart** [hɑrt] 心臟
名 **heart disease** 心臟病	名 **lung** [lʌŋ] 肺
名 **cavity** [ˋkævətɪ] 蛀牙	名 **stomach** [ˋstʌmək] 胃
名 **heart stroke** 中風	名 **belly** [ˋbɛlɪ] 肚子；腹部
動 **chill** [tʃɪl] 打寒顫	名 **pancreas** [ˋpæŋkrɪəs] 胰腺
動 **tremble** [ˋtrɛmbl̩] 發抖	名 **liver** [ˋlɪvə] 肝臟
形 **nauseous** [ˋnɔʃɪəs] 令人嘔吐的	名 **intestine** [ɪnˋtɛstɪn] 腸子
動 **throw up/ vomit** [ˋvɑmɪt] 嘔吐	名 **kidney** [ˋkɪdnɪ] 腎臟
名 **drug store** 藥店	名 **cystitis** [sɪsˋtaɪtɪs] 膀胱炎
名 **pharmacy** [ˋfɑrməsɪ] 藥房	名 **bladder** [ˋblædə] 膀胱

名	**vitamin** [ˋvaɪtəmɪn] 維他命	名	**scale** [skel] 磅秤
名	**cane** [ken] 拐杖	名	**nasal congestion** 鼻塞
名	**crutch** [krʌtʃ] 撐在腋下的拐杖	名	**high blood pressure** 高血壓
名	**tonic** [ˋtɑnɪk] 補藥	名	**hypertension** [ˌhaɪpɚˋtɛnʃən] 高血壓
名	**emergency** [ɪˋmɝdʒənsɪ] 緊急事件	名	**emergency room** 急診室

名 **HIV(human immunodeficiency virus)** 人體免疫力損害病毒；愛滋病
名 **AIDS(acquired immunodeficiency syndrome)** 愛滋病

名	**ambulance** [ˋæmbjələns] 救護車	名	**pimple** [ˋpɪmpl̩] 面皰；青春痘
形	**uncertain** [ʌnˋsɝtn̩] 不確定的	名	**skin problem** 皮膚問題
形	**suspicious** [səˋspɪʃəs] 多疑的	名	**burn** [bɝn] 燙傷；燒傷
名	**insect bite** 昆蟲咬傷	名	**frostbite** [ˋfrɔstˌbaɪt] 凍傷；凍瘡
名	**snack attack** 蛇咬傷	名	**sunburn** [ˋsʌnˌbɝn] 曬傷
名	**cut** [kʌt] 割傷	名	**suntan** [ˋsʌntæn] 曬黑
動	**drown** [draʊn] 溺死	動	**fall down** 摔落；跌倒
名	**choke** [tʃok] 噎到；窒息	動	**breathe** [brið] 呼吸
動	**overdose** [ˋovɚˌdos] 服藥過量	動	**break one's bone** 骨折
名	**bruise** [bruz] 黑青；淤傷	名	**sprained ankle** 腳踝拐到；扭傷
名	**bloody nose** 流鼻血	形	**swollen** [ˋswolən] 浮腫、脹大的
名	**infection** [ɪnˋfɛkʃən] 傳染；感染	名	**inflammation** [ˌɪnfləˋmeʃən]發炎

Reading Passage

Annoying spring is coming again. For such an unpredictable and unstable weather, the new improved Cheers Vitamin C compound will help you stop  coughing, sneezing, tearing, and feeling itchy. It increases your immunity in such a changeable weather. A series of long-term medical tests have proven that the Cheers Vitamin C compound will supply you for the essential nutrition and fiber of vegetable and fruit. Get a head start and be ready for

the coming season. Taking 300 mg of Cheers Vitamin C compound every day is able to reinforce your immunity and beneficial to your digestion. Taking 600 mg once a day can make you feel better when you have the symptoms of cold and ease your uncomfortable feelings. Cheers Vitamin C compound: only available at Sunshine chain pharmacies.

Warning: Inquire your doctor if you are taking any prescription of hypertension or antidepressant before you take Cheers Vitamin C compound.

_____ (1) What is the purpose of the passage?
A. To warn people of the danger of high blood pressure.
B. To announce a higher charge of the insurance.
C. To offer the free medical tests for the elder.
D. To promote a new health supplementary.

_____ (2) According to the passage, why is the spring season annoying?
A. There are flowers everywhere.
B. The weather changes from time to time.
C. The drug stores usually have no discount in spring.
D. Many people have heart diseases in such a season.

_____ (3) If Sam catches a cold, how should he take the vitamin?
A. Take 600 mg once a day.   B. Avoid taking it.
C. Take 300 mg instead.   D. Take other medicine.

_____ (4) Where can people buy the Cheers Vitamin C compound?
A. Go shopping online   B. Any local drug store.
C. In some clinics.   D. A chain drug store.

_____ (5) What does the ads suggest those who are taking the antidepressant medicine?

A. Avoid taking the vitamin.　　B. Taking the vitamin instead.
C. Ask for the instruction for taking the vitamin.
D. Ask for another prescription from other doctors again.

♥愛的筆記貼♥本篇文章是篇維他命的廣告文章。內容是：惱人的春天又要來了。對於這樣一個無法預測又不穩定的天氣，新改良的契爾斯維他命 C 綜合錠將會幫助你阻絕咳嗽、打噴涕、流淚和癢的感覺。它會在這樣一個多變的天氣裡增加你的免疫力。一連串長期的醫學實驗已經證明契爾斯維他命 C 綜合錠將補給你所需要的蔬菜和水果的營養素及纖維素。早點開始然後準備好面對即將到來的季節。每天服用 300 毫克的契爾斯維他命 C 綜合錠能加強你的免疫力而且有助於你的消化。當你有感冒症狀時，一天服用一次 600 毫克可以幫你好很多而且舒緩你不舒服的感覺。契爾斯維他命 C 綜合錠：只在陽光連鎖藥局才買得到。**警告：如果你正在服用任何高血壓或抗憂鬱劑的處方藥，在你服用契爾斯維他命 C 綜合錠前請詢問你的醫生。 **解答：1.(D)** 這段文章的意圖是『推廣一種健康補給品』。 **2.(B)** 根據本文，因為春天的天氣時常變化所以很討厭。 **3.(A)** 如果 Sam 感冒了，他應該要服用多一點的維他命劑量，也就是一天 600 毫克以舒緩感冒症狀。 **4.(D)** 要到一個連鎖藥局才能買到這種維他命。**5.(C)** 這個廣告建議正在服用抗憂鬱劑的人要詢問指示才能服用這種維他命。

Vocabulary Challenge

_____ 1. There were 23 people injured in this car accident last night, and they were sent to the _____ room right away.

　(A) urgent　(B) emergency　(C) dining　(D) dressing

_____ 2. One of his legs had been cut because of the _____ of a wound.

　(A) inflammation (B) immunity (C) community (D) affection

_____ 3. Martin sprained his ankle in the game and it got _____.

　(A) sunburn　　(B) frostbite　(C) swollen　(D) swallow

解答：(1) B (2) A (3) C

延伸閱讀

　　對於程度比較好的同學，現在網路這麼方便，老師建議大家，以下的多媒體學習方式，只要我們自己願意下工夫去接觸，處處都是英語學習的資源：

◎　閱讀加強：

www.mail.com

很多人會建議 CNN 及 BBC 的新聞網站，不過在此為了初級及銜接中級程度的同學，老師比較建議這個網站，因為它不僅提供免費的英文 e-mail 信箱，它還提供了即時的全球新聞。文章內容長度適中，且有各種話題，也有八卦新聞或運動報導，內容很多元，較符合同學的興趣。

http://answers.yahoo.com/

同學愛用雅虎奇摩知識嗎？那你不能錯過英文版的知識家喔！在這裡，你可以學到很多最 in 的英語及背景知識。

◎　聽力加強：

網路上是有很多英語聽力練習網站，在此建議同學可以去 www.apple.com 蘋果電腦網站上下載 itune 這個音樂播放軟體來使用，它的廣播可以依音樂類型來收聽很多國外的電台。老師的母校所在地也有個電台跟多益考試相關的是廣播中也會出現商業廣告或播報氣象，也有即時幾分鐘的新聞插播，同學可以一邊放鬆，一邊也練習聽力。其他像是 BBC 的 Radio 網站也不錯，只是有英國腔，適合要去英國唸書的同學們適應口音專用。☺

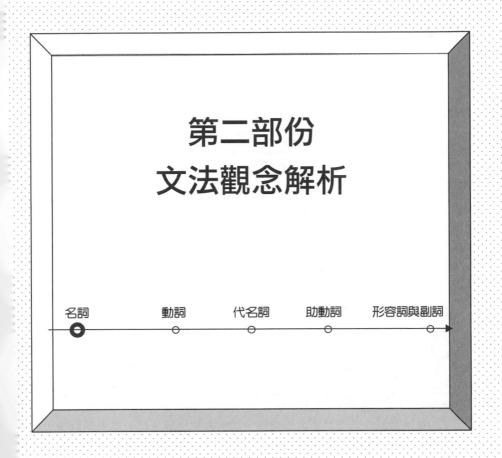

第二部份
文法觀念解析

名詞　　　動詞　　　代名詞　　　助動詞　　　形容詞與副詞

Grammar session 1 | 名詞及名詞片語
 Noun and Noun phrase

❧ 本課學習要點 ❧

1. 名詞可分可數名詞、不可數名詞，牽動『動詞變化』
2. 名詞可簡可繁，可長可短的原因是加上了冠詞、所有格、形容詞或介系詞。
3. 動詞也可變化為名詞，將『動作』轉為『一件事情』，只要將動詞後加上 **ing** 即可。

---

① 名詞可分可數名詞、不可數名詞，牽動『動詞變化』

 常見疑問 1 | 如何分可數和不可數名詞呢？

♥愛的筆記貼♥

  在課堂上同學發問最高的問題，以及考試中最苦惱的是動詞什麼時候該加 s 什麼時候不加 s，還有 be 動詞與動詞的使用搭配，都是因為名詞的單、複數觀念不清楚而混淆用法了。很多人以為名詞的觀念很簡單而忽視它，卻讓它成為了根基的薄弱因素。要學好英文，文法上要正確，絕對要學好名詞和動詞的觀念，因為英文最基本的句子組成要項就是 S+V，主詞(主要名詞)+動詞。

◎ **先講名詞為什麼是單數的情形。**

  名詞是單數可能是❶名詞是可數狀態，但要敘述的主體只有一個，單獨存在的情形。❷名詞本身的性質是不可數狀態，像 water 水。換句話說：<u>只要是可數名詞單一狀態，或名詞不可數的狀態下，這樣的名詞就是單數形。那麼可數名詞是很多個的狀態下，就是複數形，名詞後要加 s 或 es。</u>

◎ **不可數名詞有哪些？如何分辨？**

大部份同學為認為分辨不可數名詞最好就是查字典，單字後有(C)就是可數名詞，單字後有(U)就是不可數名詞，但沒有帶字典的時候呢？這裡老師幫大家整理了一些常用的分辨原則：

● **物質名詞：**

物質、材質通常是不可數的，例如剛剛提到的 water 水，水本身無固定形狀，又會因溫度變化產生形態變化，屬於流質的，拿也拿不起來，正所謂覆水難收，除非你用到第二個名詞：可數的容器，將它裝起來，像 bottle 瓶子，你就可以一瓶一瓶的數了，a bottle of water 一瓶水。所以太冷就結冰 ice，也不可數。太熱變成水蒸氣 steam 不可數。飄到 air 空氣裡，空氣無色無味當然也就不可數。飄上 sky 天空，全地球的 sky 概念是相通的，我們也只有一個天空所以不可數。水氣凝結成 rain 雨，rain 當做雨的意思時也不可數，沒有人一滴雨滴來數雨的。物質變化還有一個和日常生活相關的就是牛奶 milk，本身是液體就不可數，凝固結成 cream 奶油、起司 cheese，這些製品本身可以依容器形狀及裁切方式變成各種形態，當然也不可數。(其實 cream 和 cheese 本來也就是流質的。)這讓我想到 soap 肥皂這事，有 DIY 親手製肥皂的同學就知道，肥皂本身也是流質的，依容器形狀而凝固成各種形狀或被切成各種形態。其他例如是 wood 木頭、salt 鹽、sugar 糖、oil 油、gold 金、silver 銀、sun 陽光，這些都屬於不可數名詞。

● **抽象名詞：**

顧名思義『抽象』abstract，不是實體的物體怎麼數呢？這類的名詞通常是指概念、感覺，例：happiness 幸福、wisdom 智慧、peace 和平、belief 信仰、history 歷史、culture 文化、custom 風俗習慣、health 健康、wealth 財富、fortune 財富或運氣…等等。

● **專有名詞：**

專有名詞也就是說世上只有一個，所以天生就是獨孤星、單數。例：Taiwan 台灣、Taipei 101 台北 101、New York 紐約、Obama Barack 歐巴馬、June 六月、the Pacific Ocean 太平洋、the Atlantic Ocean 大西洋…等等。一個名詞就對應著一個特有的物件。

● **代表『物質群組名稱、類別』的名詞：**

剛剛有提到 water、milk、cream、oil 這些物質，它們本身還有一個任務就是代表群組的名稱。水有很多種，牛奶、奶油、油品類下面都有所屬的物質。舉 meat 肉類來說，肉類分為 beef 牛肉、pork 豬肉、chicken 雞肉、lamb 羊肉，不僅這些肉的名稱不可數，代表類別的 meat 也不可數。其他例如：vegetable 蔬菜、fish 魚、seafood 海鮮、money 錢(錢的形態也有很多種，所以是類別。)

◎ **集合名詞通常是複數形。**

　　這裡介紹的幾個常考的集合名詞如 people 人們、the police 警察、family 家庭或家人、staff 職員、clothing 穿著、jewelry 珠寶。集合名詞指整體時當做單數，指其中的個體成員時當做複數。people 通常當做複數名詞用，我們會數 one person, two people, three people…以此類推，people are、many people 的用法。The police 警察通常也是複數名詞的使用法，警力表示有很多警察。不過因為有一個樂團叫警察樂團很有名，所以當警察樂團時 the police 當然就視為單數名詞。還有 family 這個字，例：There are six families in my family. 意思就是 We have six family members. 有六個成員在我的家庭裡。/ 我們有六個家庭成員。

<Practice 練習時間> **請將以下的名詞分為可數及不可數兩種名詞：**

water　　mouse　　car　　tree　　seat　　vegetable　　dog

people　　human being　　planet　　cheese　　juice　　milk

tooth　　bed　　room　　space　　parking lot　　money

coin　　bill　　air　　aircraft　　airport　　MRT　　train

event　　culture　　belief

可數 countable	不可數 uncountable

**不確定是可數或不可數的單字，可以查字典來學習更多的名詞狀況

常見疑問2 │ 名詞 + s 和動詞 + s 的差別？

♥愛的筆記貼♥

　　初學英語的同學們會有這樣的疑問是很正常的，至少勇於解開心中的疑惑，並且知道自己不懂的在哪裡。現簡要說明如下：

◎名詞後加 s 或 es，表示兩個以上的複數型態。

◎動詞後加 s 或 es，則是一種動詞變化，是配合前面的主要名詞而加的。當主要名詞是第三人稱單數，而動作的時態是現在式，動詞就要加 s 或 es 了。(其實也就是說當名詞是第三人稱單數時，這時動詞需配合變化加上 s 或 es，但是這樣的動詞變化反而證明了主要動詞是第三人稱單數型態，例：The man _____ (laugh) at her. 此時空格中的動詞因為前面的主詞是第三人稱單數，這個男人，所以答案是 laughs。這男人嘲笑她。反過來看這題 The _____ (man/men) laughs at her. 因為我們看到主要名詞後跟著的動詞變化是 laugh+s，表示主要名詞是第三人稱單數，所以要選單數型的 man，是指一個男人而不是很多男人。)

◎至於加 s 還是 es 這是發音的問題，一般來說不管是名詞還是動詞，單字字尾若是子音-s, -sh, -ch 或母音-o 結尾的多加 es。例如 buses, glasses, bunches, polishes, potatoes, tomatoes 等等。但是要注意：photo，不加 es，複數型為 photos。

　　希望以上詳盡的解說，可以幫助同學們對於名詞單複數形有更清楚的認知。

常見疑問3 │ 何時該用 be 動詞？

♥愛的筆記貼♥

　　網路搜尋名列前茅的還有這個問題，一個跟名詞關係密切，在學英文的路上遇到的第一位朋友，偏偏也是最容易被遺忘或錯用的 be 動詞。be 動詞有著特殊的身份，它很類似於中文中的『是』，也是個具有『連繫』功能的詞。它雖然算是動詞，卻不像 run 跑、jump 跳那樣的實際動作產生。be動詞的主要功能是『用來敘述事物，用來連接名詞和名詞之間，或名詞與形容詞，做為一個句子中的主要動詞』。

例：Mr. Lin is a nice man. 林先生是個好男人。(名詞+is+名詞)

　　Mr. Lin is handsome. 林先生很帥。(名詞+is+形容詞)

BE 動詞與各人稱之間的配合用法

單數	主詞	現在式	過去式	複數	主詞	現在式	過去式
一	I 我	am	was	一	We 我們		
二	You 你	are	were	二	You 你們		
第三人稱	He 他 She 她 It 它 Mr.Hank	is	was	第三人稱	They 他們 Students People	are	were

<Practice 練習時間> 名詞單複數牽動 be 動詞變化練習

(1) Lisa _____ my best friend.　　(2) Billy ____ a tall boy.

(3) I ___ a student.　　(4) They _____ my cousins.

(5) People _____ forgetful. → _____ _____ forgetful.

(6) Yesterday, we _____ in the Starbucks coffee shop.

<Practice 練習時間> 名詞單複數牽動動詞變化練習

(7) My cousin _____ (have/ has) many toy cars on his bookshelf.

(8) There _____ (is/ are) many apple trees in the garden.

(9) Many cars just _____ (run/ runs) through the red light here
　　every day.

(10) Julie _____ (want/ wants) to buy a brand new car this month.

(11) There _____ (is/ are) too much trash in the pond. The water in
　　it ____ (is/ are) very stinky and dirty.

(12) We _____ (don't/ doesn't) believe in god here. We
　　_____ (believe/ believes) in Guanyin Mom.

♥愛的筆記貼♥

解答：**(1) is / Lisa 是我最好的朋友。(2) is /** 比利是個高個子的男孩。

(3) am / 我是一個學生。 (4) are /他們是我的堂兄妹。

(5) are / 人們是健忘的。→ They are

(6) were / 昨天，我們在這家星巴克咖啡店。

(7) has / 我表弟有好多的玩具車放在他的書架上。

(8) are / 在這花園裡有好多蘋果樹。

(9) run / 在這每天都有很多車闖紅燈。

(10) wants / 茉莉這個月想要買一台新車。

(11) is/ 這個池塘裡有好多垃圾。is/ 這個池塘裡的水好臭好髒。

(12) don't / 在這我們不相信上帝。believe / 我們相信觀音媽。

(**12 題其實是一位新加坡朋友模仿電影時講的笑話，並無惡意，當然我們也可以用來回答我們自己的信仰。)

2 名詞可簡可繁，可長可短的原因，是前後加上了冠詞、所有格、形容詞或介系詞，就成了『名詞片語』。不管是名詞片語有多長，它還是屬於名詞的用法。

語言實驗室

Step 1 名詞片語基本組成要項

冠詞(a/ an/ the) 所有格(my/ your/ his/ her/ its/ our/ your/ their)	形容詞	名詞
the	tall	girl
my	cute	puppy
the	unforgettable	event
his	emotional	character

Step 2 接上了連接詞，就可以連接兩個以上的形容詞，使名詞片語變得再長點：

冠詞所有格	形容詞	連接詞	形容詞	名詞
the	tall	and	thin	girl
my	cute	and	furry	puppy
the	unforgettable	or	regretful	event
his	emotional	but	creative	character

Step 3 接上了介系詞 in/at+地方、時間，on 日期，of 表從屬關係，就更長了：

冠詞所有格	形容詞	連接詞	形容詞	名詞	介系詞	冠詞	名詞
the	tall	and	thin	legs	of	that	girl
my	cute	and	furry	puppy	in		Kaohsiung
the	unforgettable	or	regretful	event	in	Taiwan's	history
his	emotional	but	creative	character	on	his	music

<Practice 練習時間>

自己動手寫寫看以下的 **2** 個練習，體驗一下名詞片語的魅力吧！

1. 我的女朋友(或男朋友)	2. 一個故事
我美麗的女朋友(或我帥氣的男朋友)	一個有趣的故事

我美麗又溫柔的女朋友(或帥氣又體貼的男友)	一個有趣而鼓勵人心 (encouraging)的故事
我那來自日本美麗又溫柔的女朋友 (我那來自韓國帥氣又體貼的男友)	一個在每個人心中有趣而鼓勵人心的故事

♥愛的筆記貼♥

　　經過以上的練習，有沒有發覺自己也挺有文藝青年風範？語言本來就是用來敘事的，可抒情也可寫實，這也是語言感動人心的一面。希望同學們發揮實驗的精神，除了此章提到的練習，平時也可以試試用名詞片語不斷加長的模式，來敘述自己周遭的人事物喔！

1. 我的女朋友(或我的男朋友)	2. 一個故事
-my girlfriend (my boyfriend) -my beautiful girlfriend (my handsome boyfriend) -my beautiful and tender girlfriend (my handsome and thoughtful boyfriend) -my beautiful and tender girlfriend from Japan (my handsome and thoughtful boyfriend from Korea)	- a story - an interesting story - an interesting and encouraging story - an interesting and encouraging story on everyone's mind

◎呈以上所述，連接詞可以連接好幾個形容詞來敘述名詞的狀況下，就會衍生出形容詞順序的問題。常用來修飾同一名詞的形容詞排序如下：

主觀感覺	大小	年齡長幼	顏色	國籍;城市	材質
wonderful	big	young	red	American	wooden
beautiful	small	middle-age	yellow	Chinese	plastic
great	tall	old	blue	Japanese	leather

<Practice>

A. She has a _____ hair.
(curly / blonde/ beautiful)

B. Lucia is a _____ girl.
(American/ wonderful/ young)

C. The dress is elegant with the _____ belt.
(leather/ gold/ wide)

D. My husband was satisfied with the _____
_____ food in your restaurant. (Italian / creative/ creamy)

E. Do you see my _____ sweater?
(woolen/ loose/ blue)

解答：**(A) beautiful curly blonde /** 她有一頭美麗的金色捲髮。

(B) wonderful young American / 露西亞是一位美好的年輕美國女孩。

(C) wide gold leather / 這件洋裝和這條金色粗皮帶搭配起來很優雅

(D) creative Italian creamy / 我的丈夫很滿意你們餐廳的創意義大利奶油食物。

(E) loose blue woolen / 你有看到我那件寬鬆的藍色羊毛衣嗎？

常見疑問 4　不可數名詞如何形容數量？

♥愛的筆記貼♥

　　不管是可數或不可數名詞，都有兩種數量的表達方式。不可數名詞雖然和可數名詞不同，前面無法直接加數字來數，但也可用以下所提的兩種數量表達方式來敘述。

◎ **用數裝盛的容器來表達**

a bar of soap 一塊香皂	three boxes of candy 三盒糖
a pack of potato chips 一包洋芋片	a bunch of bananas 一串香蕉
some sacks of flour 好幾袋麵粉	a bouquet of roses 一束玫瑰花
a bag of salt 一包鹽	five jars of marmalade jam
a bottle of juice 一瓶果汁	五罐橘子果醬
two cans/ tins of tuna 兩罐鮪魚	a cup of tea/ coffee 一杯茶或咖啡

a tube of toothpaste 一條牙膏	a glass of water 一杯水
a carton of milk 一紙盒裝牛奶	a sheet/ piece of paper 一張紙
a bowl of rice 一碗飯	a stack of documents 一疊文件
a loaf/ two loaves of bread/ toast 一條/ 兩條麵包或吐司	a slice of ham 一片火腿
	a piece of cake 一塊蛋糕
a herd of rhinos 一群犀牛	a crowd of people 一群人
a pile of clothes 一堆/一排衣服	a flock of ducks 一群鴨子

◎ **用專門講可數或不可數的量詞來表達**

用量詞來表達『其中之幾』，強調某個指定範圍中的一部份，則用量詞+of+the+名詞來表示。

Much of his advice is quite useful to me.

  (2)   (1)   (3)   (4)

(1) 先判別主要名詞為可數或不可數。→ advice『建議』是不可數
(2) 再看量詞要選用可數或不可數量詞。→所以用不可數的『多』
(3) 往後看動詞變化，要搭配前面的名詞做單數或複數變化。
    → 不可數名詞片語 much of his advice，be 動詞用單數變化。
(4) 貫徹始終：最後的補語也要檢查，如果是名詞也得和前面的主詞做一致的變化。→這裡是形容詞所以沒有單複數變化

可數	不可數	兩者都可以
每一個 Every(單數)	多 Much	大部份 Most
一個 One(單數)	少 Little	多 A lot of
兩個 Two	一些 A little	多 Lots of
兩者都 Both		一些 Some
多 Many		任何 Any
少 Few		全部 All
一些 A few		

<Practice>

A. _____ (Many/ Every/ Some) of the water is poisonous and undrinkable in this area.
B. Many of them _____ (is/ are) my friends.
C. One of the students _____ (raise/ raises) his hand.
D. _____ and _____ people (fewer/ less) _____ (buy/ buys) the plastic products.

E. Both of them _____(is/ are) my _____ (son/ sons). One
    is Jeff, the other is Kevin.
F. Neither of them _____ (is/ are) _____ (a doctor/
    doctors).
G. We can digest _____ (some/ any/ many) of the vegetable
    directly. However, _____ (few/ little) of it _____ (has/ have)
    certain medicinal reaction.

解答：(A) Some /主要名詞是 water 屬於不可數名詞，所以量詞也要用
可數和不可數都可以用的 some。/這個地區的有些水是有毒的且不能
飲用的。(B) are /主要名詞是『他們』加上量詞為可數的『many』，所
以動詞應為複數的 be 動詞 are。他們其中的很多人都是我的朋友。(C)
raises / 雖然主要名詞是複數型的學生，但量詞 one 表示是其中一位，
所以動詞應選用第三人稱單數的動詞變化 raise+s。其中一位學生舉手
了。(D) Fewer, fewer, buy /主要名詞是 people，是複數型的集合名詞，
所以要搭配可數的量詞 fewer，fewer and fewer 是 few+er 比較級形容
詞的用法，意思是『愈來愈少的』，即使是少，還是算複數，所以動
詞要用複數形動詞變化 buy 不加 s。愈來愈少的人購買塑膠製品。(E)
are, sons / 主要名詞是他們，且量詞 both 是兩者都，屬於複數，be
動詞用 are，後面補語的部份也要選擇複數型名詞 sons。他們兩個都
是我的兒子。一個是傑夫，另一個是凱文。(F) is, a doctor/ Neither 這
個量詞是兩者都不是，所以是單數。他們兩個都不是醫生。(G) some,
little, has/ 這句中決定量詞的名詞是 vegetable 蔬菜，本身不可數，所
以要選可數和不可數都可以，且用於肯定句的 some，any 通常用於否
定或疑問句。後句的 it 代名詞指得也是 vegetable，所以量詞要用不可
數的 little，動詞要用單數變化的 has。我們能夠直接消化這些蔬菜的
其中一些。但是，這些蔬菜中的少部份有某種藥物反應。

3 動詞也可變化為名詞，將『動作』轉為『一件事情』，
   只要將動詞後加上 ing 即可。即現在分詞當做名詞使用。
   例：collect 收藏→ collecting 收藏這件事
       learn 學習→ learning 學習這件事
   Reading magazines is helpful for me to relax.

(閱讀雜誌這件事對於我放鬆情緒很有幫助。)

這句中的 reading magazines 是一個名詞片語，指得是『閱讀雜誌』這件事，所以是一件事。因爲沒有特別講是那一本雜誌，所以雜誌這個名詞 magazine 是複數型，但即便是這樣，這句話中指得就是閱讀雜誌這件事。所以 be 動詞用單數的 is。這種句型常考，不管是多長的名詞片語，都得認清到底這個名詞片語是單數還是複數，再判斷動詞變化。

<Practice>

A. Collecting coins _____ (is/ are) _____ of my hobbies.

B. 聽音樂和騎自行車對我來說都很放鬆且愉快的。

♥愛的筆記貼♥

解答：**(A) is, one / 收藏錢幣是我的嗜好之一。**
(B) Listening to the music and cycling are so relaxed and
**　　 pleasant for me.**

Grammar Challenge

_____ 1. Drinking too much alcohol ___ not good for both your health
and your mind.　 (A) be　 (B) is　 (C) are　 (D) been

_____ 2. She is allergic to _____ of the seafood. She only accepts tuna.
(A) most　 (B) many　 (C) few　 (D) one

_____ 3. There are _____ of files on the desk.
(A) groups　 (B) piles　 (C) bunches　 (D) flocks

_____ 4. The air pollution in the city is getting more and more serious
because of _____.

(A) the increasing number cars　 (B) the number of increasing cars

(C) the cars number increasing　 (D) cars increasing the number

_____ 5. _____ of my classmates suggests that we may have a trip to
Hualien this summer. And everybody agrees with her.

(A) One　(B) None　(C) Neither　(D) Any

_____ 6. Both of you _____ in the meeting room yesterday. What
happened? (A) is　(B) are　(C) was　(D) were

_____ 7. The case ___ approved by all of the managers.

(A) is　(B) are　(C) be　(D) been

_____ 8. Cabbages is a kind of _____.

(A) vegetable　(B) vegetables　(C) fruit　(D) fruits

_____ 9. Jennifer spent _____ money buying the house.

(A) many　(B) much　(C) lot of　(D) few

_____ 10. None of the birds in the cage ____ able to sing and talk.

(A) is　(B) are　(C) can　(D) be

_____ 11. Please don't throw away the _____ of paper on my table.
The documents are quite important to me.

(A) piece　(B) corner　(C) stack　(D) bottle

_____ 12. The hotel is well-known about their good _____.

(A) staff　(B) staffs　(C) fames　(D) airs

_____ 13. Living in a big city ___ much different from a small town.

(A) is　(B) are　(C) do　(D) does

_____ 14. They put too _____ sugar so that the coffee tastes sour and
too sweet.　(A) many　(B) a lot　(C) lot of　(D) much

_____ 15. Would you like _____ orange juice?

(A) any　(B) some　(C) every　(D) many

_____ 16. I want some _____ and a glass of juice.

     (A) salad   (B) salads   (C) fishes   (D) side dish

_____ 17. There are some _____ in the _____.

     (A) skies; clouds   (B) clouds; skies

     (C) sky; cloud   (D) clouds; sky

_____ 18. Do you know _____ of the trains is to Brighton?

     (A) some   (B) any   (C) none   (D) part

_____ 19. Your _____ will be _____ appreciated and we will reply

    your mail as soon as possible.

     (A) advices; many   (B) advice; much

     (C) advice; many   (D) advices; many

_____ 20. Which of the following sentences is correct?

     (A) No one can stop her believes.

     (B) We only have a few water in the refrigerator.

     (C) There is a flock of crows on the grass.

     (D) We need many flours and butters to make the cakes.

Grammar session 2 ｜ 動詞及動詞片語 Verb and Verb phrase

❧ 本課學習要點 ❧

1. 動詞依『時態』和『語態』，而有動詞常用的三態變化形：
   原形動詞、過去式、過去分詞。
2. 動詞可分『及物動詞』及『不及物動詞』，不及物動詞後要加介系詞來搭配使用。
3. 動詞變化在敘述『現在簡單式』時態時，要特別注意與主詞的單複數形變化需一致。

1 動詞依『時態』和『語態』，而有動詞三態的變化形：
　　原形動詞、過去式、過去分詞。

　　　在前一章名詞單元時，我們曾提到 Be 動詞的用法，再複習一下，Be 動詞並沒有實際的動作發生，它的功能，主要是用來『連繫』名詞與名詞間，及名詞及形容詞。如果真要給它翻成中文意思，可以當作『是』的意思。基本上也就是繫詞的功能了。所以我們也可以稱它為『連繫』或『連綴』動詞的用法。這個動詞類別的用法我們會在此章後段詳加說明。Be 動詞基本上也是動詞，所以它也會有動詞變化：

原形	現在式	過去式	過去分詞	現在分詞
be	am is are	was was were	been	being

語言實驗室

　　緊接著，在我們要談到實際講『動作』的動詞前，我們先來複習，在我們腦海中，對以下這些動詞的三態是否都很熟悉了。動詞三態變化，又分為規則動詞及不規則動詞變化。規則變化在過去式及過去分詞中，多半後面加 ed 就可以。但是惱人的是不規則動詞變化就難記了。

　　以下精選了 30 個常用而且必會的動詞，請同學們試著找出這些動詞的變化規則是否有相似之處呢？

中文	原形	過去式	過去分詞	中文	原形	過去式	過去分詞
有	have	had	had	做	do	did	done
去	go	went	gone	來	come	came	come
得到/變成	get	got	gotten	變成/成為	become	became	become
忘記	forget	forgot	forgotten	說	say	said	said
睡覺	sleep	slept	slept	付費	pay	paid	paid
保持	keep	kept	kept	帶來	**br**ing	**br**ought	**br**ought
開車	drive	drove	driven	買	**b**uy	**b**ought	**b**ought
騎車	ride	rode	ridden	選擇	choose	chose	chosen
喝	drink	drank	drunk	冷凍	freeze	froze	frozen
唱歌	sing	sang	sung	搭乘	take	took	taken
跑步	run	ran	run	搭乘	catch	caught	caught
看	see	saw	seen	教導	teach	taught	taught
掉落/摔倒	fall	fell	fallen	賣	sell	sold	sold
聽到	hear	heard	heard	告訴	tell	told	told

握住/舉行	hold	held	held	見面	meet	met	met

如果同學發現，以上的有些動詞，因為變化的方式很類似，可以圈起來成為一組一組的，那這樣記憶起來就更有效率。

<Practice 練習時間>

1. 『站著』的動詞三態為 stand/ stood/ stood，『了解、懂得』的動詞三態為 understand/_____ /
   _____。『誤解』的動詞三態為 misunderstand/
   _____/ _____。

2. 『騎車』的動詞三態為 ride/ rode/ ridden，所以『寫』的動詞三態就會是 write/ _____/ _____。『升起』的動詞是 rise/ _____/ risen。

3. 『喝』飲料的喝的動詞三態是 drink/ _____/ _____，所以『唱歌』的動詞三態是 _____/ _____/
   _____ ， 而『搖鈴』或電話『響起』的動詞三態是 ring / _____/ _____。

4. 『知道』的動詞三態是 know/ knew/ known，所以『丟掉』的動詞三態是 throw/ _____/ _____。

5. 『寄送』的動詞三態是 send/ sent/ sent，所以『花費』的動詞三態是 spend/ _____/ _____。

♥愛的筆記貼♥

　　經過以上的練習，同學們還覺得不規則動詞很難記嗎？應該多少會容易一些了吧！至少我們透過以上的練習會發覺，其實英文蠻有邏輯性的，雖然英文這種拼音文字語言對我們來說，要記好多拼字，字義也要另外記，但它的字母只有 26 個，發音和拼字也有一定的規則。看看你的電腦鍵盤就知道，通常相鄰近的字母就是常會被拼在一起的字母。如果你了解這個基本規則，英打的速度也會變得快一些喔！年紀愈長，我們的記憶力通常沒有小時候來得好，但是邏輯推理的能力、關聯能力相對的會比較高，所以只要用有效率的方法來學習，你一定會很快學會英文的。現在有沒有比較有信心了呢？就像星爺的『食神』電影裡提到的：『只要有心，人人都可以是食神。』那我們就是『只要有心，人人都可以變成英文達人喔！』一字記之若『心』啦！

解答：❶understand/ understood/ understood, misunderstand/ misunderstood/ misunderstood (understand 是了解，前面若加上表示『錯過』、『不』、『失誤』的字首，就代表『不甚了解』，也就是『誤會』。這樣的字彙原則讓我想到另一個單字 mistake，意思就是『拿錯了』，所以是『錯誤』的意思。❷ write/ wrote/ written, rise/ rose/ risen。升起 rise 的過去式是 rose，所以同學們看到文章中有 rose 時，不要再大目地、直線條地以為是『玫瑰』或是『蘿絲』囉！要看前後文還有在句中的位置來判斷 rose 是名詞還是動詞變化。不然翻譯和理解上可就 You jump, I jump 了喲！❸ drink/ drank/ drunk, sing/ sang/ sung, ring/ rang/ rung。❹ throw/ threw/ thrown。❺ spend/ spent/ spent。

有些不規則動詞超級划算的，背一個等於背全家，全家就是我家的意思。這麼好康的動詞，那不背起來真的對不起自己了。The winner is…

中文	原形	過去式	過去分詞	中文	原形	過去式	過去分詞
讓	let	let	let	放	put	put	put
閱讀	read	read*	read*	剪/切	cut	cut	cut
設置	set	set	set	價值	cost	cost	cost
傷害	hurt	hurt	hurt	打擊	hit	hit	hit

* read 這個字動詞三態雖是一樣，但讀音為 read[rid]/ read[rɛd]/ read[rɛd]。

常見疑問 1 ┊ 規則動詞過去式-ed 的唸法？

♥愛的筆記貼♥

　　由於現在許多英檢中都加考口試的部份，近年來大家對發音也相對的較重視了起來。規則動詞 ed 的發音，通常在對話中不是那麼容易清楚的聽見，因為我們不會為了特別要將這個尾音發清楚，而讓整句話因中斷而聽起來不順暢。在對話中，說話者常常也會因為話講得快因此會有『連音』的現象出現，像本來沒有 gotta 這個字，這也是因為 got to 連音而來的。但是在初級英檢中，因為要測試同學們對於一些基本發音的認識，所以口說時要注意這項發音要素。規則動詞過去式的變化就是在字尾加 ed，唸法其實是跟隨著單字本身字尾來做發音的調整，我們只要記得三大原則；

◎ **有聲唸有聲。** 字尾是有聲子音或母音的話，就唸有聲的[d]。
　　例：listened, studied, played, enjoyed
◎ **無聲唸無聲。** 字尾是無聲子音的話，就唸無聲的[t]。
　　例：walked, watched, looked, cooked, jumped
◎ **遇到[t], [d]唸[Id]。**
　　字尾是有聲子音[d]的話，如果再唸有聲的[d]，就會造成重覆的讀音，好像 lag 唱片跳針一樣，所以要唸[Id]來避免重覆。
　　例：started, wasted, wanted

<Practice 練習時間> **請將以下的動詞依字尾來分辨 ed 的讀音：**

finished　　　stopped　　　remembered　　　decided　　　practiced
loved　　　liked　　　sounded　　　tasted　　　turned
touched　　　smelled　　　tried　　　helped　　　planed

字尾唸[d]	字尾唸[t]	字尾唸[Id]

♥愛的筆記貼♥

解答：

字尾唸[d]	字尾唸[t]	字尾唸[Id]
remembered, loved, turned, smelled, tried, planed	finished, stopped, practiced, liked, touched, helped	decided, sounded, tasted

常見疑問 2 ┊ 動詞之後什麼時候要加 s 和 es？

在前面的名詞章節中，我們有為大家區分名詞後加 s 和動詞後加 s 的意義。在這裡要講得是什麼時候動詞後要加 s 或 es 來做動詞變化。其實事情很單純，就是動詞前面所搭配的主詞(即名詞)是第三人稱單數型時，又是要表達『現在式』時態的時候，動詞就要加 s 或 es 來表現動詞變化。而何時加 s 何時加 es 就要看動詞字尾的發音，這我們在前面名詞章節的相關問題有討論過。

所以在『現在式』的句子裡，do 這個動詞，前面遇到第三人稱單數的名詞，就要改成 does。同理可證，go 也是一樣，遇到第三人稱單數的名詞，就要改成 goes。還有 have 比較特別，遇到第三人稱單數名詞，現在式句子，就要改成 has。其他的動詞也都是如此。用例句來解釋說明如下：

Dora <u>does</u> her homework by herself. (朵拉靠自己做她的功課)。

Gary <u>has</u> three brothers, Tom, Bill, and Sam.

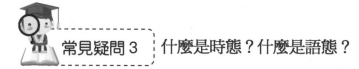

（蓋瑞有三個兄弟，湯姆、比爾和山姆。）

Their teacher <u>asks</u> them to do the math practices every day.

（他們的老師要求他們每天都要做數學功課。）

The DJ <u>wants</u> to tell an English joke for the audience every day.

（這個廣播員想要每天為聽眾講一個英語笑話。）

One of my friends, **George**, <u>watches</u> the ESPN channel on

weekends. （我有個朋友喬治每個週末都會收看 ESPN 體育台。）

　　　所以只要是主詞是第三人稱單數，又遇到現在式的時態，動詞就要加 s 或 es。

　　常見疑問 3　什麼是時態？什麼是語態？

　　　英文主要分為兩大語態及三大時態。兩大語態就是主動語態及被動語態。通常以主詞開始一句話的是主動語態。用受詞開始一句話的是被動語態。被動語態通常中文都會翻譯成『某件事物被誰…』。三大時態是依事物發生的『時間觀念』而分為過去式、現在式、未來式。在三大時態下因為『動作進行的狀態』又分為完成式、簡單式、進行式。

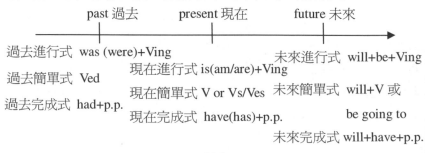

past 過去	present 現在	future 未來

過去進行式　was (were)+Ving　　　　　　　　　　　未來進行式　will+be+Ving

過去簡單式　Ved　　　　　現在進行式 is(am/are)+Ving

過去完成式　had+p.p.　　　現在簡單式 V or Vs/Ves　　未來簡單式　will+V 或

　　　　　　　　　　　　　現在完成式　have(has)+p.p.　　　　　　　　be going to

　　　　　　　　　　　　　　　　　　未來完成式 will+have+p.p.

　　　　學英文時文法架構(frame)，主要是時態及語態的觀念架起了一個人的骨骼，而說話的內容就需要靠字彙量來充實了，就像身上的血液(blood)一樣。兩者都是根基(base)，也是本書希望幫助同學建立的部份。至於要怎麼強身健體？就跟某位小天王說的一樣，每天一罐雞精吧！什麼是學好英文的雞精或補藥(tonic)呢？當然就是你對英文的興趣囉！我們先來了解英文的架構吧！

◀ 現在式 ▶

現在簡單式 V or Vs/Ves (動詞變化)
現在進行式 is(am/are)+Ving (現在分詞)
現在完成式 have(has)+p.p. (過去分詞)

現在簡單式	通常是指現在發生的事，或每天都會發生的事，表命令的祈使句，或者是常理。

Ex. Betty <u>is</u> my young sister. (貝蒂是我的妹妹。)
　　We <u>have</u> 4 classes every day. (我們每天有四堂課。)
　　The sun <u>rises</u> from the east. (太陽從東方升起。)
　　<u>Clean</u> up your room right now. (現在馬上清理你的房間。)

現在進行式	敘述現在正在發生的動作。

Ex.　My brother <u>is swimming</u> in the pool. (我哥正在泳池游泳。)
　　Mr. Jones <u>is talking</u> on the phone. (瓊斯先生正在講電話。)
　　They <u>are having</u> a meeting now. (他們現在正在開會。)

現在完成式	敘述『已經』完成的動作，從過去到現在持續的動作，以及表示『曾經』有的經驗。

Ex. We <u>have completed</u> the work. (我們已經完成了這項工作。)
The song <u>has been</u> popular for 20 years. (這歌已流行了 20 年。)
Kevin <u>has been</u> to Guatemala before. (凱文以前曾去過瓜地馬拉。)

名詞　　　動詞　　　代名詞　　　助動詞　　　形容詞與副詞

◀ **過去式** ▶　過去簡單式 Ved (動詞變化)
　　　　　　　過去進行式 was/ were +Ving (現在分詞)
　　　　　　　過去完成式 have(has)+p.p. (過去分詞)

過去簡單式　通常是指過去發生的事。

Ex. She used to work in our company. (她過去曾在我們公司上班。
　　Nancy was a nurse before. (南希以前是個護士。)
　　I ran into my classmate on the street. (我在街上遇到我同學。)

過去進行式　敘述在過去的某個時間點正在發生的事。

Ex. He rang the doorbell while I <u>was talking</u> on the phone.
　　(當我正在講電話時他按了門鈴。)
　　The party <u>was</u> still <u>going</u> on around 2 a.m. in the early
　　morning. (在凌晨 2 點左右這舞會仍在進行中。)

過去完成式　敘述『已經』完成的動作，在過去一個時間點發生過的事，或者是在一個有兩個動作的句子裡，用來敘述較早發生的動作。

Ex. The department store <u>had shut</u> down two months ago.
　　(這家百貨公司已經在 2 個月前歇業了。)
　　Before he arrived at the town, his family <u>had been</u> there.
　　(在他到達這鎮上之前，他的家人已經在那了。)
　　Sally was so sad because her husband <u>had sold</u> her
　　favorite car. (莎莉好難過因為她的丈夫已經賣掉她最愛的車。)

◀ **未來式** ▶　未來簡單式 will+V 或 be going to+V
　　　　　　　未來進行式 will+be+Ving (現在分詞)
　　　　　　　未來完成式 will+have+p.p. (過去分詞)

未來簡單式　通常是指未來『將要』發生的事。be going to 通常用於表示對未來的事有計劃去做。

Ex. We <u>are going to have</u> a party to celebrate his promotion.
　　(我們將為他舉辦個聚會來慶祝他的升職。)
　　If it rains tomorrow, they <u>will cancel</u> the picnic.
　　(如果明天下雨的話，他們將會取消野餐。)

I <u>will arrive</u> at there as soon as possible.
(我會盡可能快點到那裡。)

未來進行式　敘述在未來的某個時間點，即將正在發生的動作。

Ex. In the afternoon, our manager <u>will be reporting</u> the sales performance of the quarter to the board.
(在下午的時候，我們經理將正在對董事會進行本季的業績報告。)
Don't call me later. I <u>will be riding</u> on my way home.
(等一下不要打給我。我將正在騎車回家的路上。)

未來完成式　敘述未來『已經將會』完成的動作，或者是在一個有兩個未來動作的句子裡，用來敘述較早發生的動作。

Ex. Judy and I <u>will have saved</u> 2 million by the end of this year. (茱蒂和我在今年年底將會已存到 200 萬了。)
The customer <u>will have gone</u> when you finally decide to say something to her.
(等到你終於決定要和顧客說些什麼時，她將早就不見了。)

　　以上說明完三個時態，九個式子的文法概念。但既然英文時態是跟著時間去定義的，我們就必需了解時間的說法，這樣一來同學以後只要一聽到相關的時間字彙就可分辨出應該要用什麼時態比較適合了。

◀ 時間單位由小到大的排列 ▶

second→minute→hour→morning, noon, afternoon, evening,
　秒　　分鐘　　小時　　早晨　　中午　　下午　　傍晚/晚間
night, midnight, wee hours→ day→a couple days→ week→
夜晚　午夜　　凌晨時分　　天　　兩三天　　星期
weekend→ a couple weeks→ month→season(quarter)→year
週末　　兩三個星期　　月　　季節　　年

→decade→century(age)
　十年　　一百年=世紀

♥愛的筆記貼♥

◎ **quarter** =4 分之 1

　　　　=15 minutes(一小時的四分之一)

　　　　=3 months (一年的四分之一，即一季 season)

◎ **half** = 2 分之 1

half an hour = 30 minutes(一小時的二分之一)

half a year = 6 months (一年的二分之一)

◎ **There are 7 days in a week.** 一週有七天，分別是：

週一 Monday, 週二 Tuesday, 週三 Wednesday, 週四 Thursday, 週五 Friday, 週六 Saturday, 週日 Sunday

on Mondays 為『每逢週一』之意，依此類推，每週五是 on Fridays, 每逢週末就是 on weekends。every other day 是指每隔一日。

◎ **There are 12 months in a year.** 一年有 12 個月。

1 月 January, 2 月 February, 3 月 March, 4 月 April,

5 月 May, 6 月 June, 7 月 July, 8 月 August,

9 月 September, 10 月 October, 11 月 November, 12 月 December

◎ **There are 4 seasons in a year.** 一年有四季。

　　spring 春　　　summer 夏　　fall(autumn)秋　　winter 冬

◎ **last** 上一個、**this** 這一個、**next** 下一個(前面均不加介系詞)

　屬於過去的時間點　last Monday 上週一、last month 上個月、last night 昨晚、last year 去年、last summer 去年夏天、this morning 今天早上(通常我們說到今天早上發生的事，都是已經發生過了，所以多用過去式。)、yesterday 昨天

　屬於現在的時間點　this month 本月份、this week 本週、this year 今年、this season(quarter)本季、today 今天、now 現在。

　屬於未來的時間點　next month 下個月、next week 下週、next year 明年、tomorrow 明天。

◎ **Nowadays** 也是『今日、現在』之意，用現在式。

◎ **Before, after, ago, later** 表示『在…之前』、『幾天前』及『在…之後』、『幾天後』的時間說法。

Something happened <u>before</u> the 3 days.(在這三天前有某事發生了。)
3 days <u>ago</u>, something happened. (三天前，有某事發生了。)

She admitted everything <u>after</u> 3 days. (在三天後她承認了所有事。)
3 days <u>later</u>, she admitted everything. (三天後，她承認了所有事。)

◎ **關於時間的介系詞用法**

in – in a year 一年內, in spring 在春天, in February 在二月, in the morning 在早晨, in 3 days 在三天內

on–特定的日期, on Monday 在週一, on Jan. 21st 在 1 月 21 日, on holidays 每逢假日, on vacation 渡假, on Christmas 在聖誕節

at–時間, at 3 p.m.在下午 3 點, at night 在夜晚

during–在一段期間內, during the summer vacation 在暑假期間, during my stay in Taipei 在我於台北停留的期間

from_____ to_____–從…到…, from 8 a.m. to 5 p.m. 從早上 8 點到下午 5 點

since–自從，since last year 自從去年起, since 1985 自從 1985 到現在, since his left from our hometown 自從他從我們鎮上離開起 (since 後接過去的時間點，從過去的時間點開始到現在，所以多和現在完成式一起使用)

for-有一段時間了, for 3 years 三年了, for a long time 有好一段時間了，多和完成式一起使用。

◀ 需特別注意但不常用的時態 ▶

現在完成進行式	have(has)+been+Ving 通常指得是已經進行一段時間，而到目前還正在進行的動作。

The construction of the new parking lot <u>has been progressing</u> since last spring. (新停車場的施工從去年春天一直進行到現在。)

<Practice 練習時間> **判別時態測驗題**

(　　) 1. Jane _____ in the park every morning.

(A) is jogging　(B) jogged　(C) jogs　(D) has jogged

(　　) 2. Last summer, they _____ the best memory in the Disney Land in the United States.

(A) have　(B) were having　(C) had　(D) is having

(　　) 3. This time, the medical team _____ from Kobe, a city in Japan, which had ever been ruined by a famous earthquake. (A) was　(B) is　(C) has　(D) had

(　　) 4. Have you ever _____ of the "La la la la song" before?

(A) heard　(B) hear　(C) hears　(D) hearing

(　　) 5. There _____ some water in the glass few minutes ago, but there _____ no water now. The water had vapored.

(A) are; is　(B) were; is　(C) is; were　(D) was; is

(　　) 6. Jamie went home while his mother _____.

(A) was cooking　　　　(B) cooked

(C) is cooking　　　　(D) cooks

(　　) 7. Now you _____ to the most popular radio program in town ACBC.

(A) listen　　　(B) are listening

(C) listened　　(D) are listened

(　　) 8. The bus _____ in five minutes, and please line up in front of the bus stop.

(A) will come　　　　(B) is coming

(C) is going to come　(D) comes

(　　) 9. Our teacher _____ us the Lesson 5 this morning, and
the course for tomorrow will be lesson 6.

    (A) taught　　　　　　(B) was teaching

    (C) teaches　　　　　　(D) is teaching

(　　)10. By the time you come tomorrow, we _____ the work
and will hand over it to you.

    (A) will do　　　　　　(B) will done

    (C) did　　　　　　　　(D) will have done

♥愛的筆記貼♥ ❶看到 every morning 每天早上，知道這是件每天
都會做的事，所以是用現在簡單式，又配合 Jane 第三人稱單數，動詞
後加 s。題意：Jane 每天早晨都在公園慢跑。答案是：(C)。❷ 看到
Last summer，去年夏天，過去的時間點要用過去式來敘述。題意：去
年夏天，他們在美國迪士尼樂園有一段最好的回憶。答案是：(C)。❸
看到 this time 這一次，是現在時間，所以要用現在式。題意：這一次，
來自日本神戶的醫療團隊，這個城市曾經被一個有名的地震毀壞。答
案是：(B)。❹看到問句句首為 Have 助動詞開頭，所以後面要加過去
分詞。題意：你以前有聽過『啦啦啦啦歌』這首歌嗎？答案是：(A)。
❺第一句話後面有 few minutes ago 幾分鐘前，所以知道是過去式，而
名詞 water 是不可數名詞，所以要用 was。後面這句有 now，所以表
示現在式的 is。題意：在幾分鐘前這玻璃杯內有一些水，但現在杯裡
沒有水了。水已經蒸發了。答案是：(D)。❻看到 while 後面多半是接
Ving，前面主要子句的動詞是過去式 went，所以後面要選過去式的 be
動詞。題意：Jamie 回家時，他媽媽正在煮菜。答案是：(A)。❼看到
Now 現在，依句意應選擇現在進行式。題意：你現在正在收聽的是鎮
上最受歡迎的廣播節目 ACBC。答案是：(B)。❽看到時間副詞 in five
minutes 在五分鐘內，所以要選擇未來式。有些動詞像 come 來, go 去,
arrive 到達, leave 離開都可用現在進行式來表示未來式。題意：巴士
在五分鐘內就要來了，請在站牌前排好隊。答案是：(B)。❾看到 this
morning 今早是過去時態，所以要選過去式的動詞。題意：今天早上
我們老師教了我們第五課，而明天的課將是第六課。答案是：(A)。❿

看到 tomorrow 明天，要選擇未來時態。依題意：在你明天來的時候，我們將會已經完成了這個工作，而且將交給你。因為後面有 will hand over，表示工作已經完成。所以此題要選未來完成式的(D)選項。

◀ 主動語態與被動語態 ▶

　　主動語態是以主詞主動做動作的句子。被動語態是以受詞開始被做動作的句子。以下用『我做了一個蛋糕』，和被動語態『這個蛋糕是由我做的』句子來表現各時態下的主、被動語態句子。主動語態的公式為主詞(S)+動詞(V)+受詞(O)。被動語態的公式為受詞(O)+be 動詞+動詞的過去分詞+by+主詞(S)。

現在簡單式	主動：I make a cake.
	被動：The cake is made by me.
現在進行式	主動：I am making a cake.
	被動：The cake is being made by me.
現在完成式	主動：I have made a cake.
	被動：The cake has been made by me.
過去簡單式	主動：I made a cake.
	被動：The cake was made by me.
過去進行式	主動：I was making a cake three hours ago.
	被動：The cake was being made three hours ago.
過去完成式	主動：I had made a cake.
	被動：The cake had been made by me.
未來簡單式	主動：I will make a cake.
	被動：The cake will be made by me.
未來進行式	主動：I will be making a cake next Friday.
	被動：The cake will be being made by me next Friday.

未來完成式	主動：I <u>will have made</u> a cake next Friday.
	被動：The cake <u>will have been made</u> by me next Friday.

同學們有沒有發現，這樣推論下來，其實主動語態轉被動語態基本上只要注意(1)受詞和主詞調換位置，(2)原本主動句的時態加上被動語態的基本型 be+過去分詞(p.p.)來相互作用，也就是時態+語態。例如：過去完成式在主動語態裡是 had+p.p.，加上被動語態的基本式 be+p.p.：

had + p.p.時態

+)   be + p.p.語態

had + been + p.p.

<Practice 練習時間> **時態+語態測驗題**

( ) 1. There is a poor kitty _____ in the rain, do you want to bring it in? (A) sat (B) sit (C) is sitting (D) sitting

( ) 2. Have you ever _____ by your best friends? It really made me feel hurt.

   (A) laughed   (B) been laughed

   (C) be laughed   (D) laugh

( ) 3. Joanna has lost her favorite book since last summer, but it _____ on the table this morning.

   (A) shows (B) showed (C) is showed (D) was showed

( ) 4. I just want to know who ____ my cake. It was overdue!

   (A) ate (B) eats (C) eat (D) was eating

( ) 5. I can tell that the thieves must have come already. Some things _____ slightly.

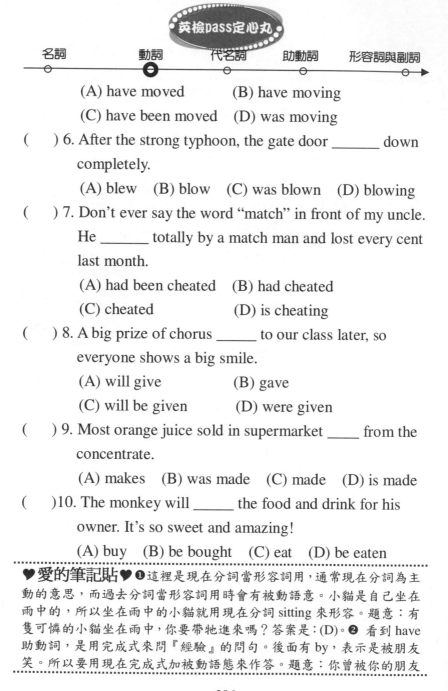

(A) have moved　　　　(B) have moving

(C) have been moved　(D) was moving

(　　) 6. After the strong typhoon, the gate door _____ down completely.

　　(A) blew　(B) blow　(C) was blown　(D) blowing

(　　) 7. Don't ever say the word "match" in front of my uncle. He _____ totally by a match man and lost every cent last month.

　　(A) had been cheated　(B) had cheated

　　(C) cheated　　　　　(D) is cheating

(　　) 8. A big prize of chorus _____ to our class later, so everyone shows a big smile.

　　(A) will give　　　　(B) gave

　　(C) will be given　　(D) were given

(　　) 9. Most orange juice sold in supermarket _____ from the concentrate.

　　(A) makes　(B) was made　(C) made　(D) is made

(　　)10. The monkey will _____ the food and drink for his owner. It's so sweet and amazing!

　　(A) buy　(B) be bought　(C) eat　(D) be eaten

♥愛的筆記貼♥ ❶這裡是現在分詞當形容詞用，通常現在分詞為主動的意思，而過去分詞當形容詞用時會有被動語意。小貓是自己坐在雨中的，所以坐在雨中的小貓就用現在分詞 sitting 來形容。題意：有隻可憐的小貓坐在雨中，你要帶牠進來嗎？答案是：(D)。❷ 看到 have 助動詞，是用完成式來問『經驗』的問句。後面有 by，表示是被朋友笑。所以要用現在完成式加被動語態來作答。題意：你曾被你的朋友笑過嗎？這真的讓我覺得很受傷。答案是：(B)。❸看到 this morning 今早是過去時態，所以要選過去式的動詞。然而書不會自己出現，應該是被放在桌上，然後被大家看到，所以要選被動語態。題意：Joanna 最愛的書自從去年夏天就不見了，但今天早上它出現在桌上。答案是：(D)。❹看到後面 was overdue 是過去動詞，已經有人吃掉蛋糕了，所以要選過去式動詞。題意：我只想知道是誰吃了我的蛋糕？它早就過期了。答案是：(A)。❺前一句話 must have come already 表示『一定已經來過了』，所以知道是現在完成式，而東西不會自己移動而是被移動，所以要用被動語態。題意：我可以分辨得出來小偷一定已經來過了。有些東西已被稍微移動過。答案是：(C)。❻颱風來過了，所以是過去式。大門不會自己吹倒，而是被吹倒，所以是被動語態。題意：颱風過後，大門被完全地吹倒了。答案是：(C)。❼首先看到 and 這個對等連接詞後面接的是過去式動詞 lost『失去』，時間副詞是 last month 上個月，所以空格中的動詞要用過去式。因為是被騙，所以是被動語態。題意：不要在我叔叔面前提到『火柴』這個字。他上個月曾經被一個火柴人(金光黨)騙過而且失去了他的每一分錢。答案是：(A)。❽看到時間副詞 later，等一下、稍晚的意思，所以要選擇未來式。獎項是被頒而不能自己頒，所以要用被動語態。題意：一個合唱的大獎將要被頒發給我們班，所以每個人臉上都展露笑容。答案是：(C)。❾柳橙汁是被製造而不能自己製造，所以用被動語態。又依題意，是個事實，所以要用現在式。果汁是不可數名詞，故 be 動詞要用單數的 is。題意：大部份在超市販售的柳橙汁都是由濃縮果汁製造而來。答案是：(D)。❿猴子可以主動做動作，所以用主動語態。依題意：這猴子會為主人買食物和飲料。真是很溫馨且令人驚訝。所以此題要選未來原形動詞的(A)選項。

<Practice 改寫句子寫作題練習時間>

1. Yes, I <u>bought</u> the CD last week. (請依劃線部份造原問句)。

_____

2. Mr. Williams drove to work yesterday. (請依提示改寫句子)。

_____every day.

3. Sally went to <u>the hospital</u> this morning. (請依劃線部份造原

問句)。

---

4. Henry does the dishes every day. (請改爲被動式的句子)。

---

5. They teach the children how to read Chinese. (請改爲被動
式的句子)。

♥愛的筆記貼♥以上的練習題型在全民英檢初級寫作考試時常
考，同學比較容易出錯的部份是造過去式的原問句，以及被動語態的
轉換。希望同學可以多多練習，更上一層樓。❶造原問句時需注意劃
線部份劃在哪裡。此句劃線在動詞上，表示我們要注意動詞時態。此
句是 Yes/ No 的回答，所以我們知道要用助動詞開頭的問句。動詞時態
是過去式，所以選擇用 Did 開頭。在助動詞後的動詞均爲原形動詞，
所以 bought『買』這個動詞要還原成原形的 buy。這種題型也最喜歡
考 I 和 You 的轉換，回答句是『我』，那麼原問句應該就是問『你』。
所以答案爲 Did you buy the CD (last week)? 你(上星期)買了這片 CD
嗎？要注意的是，buy 的過去式 bought 和 bring 的過去式 brought 常常
會混淆，差別就在有沒有那個 r 了。❷此題爲依提示作答的句子，要注
意答案線前後是否有提示文字出現。此題的提示文字爲句尾的
yesterday 改爲 every day 來做答。因爲時間從過去式改爲現在式，動詞
變化上當然需做現在式的變化。不規則動詞在這種時態變化的題型上
就是常考重點了，因爲同學們常常會忘記不規則動詞的三態變化。所
以這題應改寫爲 Mr. Williams drives to work every day. 威廉先生每天開
車去上班。因爲每天是慣性動作，所以用現在簡單式，而 Mr. Williams
是第三人稱單數，所以動詞要還原成原形 drive 再加個 s。❸本題動詞
是過去式，而劃線部份在 the hospital 醫院，是個地點。句子前面並沒
有 yes/ no，所以不是助動詞開頭的問句，而是表示地方疑問詞的 where
開頭的問句。本題應該爲：Where did Sally go this morning? 莎莉今天
早上到哪裡去了？❹改成被動式的句子，首先要看受詞是 dishes 碗盤，
第三人稱複數形，be 動詞要用 are/ were。然後看動詞 does，是現在簡

單式。所以 bc 動詞要選現在式的 are。而原動詞 does 要改為過去分詞的 done。Henry 是原本的主詞。改為被動式時，受詞要放在前面，成為 <u>The dishes are done by Henry every day.</u> 碗盤每天都是由亨利洗的。(do the dishes 為『洗碗盤』之意。) ❺ 承上題，被動式語態要以主動式句子中的受詞為開頭。受詞是 The children。孩子的複數型。所以 be 動詞在此處要選現在式的 are。原動詞 teach 要改為過去分詞的 taught。事情是 how to read Chinese，所以擺在動詞後面。主詞 they 因為放在句尾當 by 的受詞，所以應改為受詞 them。整句話應改寫為 <u>The children are taught how to read Chinese by them</u>。這些小孩們被他們教導如何讀中國字。

 ▶ **進階練功坊** ◀

1 四大動詞體系----感官動詞

a. 感官動詞有 look, see, watch 表示『看』, smell『聞』, taste『嚐』, hear, listen 表示『聽』, feel『感覺』, touch『摸』。

b. 所謂感官動詞，是以人為出發點，『感覺』事物的動詞。

c. 用法： **感官動詞 + 原形 V / Ving**

一般用法為後接原形 V，但若要表達當時所感覺的那一瞬間動作，有正在進行之意義，則後面動詞用 Ving 來做強調。

中文	原形	過去式	過去分詞	中文	原形	過去式	過去分詞
看	look	looked	looked	嚐	taste	tasted	tasted
看	see	saw	seen	聽	hear	heard	heard
看	watch	watched	watched	聽	listen	listened	listened
聞	smell	smelled	smelled	感覺	feel	felt	felt
摸	touch	touched	touched				

Ex. I <u>saw</u> Wendy <u>walk</u> in the rain last night.

（我昨晚看到溫蒂走在雨中。）

<Practice 練習時間>

1. 今天早上當Tom經過教室時，他看到Wendy正在那兒哭泣。

_____

2. 每天早上我們都能聽到鳥叫聲。

_____

♥愛的筆記貼♥

解答： ❶ When Tom walked through the classroom this morning, he saw
　　　　 Wendy crying (weeping) there.
　　　 ❷ We can hear the birds sing every morning.

---

2 四大動詞體系----連繫(綴)動詞

a. 連繫動詞有哪些？

　(1) 『變得』：get, become, turn, seem，等等。

　(2) 『感覺』起來如何？look, smell, taste, sound, feel,
　　　　touch，等等。

b. 所謂連繫動詞，是用來『描述事物』的另一種句型，形
　　容事物變得如何，感覺起來如何。所以後面加形容詞，
　　而這樣的動詞用法就類似 **be 動詞**。

c. 用法： **連綴動詞 + adj.形容詞**

中文	原形	過去式	過去分詞	中文	原形	過去式	過去分詞
變成	get	got	gotten	聞	smelled	smelled	smelled
變成	become	became	become	嚐	taste	tasted	tasted
變成	turn	turned	turned	聽	sound	sounded	sounded
似乎	seem	seemed	seemed	感覺	feel	felt	felt
看	look	looked	looked	摸	touch	touched	touched

Ex. The song **seems** <u>familiar</u> to me. (這首歌對我來說似乎很熟悉。)

Ex. It suddenly **turns** <u>dark</u>. It might rain later.

(天色突然間變暗了。等一下可能會下雨。)

感官動詞 look, smell, taste, sound, feel, touch 等，當做『感覺』起來如何時，後面直接加形容詞，或加 like+名詞，就是連繫動詞的用法。比較說明如下：

👁	He **looks** so handsome. (他看起來好帥。)
	He **looks like** Tom Cruise. (他看起來像湯姆克魯斯。)
👃	It **smells** awful. (它聞起來好糟。)
	It **smells like** the stinky tofu. (它聞起來像是臭豆腐。)
😋	The steak **tastes** dry and hard. (這牛排嚐起來又乾又硬。)
	The steak **tastes like** plastics. (這牛排嚐起來像塑膠。)
👂	The song **sounds** familiar. (這歌聽起來好熟悉。)
	The song **sounds like** our song. (這歌聽起來是我們的歌。)
✋	The floor **touches** so cold. (這地板摸起來好冷。)
	The floor **touches like** ice. (這底板摸起來像冰一樣。)
❤	Your words **make me feel** so warm. (你的話使我感到好溫暖。)
	Your words **make me feel like** drinking a cup of hot chocolate in winter. (你的話使我感到像是在冬天喝上一杯熱可可一樣。)

<Practice 練習時間>

1. 最近天氣變冷了，媽媽要我們穿上夾克。

_____ recently, and my mother wants us to put on our jackets.

2. 這個主意聽起來很棒。你覺得如何？

_____. How do you feel?

3. 這瓶牛奶嚐起來是酸的，它應該是過期了。

_____, and it should be out of date.

♥愛的筆記貼♥

解答：❶ It turns(gets/ becomes) cold　❷ The idea sounds great.
　　　❸ The bottle of milk tastes sour.

---

3 四大動詞體系----使役動詞

a. 使役動詞有哪些？

　　第一類：有『要、叫、使、讓』之意的動詞 have, make, let。

　　第二類：有『要求』之意的動詞 ask, tell 等等。

　　第三類：『幫助』help

b. 所謂使役動詞，是要表達『令、使、讓、幫助+名詞(人事物)+做什麼動作』。

c. 用法：　第一類：**使役動詞 +N 名詞 + 原形動詞**

　　　　　第二類：和 to 連用，即 ask someone to 原形動詞, tell someone to 原形動詞。

　　　　　第三類：help 後的 to 通常可省略。

中文	原形	過去式	過去分詞	中文	原形	過去式	過去分詞
要/叫	have	had	had	讓	let	let	let
使	make	made	made	幫助	help	helped	helped
要求	ask	asked	asked	要/叫	tell	told	told

Ex. 我姐姐要我們整理今天下午整理好房間。

　　<u>My sister</u> had <u>us</u> clean up the rooms this afternoon.

　　(主詞)　　(受詞)

**但用在被動語態時，由於受詞 us 被移到句首，had 和 clean

- 212 -

兩個動詞將會碰在一起，故用 to 隔開，於是變成：

<u>We</u> were had to clean up the rooms by <u>my sister</u> this afternoon.

(受詞當主詞用)　　　　　　　　　　　(原主詞)

意思是：今天下午我們被我姐姐叫去清理房間。

**使役動詞多半後面是接原形動詞,若後面接過去分詞,則是使役動詞+被動語態的用法,指得是讓…被…。

Ex. 我去剪頭髮了。

　　→ I **have** my hair <u>cut</u>.

　　　(使役動詞)　　(cut 的過去分詞)

　　　並不是我自己剪,而是我讓我的頭髮被剪了。屬於被動語態的用法,cut 動詞三態都一樣。

(主動語態) → I **have** the hair dresser <u>cut</u> my hair.

　　　　　(使役動詞)　　　　　(原形動詞)

　　　　　意思是『我讓髮型師剪我的頭髮。』

<Practice　練習時間>

1. 我送車子去洗。

　　(主動語態) I have the workers _____ my car.

　→ (被動語態) I _____.

2. Frank 經常幫助長者(elders)過馬路。

_____.

3.讓我告訴你一個鬼故事。

_____.

4.很多年前這裡大多數的人都被他幫忙搬家過。

_____ .

♥愛的筆記貼♥

解答： ❶ wash, I have my car washed by the workers. 此句被動語態的
句子比較複雜，因為一個句子裡有三個名詞：I, my car, the
workers. 在寫被動語態的句子時，要表達什麼概念，是誰
被怎樣了一定要先搞清楚。像題目中的被動語態句是以 I
開頭，所以我們會寫成 I have my car washed by the workers.
我讓我的車被工人們洗。如果要表達『這些工人們被我叫
來洗車』，則為另一種被動語態+使役動詞的句子：The
workers are had to wash my car by me. 此時因為 had 和 wash
兩個動詞直接碰到，所以用 to 這個不定詞隔開。語意上是
有些不一樣的。

❷ Frank often helps elders walk through the roads.

❸ Let me tell you a ghost story.

❹ Most of people here were helped to move by him many years
ago.

---

4 四大動詞體系----授與動詞

a. 授與動詞有哪些？

  (1) 表示『給予』的 give、『買』 buy、『帶來』的 bring。

  (2) 表示『寄給』的 send、『寫給』write、『展示給、秀
  給』show

b. 所謂授與動詞，是要表達『**給某人某件事物**』，句中會有
3 個名詞，需區分誰是**主詞(施與者)**、誰是直接受詞(**事
物**)、誰是間接受詞(**接受者**)。(1 主 2 受的說法)

c. 用法： **(1) 授與動詞 + 人 + 物**

  → <u>**My father** brought <u>me</u> <u>a birthday present</u></u>.

  (主詞) (人) (物)

  (我爸爸帶給我一份生日禮物。)

(2) <u>授與動詞 ＋ 物 ＋ to 人 (給某人)</u>

<u>授與動詞 ＋ 物 ＋ for 人(為了某人)</u>

→ **<u>My father brought a birthday present</u> to <u>me</u>.**

(我爸爸帶了一份生日禮物給我。)

→ **<u>My father brought a birthday present</u> for <u>me</u>.**

(我爸爸為我帶了一份生日禮物。)

d. 當『直接受詞』(物品)或『間接受詞』(接受者)其中有一個是代名詞時，需注意以下用法：

(1) 當『直接受詞』(物品)是代名詞時：

不適宜用授與動詞+接受者+物品。

Ex. We gave them to Lisa. (正確) (我們把他們交給麗莎。)

We gave Lisa them. (不正確) (我們給麗莎他們。)

(2) 當『間接受詞』(接受者)也是代名詞時：

不適宜用授與動詞+接受者+物品。

Ex 1. Lisa's friends sent them to her. (正確)

(麗莎的朋友把他們交給她。)

Lisa's friends sent her them. (不適當)

(麗莎的朋友交給她他們。)

Ex 2. We gave them to her. (正確) (我們把他們交給她。)

We gave her them. (不適當) (我們給她他們。)

　　從以上兩組例句可看出，一個句子裡若出現了兩個代名詞，就會造成句義交待不清楚的感覺。第一組句子 Lisa's friends sent them to her.主詞是麗莎的朋友，可能讓人直接聯想接受者 her 就是麗莎。在閱讀文章時，需視前後文來做判斷。再加上物品也是代名詞，是什麼物品也需視前後文來做判斷。所以當『直接受詞』(物品)是代名詞時，或『直接受詞』和『間接受詞』(接受者)兩者都是代名詞時，兩個受詞間應用 to 或 for 隔開，在語法上比較清楚一些。

中文	原形	過去式	過去分詞	中文	原形	過去式	過去分詞
給予	give	gave	given	寄給	send	sent	sent
買	buy	bought	bought	寫給	write	wrote	written
帶來	bring	brought	brought	展示	show	showed	shown

Ex. 我的爺爺前幾天給我寫了一封信。

_____

Ex. 郵差帶來了好消息給 Lisa。

_____

Ex. 我爸爸為我買了一台腳踏車。

_____

♥愛的筆記貼♥

解答： ❶ My grandfather wrote me a letter few days ago.

　　　　　授與動詞中都有三個名詞，某人把某件事物交給了另一個人。重點是接受動詞的人與動詞之間不加 to。此句也可以寫成 My grandfather wrote a letter to me. 物品與接受人之間就要加 to 了。

❷ The mailman brought a good news to Lisa./ The mailman brought Lisa a good news.

❸ My father bought me a bicycle./ My father bought a bicycle to me.

▼ 花費的四大動詞 ◀
spend、pay、take、cost

以『人』爲主詞	以『物』爲主詞
spend 花錢、花時間都可用 (花費)	**cost** 某事花了某人多少錢 (價值)
【用法】	【用法】
人 + spend + 錢 + on 事物(名詞) 時間+Ving (動名詞)	物 + cost + 人 + 錢
例：Henry spent 2 hours washing the dishes. (亨利花了兩小時洗這些碗盤。)	例：The new bike will cost me 20,000 dollars. (這台新腳踏車將花費我 2 萬元。)
pay 花錢；付費　pay for	**take** 某事花了某人多少時間
【用法】	【用法】
人+ pay + 錢+ for 事物(名詞)	物 + take + 人 + 時間
例：Ronda paid 3 thousand dollars for the bill. (汪達付了三千元的帳單。)	例：Reading the book took me 3 days. (看完這本書花了我三天時間。)

中文	原形	過去式	過去分詞	中文	原形	過去式	過去分詞
花費	spend	spent	spent	價值	cost	cost	cost
付費	pay	paid	paid	花費	take	took	taken

Ex. 這趟東京之旅花了我 2 萬元。

_____

→ 我爲了這趟東京之旅花了 2 萬元。

_____

Ex. Sally 會花兩個星期停留在台北。

_____

Ex. 這個企劃案花了我們一個月才完成。

_____

英檢pass定心丸

♥愛的筆記貼♥

解答：

❶ 主詞是『東京之旅』是事物，所以花費的動詞不可以使用 spend 或 pay，花了 2 萬元是『花錢』，所以要用主詞是事物，花錢要用 cost 這個動詞。cost 的過去式亦為 cost。答案即為：The trip to Tokyo cost me 20,000 dollars (twenty thousand dollars). 當整句轉換為『我為了這趟東京之旅花了 2 萬元』時，主詞為『人』，花錢花時間都可用 spend 這個動詞。spend 過去式為 spent，所以答案為：I spent twenty thousand dollars on the trip to Tokyo. 因為『東京之旅』是一件事物，屬於名詞，所以前面加 on 這個介系詞。如果改為『旅行』travel 這個動詞，就要用動名詞的形式而改為：I spent twenty thousand dollars traveling around Tokyo.

❷ 主詞是 Sally『人』，花錢花時間都用 spend 這個動詞。時態是未來式，句後接的動詞是『停留、待在』stay 這個動詞，要變成動名詞 Ving 形式。答案即為：Sally will spend 2 weeks staying in Taipei.

❸ 主詞是企劃案是『物』，花時間要用動詞 take。時態應是過去式。take 的過去式是 took。答案即為：The project took us one month to accomplish.

....

<Practice 練習時間>

_____ 1. The quilt for rent _____ me 50 pounds a week there. It's very expensive!

　　　(A) took　(B) spent　(C) paid　(D) cost

_____ 2. Be my guest. I'll _____ for the bill.

　　　(A) take　(B) spend　(C) pay　(D) cost

_____ 3. How many days did it _____ you to finish the work?

　　　(A) take　(B) spend　(C) pay　(D) cost

_____ 4. Mary and I will _____ one night in Hong Kong, and then we will stay in Shanghai for one month.

　　　(A) take　(B) spend　(C) pay　(D) cost

_____ 5. A: Wow, nice camera! How much does it cost?

B: Sure. I _____ a lot ___ it.

(A) took; for   (B) spent; for

(C) cost; on   (D) spent; on

_____ 6. Many people know family is important, but they still

_____ little time _____ together with their family.

(A) pay attention; to   (B) spend; to get

(C) spend; getting   (D) take part; in

_____ 7. A: How long will it ____ from Taipei to Yilan?

B: It's around 1 hour.

(A) take   (B) cost   (C) pay   (D) spend

♥愛的筆記貼♥

解答：

❶ 答案是(D)。語意：在那裡出租的棉被花了我一星期 50 英磅。真是非常貴。依主詞是『棉被』(物)，花錢用 cost。

❷ 答案是(C)。語意：我請客。我會付這筆帳單。依主詞是『我』(人)，空格後有 for，和 for 連用的是 pay，『付錢』之意。

❸ 答案是(A)。語意：完成這項工作花了你多少天？依此問句助動詞後是虛主詞『it』(物)，代表後面 to finish the work 這件事，花了多少天是『時間』，所以動詞要用 take。

❹ 答案是(B)。語意：瑪莉和我將會花一個晚上停留在香港，然後我們會在上海待上一個月。依主詞是『瑪莉和我』(人)，花錢花時間都用 spend。

❺ 答案是(D)。語意：A: 哇，很好的相機。它價值多少錢呢？B: 當然囉！我花了很多錢在它身上。依主詞是『我』(人)，花錢花時間用 spend。時態是過去式所以用 spent。後面接的是名詞，所以名詞前要加介系詞 on。

❻ 答案是(C)。語意：很多人知道家庭是很重要的，但他們仍然花很少時間和他們的家人聚在一起。依主詞是『他們』(人們)，花錢花時

間用 spend。spend 後接動詞 get 要改為動名詞 getting，所以要選(C)。
pay attention to 是『注意某事』之意。take part in 是『參與』之意。

❼ 答案是(A)。語意：A: 從宜蘭到台北要花多久時間？B: 大概要 1
小時。依主詞是『從宜蘭到台北的這段路程』(事物)，花時間用 take。

 **▶動詞後加 to 的動詞◀**

中文	原形	過去式	過去分詞	中文	原形	過去式	過去分詞
希望	hope	hoped	hoped	希望	wish	wished	wished
想要	want	wanted	wanted	計劃	plan	planed	planed
學習	learn	learned	learned	計劃	manage	managed	managed
要求	ask	asked	asked	告訴	tell	told	told

<Practice 練習時間>

1. I _____ have a nice car in the future.
   (我希望未來有一台好車。)

2. Everyone _____ have a better life.
   (每個人都希望有更好的生活。)

3. Peter _____ write a song for her.
   (彼得想要為她寫一首歌。)

4. My family _____ move to Canada last year.
   (我的家人們在去年就計劃要搬到加拿大。)

5. I _____ repair computers from the magazine.
   (我從這本雜誌上學會修理電腦。)

6. They _____ save the poor drifting creature back to the
   shore. (他們計劃拯救這隻可憐而漂流的生物回到岸上。)

7. Mr. Lin _____ us ___ remember all the words on the list.

(林老師要求我們記得在這張表上的所有單字。)

8. Kevin _____ my sister _____ go to the dangerous places.

(凱文跟我妹妹說不要去危險的地方。)

♥愛的筆記貼♥

解答： ❶ hope to　　❷ wishes to　　❸ wants to
　　　 ❹ planned to　❺ learned to　❻ manage to
　　　 ❼ asks; to　　 ❽ told; not to

第八題請注意以下語法比較，語意會有所不同：

Ex: Kevin didn't tell my sister to go to the dangerous places.
　　（凱文沒有要我妹妹去危險的地方。→他沒有這樣的意思。）

Ex: Kevin told my sister not to go to the dangerous places.
　　（凱文跟我妹妹說不要去危險的地方。→他曾提醒過妹妹。）

從以上兩個例句，可以比較一下，因為 not 放置的位置不同，
所以語意上會有所不同。請特別注意。另外如 ask to 也是一樣
的道理。

 ▼**動詞後接 Ving 的動詞**◀

◎ 有些動詞後面多半接動名詞，我們稱為『愛的進行式』

like→love→keep→practice→enjoy→spend→miss→mind
喜歡　愛　保持/持續　練習　享受　花費　錯過　介意

→stand →avoid→waste→give up→finish
忍受　　避免　　浪費　　放棄　　結束

♥愛的筆記貼♥

同學們在記這些後面加 Ving 的動詞是不是很頭痛
呢？有時我們遇到這樣需記憶的事，也可以編一個
故事來方便我們記憶。例如這裡提到的『愛的進行式』。
談一場戀愛剛開始時兩個人當然互有好感，從『喜

歡』(like)開始，進一步發展到『愛』(love)，想要跟對方告白卻又害羞不敢講，所以『持續』(keep)『練習』(practice)幾百次，告白順利了兩個人在一起當然要『享受』(enjoy)在一起的每一刻，每天約會可是要『花費』(spend)不少的呢！如果『錯過』(miss)了對方的生日，還是一些兩個人在一起的重要日子，對方可是會很『介意』(mind)的喲！兩個人在一起日子久了，難免會有些口角紛爭，有時忍(stand)一時風平浪靜，避免(avoid)吵架，但這樣子久了，可能感情就淡了，大家覺得好像是浪費(waste)時間，最後心生放棄(give up)的念頭，結束(finish)這段感情吧！

　　以上這段故事，口耳相傳已久，舉凡佳偶怨偶，無不經歷這樣刻骨銘心、難忘的(unforgettable)戀愛過程，所以我們戲稱此為『愛的進行式』，讓同學們除了回憶那段酸甘甜的初戀無限美好的滋味以外，也要記得一下以上所提的動詞後面和動詞連接時，後面的動詞多為 Ving 型態喔！

中文	原形	過去式	過去分詞	中文	原形	過去式	過去分詞
喜歡	like	liked	liked	愛	love	loved	loved
保持	keep	kept	kept	練習	practice	practiced	practiced
享受	enjoy	enjoyed	enjoyed	花費	spend	spent	spent
錯過	miss	missed	missed	介意	mind	minded	minded
忍受	stand	stood	stood	避免	avoid	avoided	avoided
浪費	waste	wasted	wasted	放棄	give up	gave up	given up
結束	finish	finished	finished				

<Practice 練習時間>

1. Diana enjoys _____(surf) the Internet every night, and chatting with friends on MSN is much fun to her.

2. Weber wants _____ (attend) the Juilliard School. He dreams of _____ (stand) on the stage of Carnegie Hall in New York one day, so he _____(keep) _____(practice) _____ (play) the piano every day.

♥愛的筆記貼♥

解答：

❶ 答案是：surfing。

　　因為 surf 上網這個動詞是接在 enjoy 喜歡或享受這個動詞的後面，所以要變化為 Ving 的形式。題意是：黛安娜喜歡在每天晚上上網，而且對她來說在 MSN 上和朋友聊天是很有趣的事。

❷ 答案是：to attend/ standing/ keeps/ practicing/ playing。

　　本題是綜合概念題。第一格 attend(上學；出席)這個動詞接在 want(想要)的動詞後面，want 只和 to 連用，所以要寫 to attend。第二格是個動名詞的用法。dream of 是慣用法，表示『夢想著某事』，of 介系詞後要接一個名詞。所以『夢想著有朝一日要站在舞台上』，就把 stand(站著)這個動詞後加上 ing，把這個動作變成一件事情，也就是動名詞的用法。一件事情，也就是和名詞的用法是一樣的。所以 standing on the stage 要視為一個名詞片語，代表『站在舞台上』這件事。第三格，因為每天持續練習，所以此格的 keep(保持；持續)動詞需和主詞 he，做第三人稱單數形現在式動詞變化，所以 keep 要加 s。後面跟著第四格 practice(練習)這個字，配合前面的 keep 而改為 practicing，而這個字也影響著後面的 play。因為 play the cello 是一件事情，所以改為 playing the cello 名詞片語。通常的用法是 keep practicing and playing the cello. practice 和 playing 之間用 and 隔開。不過如果遇到本題的形式，第四格還是要回答為動名詞較正確。題意是：Diana 喜歡在每天晚上上網，而和朋友在 MSN 上聊天對她來說很有趣。

 **▼動詞後接 to-V 或 Ving ◢**
意義有所不同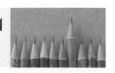

　　有些動詞例如 forget(忘記)、remember(記得)、stop(停止)，這些動詞後加 to+原形動詞，或直接加 Ving 的語意有所不同，請注意要依語意來判別用法。

名詞　　　　　動詞　　　　代名詞　　　助動詞　　　形容詞與副詞

中文	原形	過去式	過去分詞	中文	原形	過去式	過去分詞
忘記	forget	forgot	forgotten	停止	stop	stopped	stopped
記得	remember	remembered	remembered				

Ex 1. George *__forgot to hand__* in his homework on time.

(喬治忘記準時去交出他的回家作業。)→沒有做到準時交出的動作

George *__forgot handing__* in his homework this afternoon.

(喬治忘記今天下午已經交過他的回家作業。)→已做過交出的動作
但忘了曾經做過。

Ex 2. *__Remember to book__* the tickets in advance.

(記得要去事先訂票。)→還沒訂票，要記得去做。

Henry *__remembered seeing__* the same person before.

(亨利記得以前看過這同一個人。)→看過了，而且還記得看過了
這件事。

Ex 3. My mother *__stopped to answer__* the phone.

(我媽媽停下來去接電話。)→停止手邊正在做的事而去做某事。

My mother *__stopped cooking__* and answered the phone.

(我媽媽停止作菜然後去接電話。)→停止正在做的動作。

<Practice 練習時間>

1. I thought that I forgot _____(turn) the gas off before I
   went out. Then, when I returned home to turn it off, I found
   that I've forgotten _____(turn) it off already.

2. The salesmen in our office sometimes stop _____(smoke)
   in the staircase or on the balcony. Now, these places are

belonged to the public and no smoking areas. Many of them are trying to stop _____(smoke).

♥愛的筆記貼♥

解答：

❶ **答案是：to turn/ turning**

　　本題題意為：我本來以為在我出門之前我忘了去關瓦斯。然後，當我返回家中時，我才發現我忘了我已關過瓦斯。所以第一格要填 to turn，表示『忘記去關』的語意。第二格要填 turning，表示『忘了已經關過』的語意。

❷ **答案是：to smoke/ smoking**

　　本題跟『戒煙』有關的主題常常會考，請同學留心。題意是：在我們辦公室的業務員有時會在樓梯間或陽台上停下來抽根煙。現在這些場所都被歸類為公共且禁煙的區域。他們之中有許多人正在試著戒煙。所以第一格要填 to smoke，表示『停下手邊的事去抽煙』的語意。第二格要填 smoking，表示『停止正在抽煙的這個舉動』，所以有『戒煙』的意思。

常見疑問 4　take 的用法有哪些呢？

　　愈簡單的動詞有時候用法愈是多元化，而且意義也有所不同，舉 take 為例子來做練習：

小試身手：想想看，take 到底有幾個用法呢？

1. I <u>took</u> many <u>pictures of</u> the Koalas from New Zealand this summer.

2. Gary and I will <u>take</u> MRT first and then go there by bus.

3. Did you <u>take</u> my umbrella with you? I can't find it in my room.

4. It <u>took</u> me three hours to fix the alarm radio.

5. My father <u>took</u> my young sister to the Taipei City Zoo to see the pandas this morning.

6. It's too cold today. I don't want to <u>take</u> a shower.

7. My sister <u>takes care of</u> her sons carefully.

8. Do you want to <u>take</u> a break?

9. I have <u>taken</u> some pills before lunch.

10. Kevin <u>takes</u> 10 courses this semester.

11. The concert is going to <u>take place in</u> the new stadium.

12. Let Jenny and Linda <u>take part in</u> our tennis club.

請將以上 12 個句子中的 take 或 take 的片語之中文意思依編號寫在下面表格中：

1.	2.	3.
4.	5.	6.
7.	8.	9.
10.	11.	12.

take 最常見的就是以上的十二道小菜，接著請判斷以下這幾句話中各種形式的 take，語意近似於以上哪一題的用法？
(請填寫 1~12 的編號)

A. Did the work <u>take</u> you much time to finish? ＿＿＿

B. Mr. Lin wants to <u>take</u> a long vacation. ＿＿＿

C. <u>Take</u> the brand for example. They sold more cars in such a difficult time because of their successful strategies. ＿＿＿

D. My boyfriend and I like to <u>take</u> a walk together. ＿＿＿

❤愛的筆記貼❤

以上的練習句子同學們從剛開始學習英文起，應該或多或少都已接觸過，所以在此用判讀的方式帶領同學們練習。中文意思及解答如下：

1. 今年暑假，我從紐西蘭拍了好多無尾熊的照片回來。
2. Gary 和我將會先搭捷運再搭公車去那。
3. 你有拿我的雨傘嗎？我在我的房間裡都找不到。
4. 修理這台鬧鐘收音機花了我三小時。
5. 我爸爸今天早上帶我的小妹去台北市立動物園去看熊貓。
6. 今天好冷喔。我不想洗澡。
7. 我姐姐很細心地照顧她的兒子們。
8. 你想要休息一下嗎？
9. 我已經在午餐前服用了一些藥丸。
10. Kevin 這學期修了十堂課。
11. 這場音樂會將於新的體育館舉行。
12. 讓 Jenny 和 Linda 參加我們的網球社團吧。

所以 take 的常見用法有：

1. 拍攝照片	2. 搭乘	3. 拿；帶
4. 花費(時間)	5. 帶領	6. 洗澡
7. 照顧	8. 休息	9. 服藥
10. 修課	11. 舉行	12. 參加

A. __4__ B. __8__ C. __3__ D. __8__

A. 這件工作花了你很多時間做完嗎？
B. 林先生想要休個長假。
C. 拿這個品牌來做例子。他們在這樣一個艱辛的時刻賣出了更多的車子全因為他們有著成功的策略。
D. 我的男朋友和我喜歡一起去散步。
**除上所述之外，take 還有『接受』之意，例：He finally took my apology. (最後他接受了我的道歉。)還有 take a look 『看一看』。

常見疑問 5 ┊ **have** 到底是動詞還是助動詞？

以下再舉 have 為例子來說明，have 其實有當動詞，意義為『擁有』或『吃』東西。而 have 當助動詞時，和過去分詞連用，即 have+p. p. 表示『現在完成式』的時態。

小試身手：判別一下，以下的 have 到底是什麼意思呢？

1. She <u>has</u> a new job, life, and a car now.
2. We <u>have to</u> go to the company to get the document before going to the airport.
3. Do you <u>have</u> dinner yet?
4. Mary <u>had</u> me put over the car.
5. They <u>have moved</u> to the town three years ago.
6. How often do you <u>have</u> your <u>hair cut</u>?

請將以上 12 個句子中的 take 或 take 的片語之中文意思依編號寫在下面表格中：

1.	2.	3.
4.	5.	6.

have 最常見的就是以上的六道小菜，接著請判斷以下這幾句話中各種形式的 have 動詞，語意近似於以上哪一題的用法？(請填寫 1~6 的編號)

A. Joanna <u>had</u> everyone figure out an idea on this item. ＿＿＿

B. She <u>has</u> <u>had</u> lunch already. ＿＿＿ ＿＿＿

C. Bob <u>has</u> to get more support for winning more votes. ＿＿＿

D. Anyone who buys the DVD player before the end of this week will have a chance to win a Ferrari. ＿＿＿

♥愛的筆記貼♥

判別練習例句的中文意思及解答如下：

1. 她現在有了新工作、生活和車子。
2. 在去機場前我們必需去公司拿這份文件。
3. 你吃晚餐了嗎？
4. Mary 要我把車停在一邊。
5. 他們在三年前就搬到鎮上了。
6. 你多久剪一次頭髮？

所以 have 的常見用法有：

| 1. 擁有(動詞) | 2. 必需(動詞) | 3. 吃(動詞) |
| 4. 要(使役動詞) | 5. 已經(助動詞) | 6. 要(使役動詞) |

** 值得注意的是，第 2 題的 have 和 to 連用時，是必需的意思，have 還是動詞，所以要配合主詞及時態做適當的動詞變化。第 4 和 6 題都是使役動詞的用法，have 後的動詞前不加 to，且用原形動詞。第 6 題的 have someone's hair cut 是說『剪頭髮』的常用語法。有關『使役動詞』的用法，我們在本章前面已經有完整解說。第 5 題是 have+過去分詞的用法，表示『現在完成式』的時態，但 have 在當『助動詞』用的時候，還是要依『時態』及『主詞』來做動詞變化，這是比較需要注意的地方。

A. ＿4＿ B. ＿5＿ ＿3＿ C. ＿2＿ D. ＿1＿

A. 瓊安娜要每個人在這個產品項目上想出一個主意。
B. 她已經吃過午餐了。
C. 鮑伯必需得到更多的支持以贏得更多的選票。
D. 任何在這個星期結束前購買這台 DVD 播放器的人，都有機會贏得一台法拉利。

常見疑問 6　可分開和不可分開的動詞片語

　　動詞片語是由『動詞』及『介系詞』組合而成，同一個動詞因為後面搭配不同的介系詞，就會產生不同的語意。例如最常見的是 go on(繼續)、go by(從旁邊經過)和 go away(走開)，隨著動詞後面搭配不同的介系詞而改變語意。

Ex 1. They ***went on*** discussing on the project without waiting for Frank.

　　　(他們沒有等法蘭克就繼續討論這個專案。)

Ex 2. A flock of ducks ***went by*** out boat leisurely.

　　　(一群鴨子悠閒地經過(游過)我們的小船。)

Ex 3. Then he ***went away*** without saying anything.

　　　(然後他不發一語地走開了。)

　　有些動詞片語在使用時，動詞和介系詞可以分開，對語意不會有所改變。但有些動詞片語如果動詞和介系詞分開了，中間插入了別的字，就會造成語意的改變。例如：

Ex 1. We ***got on*** the bus in 5 minutes. (我們在五分鐘內上了巴士。)

Ex 2. We ***got*** the bus ***on*** in 5 minutes. (我們在五分鐘內把巴士打開。)

Ex 3. We are ***waiting for*** the bus. (我們正在等巴士。)

Ex 4. We are ***waiting*** the bus ***for***. (我們正在等這台巴士為了⋯。)

從以上的例子可以理解，為什麼有些動詞片語不能分開使用，尤其是第四句，for 放句尾感覺語意沒完全。

◎ 常見的不可分開使用的動詞片語為：

call on (拜訪) 、care about (關心)、laugh at (嘲笑)、listen to (聆聽)、look at (注視；看)、look for (尋找)、get in/ on (上車)、get off (下車)、hear from (聽到來自…消息)、take care of (照顧)、run into (偶遇)、run out of (用光；從...跑出)、wait for (等待)、work on (從事)、worry about (擔心)。

◎ 常見的可分開使用的動詞片語為：put on (穿上)、call up (打電話)、find out (找出)、give back (歸還)、give up (放棄)、keep away (遠離)、look up (查閱)、pick up (撿起、接送)、take off (脫掉)、take up (拿起)、try on (試穿)、turn on (打開)、turn off (關上)、show off (炫耀)、 wake up (叫醒)、write down (寫下)

看完以上『頗具份量』的動詞講解，從時態、語態，到各類型動詞的用法，分別為同學細部解說，就是希望同學掌握文法中考出機率最高的部份。一個句子中最基本的形態就是主詞(名詞)+動詞。『主動詞一致』的變化，從英檢初級到托福考題，不管難易度如何，都是必考的題型，而且不只是閱讀，就連聽力中也會影響答案的選擇，因為時態或動詞形式往往也影響了語義判讀。從語態中也可看出作者所想要表達的意向與概念。所以這樣基礎的概念，卻是想要通往成功的關鍵，請同學們務必耐心練功喔！基礎不穩的話，往往會走一步退好幾步的，希望這兩章名詞及動詞的大還丹，幫助

英檢pass定心丸

同學們穩住基礎盤。現在我們就用以下的練習題，來考驗一下實力吧！

Grammar Challenge

_____ 1.Our supervisor hopes us _____ the sales goal each quarter.

(A) to achieve　　　(B) achieving

(C) achieved　　　(D) achievement

_____ 2. How much did it _____ you to buy the return flight tickets from London to New York?

(A) spend　(B) pay　(C) take　(D) cost

_____ 3. Not many people _____ their whole life on fighting for the unjust cases nowadays. (A)spend (B) pay (C) take (D) cost

_____ 4. When I saw the picture, I _____ by the bloody and cruel images.　(A) astonished　　　(B) am astonishing

(C) was astonished　(D) did astonished

_____ 5. You may enjoy _____ the facilities after you check in the hotel.　(A) to use　(B) use　(C) using　(D) used

_____ 6. I _____ my best friend Nancy more than three years since I moved to here.　(A) didn't see　　　(B) don't see

(C) haven't been seen (D) haven't seen

_____ 7. The concert on the beach _____ for three days so far. It will continue until Friday.

(A) is last　(B) had last　(C) has been lasting　(D) has lasting

_____ 8. We _____ reply the questionnaires before Monday.

(A) asked to　(B) were asked to　(C) ask　(D) had asked

_____ 9. The board had decided to deny his proposal because the case has wasted too much time and money _____ the property of lands.

(A) to purchase   (B) purchased   (C) purchase   (D) purchasing

_____ 10. As a zoologist, Mr. Williams never stop _____ how to preserve the natural habitat for the wild animals.

(A) to think   (B) thinks   (C) thinking   (D) thought

Question 11~16

With the __11.__ unemployed population, more and more families can't afford their loans and has __12.__ their houses. The economists __13.__ that the opportunists whether in the stock market or in the banking system should __14.__ this huge crisis. They also expect the new government __15.__ the bailout to the biggest insurance firm. It could make millions of families avoid __16.__ the financial disaster again.

___ 11. (A) to grow   (B) grew   (C) grown   (D) growing

___ 12. (A) lose   (B) loss   (C) lost   (D) losing

___ 13. (A) to claim   (B) claiming   (C) claim   (D) claims

___ 14. (A) respond   (B) be responsible for

(C) to respond   (D) be response

___ 15. (A) to offer   (B) offering   (C) offered   (D) offer

___ 16. (A) to encounter   (B) encounter

(C) encountering   (D) encounters

B (9I) V (SI) B (ħI) C (EI) C (ZI) D (II)
C (0I) D (6) B (8) C (L) D (9)
C (S) C (ħ) V (E) D (Z) V (I) : 答解

Grammar session 3 代名詞及關係代名詞 Pronoun and Clauses

～ 本課學習要點 ～

1. 『人稱代名詞』指得是代替原本『人、事、物』名稱的名詞，在文章中有避免重覆，以及精簡文句的功用。
2. 『不定代名詞』指得是代替不特定的『人、事、物』，例如某人 somebody、到處 everywhere…等等。
3. 『關係代名詞』的功用多爲連接子句成爲一長句的功能，可以加強補充『人、事、物』的訊息。

1 人稱代名詞可代替前文提過的『人、事、物』名稱。

　　和代名詞有關，且在使用上常常容易混淆，也是常常會考的，就是代名詞相關五大詞類家族，現介紹說明如下：

代名詞相關五大詞類家族

	人稱	中文	代名詞	所有格	受詞	所有格代名詞	反身代名詞
單數型	I	我	I	my	me	mine	myself
	II	你	you	your	you	yours	yourself
	III	他	he	his	him	his	himself
		她	she	her	her	hers	herself
		它	it	its	it	its	itself
複數型	I	我們	we	our	us	ours	ourselves
	II	你們	you	your	you	yours	yourselves
	III	他們	they	their	them	theirs	themselves

　　通常在文中第一次出現的『人、事、物』都會用全名出現。然後再次出現時，我們就會用到代名詞來代替，以避免重複而繁雜的感覺，亦能達到精簡文章的效果。人稱代名詞顧名思義，要依人稱及單複數型來判別使用適當的代名詞。常常和代名詞一起考的觀念就是：所有格、受詞(格)、所有格代名詞，以及反身代名詞。

所有格

　　加在名詞的前面，代替一般表示數量的冠詞 a/ an，以及表示『指定；限定』的冠詞 the(這個)、表示『指定』的代名詞 this(這個)、that(那個)、these(這些)、those(那些)，而強調是誰擁有後面的『人、事、物』名詞。所以所有格後必接名詞，不會被單獨使用。例如：my brother(我的哥哥)、her umbrella(她的雨傘)、以及 their relatives(他們的親戚)…等等。除了以上表格中所列出的所有格，另外，名詞也可在後面加上's 來表示所有格的概念。例如：

Mary's company　瑪莉的公司
Mary and Joanna's company　瑪莉和瓊安娜共同擁有的公司
Mary's and Joanna's companies 瑪莉的公司和瓊安娜的公司
The two ladies' company 這兩位女士們的公司

由上面四個例子可以看出，如果是『一個人的』，我們就直接在名詞後加's。如果是『兩個人或多人共有的』，我們就在最後面那個名詞後加上's。如果是要『列舉很多人都有同樣屬性的事物』，而『事物』本身是一樣的，因為要避免句中出現重複的名詞，所以『事物』只出現在最後面，而每個人後面加上's。如果是遇到複數型名詞，原本的名詞後就有加 s 或 es 了，為避免遇到 ladies's 這樣的問題，所以後面的 s 省略，而成為 ladies'。

<Practice 代名詞與所有格的練習>

(1) 我的車子 ＿＿ car 　　(2) 桌子(它)的腳 ＿＿ foot

(3) 這些工人們的薪水 The worker＿＿ pay

→他們的薪水 ＿＿＿ pay

(4) 張先生的太太 Mr. Chang＿＿ wife

→他的太太 ＿＿ wife

(5) Mary 的房子 Mary＿＿ house→她的房子 ＿＿ house

(6)**你和你哥哥的計劃 ＿＿ and ＿＿ brother's plan

→你們的計劃 ＿＿＿ plan

- -

♥愛的筆記貼♥

解答：❶ my (空格後面接個名詞，所以這裡要用所有格 my 表示『我的』。)

❷ its (空格後面接名詞，而人稱是桌子，是沒有生命的事物，所以用單數形的它，要用所有格 its。)

❸ s'/ their (因為是工人們的，工人是複數形本來就加 s，所以要用 s' 來表示『工人們的』所有格。換句話說，就是『他們的』薪水，所以要用 their。)

❹ 's/ his (因為是張先生的，所以在名詞後加上's 來表示『張先生的』所有格。換句話說，就是『他的』，所以要用 his。)

❺ 's/ her (因為是瑪麗的，所以在名詞後加上's 來表示『瑪麗的』所有格。換句話說，就是『她的』房子，所以要用 her。)

❻ you/ your/ your (第一格是代名詞你 you，第二格是『你的哥哥』，所以在名詞哥哥前加上 your 來表示『你的』所有格。換句話說，就是『你們的』計劃，所以要用 your。)

- -

受詞(格)

受詞是用來『接受動作』的名詞或代名詞形態，所以都是接在動詞後或 to、for 後面。一般名詞可以直接用來當做受詞，但代名詞則需要變化為受詞。

例如：Frank will sing a song for <u>me</u>.
　　　(法蘭克將要為我唱首歌。)　me 就是 I 的受詞。

例如：They will send <u>him</u> the parcel by air mail.
　　(他們將會用航空郵件寄給他這份包裹。) him 就是 he 的受詞。

　　　其他關於受詞的觀念還有『直接受詞』及『間接受詞』，這是以『接受動作』及與『動作』的關係所判別的，我們在前一章動詞的『授與動詞』部份有提及。

例如：They will send <u>him</u> <u>the parcel</u> by air mail.
　　　(他們將會用航空郵件寄給他這份包裹。)
　　　在此句中，直接接受動詞 send(寄送)的是 him(他)，而 him 在此就是直接受詞。後面的 the parcel(包裹)就是間接受詞。

\<Practice 代名詞、所有格，以及受詞的練習\>

(1) _____(Dora) mother made a cake for _____(she).

(2) _____(Jason) just lost _____(Jason's) wallet this morning, but _____(Jason's) roommates found ___(the wallet) for _____(Jason) right away.

(3) The shop might forget to send _____(we) the goods. At least, I haven't gotten _____(they) so far.

(4) The company encourages _____(the staff) to take some professional courses in _____ leisure time.

(5) Hey, it has been a long time to see _____(you) again. Do you still remember _____(I)?

♥愛的筆記貼♥

解答：❶ Dora's 或 Her/ her (朵拉的母親為她做了個蛋糕。)第一格是
　　　　所有格，第二格是受格。

　　　❷ Jason 或 He/ his/ his/ it/ him (傑森今天早上才丟了他的皮
　　　　夾，但他的室友們馬上就為他找到了皮夾。)第一格是主詞
　　　　he(他)，第二格是所有格 his(他的)，第三格是所有格(his)他
　　　　的，第四格是受格 it(它)，第五格是受格 him(他)。

　　　❸ us/ them (這家店也許忘了寄給我們這批貨品。至少我是沒收
　　　　到他們。)第一格是受詞 us(我們)，第二格是受詞 them(他
　　　　們)。『貨物』這個字是 goods，屬於集合名詞，複數形。

　　　❹ them/ their (公司鼓勵他們(這些員工)在他們的閒暇時間修
　　　　一些專業課程。)第一格是受詞 them(他們)，第二格是所有
　　　　格 their(他們的)。staff 員工是集合名詞，複數形，所以都是
　　　　用 they 來做代名詞。

　　　❺ you/ me (嘿！好久不見了。你還記得我嗎？) 第一格是受格
　　　　you(你)，第二格是受格 me(我)。

所有格代名詞

　　所有格代名詞其實就是用一個字來代替『所有格』+
『名詞』。所以當『所有格代名詞』出現時，表示它後面不
會再接一個名詞。例如：my house(我的房子)可以說成
mine(我的)。和所有格不同的是，『所有格代名詞』是名詞
的功能，可單獨存在，指得就是『某人的某樣事物』，但差
別就在於『所有格』+『名詞』很明確地表現出『誰的什麼
東西』。『所有格代名詞』若沒有前後文，就只能指出是誰
擁有的，卻不知是什麼東西。例如：Everyone prefers his.(每
個人都喜歡他的。)單純以此句來看，看不出到底大家比較
喜歡他的什麼？而 Everyone prefers his idea.(每個人都喜歡
他的主意。)就知道原來大家喜歡的是他的想法。換句話
說，通常我們使用『所有格代名詞』來表意，就像代名詞

的使用方法一樣，通常前文已有交待過全名。在一篇文章裡為了避免重覆、精簡文字所以用『所有格代名詞』來代替，並強調是『誰所擁有』的。

所有格代名詞很好記，除了我的是 mine 以外，其實就是『所有格』+something。例：your 你的+s 成為 yours，his+s 避免重覆所以還是 his，her+s 成為 hers，it+s 成為 its，our+s 成為 ours，their+s 成為 theirs。這也再次提醒了，所有格代名詞是取代了『所有格』+『名詞』兩個字。

<Practice 代名詞、所有格、受格，以及所有格代名詞的練習>

(1) Jennifer took _____ (my comb), but_____ (Jennifer) didn't return ____(the comb) to _____(I).

(2) A: Baby, don't you walk _____(the dog) today?

B: Why? _____(the dog) is _____(you) dog, not _____(I).

(3) Could you repeat _____(you) cell phone number for _____(I)? OK, I told _____(you) _____(my phone number) first.

(4) Do you need _____(I) help? If you need ____(I), I am just around here all the time.

(5) Mr. and Mrs. Cook have a house in the suburb. _____(The house) used to be _____(Amanda's house), but she sold ___(the house) out. So, _____(the house's) property was transferred to _____(Mr. and Mrs. Cook).

♥愛的筆記貼♥

解答：❶ mine/ she/ it/ me (珍妮佛拿走了我的梳子，但她並沒有把它還給我。)第一格只有一格而要代表『my comb』我的梳子兩個字，所以要用所有格代名詞 mine(我的)，第二格是代名詞，第三格是代名詞，第四格是接受動作的受詞。

❷ it/ it/ your/ mine (A:寶貝，你今天不帶它出去蹓狗嗎？B:為什麼？它是你的狗，又不是我的。)第一格是代名詞 it(它)，第二格是代名詞 it(它)，第三格是所有格(your)你的，第四格是所有格代名詞 mine(我的)，代替 my dog(兩字)。

❸ your/ me/ you/ mine (你可以為我再重覆一次你的手機號碼嗎？好吧，我先告訴你我的。)第一格是所有格 your(你的)，後面有接 cell phone number(手機號碼)這個名詞。第二格是受格 me(我)，第三格是受格 you(你)，第四格是所有格代名詞 mine(我的手機號碼)。

❹ my/ me 或 mine (你需要我的幫助嗎？如果你需要我(或是我的幫忙)，我總是在這附近。)第一格是所有格 my(我的)，第二格可以是受格 me(我)，你需要我嗎？或者是你需要我的幫忙嗎？所以第二格也可以寫成代替『我的幫助』my help 的所有格代名詞 mine(我的)。

❺ It/ hers/ it/ its/ them (考克夫婦在郊區有一棟房子。它過去曾是她的(亞曼達的)，但是她將它賣掉了。這樣，它的所有權就被轉移給了他們。)第一格是代表『這棟房子』的代名詞 it，第二格是代表『亞曼達的房子』所有格代名詞的 hers，第三格是代表『這棟房子』的受格 it，第四格是『這棟房子』的所有格 its(它的)，第五格是代表『考克夫婦』的受詞 them。

反身代名詞

反身代名詞有兩個功能：

(1)直接加在主詞後，或加在句末來『強調』主詞本身。

　　例句：Nature <u>itself</u> has certain rules.
　　　　　= Nature has certain rules <u>itself</u>.
　　　　　(大自然本身就有著某種定律規則。)

(2)表示『某人自己』之意，以釐清句義。

　　例句：She was irritated by her. (她被她給惹怒了。)

　　　　→意指被另一個人給惹怒。

　　　　She was irritated by herself. (她被她自己給惹怒了。)

　　由以上兩句可看出，有時候我們光用受詞或代名詞，是無法表達出『自己』的語意，所以必需藉由『反身代名詞』來強調『自己』self 的概念。因為是『某人的自己』，所以通常是用『所有格』+self 就是反身代名詞。唯獨他自己 himself，以及他們自己 themselves 例外。而遇到複數形的我們自己、你們自己、他們自己，後面的 self 就必需寫成複數形 selves 了。

<Practice 反身代名詞的改寫句子練習>

(1) New York City has a lot to offer. (請在句中加入 itself)

_____

(紐約本質上有很多內涵可展現、提供。)

_____

(紐約有很多內涵可展現、提供給它自己。)

(2) Mr. and Mrs. Cook decorated the house.
　　No one helps them. (請用反身代名詞合併為一句。)

_____

(3) 他買了一份聖誕禮物給他自己。

_____

❤愛的筆記貼❤

解答：❶ New York City itself has a lot to offer. / New York City has a lot of offer itself.(此處 itself 當做 offer 的受詞。)❷ Mr. and Mrs. Cook decorated the house by themselves.(考克夫婦他們自己裝飾這棟房

子。)❸ He bought a Christmas present for himself.

② 『不定代名詞』指得是代替不特定的『人、事、物』。

語言實驗室

every, some, any, no 不定代名詞				
keywords	every	some	any	no
body	每個人 _____body	某人；大人物 some_____	任何人 _____	無名小卒 _____
one	每個人 _____one	某人 _____one	任何人 _____	沒有人 _____ _____
thing	每件事 _____thing	某事 _____thing	任何事 _____	沒事 _____
where	到處 _____where	某地 _____	任何地方 _____	沒地方 _____
time	每次；總是 _____ time	有時 _____times	任何時間 _____	立刻 in no time
way	無論怎樣 _____way	總算；好歹 _____	不管怎樣 _____	不行 _____ _____
day	每天的 _____day 每天 _____ day	有朝一日 _____		

**通常 any 是用於疑問句或否定句中的。

　　經過以上的練習，希望幫同學們透過推理的方式來學習理解這些不定代名詞。不定代名詞的常考重點是：當不定代名詞遇上了形容詞的修飾，排列順序會有所改變。形容詞本是用來修飾名詞和代名詞的，我們在名詞章節中提過，形容詞通常置於冠詞和名詞的中間，例：a wonderful day(美好的一天)。但如果遇上欲形容的人、事、物是不特定的對象，我們要用不定代名詞+形容詞的語法。例：something special(某件特別的事)、anything wrong(任何錯誤的事)。這就叫做『形容詞的後置修飾』。什麼情況會用到不定代名詞呢？以下有 10 題練習，請依括號中的提示字，猜猜看應該使用哪個不定代名詞呢？

<Practice 不定代名詞的練習>

1. I don't want to be _____(body). I believe I can be _____(body) in the future and have a great business.

2. Hey, Jeff. Nice to meet you. I want you to meet _____(one/ body) in the party.

3. It's emergency! Doctor Wu needs _____(body/one) to get ready _____(time).

4. A: The dress on you seems too good to do some house chores. _____(way), can you take the garbage out for me now?   B: _____(way), I have to go to a party now.

5. It's Christmas season now, so you can see many crowds _____(where) for shopping the gifts!

6. A: Did you see _____(body/ one) there last night?
    B: Well, I am not sure if it is an old man. I only saw a shadow and it disappeared right away.

7. _____(time) we misunderstand people easily.

8. What is the _____(day) routine for you? I wonder why you can live so far away from here, but you are always on time.

9. A: What's wrong? Do you forget _____(thing)?

   B: I think I lost my key _____(where).

10. Do you know _____(where) that I can have the umbrellas repaired?

♥愛的筆記貼♥

解答：① nobody/ somebody（我不想當無名小卒。我相信我在未來可以成為某個大人物而且有一個成功的事業。）

② someone 或 somebody（嗨！傑夫。很高興見到你。我想你來這個舞會裡見見某個人。→意思就是我要介紹你和某人認識的說法。）

③ someone 或 somebody/ in no time（這是緊急狀況！吳醫生需要某個人馬上準備好(要幫助他)。）emergency 緊急狀況，也有一說是 May Day 五月天代表的是『緊急狀況』之意。

④ Anyway/ No way（A: 你身上好像穿太好的衣服對於做家事來說。不管怎樣，你能幫我去丟垃圾嗎？B: 不行，我現在必需去參加派對了。

⑤ everywhere（A: 現在是聖誕季節，所以你可以看到很多一群群的人群到處都是要買禮物的人！）

⑥ anybody/ anyone（A: 你昨天晚上有看到這裡有人嗎？B:是喔，我不確定它是一位老人。我只看到一個陰影而且它很快的就消失了。）

⑦ Sometimes（有時候我們很容易誤會人們。）

⑧ everyday（冠詞 the 和名詞 routine 慣例會做的事之間缺少一個形容詞，所以此處要用合起來的 everyday 而非分開的 every day，是『每天的』之意。本題題意為：你每天的作息時間如何？我很好奇你為什麼住很遠但你總是可以準時到。）

⑨ anything/ somewhere（A: 怎麼了？你忘了什麼東西嗎？B:

我想我把鑰匙掉在某處了。)→否定或疑問句中常用 anything，而肯定句中常用 some，所以是 somewhere.在某處的意思。

⑩ anywhere (你知道我到哪可以修雨傘嗎？→讓傘被修理，用法請參見動詞單元之使役動詞說明。

常見疑問 1 ┊ **one, the other, another** 的用法。

　　在人與人之間，在兩人以上的團體中，我們要指出某些特定的對象，不一定都要說出名字來，這個時候，我們可以採取『分眾』的說法。關鍵詞主要有：one(一個)、other(別的、另一個)、another=any other(不限定的另一個)、some(一些)。用以下圖示法來表示其關係：

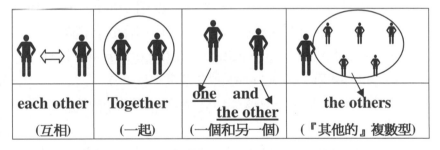

each other (互相)	Together (一起)	<u>one</u> and <u>the other</u> (一個和另一個)	the others (『其他的』複數型)

只有一個= only one、兩者都 = both、三者及三者以上稱為：全部都…= all、another= any+ other 別的；另外的、三者以上在一起：all+together 一起→ altogether 整體。

(1) 指兩人間『互相』的關係，就用 each other。

Ex. We are very close friends. We have encouraged *each other* all the time since our high school age.

(我們是很要好的朋友。自從我們在高中的年紀時,我們就一直互相鼓勵至今。)

(2) 強調『一起』去做什麼事,就用 together。

Ex. Nancy and my brother went to see the movie *together*.

(南西和我哥哥一起去看電影。)

(3) 兩人之間的指稱是 one...the other(一個是…另一個是…)

Ex. The two boys standing behind my uncle are my cousins. *One* is Jason, and *the other* is Charlie.

(站在我叔叔後面的這兩位男孩是我的堂兄弟。一位是傑森,而另一位是查理。)→用來在『兩人之間』指稱。

(4) 如果『其他的人、事、物』有很多,就用 others。the others 和 others 的差別在於有沒有『指定、限定』範圍。

Ex. Two of the books are mine, and *the others* are hers.

(這些書中的兩本是我的,而其他的書都是她的。)

→有限定在這些書 the books 之中,所以『這些書中的其他本』要用 the others 來指稱。

Ex. *Some* people prefer the horror films while *others* prefer drama ones.

(有些人喜歡恐怖片就有其他的一群人喜歡劇情片。)

→some 和 others 常用來指稱『一些…和另一些…』的比較。在都沒有指定限定範圍的情況下使用。

(5) another 用來指稱『其他的人、事、物』,通常沒有限定

範圍。

Ex. Besides this, do I have **_another_** choice?

(除了這個以外，我有沒有另外的選擇？)

<Practice 不定代名詞 one、other、another 的練習>

(1) 那隻小貓的眼睛有兩個顏色。一隻是藍色的，一隻是棕色的。

_____

(2) 讓我們互相幫忙。

_____

♥ 愛的筆記貼 ♥

解答：❶ The cat's eyes have two colors. One is blue, and the other is brown. ❷ Let us help each other.

③ 『關係代名詞』與『關係子句』。

　　『關係代名詞』是用來代替句子中重複的名詞，可以用來補充說明句子裡『前面已提過的名詞』(先行詞)，所以有『代名詞』的功能。又因為它可以連接兩個句子為一句，所以它又有『連接詞』的功能。以關係代名詞領導的句子，我們稱之為『關係子句』。『關係子句』可以當形容詞子句使用。

關係代名詞功能表

主詞	代名詞	受格	所有格
人	who	whom	whose
事、物	which	which	whose/ of which
人、事、物	that	that	

代替『代名詞』的功能

who 代替人	**_Gina_** is the tallest girl in our class. **_She_** won the racing game. **_Gina who_** is the tallest girl in our class won the racing game. (吉娜是我們班最高的女生贏了這場跑步比賽。)
which 代替 事、物	We didn't find **_that material_**. **_The material_** is necessary to make the model. We didn't find **_the material which_** is necessary to make the model. (我們找不到這種製作這個模型的必備材料。)
that 代替 人、 事、物	Jay Chou created **_a new song_**. **_The new song_** is not only popular in Taiwan but also in Japan. Jay Chou created **_a new song that_** is not only popular in Taiwan but also in Japan . (周杰倫創作了一首新歌不但在台灣受歡迎在日本也是。)

　　從以上的例句可以看出，關係代名詞可以代替重覆的名詞來合併句子，一句話中可以用關係代名詞來串連更多的語意。基本上就是，代替『人』就用 who，代替『事、物』就用 which，而 that 則可代表『人、事、物』。

代替『受詞』功能

whom who 的受詞	They have forgiven **_the girl_**. →受詞功能 **_She_** steals because her life is too stressful. They have forgiven **_the girl whom_** steals because her life is too stressful. (他們已經原諒了這個女孩她偷竊是因為壓力大。)
which 本身即可	Both of us work hard on **_the work_**. →受詞功能 **_The work_** influences our promotion.

當受詞用	Both of us work hard on ***the work* *which*** influences our promotion. (我們兩個都很努力做這份工作，它影響了我們的升遷。)
that 本身即可 當受詞用	I can't stand ***the noise***. ***The noise*** really drives me crazy.
	I can't stand the noise that really drives me crazy. (我不能忍受這噪音了，它真得快把我逼瘋了。)

　　從以上的例句可以看出，如果要代替的名詞原本是當受詞用的，則要選用當『受詞』用的關係代名詞來合併句子。也就是，『人』當受詞時，關係代名詞用 whom，『事、物』當受詞時就用 which，而 that 也可代表『人、事、物』的受詞關代。

代替『所有格』的功能	
whose who 的所有格	Everyone dislikes ***Aaron*** in the company. ***His*** attitude is quite negative and annoying. →所有格
	In the company, everyone dislikes ***Aaron* *whose*** attitude is quite negative and annoying. (在這家公司裡，大家都不喜歡艾倫相當負面又討人厭的態度。)
of which which 的 所有格	The floor ***of the house*** is made by marble. →受詞功能 ***The house*** is so luxury.
	The house* *of which the floor is made by marble is so luxury. (這房子的地板是用大理石製成這麼地豪華。)

　　從以上的例句可以看出，如果要代替的名詞原本是有『所有格』的意思，則要選用當『所有格』用的關係代名詞來合併句子。也就是，『人』是所有格時，關係代名詞用

whose，『事、物』是所有格時就用 of which。

<Practice 關係代名詞的練習>

請依劃線提示部份，選擇適當的關係代名詞來合併句子：

1. <u>The girl</u> is with a long and black hair.
   <u>Her</u> name is Silvia.

   _____

2. My young brother likes to be with <u>our nanny</u>.
   <u>She</u> used to be a kindergarten teacher.

   _____

   _____

3. <u>The project</u> was estimated as a high-profit result.
   The committee tended to support <u>the project</u>.

   _____

   _____

4. <u>Those people</u> are willing to experience the first ride of the route.
   <u>They</u> will get the one-month pass free cards.

   _____

   _____

5. The seats <u>of the new plants</u> are more comfortable.
   Many people want to take <u>the new planes</u>.

   _____

   _____

♥愛的筆記貼♥

做這種關係代名詞的合併句子寫作題時，其實第一步就是抓兩句<u>重覆的部份是哪邊</u>，第二步是分辨一下重覆的部份是<u>什麼詞性</u>，以判別使用適當的關係代名詞來合併。

解答：❶ 重覆的地方是 the girl 和 her，而 her 是所有格，所以要選用代表『人』的關係代名詞又是所有格功能的 whose 這個關係代名詞來合併句子，答案即為：<u>The girl whose name is Silvia is with a long and black hair.</u>(這位名叫 Silvia 的女孩有著一頭烏黑的長髮。) ❷ 重覆的地方是 our nanny 和 she，但 our nanny 接在 with 後，是『受詞』功能，所以要用代表『人』又有受格功能的關代『whom』來合併句子，答案即為：<u>Our nanny whom my young brother likes to be with used to be a kindergarten teacher.</u> (我弟弟很喜歡跟我們的保姆待在一起而她以前曾是一名幼稚園的老師。) ❸ 重覆的地方是 the project 企劃案，有一個 the project 接在 support 支持這個動詞後面，所以是『受詞』，但代表『事、物』的關代 which 受詞還是 which，答案即為：<u>The project which was estimated as a high-profit result the committee tended to support.</u> (這個被評估為高獲利結果的企劃案委員會傾向要支持它。) ❹ 重覆的地方是 those people 這些人和 they 他們，沒有受格或所有格的功能，所以單純地是指『人』的關係代名詞，用 who 來合併就好了。答案即為：<u>Those (people) who are willing to experience the first ride of the route will get the one-month pass free cards.</u> (那些願意體驗這路線第一次搭乘的人們將會得到一個月的免費通行卡。) ❺ 重覆的地方是 the new plane，但有一處是『物』的所有格形式，看到 of 這個介系詞，有『從屬』的關係，所以是所有格。『物』的所有格功能關係代名詞為『of which』，答案即為：<u>Many people want to take the new planes of which the seats are more comfortable.</u> (很多人想要搭這種新飛機，它們的座椅比較舒適。)

Grammar Challenge

_____ 1. Both of them are my best friends. One is Bill, and _____ is Shirley. (A) the other   (B) others   (C) other   (D) another

_____ 2. _____ is more important than my son. He means a lot to me. (A) Anything　　　(B) Something

(C) Nothing　　　(D) Everything

_____ 3. We didn't talk to _____ but bore it in our mind.

(A) together　(B) altogether　(C) other　(D) each other

_____ 4. If you remember _____ to the robbery, please report it

to the police.

(A) suspicious something　　(B) anything suspicious

(C) something suspicious　　(D) suspicious nothing

_____ 5. Karen's brother is definitely the right man _____ everyone

relies on.

(A) who　(B) which　(C) of which　(D) whom

_____ 6. Are you sure _____ the station offers the shuttle-bus service?

(A) who　(B) which　(C) that　(D) whose

_____ 7. Is there _____ possible to arrive there on time?

(A) someone　(B) anyone　(C) no one　(D) everyone

_____ 8. When I first saw Miranda, I knew she is _____ in my heart.

(A) one　(B) another　(C) the others　(D) the one

_____ 9. They made all the soap by _____, and sold it to _____.

(A) them; other　　　　(B) theirs; the other

(C) themselves; others　　(D) theirselves; some other

_____ 10. Unfortunately, they didn't vote to my idea. They voted to

_____.　(A) her　(B) his　(C) thems　(D) itself

Question 11~20

Most people want to be a __(11)__ some day while others

want to be a __(12)__ and live as usual. Oscar is one of _(13)_ little fish, which dreams of becoming a famous one some day and living at the __(14)__ of the Reef(礁岸). By __(15)__, he lies everyone that he is a "shark slayer", and everybody respects him as a hero to __(16)__ the sharks for the peace under the sea. However, he doesn't enjoy ___(17)___ so much. He is unhappy. Finally, he understands the true hero is ___(18)___ face the ___(19)___ and tell the truth. Every one should be __(20)__ to live for themselves.

```
(    ) 11.    (A) nobody    (B) anybody    (C) body    (D) somebody
(    ) 12.    (A) nobody    (B) anybody    (C) body    (D) somebody
(    ) 13.    (A) an        (B) a          (C) the     (D) X
(    ) 14.    (A) bottom    (B) top        (C) tip     (D) middle
(    ) 15.    (A) performance             (B) accident
              (C) accidentally            (D) performing
(    ) 16.    (A) beat      (B) beating    (C) beaten  (D) bit
(    ) 17.    (A) lie       (B) to lie     (C) lying   (D) lied
(    ) 18.    (A) to        (B) in         (C) at      (D) for
(    ) 19.    (A) hole      (B) bear       (C) challenge (D) channel
(    ) 20.    (A) brave     (B) dangerous  (C) difficult (D) donut
```

Grammar session 4 助動詞及連接詞
Auxiliary Verb & Conjunction

∽ 本課學習要點 ∾

1. 『語態助動詞』可以表達語氣及說話時的態度，後面接原形動詞。
2. 『語態助動詞』假設語氣的用法。
3. 『連接詞』主要是用來連接字詞或句子，分為『對等連接詞』、『從屬連接詞』。
4. 『連接詞』的句法活用。

---

① 『語態助動詞』可以表達語氣及說話時的態度，後面接原形動詞。

　　常見的助動詞 do、does、did 是用來搭配一般動詞運用，造否定句及疑問句時所使用。例：<u>Do</u> you want to have a break?(你想要休息一下嗎？)、<u>Does</u> anyone get her message? (任何人有收到她的消息嗎？)、We <u>didn't</u> go to the summer camp.(我們沒有去夏令營。)但也有肯定句中加上 do、does、did 的用法。例：We <u>do</u> really love her.(我們真得很愛她。) 這裡的 do 和 love 共存在肯定句中，表示強調動詞 love，強調的語氣。Sam <u>did</u> go there before.(山姆之前的確是有去那裡。)本句中的 did 也屬於強調的語氣。

常見的語態助動詞

1. 表示『允許』的 may 和表示『可能』的 might。

Ex. A: <u>May</u> I enter the boardroom now?　B: Yes, you <u>may</u>.
(A:我現在可以進會議室了嗎？　B: 是的，你可以。)

Ex. It <u>might</u> be difficult to have all the stars come together
in our show.
(要讓所有明星都聚到我們的演出裡可能是很困難的事。)

2. 表示『將會、願意』的 will 及其過去式 would。

will 有表示未來式、動作還沒有做但即將做的意義。
would 的用法有 will 的過去式、表示『禮貌、客氣』
的語氣，用來表示『請求』的語氣…等等。

Ex. A: <u>Will</u> you drop me at the train station?
B: Sure, I <u>will</u>.
(A: 你會讓我在火車在下車吧？　B: 當然我會。)

Ex. <u>Would</u> you leave me alone for a while?
(你願意讓我一個人靜 下嗎？)

A. would you like to +原形動詞 (想要…)
B. would you love to +原形動詞 (願意…)
C. would rather +原形動詞 (寧願…)
D. would you mind +Ving (你介意…)
E. would you mind + if I V-ed (你介意我…)

\<Practice-would 助動詞用法判別練習\>

1. _____ have some cookies?
2. I _____ ride my bicycle to work. I don't like
cars at all.
3. A: _____ doing me a favor?
B: Not at all. I _____ help you.
4. _____ if I used your color pencils?

❤愛的筆記貼❤

解答：❶ Would you like to (你想要吃點餅乾嗎？)

　　　❷ would rather (我寧願騎腳踏車去上班。我一點也不喜歡
　　　　汽車。)

　　　❸ Would you mind/ would love to (A:你介意幫我一個忙
　　　　嗎？B:一點也不。我樂意幫你忙。)

　　　❹ Would you mind (如果我用了你的彩色鉛筆你會介意嗎？)

3. 表示『能夠、允許、可能、請求』的 can 及其過去式 could。

A. <u>Can</u> we make the deadline?

B. You <u>can</u> try your best in the meeting.

C. It <u>can't</u> be Joseph. He is my best friend.

D. You <u>can</u> go upstairs now.

　　依照以上例句的句義來判斷，所以 A 的句義為：我們
可以、能夠在期限內完成嗎？B 句義為：你可以在這會議
中盡全力來表現。C 句義為：不可能是喬瑟夫。他是我最
好的朋友。D 句義為：你現在可以上樓了。

　　另外，can 和 could 都可以表示『請求』之意，但 could
的語氣更為婉轉而客氣些。例：Can I use your telephone?
和 Could I use your telephone?(我可以用你的電話嗎？)前
者較為直接，而後者較為客氣些。

　　Can 當『可以、能夠』時，還可以等於 be able to 的用
法，可以互相代換。例：Mr. Dior can meet you at 10 a.m.. =
Mr. Dior is able to meet you at 10 a.m..(迪奧先生在早上 10
點時可以見你。)

4. 表示『提議』的 shall 及其過去式表示建議語氣『應該』的 should。

should 應該

had better 最好

ought to 應該

must 一定

> 依照語氣強弱,最客氣的提議為 should 應該…,而語氣最強的是 must 一定要…。

Ex. Shall we have dinner together?
(我們要不要今晚一起吃個晚飯?)→表提議

Ex. A: The weather is getting cold. (天氣愈來愈冷了。)

B: (1) You should put on your jacket.
(你應該要穿上夾克。)→表建議

(2) You had better put on your jacket.
(你最好穿上夾克。)→表強烈建議

(3) You ought to put on your jacket.
(你應該穿上夾克。)→表示義務性的應該

(4) You must put on your jacket.
(你一定要穿上夾克。)→表命令

◎ **have to 和 must 語氣上的差別**

have to 和 must 兩者都有『必需』去做…的意思,但講話的語氣態度表現有些不同。

Ex. The meeting is going to start in3 minutes.
(會議將在 3 分鐘內召開。)

I must go now. (我必需得走了。)
→情非得已,一定得走。

Ex. OK. It's time to study in the library.

(好。是時候要去圖書館唸書了。)

I <u>have to</u> go now.

(我現在要走了。)

→比較主動的說法。自己覺得必需要走了。

5. 表示『假設語氣』助動詞有 should 萬一、must have 一定是…、would have 將可能會…、 should have 早就應該…

Ex. If the picnic <u>should be canceled</u>, we <u>would go</u> to sing the Karaoke. (萬一野餐被取消了,我們就去唱卡拉 OK。)

Ex. It <u>must have been</u> an accident, and no one <u>could have predicted</u> it precisely. (那一定是個意外,沒有人能夠精準地預測到它。)→意外已經發生了。

Ex. Doris <u>should have seen</u> the doctor, but she didn't.
(朵莉絲應該已經去看過醫生了,但她並沒有。)
→早就該去做的事,結果沒做。

▼ 連接詞 ◄

③『連接詞』主要是用來連接字詞或句子,分為『對等連接詞』、『從屬連接詞』。

1. <u>對等連接詞 and, but, or</u>

　　and 和,but 但是,or 或者/否則,是對等連接詞的功能。連接詞用來連接名詞與名詞之間,形容詞和形容詞間,或動詞與動詞之間。對等連接詞的前後詞性對等,例 jump and run(又跳又跑),Mary and Jane(瑪莉和珍),不可以連接不對等的詞性 jump and Mary(跳和瑪莉),但 Jane's jump and Mary's run(珍的跳躍和瑪莉的跑步)是可以的,兩者均是名詞。第一、文法上詞性對等,第二、語意上對等。

<對等連接詞的練習>

(1) They don't have wings _____ tails.

(2) I am a quiet girl, _____ Mary isn't (a quiet girl).

(3) A: Coffee, tea, ___ me?

    B: No kidding. Coffee, please.

♥愛的筆記貼♥

解答: ❶ and (他們沒有翅膀和尾巴。)

      ❷ but (前後語義相反,故填 but。題義是:我是一個安靜的女孩,但瑪莉不是(一位安靜的女孩)。)

      ❸ or (提供選擇,所以是『或者』的 or。題義是:A: 要點咖啡、茶還是我呢?B: 不要開玩笑了。咖啡,有勞了。)

◎ 連接詞 or『否則』和 and『然後、那麼』的用法說明

以下舉兩句祈使句為例說明,

語法是:祈使句+or 主詞+will+原形動詞…

Hurry up, or you will miss the bus.

(快一點,否則你將會錯過公車。)

Hurry up, and you will catch on the bus.

(快一點,那麼你將會趕上公車。)

GOOD IDEA!

小試身手 文法判別：請問是用 and 還是 or?

1. Don't be afraid, _____ you will be all right.

2. Please go away from here, _____ you will be hurt by the glass.

3. Be quiet, _____ the teacher won't be angry.

4. Put on your jacket, _____ you will catch a cold.

5. Be polite, _____ your mother will get angry with you.

6. Drive carefully, _____ you won't get the fine ticket.

7. Wait a minute, _____ you will see her later.

♥愛的筆記貼♥

解答：❶ and (不要害怕，而你將會沒事的。)

❷ or (請遠離這邊，不然你將會被這玻璃傷到。)

❸ and (安靜，而老師就不會生氣了。)

❹ or (穿上你的夾克，不然你將會感冒。)

❺ or (要禮貌點，不然你媽媽會對你生氣。)

❻ and (小心開車，這樣你就不會拿到罰單。)

❼ and (等一下，你稍晚就會看到她了。)

　　有沒有發現，通常逗點後面結果好的，就是接 and，結果不好的，就是接 or 否則你將會…有不好的結果。

2. 從屬連接詞 because 和 because of 表原因，通常位於句中。

Because 後接完整句子(主詞 S+動詞 V....)

Because of 後接名詞 N 或名詞片語 NP

英文中『因為』because 和『所以』不會出現在同一句

中，王不見王。有『因為』就不會有『所以』，有『所以』就不會有『因為』。

例句：

因為這次的強烈颱風，今天的火車嚴重誤點了。

The trains delayed seriously today _____ the strong typhoon.

因為強裂颱風來襲，今天的火車嚴重誤點了。

The trains delayed seriously today _____ the strong typhoon hit.

強烈颱風來襲，所以今天的火車嚴重誤點了。

_____.

💗愛的筆記貼💗

解答：❶ 空格後面接 the strong typhoon 是名詞片語，所以前面要接 because of。

❷ 空格後面接的是 the strong typhoon hit 有主詞有動詞是一個完整的句子，所以前面要接 because。

❸ 用『所以』so 來造句，so 的後面要接『結果』。強烈颱風來襲是『原因』，火車誤點是『結果』。答案是：The strong typhoon hit, so the trains delayed seriously today.

3. (表示時間的)從屬連接詞：

從屬連接詞 when(當...時候)、before(在...之前)、after(在...之後)，用來連接**主要子句**及**時間副詞子句**。

She suddenly burst into tears `when` she got the news.
└────── 主要子句 ──────┘　　　　└── 時間副詞子句 ──┘

(當她聽到這個消息時,她突然間大哭了起來。)

→ when 前後連接的句子時態相同,表示兩件事同時發生。

They will move to the town `when` the house is sold.
└────── 主要子句 ──────┘　　　　└── 時間副詞子句 ──┘

(當這房子被賣掉後,他們將會搬到鎮上。)

→當…發生時,另一件事情將會發生。

主要子句指出『事件』,時間副詞子句指出『時間』
◎ 時間點的表示方式有以下的方式:

1. 明確的點出時間:
this morning 今早/ last summer 去年夏天/
at 5 p.m. 下午五點/ on November 17th

2. 用『事件』來點出時間,
when I was a child 當我是小孩的時候
when he gets on the bus 當他上公車的時候
when Lisa cooks 當 Lisa 烹調的時候
when it rains 當下雨的時候

用法 a.從屬連接詞 when 後面跟著時間副詞子句。

b.從屬連接詞放句中時連接前後兩句，但如果從屬連接詞及時間副詞子句搬到整句的前面先講，時間副詞子句與主要子句間，必需以逗號隔開。

例：**When it is afraid**, it goes into the sea.

c. 從屬連接詞後接現在簡單式或過去簡單式。

<Practice 從屬連接詞的練習>

(1) _____ Shelly _____ the good news, she really _____ believe it!

當 Shelly 接到這個好消息時，她真的不敢相信。

(2) Do you ever feel _____ _____ you walk at a dark night?

你曾感到害怕嗎當你走在暗夜中？

(3) _____

我們可以感受到幸福，當我們和朋友或家人聚在一起的時候。

(4) _____ the plane _____, the control tower will send it the message to permit its landing.

在飛機抵達前，塔台將會傳送允許它降落的訊息。

♥愛的筆記貼♥

解答：❶ When/ got/ couldn't（這件事已經發生了才會有這句話，所以要用過去式。在此 when 的前後時態要一致，所以前面用過去式的 got 後面也要用過去式的 could。）

❷ afraid/ when

❸ We can feel happy when we are with our friends and family together.

❹ Before/ arrives

常見疑問 1 ┊ when 和 while 的差別？

when	when 後面通常接『簡單式』
while	while 後面通常接『進行式』，強調動作正在發生的那一刻。

Ex. Debbie goes back to her room when Bill turns on the TV.

（當比爾開電視時，黛比就回到她的房間。）

→前後時態一致表示同時發生的兩件動作。

Ex. Debbie goes back to her room while Bill is turning on the TV. （當比爾正在開電視時，黛比就回到她的房間。）

→強調在比爾開電視的那一刻，動作正發生的時候，另一件事同時發生。

4. if 如果、假設語氣的句法

所謂的條件子句，也就是『在....條件下，....發生了。』表示前後句有從屬的關係。必需讀完前後句及相關文法才能判別語意。

If 子句(if clause)有好幾種用法，現說明如下：

狀況 1：陳述事實。

這時的 if，通常可作『當...的時候』解釋，用意類似 when。

重點一：陳述現在事實(Present Factual)

例：If you always <u>argue</u> with people, they <u>treat</u> you unfriendly.
　　(當你總是和人們爭吵，他們對你也不友善。)

此時在陳述現在事實，故動詞時態 argue 及 treat 均依現在式時態配合主詞做變化。***前後兩句時態一致。***

<練習> 當你加入更多的冷水到這瓶子裡，水很快變涼。

重點二：陳述過去事實(Past Factual)，

例：Last year, if I <u>learned</u> French every day, my pronunciation <u>improved</u> a lot.
　　(去年，當我每天練習法文，我的發音進步了。)

此時在陳述過去事實，故動詞時態 learn 及 improve 均依過去式時態做變化。***前後兩句時態一致。***

<練習> 去年聖誕節，當我和 Mary 說我愛她，她馬上就允諾(promise)了。

♥愛的筆記貼♥

解答：❶ If you add more water into the bottle, the water turns cold soon. (陳述現在事實，所以 add 和 turns 均為現在簡單式變化。)

❷ Last Christmas, if I said I love you to Mary, she promised me right away. (陳述過去事實，所以 said 和 promised 均為過去簡單式變化。)

狀況 2：假設語氣。

這時的 if，通常可作『如果』解釋，是『如果....發生，事情就....進行』的意思。

If+主詞+現在簡單式動詞，主詞+will+原形動詞...

對於還沒發生的狀況作假設，所以前面以 If 開頭的句子是用現在簡單式，後面跟著的句子表示即將發生的結果，所以用未來式表現。)

重點一：假設語氣之預測說法 (Predictive)

例：If it <u>rains</u>, we'<u>ll</u> play indoors.

　　(如果天氣下雨，我們將在室內打球。)

這種句子表示一種『事情尚未發生的假設』：也許天氣會下雨的情況。如果天氣真的下雨，我們將會在室內打球。故 If 子句為現在式，後面的主要子句為未來式。也可以說在下雨的預設條件發生下，我們將改到室內打球。這種句子，前後時態是不一致的。

<練習>

1. 如果我有時間，我會去。

_____

2. 如果他下午回(come)辦公室了，我會回電話給你。

_____

3. 如果你做了這事，他們將會非常生氣。

_____

4. 如果明天下雨了，我們將不會去演唱會。

_____

♥愛的筆記貼♥

　　解答：❶ If I have time, I will go.

　　　　　❷ If he comes to the office, I will call back to you.

　　　　　❸ If you do the thing, they will be very angry.

　　　　　❹ If it rains tomorrow, we won't go to the concert.

　　以上四句均是條件子句，在事情還沒發生前，先進行假設。前後時態是不一致的，『當…發生時，後面這件事將會發生』。所以 If 接現在簡單式，而主要子句用未來式。

重點二： 假設語氣之與現在事實相反

(Present Contrary to Fact)

例：If I <u>sold</u> my stocks earlier, I <u>would</u> remain more fortune.

　　(如果我早點賣掉我的股票，我可能就守住更多財產。)

這句子指得是『如果我....，我可能就(would/could/might)』。但事實上沒人知道最後到底會不會達到假設的這件事。If 子句用過去式，而後面接的主要子句也用代表『可能』語氣的助動詞的過去式。前後兩句雖說時態相同，跟前面我們提到『陳述過去事實』的句子有代表『可能』語態的助動詞之差別。可以以此來做語意上的區別。

<練習>去年聖誕節，如果我和 Mary 說我愛她，她可能馬上就允諾(promise)了。

重點三： 假設語氣之與過去事實相反
(Past Contrary to Fact)

例：If John <u>had been</u> my partner, we <u>would have won</u> the game.
　　(如果 John 是我的伙伴，我早就贏了這場比賽。)
　　→ 所以當初就是沒有贏這場比賽，與過去事實相反。

時間點是過去已經發生了的事，所以用過去完成式 had+p.p.，後面主要子句用過去式的 would+have+p.p.，表示跟事實相反。

<練習>去年聖誕節，如果我和 Mary 說我愛她，她早就馬上

允諾(promise)了。

♥愛的筆記貼♥

解答：Last Christmas, if I had said I love you to Mary, she would have
promised me right away. →所以與過去事實相反，就是事實上
他沒跟 Mary 說，所以 Mary 也沒有答應他。

5. 其他假設語法的補充：

◎ **Even if...表示即使...也。**

Even if it rained, I wouldn't give up cycling.
即使下雨了，我也不放棄騎自行車。

◎ **If only (that)...表示但願,要是...就好了。**

If only (that) Harry were here with us!
要是我父親在這就好了。

◎ **Had, should, were...表示如果...**

因為假設語氣中的副詞子句省略了 if，所以助動詞要倒
裝到主詞之前。

Should it be a good result, I would have dinner with you.
如果是個好結果，我就會跟你一起吃晚餐。

Had I been there few days ago, I would have seen A-mei.
如果我幾天前就在那，我大概會看到阿妹。

6. 表『因果』的從屬連接詞 although 雖然、but 但是

(1) 同一句中有雖然 Although，就不會有但是 but。

(2) 同一句中有因為 because，就不會有所以 so。

Ex. 雖然上星期六颱風來了，但 Anne 還是去了泰國渡假。

Although the typhoon came last Saturday, Anne still went on vacation in Thailand.

→ The typhoon came last Saturday, but Anne still went on vacation in Thailand.

Ex. 雖然我不能吃草莓，但是我喜歡吃草莓蛋糕。

_____

Ex. 因為後天是個假日，所以我們要一起去看電影。

_____

♥愛的筆記貼♥

解答：❶ Although I can't eat strawberry, I like eating the strawberry cakes./ I can't eat strawberry, but I like eating the strawberry cakes.

❷ Because the day after tomorrow is a holiday, we are going to see a movie together./ The day after tomorrow is a holiday, so we are going to see a movie together.

 ▼ 進階練功坊 ◀

接下來請同學做進階活用練習，可以測驗自己對連接詞的用法懂得多少。

◎ 先從 "也" 這個字講起，『也是』有幾種講法：

_____　　__　　____　　_____　　__

肯定句練習：Terry 喜歡看喜劇，我也是。

= Terry likes to see the comedies, _____, _____.

= Terry likes to see the comedies, _____.

= Terry likes to see the comedies, _____

= _____ Terry _____ I like to see the comedies. (兩者都)

= _____ Terry _____ I like to see the comedies.

(不只…而且)

否定句練習：Joanna 不喜歡新來的鋼琴老師，我也不喜歡。

= Joanna doesn't like the new piano teacher, _____,

_____.

= Joanna doesn't like the new piano teacher, _____.

= Joanna doesn't like the new piano teacher, _____.

= _____ Joanna _____ I like the new piano teacher.

(既不是…也不是)

♥愛的筆記貼♥

解答：❶ 『也』的說法有五種：also、too、either、so、nor。

❷ I do, too./ and so do I/ and I also like to see the comedies/
Both…and…/ not only… but also

❸ and I don't, either/ nor do I/ and neither do I/Neither…nor…

**nor 可當連接詞用，因為原本『or』就是個連接詞，但 neither 沒有單獨當連接詞用，和 nor 連用時才算是連接詞。不然和 either 一樣，只是個副詞。所以在回答 neither do I 時，如果前面有接句子，並需用 and 做連接。例：Gary didn't get up early, and neither did I.=Gary didn't get up early, nor did I.

◎ **Both …. and……　兩者都**

Both you and Brown _____ (be) qualified to this position.
(你和布朗都很符合這個職位的資格。)

**此類句型的動詞，因為『兩者都…』是複數的概念，所以就用複數型態的動詞變化，答案是 are。

◎ **Not only …. but also……　不只…而且…**

She is <u>not only</u> thoughtful <u>but also</u> just perfect for me.
(對我來說她不僅只是體貼而且就是很適合我。)

**當 Not only 放句首時，主詞和動詞要倒裝，動詞前要加上助動詞。

Ex. <u>Not only</u> |did| we <u>go</u> to Kenting <u>but also</u> had a great time in Kaohsiung.

→還原而成 We <u>not only</u> went to Kenting <u>but also</u> have a great time in Kaohsiung.

(我們不只是去了墾丁，而且我們在高雄玩得很開心。)

◎ **Either….or….. 不是…就是…**

Either you or Brown ____ (be) qualified to this position.

(不是你就是布朗是符合這個職位的資格。)

**此類句型的動詞，要選最靠近動詞的名詞來做動詞變化，例如此處是 Brown 比較靠近 be 動詞，所以就用第三人稱單數的動詞變化，答案是 is。

◎ **Neither...nor...　既不是…也不是…**

Neither you nor Brown _____ (be) qualified to this position.

(你和布朗都不符合這個職位的資格。)

**此類句型的動詞，要選最靠近動詞的名詞來做動詞變化，例如此處是 Brown 比較靠近 be 動詞，所以就用第三人稱單數的動詞變化，答案是 is。

<練習>

1. 我表哥和我阿姨都會開車去旅行。

_____

2. 不是我哥就是 Sandra 開車去旅行。

_____

3. 我哥和 Sandra 都沒有開車去旅行。

_____

4. 我去過韓國，Sally 也去過。

_____

=_____

=_____

=_____

=_____

5. 我沒去過韓國，Sally 也沒去過。

_____

= _____

= _____

= _____

6. Sally 還是 Sandra 其中一人曾經去過韓國。

_____(one of)

= _____

♥愛的筆記貼♥

解答：❶ Both my cousin and my aunt are able to drive to travel.
　　　❷ Either my brother or Sandra drives our car for traveling.
　　　❸ Neither my brother nor Sandra drives our car for traveling.
　　　❹I have been to Korea, and Sally has, too.
　　　　=I have been to Korea, and Sally also has been to there.
　　　　=I have been to Korea, and so has Sally.
　　　= Both Sally and I have been to Korea.
　　　= Not only Sally but also I have been to Korea.
　　　❺ I haven't been to Korea, and Sally hasn't, either.
　　　= I haven't been to Korea, and neither has Sally.
　　　= I haven't been to Korea, nor has Sally.
　　　= Neither Sally nor I have been to Korea.
　　　❻ One of Sally and Sandra has been to Korea.
　　　= Either Sally or Sandra has been to Korea.

Grammar Challenge

____ 1. Not only _____ an irrational status symbol, they're
　　　killing our Earth!

　　(A) cars are　　　　(B) considering the cars

　　(C) are cars　　　　(D) the cars may be

____ 2. Would you mind _____ a window for me? It's stuffy.

(A) open　(B) to open　(C) opened　(D) opening

_____ 3. I _____ a super star if I had joined the competition.

(A) want to be　　(B) am supposed to be

(C) should be　　(D) could have been

_____ 4. If I _____ you, I would do nothing but sleep.

(A) am　(B) was　(C) been　(D) were

_____ 5. Karen didn't notice the burglar in the party, _____ do I.

(A) nor　(B) none　(C) neither　(D) either

_____ 6. Either you or Lisa _____ going to win the first price in the

game.　(A) are　(B) is　(C) were　(D) be

_____ 7. What a wet day! I _____ stay at home to keep my feet dry.

(A) would have　　(B) would like

(C) would love　　(D) would rather

_____ 8. _____ the 16-week campaign, all the candidates have been

ready for facing the result.

(A) When　(B) After　(C) Before　(D) If

_____ 9. They finally quitted the idea _____ the limited budget.

(A) because　(B) although　(C) so　(D) because of

_____ 10. The glass dropped while she _____ the bread to my mom.

(A) passes　(B) is passing　(C) was passing　(D) pass

Grammar session 5 | 形容詞及副詞
Adjectives and Adverbs

∾ 本課學習要點 ∾

1. 『形容詞』是用來形容名詞及代名詞的修飾、敘述語。
2. 『副詞』可用來形容動作，修飾動詞及形容詞。

　　我們在名詞章節中的名詞片語組成要項中，有初步地介紹了形容詞的概念，在本章開始，我們要複習的是形容詞的比較級及最高級的概念。以及副詞比較級、最高級的概念。還有形容詞和副詞的區分。

1 形容詞比較級的形成規則

比較級形容詞的句型基礎為：

A 比 B 來得更…。(A+be 動詞+比較級形容詞+than+B)

<u>The girls</u> are more than <u>the boys</u> in our class.

　(A)　　　　　　　　　　　　(B)

在我們班的女生比男生多。

　　一般規則的形容詞，若單字長度為兩個音節的，比較級形容詞就是原級的字尾加 er，最高級形容詞則是原級字尾加 est。例：bright 明亮的 →brighter 更明亮的 →the brightest 最明亮的。三個音節以上的形容詞，比較級形容

詞就在單字前加上 **more**，而最高級則在單字前加上 **most**。例：important 重要的➔more important 更重要的➔the most important 最重要的。比較級形容詞前，若要再加中語氣，像『比…更重要得許多』，本來『比…更重要的』就是 **more important**，但『重要的許多』，可以在前面加上 much 這個副詞去修飾 **more important** 這個形容詞，所以『比…更重要的許多』，就是 **much more important**。

　　以下舉比較級形容詞為例，介紹形容詞變化的規則，而同學們可以依此類推最高級形容詞的變化,最高級只要把比較級的 er 換成 est，如果是三個音節以上的單字，只要把前面的 more 改成 most 即可。但要注意的是，所謂的最高級，即世界之最，所以最高級形容詞前面要加個指定、限定的冠詞『the』。例：the tallest tower in the world(世界上最高的塔)、the most spectacular scene(最壯觀的景色)…等等。

(1) 兩個音節以下的形容詞變化規則

原級字尾為 e 時，比較級直接加 r。		
nice ➔ **nicer** 更好	**strange** ➔＿＿＿＿	更奇怪
cute ➔ ＿＿＿＿ 更可愛	**fine**➔＿＿＿＿	更好
late ➔ ＿＿＿＿ 更晚	**large** ➔ ＿＿＿＿	更大

原級字尾為短母音+單子音時，比較級先重複字尾再加 er。			
hot➔ **hotter** 更熱		**big** ➔ ＿＿＿＿	更大
thin➔＿＿＿＿	更瘦	**sad**➔ ＿＿＿＿	更難過
fat ➔ ＿＿＿＿	更胖	**glad**➔＿＿＿＿	更高興
red➔＿＿＿＿	更紅	**wet**➔＿＿＿＿	更濕

原級爲母音加字尾 y，比較級直接加 er。

gray→＿＿＿＿＿＿＿＿＿＿　更灰

原級字尾爲 y，比較級爲去 y 加 ier。

angry→＿＿＿＿＿　更生氣　　pretty→＿＿＿＿＿　更漂亮

happy→＿＿＿＿＿更開心　　easy→＿＿＿＿＿　更容易

dirty→＿＿＿＿＿　更髒　　hungry→＿＿＿＿　更餓

❤愛的筆記貼❤

解答：❶ cuter, later, stranger, finer, larger

　　　❷ hotter, thinner, fatter, redder, bigger, sadder, gladder, wetter
在背第二組重複字尾加 er 的單字時，其實有個聯想法可以用。正所謂夏天減肥愈減愈肥啊！太陽又『紅』(red)又『大』(big)又『熱』(hot)，想『瘦』(thin)卻愈減愈『胖』(fat)，全身『濕』(wet)答答很『難過』(sad)。這裡就收藏了七個字要重複字尾加 er，重複字尾加 est 的形容詞了。想像力會讓你學習更輕鬆喔！

　　　❸ grayer

　　　❹ angrier, happier, dirtier, prettier, easier, hungrier

兩個音節以下的形容詞後直接加 er			
原級	比較級	原級	比較級
cheap 便宜的	cheaper	sour 酸的	
sweet 甜的		bitter 苦的	
long 長的		short 短的	
old 老的		new 新的	
cold 冷的		few 少的(可數)	
great 好的		young 年輕的	

2.大多數雙音節形容詞和三個音節以上的形容詞

三個音節以上的形容詞，前面加上 more	
原級	比較級
beautiful 美麗	
important 重要	
useful 有用	
convenient 方便	
expensive 貴	
nervous 緊張	
excellent 傑出	
boring 無聊	
difficult 困難	
interesting 有趣	

❤愛的筆記貼❤

解答：❶ cheaper, sweeter, longer, older, colder, greater, sourer, bitterer, shorter, newer, fewer, younger

❷ more beautiful, more important, more useful, more convenience, more expensive, more nervous, more excellent, more boring, more difficult, more interesting

3.不規則變化的形容詞比較級

原級→比較級→最高級	
good 好的→**better**→**best**	**bad** 壞的→**worse**→**worst**
many 多的→**more**→**most** **much**	**little** 少的→**less**→**least** (不可數的少) *at least 至少…

　　以下是有關比較級形容詞的各種句型，在觀念上大致分為兩個方向：同等比較及比較級。比較級通常是在『兩者之間』做比較的，因為三者以上的情況，我們也只能兩兩比較，或指出世界之最。例如：三個人之間一起比身高，我們講比較級時，只能講誰比誰高，但用最高級的話，就可以馬上說出最高的那一位是誰？最矮的那一位是誰？而介於中間的就不用多說一切自然明瞭了。

　　『同等比較』也就是說『A 如同 B 一般的…』，或是『A 不如 B 一般的…』。『比較級』的語法則是在表述『A 比 B 更…』，或『A 不比 B 來得更…』。以下透過公式化的練習，讓同學們更清楚比較級的語法概念。

同等比較：A 和 B 相似的程度	
優等比較 +	劣等比較 -
(A=B) A 如同 B 一樣的， 　　　　用 as…as 　A be-V <u>as</u> 形容詞原級 <u>as</u> B Helen 和她姐姐一樣可愛。	(A<B) A 不如 B… A be-V <u>not as</u> 形容詞原級 <u>as</u> B Gary 不像 Henry 一樣高。
比較級：A 比 B 更…	
(A>B) A 比 B… 　A be-V 形容詞比較級 <u>than</u> B 這隻手機比那隻貴。	(A<B) A 不如 B… A be-V <u>less</u> 形容詞原級 <u>than</u> B Gary 不比 Henry 高。

A 在 AB 中比較...	A 在 AB 中較不...
A be-V <u>the</u> 形容詞比較級(名詞) + 介系詞片語 + the + 名詞	**A be-V <u>the less</u> 形容詞原級(名詞) + 介系詞片語 + the + 名詞**
這頂帽子是這兩頂中顏色較亮的。	Gary 是兩者中比較不高的。
＿＿＿＿＿＿＿＿＿＿＿＿	＿＿＿＿＿＿＿＿＿＿＿＿
＿＿＿＿＿＿＿＿＿＿＿＿	＿＿＿＿＿＿＿＿＿＿＿＿

❤愛的筆記貼❤

解答：❶ <u>Helen is as cute as her sister.</u> (Helen 和她姐姐一樣可愛。)

❷ <u>Gary isn't as tall as Henry.</u> (Gary 不像 Henry 一樣高。)

❸ <u>The cell phone is more expensive than that one.</u> (這隻手機比那隻貴。)

❹ <u>Gary less tall than Henry.</u> (Gary 不比 Henry 高。)

❺ <u>The hat is the brighter of the two.</u> (這頂帽子是這兩頂中顏色較亮的。) 指定限定這兩頂帽子中的較亮的那一頂，所以在這種情況下，brighter『較亮的』前面要加 the，而 of the two『這兩頂中』，two 前面也要加 the 來指定、限定。

❻ <u>Gary is the less tall of the two.</u> (Gary 是兩者中比較不高的。) 承上題所講解，所以這裡的較不高的這一位，形容詞前也加 the 指定限定，這兩位 the two 前面也加 the 來指定限定。值得注意的是第 4 及第 6 句練習是屬於劣等比較，比較級已經表現在 less(little 的比較級)上，所以後面接的形容詞為原級形式。這是比較級常被考的觀念易混淆區域。

　　人們本來天生就愛比較，所以日常生活中，其實我們還蠻常用到比較級形容詞句型的。尤其我們在購物時，流行一句話叫『貨比三家不吃虧』，既然有這樣的概念，我們就來透過以下的『型錄比一比』遊戲，來『身體力行』一下比較級形容詞的句型吧！

Best Bordeaux Wine

Château Léoville-Barton since 1998	Château Lafite Rothschild since 2004
 **Origin** Medoc Château Léoville (Deuxiems Crus) ★ ★ ★ ★ **In Stock** Ships from and sold by VIP.com. **Gift-wrap** available. **Value** USD$126 /Bottle	 **Origin** Medoc Château Lafite (Premiers Crus) ★ ★ ★ ★ ★ **Oversea order** 2~3 months shipping **Gift-wrap** unavailable. **Value** USD$500 /Bottle

以上是一篇波爾多紅酒 Bordeaux Wine 的型錄，可以看到很多有關這兩瓶紅酒的訊息。同學們可以就其年份、等級、訂購時間、服務，以及價格來練習說比較級的句型。我們就用所有格代名詞來造句，所以 A 的酒 The Barton's wine 就是 The Barton's，B 就是 The Rothschild's。以下是句型提示：

1. (old/ as…as) ＿＿＿＿＿＿＿＿＿＿＿＿＿＿＿＿＿＿

   (old/ than) ＿＿＿＿＿＿＿＿＿＿＿＿＿＿＿＿＿＿＿

2. (good/ than) ＿＿＿＿＿＿＿＿＿＿＿＿＿＿＿＿＿＿

   (less/good/ than) ＿＿＿＿＿＿＿＿＿＿＿＿＿＿＿＿

3. (The order for/take/ much time/ as…as)

_____

(The order for/take/ little time/ as…as)

_____

(The order for/ soon/ than) _____

(The order for/ take/ little time/ than)

_____

4. (much/ service/ than) _____

   (little/ service/ as…as..) _____

5. (expensive/ as…as…) _____

   (little/ expensive/ than) _____

   (expensive/ of the two) _____

♥愛的筆記貼♥

各位同學，做了這些練習，有沒有點茫了呢？如果以上的觀念都清楚的話，相信你對形容詞的比較級早就瞭若指掌囉！這是有關於波爾多紅酒的一些小常識：Château Lafite Rothschild 是拉斐酒莊，是波爾多最頂級紅酒品牌，列於梅鐸區 (Medoc)五大頂級酒莊之首。Château 就是酒莊的意思。紅酒評等分兩種：一種是酒莊的等級：第一級(Premiers Crus)，所以 DM 裡給它五顆星、第二級(Deuxiems Crus) ，所以 DM 裡給它四顆星、第三級(Troisiemes Crus)第四級、(Quatriemes Crus)、第五級(Cinquiemes Crus)。另一種評等是以每年的品酒來決定，通常以同等級酒莊出的酒進行評等。酒的瓶身上都有專屬標籤，通常都會寫 since+年份，也就是自從西元幾年開始釀造窖藏至今。稍微了解一下，我們就來解答以下練習題：

解答：❶ The Barton's is not as old as the Rothschild's. (Barton 的酒不和 Rothschild 的酒一樣老。)/ The Barton's is older than the Rothschild's. (Barton 的酒比 Rothschild 的酒還要老些。)

❷ The Rothschild's is better than the Barton's. (Rothschild 的酒比 Barton 的酒更好。)/ The Barton's is less good than the Rothschild's. (Barton 的酒比起 Rothschild 的酒較沒那麼好。)

❸ The order for the Barton's doesn't take as much time as the Rothschild's. (Barton 的訂購沒有花和 Rothschild 一樣多的時間。)→ Barton 有現貨 In stock。/ The order for the Rothschild's doesn't take as little time as the Barton's.(Rothschild 的訂購時間較沒有像 Barton 的訂購時間一樣少。) / The order for the Barton's is sooner than the Rothschild's.(Barton 的酒比 Rothschild 的酒訂購的快些。)/ The order for the Barton's takes less time than the Rothschild's.(訂購 Barton 的酒比起訂 Rothschild 的酒來說花比較少的時間。)

❹ The Barton's service is more than the Rothschild's.(Barton 的服務比 Rothschild 來得多一些。)→提供 gift-wrap 禮品包裝的服務。/ The Barton's service is not as little as the Rothschild's. (Barton 的服務不像 Rothschild 來得少。)

❺ The Barton's is not as expensive as the Rothschild's.(Barton 的酒不像 Rothschild 的酒那麼貴。) / The Barton's is less expensive than the Rothschild's.(Barton 的酒沒有 Rothschild 的酒那樣貴。)/ The Rothschild's is the more expensive of the two.(Rothschild 的酒是兩者中較貴的那瓶。)

以上是比較級形容詞的基礎句型,比較的觀念上需要再多一些練習,腦子比較靈光些,就可以用很多的說法,順著說倒著說來達成自己溝通的目的。不同的句法會給人不同的感覺,所以如果把比較級的句法學好的話,也許你將來就會是個英語殺價高手或是談判專家喔!

　　以下幾個句型,是我們常在文章中見到的比較級形容詞的句子，用來強調敘述的事物狀況。

(1) the + 比較級..., the +比較級...(愈....，會愈....)
The newer the model <u>is</u>, the higher the price <u>is</u>.
型號愈新，價格愈高。
<Practice 練習>
人愈多車子就愈多。

---

(2) more and more...; 比較級 and 比較級...(愈來愈...)
There are <u>more and more</u> people use cell phones to
send messages instead of the greeting cards.
有愈來愈多的人用手機傳簡訊來取代卡片問候。
<Practice 練習>
我相信我的生活會愈來愈好。
I believe that_____.

(3) more than... /better than...(超過...)
It is <u>more</u> blessed to give <u>than</u> to receive. 施比受更有福
Two heads are better than one.三個臭皮匠勝過一個諸葛亮
<Practice 練習>
健康勝於財富(wealth)

顏色的比較級
※ <u>各位同學一定要注意，顏色的比較，要注意觀念。</u>

在日常生活中我們常會說紅一點,更紅一些更黑一些,事實上這並不是一個明確的描述法,因爲每個人的標準不同,到底紅要多紅?黑要多黑?這是敘述上的問題,跟色彩基礎概念有關。在美術的角度來說,比較適切的說法,應該要說更淡些、更濃些、更明亮些,或者是更深沉些。

形容詞原級	比較級	形容詞原級	比較級
light 淡的		**strong** 濃、強烈的	
bright 明亮的		**dark** 深沉的	

Don't you think that it is too red? (or The red color is too strong!)

Do you have brighter one?

你不覺得這好像太紅了嗎?(或者你也可以說成:這紅色太濃了。)

你有沒有顏色比較亮的?

⚫ ● ⚫ ⚫ ● ● ⚫ ● ⚫ ⚫ ● ● ⚫ ● ⚫ ⚫ ● ● ⚫ ● ⚫ ⚫ ● ● ⚫ ●

2 形容詞最高級基本句型

(1) 主詞 + the +形容詞最高級
- of 數量 : of the three
- in 地方 : in town
- in 時間 : in the 10 years

形容詞最高級主要的概念是<u>**在一個範圍內**</u>去點出最明顯的那一個。例:It is the tallest building in the world. (它是世界上最高的大樓。)

<Practice 練習>

(1) 周星馳(Steven Chow)是亞洲最受歡迎的喜劇演員。

(2) 鐵達尼號(Titanic)是有史以來最浪漫的電影。

(3) 數學是所有科目中最難的。

(4) 這六顆糖中紅色是最甜的。

♥愛的筆記貼♥

解答：❶ Steven Chow is the most popular comedy actor in Asia.
　　　❷ Titanic is the most romantic movie all the time.
　　　❸ Mathematics(Math) is the most difficult subject of all.
　　　❹ The red candy is the sweetest in the six.

(2) 最高級形容詞的問句形式

What　什麼事物
Who　　誰
Where　什麼地方
Whose　誰的　　　　+ be-V+ the +最高級形容詞…
Why　　為什麼
How　　如何

接續第一點所說的概念，所以在問『最….的人事物』時，
也要說明數量、地方或時間，後面接介系詞片語。

例句：What is the best thing <u>in your life</u>?

(在你生命中最好的事物是什麼？)

Who is your best friend <u>in your class</u>?

(在你班上你最好的朋友是誰？)

Where is the best place <u>in Taipei</u> to have a romantic date?　(在台北哪裡是最佳浪漫約會地點？)

Whose cell phone is the best now?

(現在誰的手機最好？)

Why is the best car always expensive?

(為什麼最好的車總是昂貴？)

How are your best classmates <u>in the elementary school</u>?　(你小學同學現在過得怎樣？)

<Practice 練習>

(1) 在你班上誰最有藝術家的天賦？

_____

(2) 什麼是世界上最大的動物？

_____

♥愛的筆記貼♥

解答：❶ Who is the most talented one to be an artist in your class?
　　　❷ What is the biggest animal all over the world (in the world)?

---

③ 形容詞最高級進階句型－用比較級語法來描述最高級

如果在一個限定範圍內，我們說一件『事物比其他的事物都來得更…』，換句話說就是在這個範圍內沒人比得上它，那麼也就是最高級的語意了。所以比較級形容詞搭配上『than any other + 名詞』，就等同形容詞最高級的用法。

Ex. The firework festival this year **is** much **larger** and **more spectaculor than** any other festivals in the world.

(今年的煙火盛會要比世界上任何其他的節慶活動都還來得更大且更壯觀。)

\<Practice 練習\>
(1) John 比班上任何同學都來得高。(John 是班上最高的同學)

_____

(2) Joanna 比她其他兩個姐妹還漂亮些。

　　(Joanna 是三姐妹中最漂亮的)

_____

●♥愛的筆記貼♥
解答： ❶ John is taller than any other classmates in the class.
　　　 ❷ Joanna is more beautiful than the other two sisters.

 ▼ 進階練功坊 ◀

\<Practice 形容詞綜合練習 1\>
There are three cell phones. The red one costs NT$3,500,

the price of the silver one is NT$3,000, and the black one charges for NT$4,950. Please answer questions.

(　) (1) The red cell phone is _____ the silver one.

　　　　(A) the most expensive than　　(B) the most expensive of

　　　　(C) more expensive than　　　　(D) more expensive of

(　) (2) The black cell phone is the most expensive _____.

　　　　(A) than any other cell phone

　　　　(B) than any other cell phones

　　　　(C) than the red one　　　(D) of the three

(　) (3) The silver cell phone is _____ of the three.

　　　　(A) the most cheap　　　　(B) the cheapest

　　　　(C) more cheap　　　　　　(D) cheaper than

(　) (4) The black cell phone and the red one are _____ the
　　　　　silver one.

　　　　(A) much more expensive than

　　　　(B) the most expensive

　　　　(C) cheaper and more expensive than

　　　　(D) not cheaper at all

♥愛的筆記貼♥

解答：本題的題意為：有三隻手機。紅色的手機價值 3500 元，銀色的要 3000 元，黑色的要價 4950 元。請回答下列問題：❶ (C) 紅色的比銀色的貴。❷ (D) 黑色的手機是這三隻中最貴的。❸ (B) 銀色的手機是這三隻中最便宜的。cheap 是兩個音節以下，所以比較級為cheaper、最高級是 cheapest。❹ (A) 紅色的和黑色的手機比銀色的貴上許多。

<Practice 形容詞綜合練習 2>

For the romantic Valentine's Day, Vicky, Meg and Jolin learned to make a chocolate by themselves. Their teacher tasted the chocolate one by one, and gave them the scores.

	Vicky's chocolate	Meg's chocolate	Jolin's chocolate
	☺	☺	☺
Sweet	OK	Too sweet	No sugar
Bitter	OK	No bitter	Too bitter
Score	10	7	5

(1) Whose chocolate is sweeter than Vicky's chocolate?

_____

(2) Whose chocolate is less bitter than Vicky's chocolate?

_____

(3) Whose chocolate is smaller than Meg's chocolate?

_____

(4) Is Jolin's score better than Meg's?

_____

♥愛的筆記貼♥

本題的題意為：為了過一個浪漫的情人節，Vicky、Meg 和 Jolin 三個人去學自己動手做巧克力。他們的老師一個個嘗過他們做的巧克力，然後給他們評分。表格中就是評分表。好的巧克力應該要苦甜參半，bitter 是苦味還有 sweet 甜味。

答案是：❶ Meg's chocolate is sweeter than Vicky's.
(Meg 的巧克力比 Vicky 的更甜。)

❷ Meg's chocolate is less bitter than Vicky's.
(Meg 的巧克力比起 Vicky 的較不苦。)

❸ Jolin's chocolate is smaller than Meg's.
(Jolin 的巧克力比 Meg 的更小。)

❹ No, Meg's score is better than Jolin's. Jolin's score is the
worst of the three. (不，Meg 的分數比 Jolin 好。Jolin 的分
數是三者中最差的。)

<Practice 形容詞綜合練習 3>

Henry, Judy and their parents want to travel around
Europe. They plan to spend two nights in the same castle.
It sounds a great idea! The information of the castle is as
follows, and please give them some advice to choose one
castle.

The castle　　Comments	In German	In France	In Italy
Rooms	15	23	9
History	100 years	300 years	180 years
Comfortable	★★★★★	★★★	★★★★
Price for each day	US$ 50	US$ 200	US$ 10

(1) Henry: I'm afraid of ghosts! Which one is the oldest castle of the three? I don't want to stay there!

The castle in _____

(2) Judy: Hey Henry! You are almost afraid of everything! Not like me, I am only afraid of the tall buildings. Could you tell me which one is the tallest one? I don't want to go there.

_____

(3) Father: I care neither the ghosts nor the height. I work very hard almost every day. So, just tell me which castle is the most comfortable one?

_____

(4) Mother: Thank you for your advice, but all I want to know is…which one is the cheapest one? How much should we pay for two nights?

_____

_____

♥愛的筆記貼♥

本題的題意為：Henry、Judy 和他們的父母親想要去歐洲旅行。他們計劃要花兩個晚上住在同一座城堡裡。聽起來是個好主意！這些城堡的資訊如以下表格所述，請給他們一些建議幫他們選出一個適合待的城堡。❶ Henry 說他怕鬼！這三座哪一座是最古老的，他不想住在那裡。所以要回答：<u>The castle in France is the oldest one.</u> (這座在法國的城堡是最古老的。) ❷ Judy 說：嘿！亨利，你幾乎什麼都怕好不好！不像我，我只怕高樓大廈。你可以跟我說哪一座最高嗎？我不想去那。看圖中最高的應是法國那座城堡，所以要回答：<u>The castle in France is also the tallest one.</u> (這座在法國的城堡也是最高的。) ❸ 爸爸說：我既不在意鬼也不在意高度。我每天都工作得很辛苦。這樣，只要告訴我，哪一座是最舒服的就好了。德國的舒適度有五星。所以答案是：<u>The castle in German is the most comfortable one.</u> (這座在德國的是最舒適的。) ❹ 媽媽說：謝謝你的建議，但我想要知道的只是…哪一座是最便宜的？我們待兩晚要付多少錢？所以答案是：<u>The castle in Italy is the cheapest one. Staying for 2 nights there only charges you 20 dollars.</u> (這座在義大利的是最便宜的。住在那兩個晚上只收你20美金。)

4 用『現在分詞』及『過去分詞』當做形容詞來用。

這種情形大致分為兩種，一種是本來是屬於『感覺』的動詞，改變動詞形態而成分詞，有形容詞的功能，來敘述人、事、物的感覺。例如：interest(使…感興趣)，它的現在分詞interesting(令人感到有趣的…)當形容詞用，還有過去分詞interested(感到有趣的…)當形容詞用，形容人自己產生的感覺。另一種是以『現在分詞』當做主動語態的形容詞，或是『過去分詞』當做被動語態的形容詞來用。例：The <u>canceled</u> meeting will be held again next week.(原本被取消的會議在下個禮拜會重新召開。)

(1) 感覺的形容詞

原本是動詞，意思都是『使…感到…』，但字尾加 ing，變成現在分詞當形容詞用，用來形容『人事物帶給別人的感覺』。而過去方詞當形容詞用時，是用來形容『人自己產生的感覺』。以下有 10 個常用感覺形容詞，希望同學們會有更清楚的概念：

interest (使…感興趣)	The book <u>interests</u> me a lot. (動詞) (這本書使我感到有興趣。)
	I am <u>interested</u> in the book. (形容詞) (我對這本書的內容感到有興趣。)
	It is really an <u>interesting</u> book. (形容詞) (它真是一本有趣的書。)
excite (使…興奮)	The latest action movie really <u>excites</u> me. (這部最新的動作片真得使我很興奮。)
	I feel <u>excited</u> about the latest action movie. (我對於這部最新的動作片感到很興奮。)
	The latest action movie is really <u>exciting</u>. (這部最新的動作片真的很刺激。)
surprise (使…驚訝)	Her suddenly yelling <u>surprised</u> everyone. (她突然間的大叫使每個人感到很訝異。)
	Everyone was <u>surprised</u> at her yelling. (每個人都因為她的大叫感到很驚訝。)
	Nobody knows how the <u>surprising</u> accident happened. (沒人知道這令人驚訝的意外是怎麼發生的。)
depress (使…沮喪)	The series of unfortunate events really <u>depress</u> us. (這一連串的不幸事件真得讓我們感到好沮喪。)
	She has tried many ways to change her <u>depressed</u> mind. (她已經試過很多方法來改變她沮喪的心情。)
	The <u>depressing</u> fact affected the sales performance.

	(這件令人沮喪的事實影響了銷售表現。)
frustrate (使…挫折)	All they want to do is to <u>frustrate</u> me. (他們想要做的事就是要使我挫敗。)
	The failure made him <u>frustrated</u> a while. (這次失敗讓他感到挫折了一陣子。)
	His negative attitude is really <u>frustrating</u>. (他負面的態度真的很令人感到挫折。)
bore (使…無聊)	His cold jokes <u>bore</u> me all the time. (他的冷笑話總是使我感到很無趣。)
	Mr. Lin is a <u>boring</u> man. (林先生是個無聊男子。→他讓人感到很無聊。)
	Mr. Lin is <u>bored</u>. (林先生現在感到無聊。)
confuse (使…困惑)	The logical questions really <u>confuse</u> me. (這些邏輯問題真得使我感到困惑。)
	I am so <u>confused</u> with his purpose. (我真的被他混淆不知道他的來意是什麼。)
	The situation is quite <u>confusing</u>. (現在情況是相當的困擾。)
annoy (使…生氣)	Her excuses <u>annoy</u> the teacher very much. (她的藉口使這個老師非常生氣。)
	With such an impatient personality, she always feels <u>annoyed</u> easily. (有著這樣沒耐心的個性，她總是很容易感到生氣。
	The postman kept ringing my doorbell. It's really <u>annoying</u>. (這個郵差持續按我的門鈴。這真的很令人生氣。)
disappoint (使…失望)	The politician made us <u>disappointed</u> again and again. (這個政客使我們一次又一次地失望。)
	I feel so <u>disappointed</u> at your performance. (我對你的表現感到很失望。)
	The <u>disappointing</u> feeling doesn't

	disappear until he comes. (這種失望的感覺沒有消失直到他的來臨。)
irritate (使…惱怒)	Your straightforward temper sometimes irritates people easily. (你正直的脾氣有時候很容易使別人生氣。)
	Sam tried his best to relax because he was irritated with his colleagues. (Sam 盡他的全力來放鬆因為他和他的同事在生氣。)
	I still love my irritating wife for many years. (我仍然愛著我那易怒的老婆那麼多年了。)

(2) 『現在分詞』當主動語態的形容詞，『過去分詞』當被動語態的形容詞。

Ex. The man <u>standing</u> there is going to be our boss.

(站在那裡的那個男人將會成為我們的老闆。)

→ 人是主動站著，所以用現在分詞當形容詞用。

Ex. The bicycle <u>made</u> in Taiwan is not only stylish but also comfortable.

(台灣製造的腳踏車不只是有型而且很舒服。)

→ 腳踏車是被製造出來的，而不是主動製造，所以用過去分詞當形容詞用。

看了以上的例子後，同學們有沒有對形容詞的各種形態比較有印象了呢？做題目時可以用以上介紹的一些規則，來幫助你判斷正確用法喔！

⑤ 副詞的功能是用來修飾動詞和形容詞的狀態。

　　因為副詞主要的功能是來修飾動詞，來補充說明動作做的狀態(一般副詞)、情狀副詞、動作發生的時間(時間副詞)、動作發生的頻率(頻率副詞)、動作發生的地方(地方副詞)。因為時間副詞我們在前一章連接詞中提過以 when、before、after 及 if 開頭的句子，所以我們這裡只提一般副詞與形容詞的用法分辨，以及頻率副詞的用法。

(1) 一般動詞

　　通常一般敘述動作的副詞就是將形容詞後+ly，副詞的位置通常在動詞和形容詞前後，用來就近修飾。以下是一個判別練習，同學們可以透過演練，以了解形容詞及副詞的分辨方法。

<Practice>

1. It's just an _____ (usual/ usually) thing. Don't be so surprised. OK?

2. _____(Unfortunate/ unfortunately), your flight was canceled due to the bad weather.

3. According to a _____(recent/recently) research, unhappy people have more possibilities to get cancer.

♥愛的筆記貼♥
判斷用形容詞還是用副詞的訣竅就是：形容詞多是用來形容名詞

的，所以通常是夾在冠詞和名詞之間。一個句子如果句意完整，要加強語氣，或者空格在動詞或形容詞附近的話，就八九不離十是副詞了。所以答案為：

❶ usual (一般的，是形容詞。這只是一件平常的事。不要大驚小怪的，好嗎？)

❷ Unfortunately (不幸地，是副詞。不幸地，你的班機被取消了是因為惡劣天氣的因素。

❸ recent (最近的，是形容詞。根據一項最近的研究，不快樂的人有更多獲得癌症的機會。)

(2) 頻率副詞

　　頻率副詞的概念其實我們在會話內容中曾經講解過。在此再度複習一下：

> never　從不
> rarely　稀少
> seldom　很少
> sometimes　時常
> often　時常
> usually　通常
> always　總是

Ex. My sister and I <u>usually</u> go home together, but <u>sometimes</u> we don't because we go to different clubs after school.

(我妹妹和我通常在放學後會一起回家，但是有時候我們不會一起回家是因為我們在放學後去了不同的社團。)

　　這樣的頻率副詞是用來敘述動作的經常性。從頻率副詞

通常我們可以表現出日常生活中的一些習慣。

(3) 其他副詞的觀念統整

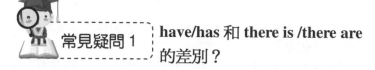

常見疑問 1　have/has 和 there is /there are 的差別？

『有』的概念 have/has 和 There is/ There are

現在式第一、二人稱單數及複數名詞用 have，第三人稱單數用 has，過去式不管第幾人稱都用 had

用 **HAVE/HAS** 的句型前面要有主詞，表示『擁有』之意。
例：Mary <u>has</u> a story book. (Mary 有一本故事書。)
例：The book <u>has</u> a red cover. (這書有一個紅色封面。)

用 **There is/ There are** 時，是用來說明某物位在某特定的地方，表示『存在』之意。
例：<u>There are</u> two trees in the yard.
　　(在這庭院中有兩棵樹。)
要注意的是，並沒有 There has/ There have 的用法，會常發生這種錯誤，主要是因為國人語用習慣的問題，在中文中，不管表示『擁有』或『存在』的概念，我們都普遍用『有』字來表示，但要記得在英文的使用上是有差異的，多做練習便能習慣此用法了。

例句分析

The camel |has| one hump. 這種駱駝有一個駝峰。

It |has| long and thick hair. 牠也有長而厚的毛髮。

|There is| a lot of sand in the desert. 在沙漠中有很多沙。

一般文句練習

(1) _____ _____ 4,000 people in Jolin's birthday party last month. 上個月有 4000 人在(參加)Jolin 的生日宴會。

(2) Do you _____ any special ideas?
你有任何特別的點子嗎？

(3) He _____ no money to help Mary, but you _____.
他沒有錢去幫助 Mary，但是你有啊。

(4) _____ _____ many students in the dorm.
這棟宿舍裡有很多學生。

♥ 愛的筆記貼 ♥

答案：❶ There were　❷ have　❸ has/ have　❹ There are

常見疑問 2　**So v.s Such 的用法**

　　so 是很經典的副詞修飾形容詞的用法，而 such 其實是形容詞，所以是用來修飾名詞。由以下的例句來理解用法：
Ex. You are so beautiful. 不是有首歌這樣唱的嗎？所以 so 後

面都是接形容詞，表示『如此；這般』之意。Ex. Such a wonderful day!這樣美好的一天！所以 such 的用法就是後面接一個完整的名詞片語，也就是冠詞+形容詞+名詞。

常見疑問 3　　too...to 和 so...that 的句型

『too...to』指得是『太…以致於不能…』，而『so...that...』是『如此…以致於…』的用法。例句如下：

Ex. 路程太遠我們無法走路過去。

→ The way is **too** far **for** us **to** walk there.

　　　→ 太(形)/對(人)來說/去(動作)

= The way is **so** far **that** we can't walk there.

　　　→ 如此(形)/以致於+(句子)

常見疑問 4　　enough 和形容詞的搭配用法

　　一般副詞都是接在形容詞前去修飾形容詞，例 <u>so</u> beautiful、<u>very</u> much、<u>much</u> more beautiful。但是遇到 enough 『夠了；足夠』，形容詞要放在 enough 的前面。

Ex. You are <u>smart</u> **enough** to be a shop owner.

　　(你很聰明足以勝任當一個店主了。)

　　 Mark is <u>tall</u> **enough** to play basketball.

　　(Mark 已經長得夠高可以打籃球了。)

　　Salina is <u>beautiful and slim</u> **enough** to be a model.

（Salina 長得美且苗條足以當一位模特兒。）

Grammar Challenge

____ 1. Lisa was so _____ that she didn't get any birthday
presents this year.

(A) surprise   (B) surprising

(C) surprised   (D) surprises

____ 2. The new American president, Obama, received _____
support from the public in the 2008 vote.

(A) efficient   (B) effectively

(C) overanxiously   (D) overwhelming

____ 3. My sister is 5 years _____ I.

(A) the oldest   (B) order more

(C) old enough   (D) older than

____ 4. The twins are living _____ any other people in the
world. (A) as longer as   (B) the least long

          (C) longer than   (D) longer better

____ 5. This is an _____ fact that everyone understand it.

(A) obvious   (B) apparently

(C) obviously   (D) appearance

____ 6. She danced _____ and it was really unforgettable.

(A) beautiful   (B) beautifully

(C) beauty   (D) beautify

解答：(1) C (2) D (3) D (4) C (5) A (6) B

國家圖書館出版品預行編目資料

英檢pass定心丸：英檢重要基礎觀念攻略
／王璟琪著，--第1版.—
臺北市：金星出版：紅螞蟻總經銷，
2009年3月[民98]
面； 公分--（語言學習叢書；01）

ISBN: 978-986-6441-00-4（平裝）

1. 英語　2. 讀本
805.18　　　　　　　　　　98002467

英檢pass定心丸
英檢重要基礎觀念攻略

作　　　者： 王璟琪
發 行 人： 袁光明
社　　　長： 袁靜石
編　　　輯： 林欣美
總 經 理： 袁玉成
出 版 者： 金星出版社
社　　地址： 台北市南京東路3段201號3樓
電　　電話： 886-2-2362-6655
傳　　FAX： 886-2365-2425
郵政劃撥： 18912942金星出版社帳戶
總 經 銷： 紅螞蟻圖書有限公司
地　　　址： 台北市內湖區舊宗路二段121巷28．32號4樓
電　　　話： (02)27953656(代表號)
網　　　址： http://www.venusco555.com
E-mail ： venusco@pchome.com.tw
　　　　　 venus@venusco.com.tw
版　　次： 2009年3月 第1版
登 記 證： 行政院新聞局局版北市業字第653號
法律顧問： 郭啟疆律師
定　　價： 350 元